Freeman Wills Crofts was born in Dublin in 1879 and died in 1957. He worked for a Northern Irish railway company as an engineer, writing in his spare time. In 1929 he moved to England and turned to writing detective fiction full-time.

His plots reveal his mathematical training and he specialised in the seemingly unbreakable alibi and the intricacies of railway timetables. He also loved ships and trains and they feature in many of his stories.

Crofts' best-known character is Inspector Joseph French, a detective who achieves his results through dogged persistence.

Raymond Chandler praised Crofts' plots, calling him 'the soundest builder of them all'.

BY THE SAME AUTHOR
ALL PUBLISHED BY HOUSE OF STRATUS

FREEMAN WILLS CROFTS

The Hog's Back Mystery

HOUSE OF
STRATUS

This edition published in 2001 by House of Stratus, an imprint of House of Stratus Ltd, Thirsk Industrial Park, York Road, Thirsk, North Yorkshire, YO7 3BX, UK.

www.houseofstratus.com

Typeset, printed and bound by House of Stratus.

A catalogue record for this book is available from the British Library and the Library of Congress.

ISBN 1-84232-396-2

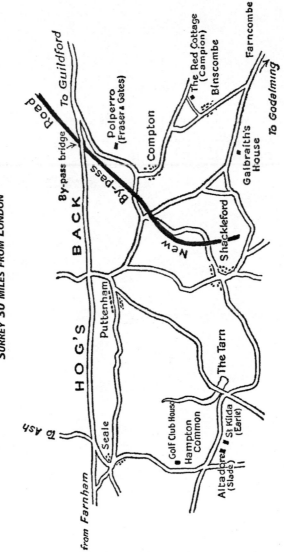

THE SETTING OF THE STORY
SURREY 30 MILES FROM LONDON

To Guildford

Road

By-pass bridge

By-pass

Polperro
(Fraser & Gates)

Compton

New

Shackleford

Galbraith's House

The Red Cottage
(Campion)

Binscombe

Farncombe

To Godalming

HOG'S

BACK

Puttenham

Seale

To Ash

from Farnham

Golf Club House

Hampton Common

The Tarn

Altadore (Slade)

St Kilda (Earle)

APPROXIMATE SCALE – HALF-INCH TO MILE

CONTENTS

ST KILDA

"Ursula! I *am* glad to see you!"

Julia Earle moved forward to the carriage door to greet the tall, well-dressed woman who stepped down on the platform of the tiny station of Ash in Surrey.

"Julia! This *is* nice!" They kissed affectionately, then the new arrival swung round to a second woman who had followed in the wake of the first.

"And Marjorie! My goodness, Marjorie," – they also kissed – "when I remember the last time I saw you! I declare we haven't met since Bolsover. How many years ago is that?"

"Don't let's think. You're not much altered, Ursula. I should have known you easily."

"Nor are you; wonderfully little." She turned back to the first woman. "And how's the world, Julia?"

The interchange of reunion was interrupted in order to superintend the removal by a porter of Ursula Stone's two suitcases from the carriage and their conveyance by the same agency to a waiting car.

"Where will you sit?" went on Julia: "in front with me or behind with Marjorie?"

"Oh, in front. I always like this drive. A lovely country, isn't it, Marjorie?"

"In its way, yes. Of course where I'm living is much finer, but this Surrey landscape is more restful."

"I forget your headquarters now, Marjorie. San Remo, isn't it?"

"Rocquebrune; close to Rocquebrune, that is. You know it perhaps; just beyond Monte Carlo?"

"I've passed it in the train. I love all that coast."

Meanwhile Julia had started up the Morris saloon and they were soon bowling along towards the ridge of the Hog's Back, which presently came into view as their southern horizon. Julia Earle and her husband, a retired doctor, had settled down in the heart of wild Surrey, though, as they were only some four miles from Farnham, and little more from Guildford and Godalming, they could not be said to be entirely divorced from civilisation. Though she had made many friends in the neighbourhood, Julia found the life lonely, and to have two visitors simultaneously was a pleasure she had not enjoyed for a long time.

Of these two, Marjorie Lawes, her unmarried sister, was the greater stranger. Marjorie liked heat and sunshine and she ordered her goings to the vagaries of Nature in this respect. She was a migrant. Winter drew her to Egypt; spring and autumn she spent on the Riviera, while in summer she penetrated as far north as Switzerland or the Dolomites. She lived by her pen. "Not serious stuff, you know, my dear," she would truly say. Sentiment, splashed lavishly on in huge purple patches, was her standby. Her simple tales of the loves of earls and typists, turned out in bulk, paid well enough for her needs and a little over, and formed just the interest required to keep her mind keen and fit.

Ursula Stone was no relation of the sisters, but at school the three had been inseparable and they had kept up their intimacy. Ursula had not married and now she lived a placid life at Bath, where she was popular enough in the local society. An occasional letter had prevented her getting entirely out of touch with the sisters, and after the Earles had moved to their present house Julia had asked her to pay them a visit. That was four years ago. This time she had been invited specially to meet Marjorie, who was spending a few weeks in England.

Julia, reaching the top of the hill up which they had been climbing, cautiously nosed the car out on to the high-speed Guildford–Farnham road which here runs along the spine of that curious narrow ridge known as the Hog's Back. The others instinctively paused to watch for approaching traffic; then as they turned west, their voices broke out again.

"Tell me about yourself, Ursula," Marjorie went on. "You're living at Bath?"

"Yes, I've got a cottage perched up on Bathwick Hill. It's a nice position. The town lies in the valley and you see across it to the hills beyond."

"And what do you do with yourself?"

Ursula smiled. "My hospital! I call it mine because I like working for it so much. It's a children's hospital and I'm honorary secretary. It's fascinating work, though it would make you weep tears of blood to see some of the little mites that are in it."

Marjorie shrugged. "More useful than my job. But then I couldn't afford it. Tell me, have you ever come across the Bantings?" And the talk went back to school days.

Except from the point of view of age – none of them would see thirty-five again – the three women contrasted both in appearance and manner. Ursula Stone was tall and slight with a facial angle approaching the vertical. All her lines indeed were vertical. Her narrow forehead was high, and instead of retreating seemed to project further forward as it rose, her nose was thin and aquiline, and her pointed chin was set well forward. Good features, all of them. With her very erect carriage and well-cut clothes she was an interesting, indeed a striking figure. Her manners were old-fashioned, courteous and unworldly, and she had the air of living in an age that has gone.

Julia Earle was also a handsome woman, tall, fair, with a commanding presence, and extremely well dressed. She was the sort of woman whom men turn to look at in the street. She did not look her age, not by a dozen years. A kind of competence radiated from her. One felt instinctively that she would hold her own in any company and deal efficiently with any situation that might arise. There was indeed too marked a hardness in her face, a hardness notably absent from Ursula's.

Her sister, Marjorie Lawes, while neither so good looking nor so well dressed, gave an impression of greater kindliness. Marjorie was smaller and thinner and had grown slightly wizened. Her skin was darkened from southern suns, showing up more prominently her greying hair. She was the only one of the three to wear glasses, through which gazed out upon the world a pair of extremely intelligent greenish-grey eyes.

They had turned south from the Hog's Back through the quaint old-world village of Seale, and now were passing through the dense pinewoods of Hampton Common. At a crossroads they turned to the left through a still thicker wood of oak, beech and ash, with plenty of birch and nut trees; an almost impenetrable thicket. Presently Julia slowed down.

"Here we are," she said, turning the car into a narrow gateway which bore on a plate the name "St Kilda".

A short curving drive brought them to the house, a typical modern South of England cottage, with lower walls of purple brick, upper story and roof of "antique" red tiles and steel-framed casement windows. In front and at both sides the trees had been cleared back to leave room for a small garden. All round was the wood. The place had struck Ursula on her one former visit as small but fascinating, and immediately she felt once again its restful charm.

But what had most impressed her then, and now impressed her more than ever, was the isolation of the house. As far as appearances went it might be the only dwelling in the world.

"Oh no," Julia said when she commented on this; "Colonel Dagger lives just down the road and the Forresters are close to him. There are plenty of houses about, but you don't see them because of the trees."

Ursula was tired from her journey. It had been good up to Reading, where she had changed. But the local train through Farnborough took a leisurely interest in the surrounding country, stopping whenever possible and being in no hurry to restart.

Not till she came down dressed for dinner did Ursula see her host. Dr Earle was a small, rather insignificant-looking man of about sixty with a round face of that high colour so often associated with heart affections. He had lived and practised in Godalming until some six years earlier. Then he had come into a little money, and hating general practice and loving research, he had obtained a partner, a Dr Campion, to take over the heavy end of the work. He had bought St Kilda for himself, intending to devote himself to writing a book on some abstruse theory he had formed on the culture of germs. Before, however, he had moved out, he had met with an accident and gone to Brighton to recuperate. There he had met and married Julia Lawes. Now he greeted Ursula with a shy cordiality which somehow convinced her that he was really pleased that she had come.

"So glad to see you again, Miss Stone," he said with a smile. "I hope you had a comfortable journey?"

Ursula reassured him and they began to chat. On her previous visit she had liked James Earle. She had found him unassuming and retiring and anxious to do what he could to make her visit pleasant. Also though surprisingly ignorant of books other than scientific treatises, he was fond of light reading, and she had enjoyed the appreciation he had shown when introduced to some of her favourites.

"What have you been doing with yourself lately, Dr Earle?" she asked.

"Nothing very much, I'm afraid," the little man smiled. "A little golf, a little writing, some work in the garden, still unhappily a few patients – I've tried to get rid of them without success – some books: particularly some books. Have you read – ?" And they seemed quite naturally to slip into their relations of four years earlier. But it didn't last long. Julia and Marjorie soon came in and they moved to the dining room.

During dinner Ursula realised with some small feeling of regret that what she had anticipated during her previous visit had come to pass. Then the Earles had not long settled down at St Kilda: it was just a couple of years since their marriage. Though both were advanced in age, they had been very much Mr and Mrs Newly-Wed: Julia was evidently newfangled and amused with her unwonted position and was fond in a maternal sort of way of her elderly boy, for James Earle was just a grown-up boy. As for him, he obviously doted on her. Now things were changed.

Earle clearly had not stood up to his wife, with the result
that she had taken command and now appeared to give him
but little consideration. Inevitable, Ursula thought, from
their respective temperaments, but rather distressing. Not
that Julia was at all unpleasant to her husband; simply she
did not appear to consider him of any account in her
scheme of things. But Earle did not seem at all unhappy. It
was just that Ursula thought they had missed a
companionship which they might so easily have had.

The evening passed uneventfully in bridge, and when
Ursula went to bed it was with feelings of satisfaction that
she had come. She had enjoyed her previous visit to this
charming country and she believed she was going to enjoy
the coming fortnight. Marjorie's presence was an added
pleasure. Ursula had always liked Marjorie better than
Julia. Julia she had found a little bit too conscious of the
side on which her bread was buttered, but Marjorie would
have shared her last crust with a stranger.

The next day the weather seemed to confirm Ursula's
optimism. It was one of those charming autumn days which
are not uncommon in south-eastern England. The sun
shone placidly with a comfortable warmth, reflecting
mellow lights from the rich colouring of the turning leaves
and drawing delightful aromatic scents from the woods.
The twittering of birds cut sharp across the soft cooing of
distant pigeons. Stretched lazily on its side on the grass lay
the Earles' big black cat, the epitome of luxurious ease, yet
with a wary eye on the birds and an occasional thump of its
tail on the ground as a protest against their presence. No
wonder Ursula felt optimistic. Yet had she been able to
foresee the future she would have recoiled with horror and
without a moment's delay would have fled from St Kilda
and all connected with it.

It was indeed on that very day that the first of those small incidents occurred which were to lead up to the awful culmination which spelled tragedy for the party and gave a thrill to the entire country. The occupants of St Kilda had dispersed on their lawful occasions. Earle had gone to play golf, walking: the clubhouse was only some half-mile back along the road to the station. Marjorie had disappeared to her room to write, while Julia was busy with household chores. Ursula, finding a deckchair in the hall, had fixed it in a shady corner of the garden and opened a new novel. But she didn't read with diligence. The sun and air were soporific and with closed eyes she lay in dreamy content.

Presently she became faintly conscious of a movement behind her. Julia, she supposed, and she prepared to congratulate her on the perfect setting of her home. But the movement ceased and Ursula sleepily imagined she had been mistaken. Then suddenly she felt a presence and opened her eyes.

A startled-looking young man was bending over her. His face was nearly on a level with her own and Ursula realised that he had been about to kiss her, in fact that she had missed the salute by a fraction of a second. He was a tall young man, tall and thin and rabbit-faced, with protruding mouth and retreating forehead and chin. He was obviously very much perturbed.

"Beg pardon, I'm sure," he muttered, drawing hastily back. "I thought it was" – he checked himself quickly, adding, "someone else."

"Oh," said Ursula frigidly.

"Yes," he went on, regaining confidence; "only saw your feet, you know; your face was hidden by the back of the chair. And that red dress" – again he broke off in confusion. "I mean – it was an accident. Sorry and all that."

"There's nothing to be sorry about," Ursula said very distinctly.

"No, no, of course not," he agreed. Ursula could have boxed his ears. "But I waked you up, you know. Shouldn't have done that. By the way, my name's Slade, Reggie Slade. Live next door, you know." He pointed vaguely to the trees ahead. "D'you happen to know if Mrs Earle's about?"

"I don't know where Mrs Earle is," Ursula answered unhelpfully.

He took out his cigarette case, selected a cigarette and slowly lit it.

"No?" he said. "I expect she's indoors. Have a message for her, you know." He paused, hung about undecidedly on one leg, then went on: "You're Miss Stone, I suppose? Heard you were coming. Julia – I mean, Mrs Earle – has been looking forward to your visit."

Ursula wondered who this young man could be who seemed on such familiar terms with Julia Earle, for she had just grasped the significance of the reference to her dress. Julia had a dress of much the same colour; she had seen it in her wardrobe when in her room on the previous afternoon. Slade was certainly on very familiar terms; there was no doubt he had been going to kiss Julia, and what was more intriguing, Ursula was satisfied he would never have dared to do so unless he knew Julia would be a consenting party.

"I expect you'll find Mrs Earle in the house," she said coldly, opening her book in a marked way.

But the young man showed no signs of taking the hint.

"Oh, come now, Miss Stone," he said, looking round as if for a seat; "don't be mad with me for a mistake, specially when I've apologised. Couldn't have known it was you, you know."

"I'm not in the least annoyed. Kindly allow me to get on with my book."

"That means you are annoyed," he grumbled. "It wasn't as if – " He broke off and his face and tones grew suddenly eager as he added, "Here's Julia!"

Ursula felt a little shocked as she looked at him. There was no mistaking the expression in his eyes. They had the adoring, worshipping look of a dog which fawns on its master. Whoever or whatever Reggie Slade might be, one thing about him was certain: he was utterly, over-whelmingly in love with Julia Earle.

Julia took no notice of him at first. She spoke cheerily to Ursula, asking her if she was cold and saying that if so there were rugs in the hall. Then she glanced at her other visitor frowningly.

"What on earth do *you* want?" she asked unpleasantly. "If it's my husband, he's gone out."

The rabbit-faced young man looked so crestfallen that soft-hearted Ursula was sorry for him in spite of herself.

"It was only," he stammered, "that I've – er – got the Bentley back. Just been into Farnham for her. She's – er – going better than ever. I wondered if perhaps – "

"Oh, you were going to take James to play golf?" Julia mocked. "Well, he's gone already."

"Then there was that book," the young fellow pleaded desperately.

"Oh yes, the financial book for Colonel Dagger. Yes, I'll get it for you if you come in. Sure you're all right, Ursula?"

"In heaven," Ursula declared dreamily, and the others disappeared.

Ursula felt more than a little distressed at this development, though not wholly surprised. She was not taken in by Julia's manner. That Julia had encouraged and was encouraging the young man she hadn't the least doubt. Probably, thought Ursula, not at all cynically, but with the humorous toleration with which she had trained herself to look on life, Reggie Slade was bestowing that selfsame kiss at the present moment. Probably also he was receiving value for it. Julia had always been like that, ever since Ursula knew her. She couldn't live without male admiration. Admittedly wherever she went she received it. And yet, until James Earle appeared, no one, so far as Ursula knew, had wished to marry her. Men were ready enough for a flirtation, but when things began to grow serious a bar to matrimony invariably appeared. Sometimes it was an existing wife, but usually that they suddenly found they had no money. For all of them knew that a poor man's love was no good to Julia.

Ursula had indeed been surprised to hear of her friend's marriage. She wondered, as she had wondered before, if it was Earle's money which had proved the attraction. Earle was by no means rich, but he was comfortably off. Or was it that Julia thought she could so dominate a man of Earle's temperament that she would be left free for any deviations from the narrow path to which she felt a drawing?

Suddenly Ursula felt ashamed of herself. This was no way to be thinking of her hostess, of her friend indeed, for during those years at school, and since, Julia had proved herself a real friend. Besides, though Julia had these little weaknesses, she was in other ways a real good sort. She was attractive socially, a pleasant companion, and good-natured – at least, so long as her good nature did not inconvenience herself.

All the same Ursula could not help feeling extremely sorry for James Earle. At his age and after his life of uncongenial work, he must have wanted to settle down and have a home. It looked as if he was scarcely getting all he had bargained for.

With a little sigh and a mental note to mind her own business instead of her neighbours', Ursula resumed her book. But she had not read many pages before she was again interrupted. This time it was Marjorie.

"I saw you out here," Marjorie announced, "and I felt I must come out and enjoy the day with you. There's something mild and soothing about this English sun that you don't get abroad. At home, or what I call home for this time of year, the light's harder; there's more glare."

Marjorie had brought her writing-pad, but she did not seem in any hurry to resume work. The two women dropped into a desultory conversation. It was many years since they had met and there were multitudinous confidences to be exchanged.

The talk was at first about their various experiences during that long period of separation, then at last it turned to the present.

"You know, Ursula," Marjorie said, staring before her into the distance and speaking more confidentially, "I'm not very happy about Julia and James. I'm afraid things are not going as well as one would have liked."

"In what way, Marjorie?"

Marjorie moved uneasily. "I don't exactly know," she answered. "There seems to be a strain between them that shouldn't be there. You haven't noticed anything?"

"I think Julia's a little bit too high-handed with Dr Earle," Ursula declared. "You remember last night at dinner. He wanted to go up to Town to some meeting, but no, he couldn't do so. She wanted him to go with us to East Grinstead so that he could drive to that nursery for the shrubs while we were seeing the Leathems. It seemed a pity to me. There was no hurry about the shrubs, and why couldn't he have gone to his meeting if he had wanted to?"

"It isn't that; James didn't mind about that. As a matter of fact I happen to know he wasn't really particular whether he went to the meeting or not. Besides," – she paused and glanced sideways at Ursula – "James is not so meek and mild as you think. He can be quite nasty to her if he wants to. I've heard him: quite nasty. I was surprised."

Ursula smiled. "You don't say so? I shouldn't have believed it."

"Well, it's quite true. But she deserved it." She paused again, then drew closer and sank her voice confidentially. "It's Julia's fault. I daren't say anything: she wouldn't take it from me. But you're different. She's always had an immense opinion of you and she'd listen to what you said. It's just what you'd expect from Julia, it's what she's always done. She – well, she has men hanging about. That's what annoys James so much."

"Dear Marjorie, what could I say? It's not my business. I suppose you mean Reggie Slade?"

Marjorie stared. "Goodness, Ursula! You almost frighten me. How could you possibly have known that?"

"I've become a detective in my old age," Ursula smiled. "I've met the gentleman. He came up and introduced himself. He thought I was Julia. Then Julia came out and I could see from his face."

"Did she encourage him?"

Ursula laughed outright. "Encourage is not exactly the word I should have used," and she repeated Julia's greeting.

Marjorie grunted. "She shouldn't do it," she protested. "James is the mildest of men, but even a worm will turn. I sometimes imagine that only for his patients he'd go away."

"I thought he'd given up his practice?"

"So he has really, but some old patients insist on having him still. Besides, Dr Campion – that's the partner, you know – calls him in occasionally in consultation. Just after I came old Mr Frazer died, and Dr Campion had called him in there two or three times. I heard them talking about it. You know who I mean? Old Mr Frazer of Frazer's, the theatrical booking people?"

"That was the owner of that fine place near Compton?"

"Yes, a lovely place and a lovely house. They say he left pots of money; most of it to his wife, but a big chunk to his nephew, Mr Gates, who lives there. I don't care for them much."

"Oh, then you know them?"

"Slightly. They were over here to see James the other day and I met them. She's a rather polite icicle and he's a rough diamond, with the emphasis on the adjective. Julia said he's been a labourer in Australia, and he just sounds like it."

"Seen life?"

"Perhaps, in its less civilised manifestations. People are talking about them already, staying on alone there in that big house. However, that's their own business. We were talking of James and Julia. I wish, Ursula, you'd give Julia a hint. I believe she'd take it from you."

Ursula didn't think she would be given an opportunity, but agreed to do what she could, and the subject dropped.

"Funny that Dr Campion should have come as assistant to James," Ursula said presently. "You know they used to live at Bath; Howard – that's Dr Campion – and Alice and Flo, his sisters. I knew them well, or at least the girls."

Marjorie nodded. "So Julia told me. I heard her speaking of Miss Campion. She was talking of asking her over. She said you would be sure to want to see her."

"That's good of Julia; I should like to."

"I like Miss Campion."

"Yes, Alice is a good sort. Tell me, Marjorie – " and the talk reverted once again to old acquaintances.

The day passed uneventfully. Earle did not appear at lunch, but he was home for dinner. Things seemed to go quite smoothly, and afterwards there was another game of rather mediocre bridge. They retired early, and next morning Ursula felt that she had quite settled down and that she was going to enjoy her fortnight with her old friends.

She little knew what the next few days would bring forth.

– 2 –

THE RED COTTAGE

It happened that Alice Campion was unable to come to the Earles on the afternoon on which Julia had asked her, and a couple of days later Ursula took advantage of a visit of Julia and Marjorie to Dorking to go over and lunch with her old friend. The Red Cottage was situated in the little village of Binscombe, some two miles from Godalming and five from St Kilda. There was no direct railway, but the bus which passed St Kilda ran within half a mile of the Red Cottage. In little more than half an hour after starting Ursula rang at the door.

Alice Campion was unfeignedly glad to see her visitor. "I was so sorry I couldn't go over to St Kilda," she explained. "Some people were coming here whom I couldn't very well put off. But I'm all the better pleased now, for I have you to myself."

Miss Campion was small, stout, round-faced and jolly; good-tempered, a great talker and a staunch friend. When Ursula could get in a word she asked after Dr Campion.

"Howard will be sorry to miss you," his sister answered. "He's out on his rounds and always lunches at Godalming. But all the better for me again. Now tell me what you have been doing with yourself since I saw you. Let's see, how long ago is that? Why, it must be four years since you were here. The Earles went to St Kilda six years ago – that's two years before we came out here – and you paid your visit to them the year we arrived."

Dr Campion had, in fact, followed Dr Earle's example in taking a partner to live over the surgery in Godalming, while he moved out into the country at Binscombe.

Alice rattled on, not waiting for a reply. Ursula, who was really attached to her, sat smiling and putting in a word now and then, not to stem, but to direct the torrent. Listening indeed with somewhat wandering attention to the flow, Ursula presently became aware that she was being asked a question.

"How long am I staying?" she repeated. "Till Monday week, I think."

"A pity it's not longer. Flo's coming on Saturday; I mean Saturday week, the Saturday before that Monday. You must wait and see her."

Flo was the third member of the Campion family. She had lived with the others in Bath, and she and Ursula had been close friends.

"Flo! Is she really? Oh, I certainly must see her. I don't like to think how many years it is since we met. But I'm afraid I couldn't stay longer. I have to be home on Tuesday."

"Put it off, whatever it is," Alice urged. "It can get on quite well without you."

"No, I really think I ought to go home. What about Sunday? Suppose I were to come over in the afternoon?"

"Come and spend the day on Sunday. That would be better than nothing."

"Oh I couldn't, Alice. I couldn't leave Julia for the whole of my last day. But I'll come in the afternoon."

After some grumbling on the part of Alice Campion it was arranged that Ursula should go over in time for tea and stay for the evening, when Dr Campion would run her back to St Kilda.

"You must see the house," Alice declared. "I don't think we were settled in last time you were here."

They went through all the rooms, of which Alice was evidently extremely proud. Ursula duly admired everything she saw, though to herself she admitted that the furniture was all very ordinary. Indeed, she was surprised that Alice had not shown better taste. However, she told herself that if it pleased Alice, it was efficiently serving its purpose.

One new and elaborate piece of furniture formed an exception to the rule, an inlaid and beautifully carved radio gramophone; really an ornament to any room. Ursula cried out with genuine delight when she saw it.

"Say that to Howard," Alice answered. "He's just finished making it and it's the apple of his eye at present. If you praise it he'll take you to his heart at once."

"*Making* it?" Ursula repeated in astonishment. "You don't mean that he made that case?"

"He made everything you see and fitted in all its works. And it has a very good tone too. Listen." She turned a switch and the room was filled with the sickly pulsating throbs of a cinema organ.

"You must see his workshop," Alice went on; "only he'd like to show it to you himself. He really can do anything with his hands. But of course he's got good tools. I don't know what that place hasn't cost him," and she produced further samples of Campion's skill. Ursula was fond of anything mechanical and she took a mental note to remember to see the workshop on her next visit.

In discussing old times the day slipped quickly away, and evening had come and Alice had driven her guest to the St

Kilda bus before they had finished half what they wanted to say.

Ursula was enjoying her visit to the Earles. She had quite settled down into their ways, and she had the freedom to amuse herself that she so much liked. In the forenoon she lay about and read, while Marjorie added page after page to the latest tale of love and longing and Julia busied herself about the house. In the afternoon they usually went exploring, either in the car or on foot. James Earle spent a good deal of his time on the golf links, but sometimes he stayed working in his study or amusing himself in the most leisurely way with odd jobs about the place. After dinner they usually played bridge.

No discord had so far marred the visit. On several other occasions Reggie Slade had put in an appearance, after which he and Julia generally somewhat mysteriously vanished. In spite of Marjorie's request Ursula had not spoken to Julia on the subject of Slade. She felt it would be a useless impertinence. It was not as if Julia were a girl. She was a woman of very nearly Ursula's own age, and she knew what she was doing and how far she intended to go without advice from any other person. Ursula indeed felt that her interference would cost her her friend, and she did not see why she should pay this price for no adequate return.

Then one day a trifling but unpleasant incident took place which worried Ursula and made her fear that affairs at St Kilda were in a more parlous state than she had supposed.

It occurred towards the end of her visit – on a Thursday, and she was leaving the following Monday. That morning Dr Earle had said he was going to play on the Merrow links, near Guildford, and that he would stay afterwards for bridge, returning only in time for dinner. This had happened twice before since Ursula's arrival and the intimation was received without comment. Shortly after breakfast he set off in the car.

He had scarcely gone when Ursula was called to the telephone. A great friend of hers, whom she had not seen for years, was passing through London that day on her way from South Africa to Yorkshire. Would Ursula come up and lunch with her?

Ursula would. Nothing special had been arranged for that afternoon. Julia, however, was overwhelmed with regrets. If only the message had come ten minutes earlier James could have taken her to Guildford. Now Ursula would have to walk to the Shackleford road for the bus. She could, of course, get the train at Godalming and she would be in plenty of time. But it was too unfortunate that the car had gone...

Ursula really did not mind in the least. She reassured Julia, said she would be back to dinner, and started off.

Again it was a lovely day and she enjoyed her journey. At Waterloo her friend met her, and as it was early for lunch, they decided to carry out one or two small commissions first. One of these took them to Marylebone Station, and it was when they were returning to the Marble Arch that the incident happened.

They were walking along the east side of Seymour Place, when near the crossing of Upper George Street a car overtook them, travelling at a very slow speed. Ursula glanced at it casually and instantly became rigid.

The car was Dr Earle's and in it sat Earle himself. For a moment Ursula could not believe her eyes and almost stopped, staring. But she had not been mistaken. It was James Earle beyond any shadow of doubt.

In a dream she watched the car. It pulled in to the pavement a few steps beyond where she and her companion were walking, and came to a stand. As it did so a lady whom she had vaguely noticed waiting on the footpath, stepped forward. Earle opened the door, the lady entered, and the car drove off, turning westwards at Upper Berkeley Street. It must have been held up at the Edgeware Road crossing, for when Ursula reached Upper Berkeley Street she glimpsed the car disappearing westwards into Connaught Street.

The little incident had taken place not more than a dozen feet from Ursula, and she had a good look at the woman. It was someone she had never seen before. She was young and rather plainly dressed in grey and was good-looking after the classical Grecian fashion. She seemed to know Earle well.

Scarcely hearing the "Someone you know?" of her friend, Ursula gazed after the retreating vehicle. James Earle! That quiet meek little man, with his uncomplaining acceptance of his wife's vagaries, his shy friendship with herself and his unobtrusive interest in books! Here was another side to his character! She could not have imagined his taking the law into his own hands like this.

There was, of course, no earthly reason why her host should not come up in his car to Town, meet a lady, and drive her wherever she wanted to go. If that were all neither Julia nor anyone else could have had the least objection. But the fact that Earle should have thought it necessary to hide his action made all the difference. He had said that he was going to spend the day playing golf at Merrow. That statement changed an innocent meeting into a guilty one. He would have had no need to tell that story unless he had something to hide.

For Julia Ursula had no sympathy whatever. Julia had only got what she very richly deserved. At the same time, Ursula was sorry. She had no special moral scruples on these subjects, but her experience told her that such a state of affairs could lead only to unhappiness. Ursula wanted everyone to be happy, and it hurt her when she saw possible happiness being missed.

However, the affair was no business of hers. Dismissing it from her mind, she lunched with her friend, saw her off to the north and returned to Waterloo. But in the train the matter recurred to her. Gradually she began to wonder could she not have been mistaken. There really was something in that theory of doubles. She remembered how on one occasion at a musical festival at Cheltenham several people had come up and spoken to her, calling her Miss Oliphant. A strange and disconcerting experience! Probably this was a similar case. The man was exceedingly like Earle, but he was not Earle. Of course, on the other hand, there was the car...

Then Ursula thought that she was merely making a fool of herself; building up this vast edifice of distrust and suspicion on no real foundation whatever. Why should not the same thing have happened to Earle as had happened to herself? Why should not he too have received an unexpected message requiring his presence in Town?

This, she felt, was the explanation of the mystery. She was now curious to meet Earle, to hear him tell of this unexpected change in his plans.

When, however, they met for dinner Earle made no reference to his day. Ursula, however, watching him covertly, thought he seemed restless, as if trying to hide some repressed excitement. She could not control her interest in the affair, and in spite of her decision that it was not her business, she felt she must obtain some information.

"Did you have a good day's golf, Dr Earle?" she asked at the next pause in the conversation.

He started, unmistakably; started and paused before replying. Then with an evident effort he said: "Quite good. In fact, though I say it who shouldn't, I covered myself with glory in going round in three less than I had done before. I don't suppose I shall ever do such a thing again."

Ursula was unhappily satisfied. Earle had spoken in a self-conscious way that left no doubt that he was lying. Indeed, it was his usually straightforward character which had prevented him from hiding it.

It was not then an unexpected call to Town. Ursula's common sense warned her to let the thing alone, but her curiosity would not allow of this.

"I had an unexpected journey today," she went on conversationally. "I was in Town. I lunched there."

Earle was evidently suspicious, and though he achieved a creditable reply, it had no conviction. Disappointed, Ursula with an effort turned the conversation to the views visible from the train, and they began to discuss the country.

Sunday came without further incident, and after lunch Ursula took the Godalming bus and walked up from the Shackleford road to the Red Cottage. It was another splendid day, warm and summery as early September. Ursula was looking forward with a good deal of eagerness to seeing Flo Campion. Flo had been her special pal and for a dozen years they had not met. Flo was companion to a wealthy old lady, a great traveller. With her she had been twice round the world, and had spent months in China, Japan, the South Sea Islands, and other places out of the beaten tourist track.

The meeting proved as satisfying as Ursula had anticipated. Flo Campion was but little changed. No reserve had grown up which required to be thawed, and the two women were able to pick up their friendship at the point at which they had laid it down. Flo had seen much during her travels, and as she had the gift of putting her experiences in an interesting way, time passed quickly and pleasantly.

Shortly before dinner Howard Campion came in. He was a tall man, of rather slight build, though evidently healthy and muscular. His manners were quiet and direct, and though he was retiring rather than pushing, in his personality there seemed to Ursula latent force. She felt that he would be a good man in a tight place.

When they had chatted for some time Ursula turned the conversation to the radio gramophone. "Alice tells me you made it, Dr Campion. I do think it's a wonderful piece of work. I've never seen one which was a greater ornament to a room."

Campion was obviously delighted. "Won't you come and see my workshop, Miss Stone? I have a rather good lathe which might interest you, if you care for such things."

The workshop was outside, a wooden shed, an extension of the garage. It was not large, but the most had been made of the space and it was scrupulously clean and tidy. There were several machine tools, all small, but all polished till they shone. In the centre was a tiny circular saw and planing machine. A mortising machine and a vertical drill stood against one wall, while against another was the lathe. Ursula did not understand all the gadgets of the latter, though the doctor explained them patiently. But she could see that it was a beautiful piece of work and admired it accordingly. Beside the circular saw was a well-equipped bench with above it rows and rows of shining tools.

As they moved round Campion picked up a brown paper parcel from one of the shelves.

"Ah," he said, "I had forgotten all about this. It just occurs to me that you might like it."

"I, Dr Campion? What is it?"

He unwrapped the paper. Within were some strangely shaped bits of three-ply wood, tiny hinges and other small metal objects, together with coloured and patterned papers.

"It's a dolls' house," he explained. "One of those packets that the Handicrafts people put out. You know, the Weedington Street people, NW3. You have nothing to do but stick the pieces together. Here are the parts of the house, the windows, doors and so on, and this is brick paper for the walls and tile paper for the roof. I got it for a patient, a little girl of six, but before I could put it together the poor little mite died. Now it occurs to me that you might like it for your hospital."

Ursula was genuinely grateful. "Oh, Dr Campion, how good of you!" she said warmly. "I'd be just delighted. But can you send it after me? I'm afraid I'm going home tomorrow."

"No need to do that. I'll slip it together after dinner."

"Can you really? In so short a time?"

Campion smiled. "Bless you, yes; it's nothing of a job. I use a cold glue that sets very quickly. I'll do it after dinner and you can take it with you." He put down the bits of wood and pointed to a half-finished frame. "Here's something that may interest you also. It's supposed to be a combined tea table and cake-stand. The tea will be here"; and he went on to describe the affair, which folded, and which was evidently an idea of his own of which he was very proud.

Ursula was interested and she talked about the scheme till Alice came out to say that dinner was ready.

Campion had not much to say at meals. Indeed, neither he nor either of the visitors had much chance to say anything. Alice's tongue seldom ceased. Ursula indeed wondered how she was able to eat anything and keep the flow of conversation going. But all that she said was both interesting and kindly. Ursula enjoyed listening to her, though how long she would continue to do so she would not have prophesied.

After dinner the women returned to the drawing-room, while Campion went to his workshop to assemble the dolls' house. Ursula got into an argument with Alice as to how she should go back to St Kilda.

"I will not have Dr Campion take out the car," Ursula insisted. "There is a bus about nine and I'll go by it. Why shouldn't I?"

"Indeed, you'll do nothing of the kind. You mustn't go so early for one thing. *Of course* Howard will run you over. That was the arrangement from the beginning."

Ursula gave in and they settled down to chat. Flo was full of a new tour her old lady was about to undertake. She was certainly a wonderful old woman, nearly seventy, and with the *wanderlust* of a girl of twenty. She wanted, it appeared, to cross the Andes before she died. It had been a dream with her for many years and now she was going to do it. She would go direct to Buenos Aires, then cross the continent to Valparaiso, and so up the coast, returning via the Panama Canal and New York.

Presently the doctor came in. He was carrying the assembled body of the dolls' house, but without windows, fittings and decorative papers.

"This'll give you an idea of what it's going to look like, Miss Stone," he said. "I wondered if you would like a brick house and a red roof, or a stone house with slates. I've got papers for both. Personally I like the brighter colours, but I think in Bath the others are the rule. What do you say?"

Ursula was delighted with the tiny structure. "Oh how splendid!" she cried enthusiastically. "The children will simply love it. It *is* good of you, Dr Campion." She turned to the others. "See what I'm getting for the hospital. What do you both think: bright colours or dull? Bright, I suggest."

"You should have a red cottage," said Flo, "to remind you of where it came from," a suggestion which was unanimously agreed on.

"I'm running you over in the car of course," Campion said, pausing as he reached the door. "Don't forget that and try and slip off by the bus."

"She was trying," Alice put in; "in fact, she wanted right or wrong to go. But I wouldn't let her. I told her you'd run her across."

"Of course. It won't take any time."

"Very good of you all, I'm sure," Ursula declared as Campion disappeared.

"There now," said Alice, who never missed an opportunity of proving herself in the right, "you see you couldn't have caught the bus even if you'd wanted to. You'd have had to leave now – without your dolls' house."

Ursula admitted it and took advantage of the change of subject to urge Alice and Flo to visit her at Bath. "Run over in the car," she begged, "even if you only stay the night. Let's have a walk over some of the old places."

They both said that they would love it. Alice promised she would try to do it in the summer and Flo when, if ever, she got back from South America. This restarted the matter of the tour, and they discussed routes and ports of call and shore excursions till Campion again entered, this time with the completed house.

When the little building had been duly admired, Ursula said she must go.

"We'll all go," Alice declared. "It's not a very big car, but we'll manage it. Come on, Flo; you needn't put on a hat. Bring round the car, Howard. Have you got your things, Ursula?"

That was Alice all over, arranging everything and everybody. But no one minded, and presently they all packed into the doctor's small Standard and started on the five-mile run to St Kilda.

3

MISSING FROM HIS HOME

It was fine but cold as the party set out. The sky was clear and a brilliant three-quarter moon blotted out all but the brightest stars and threw the shadows of the trees black as ink across the road. There was no wind and save for the purr of the car everything was still. A fitting night to follow so splendid a day.

Campion drove quickly and in a few minutes they turned into the gate of St Kilda. Then while Ursula slowly disentangled herself from her seat, Campion got out and rang the bell. Julia opened the door.

"Oh, is it you, Dr Campion?" she greeted him, and her voice was sharp as if from anxiety. "Is James there?"

"No, Mrs Earle, I've not seen him. I was just running Miss Stone back, and Alice and Flo came for the drive. What about Earle?"

"I don't know," she answered. "He's gone out, or I think he must have. But he didn't say he was going out and all his hats are in the hall."

"Or," Campion returned, "he's gone to see Dagger or the Forresters. When did this happen?"

A shadow cut across the light from the hall and Marjorie appeared.

"Is it James?" she asked.

"No," said Julia. "It's the Campions bringing back Ursula."

By this time, hearing the discussion, all three women had got out of the car.

"What is it, Mrs Earle?" asked Alice. "Is there anything wrong?"

"Earle's gone out and they don't know where he is," Campion explained. "When did this happen, Mrs Earle?"

"An hour and a half ago: at twenty minutes to nine. Marjorie and I were able to fix the exact time."

"And what exactly happened? Tell us the details."

Julia stepped back into the hall. "Won't you come in?" she invited. "Come into the sitting-room, Miss Campion. Come in" – she turned to Flo. "It's cold out here at the door."

The party moved slowly in and stood grouped about Mrs Earle.

"He said nothing? Just walked out?" the doctor questioned.

"We didn't hear him go out," Julia went on. "I'll tell you. We were alone, he and Marjorie and I. On Sunday evening Lucy goes out and I get supper. Well, we had supper as usual and then Marjorie helped me to wash up: I never like to leave the dirty things for the maid. Supper was about eight and I suppose was over about half past eight."

"Just half past eight," Marjorie interposed.

"Yes. Then we washed up and Marjorie went into the sitting room. Tell them, Marjorie."

Marjorie took up the tale. "When we were finishing washing up I remembered that I had seen one of the cups we had used at tea on the piano in here. The Bannisters came to tea and someone had put this cup away and it had been forgotten. So I came in for it. James was sitting in that

chair before the fire reading the *Observer*. I noticed
particularly that he had his slippers on. He looked up as I
entered and asked me had I read about a motor accident
which had taken place the day before near Dorking. 'It's a
regular death-trap, that corner,' he said. 'We were nearly
sent to Kingdom Come ourselves at that very place. You
can't see, and as we were trying to cross the road a bus
came charging down on us.' I murmured something and
took the cup out to the kitchen and washed it. I don't
suppose I was three minutes out of the room, certainly not
more. As I came in again I went on talking about the
accident. I said: 'Is that the corner near the school where we
met Janie Holt?' There was no reply, and when I looked
over, James was gone. His newspaper was there on the
chair, but he was gone."

She paused. "And what did you do?" Campion asked.

"I didn't do anything. Why should I? I thought it funny
just for a moment, you know, but I didn't really pay any
attention to it. I supposed he had gone upstairs. But then
when he didn't come down again Julia – "

"When I came in ten minutes later," Julia interrupted, "I
asked where he was, because once he sits down to read the
paper he usually doesn't move till he's finished it. After
another half-hour he hadn't turned up and I said again,
'Where can James be?' At first we thought he had gone
upstairs, but Marjorie said she had not heard him pass the
kitchen door, and you know you could scarcely go upstairs
without being heard. However, we supposed he must have
done so, but as time still went by and he did not come
down I got anxious and went up to look. He wasn't
upstairs: I both called and looked. Then we thought he
must have gone out. But I looked and found that all his
walking shoes were upstairs and all his hats in the hall. If he

had gone out it must have been without a hat and in his slippers. All the same, we went round the place, calling, but we could find no trace of him. He was not in the garage nor the greenhouse, nor anywhere about."

"Some patient," Campion suggested. "Are you sure the telephone didn't ring?"

"Absolutely certain. We couldn't have helped hearing it. Besides, with slippers and no hat!"

"He's gone in to Dagger or the Forresters, as I said," the doctor remarked again. "Ring them up on the ground that he's wanted on the telephone."

"Yes, do, Mrs Earle," Alice exclaimed. "You'll find that's what happened. You see, it's such a lovely night that he might easily walk a short distance in slippers and without a coat or hat. You'll find he'll turn up directly."

"I don't want to make a fuss about it," Julia declared, "because he'd be so annoyed. What you suggest is a good idea, Dr Campion. I'll ring up."

"I don't like it," said Alice in a low voice as Julia left the room. "I don't like it all. I never liked his colour. You know; *heart*. That high florid sort of colour always means something wrong with the heart. He's gone out and fallen somewhere and not been able to get up again. You'll have to search, Howard."

The doctor made a gesture of impatience. "My dear Alice," he grumbled, "do for pity's sake control your imagination. Can't a man go in to pass the time of day with a neighbour without raising the entire country? He's all right. Don't make such an unholy fuss."

"It's not making a fuss to take reasonable precautions." She turned from her brother. "Don't you see, Ursula? Don't *you* see, Flo? What I say is not making a fuss; it's *most* likely. No one goes off like that without a word. You wouldn't do it. I wouldn't do it. Even Howard wouldn't do it. Would you, Howard? Would you go – "

"He's not at the Forresters," came Julia's voice from the hall. "I'll try Colonel Dagger."

Campion moved out into the hall, possibly to escape his sister's catechism. The others slowly followed.

"Oh, is that Colonel Dagger?" they heard. "Is James there by any chance? Someone wants to speak to him on the telephone. He's gone out and I rather imagined he was going in to see you. No? Oh well, it doesn't matter. Thanks. So sorry to have troubled you."

"He hasn't been there," Julia went on as she replaced the receiver.

"Where else could he have gone?" Campion asked. "What about the golf club?"

"He would never have gone to the club in his slippers," declared Julia, "but I'll ring up all the same. No," she went on a few seconds later. "He's not been there."

"Is there no other place close by at which he might have called?"

"I don't think so," Julia returned anxiously. "No, I don't understand it. What do you think about it yourself, Dr Campion?"

"I don't think you need be in the least anxious, Mrs Earle. He's gone out for a stroll, and the night's so fine it has tempted him further than he intended. At the same time, if it would be an ease to your mind, we might have another look round. Of course it's just conceivable that he has tripped and fallen and perhaps not been able to walk home. If you would go through the house thoroughly again, I'd have a look outside."

"Hadn't we better divide and do the thing properly?" Alice suggested. "If you, Julia, and Ursula would do the house, the rest of us could help Howard outside. What do you think?"

This was agreed to and the two little parties set to work. Julia was now looking very frightened, and even Ursula was beginning to fear some mishap. Alice's theory did not seem at all impossible to her, and she would not have been very surprised to come on Earle at any moment, unconscious or even dead. She herself had often thought how like a heart subject he was.

Carefully she and Julia went from room to room. When they had finished no doubt remained. Earle definitely was not in the house.

They put on wraps and went out and joined the other searchers. The out-offices had been done without result – garage, car, electric power hut, greenhouse, tool-shed and summerhouse. So had the lawn and garden.

"When we're here," the doctor said (Ursula could see that he was making light of it to Julia), "when we're here we might as well look into the wood a little way. Are there any paths through it that Earle was accustomed to use?"

"There are paths of course; the usual mere tracks that cover the heath, but none that James would have gone along at night. In fact, he didn't like being in the wood at night; I've often heard him say so."

"Few people do," Campion returned. "All the same, the fine night might have tempted him. We'll just have a look."

He divided the surrounding wood into areas and his party into twos, allocating an area to each party. He himself undertook the road.

"I think we'd better have the car," he said to Ursula, who chanced to be his partner. "If I ran slowly you could examine the near side of the road while I looked at the other. He might have gone for a walk and felt faint and be resting on the bank."

They went for a couple of miles in each direction, returning to find that a search of the wood surrounding the house had yielded no better result. None of the party now made any pretence of being free from anxiety.

"There's half past eleven," said Julia, "and he disappeared at twenty to nine; nearly three hours ago. Something dreadful has happened. I'm frightened. What should we do?"

It was easy to ask the question; it was anything but easy to answer it. Everyone thought of the police; no one liked to suggest calling them in.

"Has he ever gone out like this before?" Flo Campion asked, as if in an effort to postpone the inevitable suggestion.

"Never," Julia declared. "James is good that way. He always says when he's going out and when I may expect him back. And if he can't come he always telephones."

"I cannot help thinking he has gone into some house," Campion put in. "Is there no one who could have called for him, say with a car?"

"Yes, Julia." Alice nodded emphatically. "That would explain the whole thing. Who might have called for him with a car?"

Julia shook her head. "No one," she declared. "That wouldn't account for it at all. James would not have gone off in a car without telling me. Besides, there was no car. I was in the kitchen at the time and the window was open, and if there had been a car I should have heard it."

"You mightn't have noticed it," Alice urged.

35

"Oh yes I should. The night was calm and everything was quiet. I should certainly have heard it. Marjorie agrees with me."

"Oh yes," said Marjorie, "there wasn't a car. I should have heard it too, and there simply wasn't one."

"Don't you lock the French window at night, Mrs Earle?" Campion asked. "You're sure it was open when he disappeared?"

"Oh yes, it was open. That was one of the first things we tried. We do lock it, of course, but not necessarily at dinnertime. Often it lies unfastened in the evening, but James always locks it before going to bed."

Campion cleared his throat nervously.

"I hardly like to suggest it, Mrs Earle," he said, "but I'm not sure that it mightn't be well if I were to run into Farnham and tell the police. We mustn't shut our eyes to the possibility of Earle's falling over something in the dark and perhaps twisting his ankle and being unable to return. The police would help in making a search in case something of that kind had happened. What do you all think?"

"I think he should go, Mrs Earle," Alice said at once. "I think we all felt that the police should be told, but none of us liked to say so. What do you think?"

Julia appeared unwilling to take so drastic a step. "I'd simply hate having the police in," she declared. "But if you all think it's the right thing, let's do it. You haven't said anything, Ursula. What do you think?"

For a moment Ursula did not reply. An unpleasant suspicion had for some time been shaping itself in her mind, a suspicion founded on the knowledge she had so unexpectedly gained during her visit to London. Had Earle really left St Kilda, but voluntarily? Had he slipped away according to some prearranged plan, to join the woman of the car? Was it really a case of desertion that they were considering? This solution had not occurred to the others, because they didn't know what she knew.

But if she were right, if Earle had quietly departed, would Julia want the police to be called in? Would she not rather wish to keep the unhappy affair private? Would she not prefer to give out that Earle had been called away on business, and perhaps afterwards herself move to some other locality where she would be a stranger?

Ursula saw that she was letting her imagination run away with her. She had no real reason to suppose her idea correct: Alice's theory of a heart attack was much more probable. However, she thought she ought to put the point to Julia before this decision about the police was taken. Could she get her alone?

"I think you should look again in his room before you make a move. There might be a note in an engagement book or something." She got up. "Come along, Julia, and I'll help you. We won't keep you others a moment."

Alice and Marjorie stared, but neither spoke, and Julia suffered herself to be led from the room. They went into Earle's study and Ursula, summoning all her courage, closed the door and turned to her friend.

"Dear Julia," she said, "I asked you to come away from the others because there's something that you should know before you decide about calling in the police." She hesitated. In spite of Julia's own little failings it wasn't going to be easy to suggest to her that her husband was unfaithful. Nor that he was callous enough to leave her in this cruel doubt as to his fate and her own. Suddenly Ursula saw that she had been wrong. Earle would never have done it. If he were infatuated with that other woman he might desert Julia for her, but he would at least have left a note telling his wife the truth.

But it was too late to change her mind now. Besides, Julia ought to know in any case.

"I'm afraid, my dear, you'll be very much hurt and upset by what I have to tell you, but I do think you ought to know. I don't think it has any connection with this affair, but it just possibly might have. When I went up to London last Wednesday" – And she went on and told in the simplest and most direct way just what she had seen. "What I thought, Julia, was this," she went on. "If by any chance he was momentarily overcome by his infatuation, it's just conceivable he might have gone off to see this woman, and in that case, would you like the police to be brought in? I thought you should know about it, so that you might be able to decide."

Ursula was surprised at the way her friend took the news.

"Dear Ursula," she said, "how you must have hated telling me that! But you needn't have minded. I didn't suspect anything of the kind, I admit. But I can't blame him. I may tell you now that we're talking in confidence that our marriage was a mistake. I don't think it was our fault; just we didn't suit each other." She paused, then went on in a burst of confidence: "If he hadn't looked elsewhere, I might have." Again she paused, as if regretting her admission, then continued in a tone of greater conviction: "But, Ursula, you're wrong. It's not that. If he had wanted to go to another woman he could have done so at any time without making a mystery about it. I do appreciate your telling me, but I'm sure you're wrong. No, what I'm really afraid of is his heart. His heart is not strong. He has gone out and got an attack and he's not able to come back. I think we should tell the police and I think we should organise a more thorough search."

Ursula, so far as she was concerned herself, was profoundly thankful. She had done a horrible duty because she believed it was her duty, and she had not lost her friend.

"Then by all means ask Dr Campion to go at once," she agreed. "If you feel that way, there's no time to be lost."

They returned to the others.

"We've not found anything," Julia told them, "and I think if you, Dr Campion, would be so good, the police should be told. As I was saying to Ursula, James' heart is not very strong and he may have become faint and be unable to come back. But I don't like your going off to Farnham at this hour. Why not telephone?"

"I thought it would be quicker if I had the car there to drive the men out, but of course they can get their own car. Yes, I'll telephone." Campion disappeared into the hall and they heard his muffled voice as he put through the call.

"I rang up Margaret also," he said to his sister, returning presently.

"Our servant, Mrs Earle," Alice explained. "She needn't wait up for us."

After what seemed an age, but what was really only a few minutes, the sounds of an approaching car became audible. It stopped at the door. Campion went out and the murmur of voices followed. Then he returned with two police officers, a sergeant and a constable. The sergeant saluted as they entered.

"This is Mrs Earle," said Campion. "Sergeant Sheepshanks has very kindly come out to help us."

"Dr Campion has told me what has taken place, madam," Sheepshanks began. "He says that while not diseased, Dr Earle's heart was not strong, and that you think he may have had an attack which would have prevented him returning?"

"That's putting it a little strongly," Julia answered. "I only suggested a heart attack because I can't explain his disappearance in any other way. I don't, of course, know anything about it."

"Quite so, madam." The sergeant nodded sagely. "Now before we go any further I should like a word or two with you. Perhaps you could give me an interview in another room? Just you, madam."

Campion moved forward. "But what about a search, sergeant?" he said. "If Dr Earle really is ill, every moment might be of value."

"I've not overlooked that, sir," Sheepshanks answered civilly; "but we'll get on better if we know just how we stand. Will you come along, madam?"

They disappeared, accompanied by the constable.

"He's got it into his mind that Earle has gone off voluntarily," Campion explained. "He said, 'You'll hear of him all right. He just wants a change of establishment. You'll find there'll be a letter from him in a day or two.' "

"Nonsense," Alice declared sharply. "If it were that, why didn't he leave a note? Besides, I don't think Dr Earle's that way inclined. And again, why didn't he take a hat and outdoor shoes?"

"That's what I said," Campion returned, "but it didn't seem to convince Sheepshanks. Well, he's here at all events. I wonder what he'll do."

Before anyone could reply the sergeant reappeared.

"We're going to have a search round the place," he said, "and if we find nothing we'll come out and have a better one as soon as it's daylight. Perhaps, sir, you could stay and give us a hand? The ladies may go to bed; there's nothing that they can do. Have you a torch in your car?"

This programme was carried out. Both sergeant and constable were quick and thorough. Armed with powerful torches they went over the entire ground surrounding the house, as well as following for a considerable distance the various paths through the wood. The sergeant also carefully examined the path from the French window and the road near the gate, but nowhere could they find any traces of either Earle or anyone else. If the man had dissolved into thin air he could not have more completely vanished.

It was getting on to two in the morning when Campion drove his party home. Nothing more could be done but wait for the morning, and though Julia declared she would not undress, all agreed there was no use in sitting up.

Before starting on his round next morning Campion drove back to St Kilda, to find the sergeant and three policemen already at work. But no faintest clue had so far rewarded their efforts. Earle had simply vanished without trace.

The search was kept up till nearly midday, and then Sergeant Sheepshanks took formal statements from each member of the household, with Julia's permission looking through Earle's papers. One of the questions he asked Ursula was whether she had ever had any suspicion that Earle might have been attached to or had relations with any other woman, and in view of the direct question, she very unwillingly told him what she had seen in London. Somewhat to her relief he didn't seem to think much of it, though he took details of the story. He left with a civil word of thanks for her information, but without any expression of his own opinion.

Slowly the hours of that day dragged away without bringing to light the slightest information about the missing man. Earle had utterly and completely vanished – vanished instantaneously. At one moment seated in his chair, settled down for the evening, entirely normal, dressed for the house: three minutes later, gone. Neither sight nor sound of his going: no trace left: no hint either of cause or method: no suggestion of motive: no explanation anywhere of any part of it. Spirited away! The old phrase seemed to take on a new meaning. It was like seeing the impossible happen before one's eyes.

Nor did the sergeant's prognostication prove correct. There was no letter from Earle, neither that day nor the next. No intimation of any kind was received to prove that he was still alive. Julia indeed was convinced that he was dead. She said that whatever her husband might or might not do, he would never have left her in such a painful state of doubt. Marjorie held the same view, and even Ursula found herself forced to a similar conclusion. Ursula had cancelled her departure, deciding to stay on with Julia for a few days longer.

What the police were doing, if anything, the ladies did not know. The sergeant had returned after lunch to Farnham, saying that he would keep them advised how things went on. But he had told them nothing.

Two days later, however, they found that the police had not been idle after all. A pleasant-looking, keen-eyed man of slightly under medium height called. He presented a card bearing the legend, "Detective Inspector French, CID, New Scotland Yard," and said he wished to ask some questions relative to the disappearance of Dr Earle.

Instantly to the inmates of the house the mystery grew darker and more sinister.

4

INSPECTOR FRENCH TAKES HOLD

About ten o'clock on the morning of that same day Inspector Joseph French had alighted from the train at Farnham Station and turned his steps towards police headquarters. He knew the town well, as also the local officers, having worked with them only a few years earlier in connection with a number of burglaries which had taken place in the surrounding country, and which were supposed to be the work of a gang from the East End.

He had had a rather humdrum existence since in the beginning of the year he had investigated that nasty case on the Whitness Widening. That case, in spite of its puzzles and anxieties, he had enjoyed. The railway atmosphere in which he had worked was to him a new and fascinating feature. He had become interested in the technical work of the Widening and had liked watching the slow progress of the job. Moreover, in spite of his calling, he had found the people down there in Dorset pleasant and friendly, and the hotel had been particularly comfortable. The weeks spent on the case had formed a welcome relief from the somewhat drab routine of Town.

So much, indeed, had he liked the district that when the blissful time of his summer holidays came round, he and Mrs French had spent them at Redchurch. There he had renewed his acquaintanceship with Lowell and Brenda

Vane, now Mrs Lowell, with Bragg, Pole, Ashe, Mayers, and the other people whose acquaintance he had made in the winter. Also, he had a walk over the Widening, admiring what had been done since his previous visit, and now seeing the *raison d'être* of a good many things he had not then understood.

Except for the break of the holiday, he had been engaged in London ever since the Widening case. Four seemingly endless months he had spent on a case of forged ten-shilling notes, thousands of which were passed out before he and his fellow-labourers succeeded in laying their hands upon the forgers. Then he had been on a murder in Whitechapel, a sordid affair without any features of interest, requiring for its clearing up dogged hard work, but neither skill nor intelligence. Lastly, he had just recovered two thousand pounds' worth of jewels, stolen from a Mayfair flat. Now he welcomed the instructions which seemed to promise a change of scene.

On reaching the police station he was smilingly saluted by the constable on duty, and shown at once to the room of Superintendent Sheaf.

"Hullo, inspector! Here you are," Sheaf greeted him, holding out a hand massive as an Epstein carving. "It's what I always say; no one who had ever been to Farnham can keep long away."

"Always glad, super, to come and give you a lift when you're in trouble," French rejoined slyly. They had become good friends, these two, and liked and respected each other.

"Oh," Sheaf returned, "so you think you're coming down to teach us our job, do you? Well, so that there'll be no mistake, I'd better tell you at once that you're not. You're coming to do a job for the Yard, in London. We'll tell you what to do and then you can go and do it." The superintendent held out a cigarette case. "Seriously, I think our trouble may lie in Town. It's not, I may tell you, a very satisfactory case. There may be nothing wrong. But there are certain suspicious circumstances, and after consultation with the Chief Constable we've decided it's worth while having the thing looked into."

"A disappearance, isn't it?"

"Yes; man called Earle. Lives or rather lived about four miles out in the country. Sergeant Sheepshanks was sent for in the night to help to look for him. There's mighty little evidence of any kind, but there is a certain amount of suspicion. We'll have Sheepshanks in and he'll tell you about it."

Superintendent Sheaf rang and presently the sergeant made his appearance. He also smiled at sight of French, and shook hands with some warmth.

"Now, sergeant," said Sheaf, "the inspector knows nothing of this case. Get ahead and tell him about it. Have a cigarette?"

The sergeant deposited his huge bulk on a chair, took and lit a cigarette, and addressed himself to French.

"About 12.15 on Monday morning last, sir, I was called out of bed by a 'phone from here. There was a message from Dr Campion, who lives at Binscombe, a couple of miles from Godalming. It stated – " And Sheepshanks repeated the story and described his visit to St Kilda, his search there during the night, his return next day and the further enquiries made. "There, sir," – he handed over some typewritten sheets – "are the statements of those concerned, so far as I was able to get them."

The man had spoken well and French was able to visualise the happenings almost as if he had been present.

"That's very clear, sergeant," he said. "Were you able to check up these statements?"

"In a general way, yes, sir. At least as far as I was able to go, I found no discrepancies."

French nodded and Sheaf struck in, "Better read the statements, French, and then we'll talk about it."

French did so while the local men conversed on other business. At last French signified that he had finished.

"Well," said Sheaf with a keen glance, "what does it look like to you?"

This was the sort of question which on principle French never answered. He was certainly not going to give an opinion until he had had time to think over the facts and come to a reasoned conclusion.

"I don't know," he said cautiously. "At first sight I should say this Earle had gone off to his lady friend in Town, but I see there are some objections to that theory: that is, assuming that all these statements are true."

"You're not going to commit yourself too irrevocably, are you? Still, speaking quite broadly, does nothing strike you about it?"

"In what way, super?"

"Nothing does, you mean. Well now, look here: is it *likely?* The whole story, I mean. Just think of it. Assume first that Earle intended to disappear. Would he go off in his house-shoes and without a hat or coat? Would he go off without saying where he was going to; I mean, telling some plausible story? More important still, would he not have gone away openly, say for the night? Do you see what I'm getting at?"

"You mean that he was making things unnecessarily difficult for himself?"

"Quite; much more difficult than they need have been. According to this story he chose a method which would arouse suspicion and cause enquiry. At once, I mean. Why should he do that when he could equally easily have got twelve or twenty-four hours' start, or even a week? He would know enough to understand that the hotter the trail, the more likelihood of its being followed up."

French crushed out the stub of his cigarette and produced his own case.

"It's a point, certainly," he admitted as the others helped themselves.

"If you or I had been Earle and had wanted to make another start, what would we have done? I fancy both of us would have said to Mrs Earle: 'I'm going to play golf today,' or 'I'm going up to Town and I won't be back till dinner.' That would have given him another twelve hours. See the difference? Acting in that way he could have been across the Channel without a question being raised, whereas if he did what these statements suggest he would have been spotted at the boats from the details we sent early on Monday."

French amiably agreed that there was a good deal in the superintendent's argument. He was always pleased to engage in discussions of this kind, for he had found that in allowing other people to theorise on his cases he occasionally came on an idea of value. The more thought Sheaf had put into the affair and the more he could be induced to air his conclusions, the more of the preliminary spade-work French would be saved.

"There's a good deal of testimony backing up Mrs Earle's statement," French asserted to draw the superintendent further.

Sheaf shook his head. "That's just what there's not, French. Don't you see? There's only the sister's. The maid was out and the visitor, Miss Stone, was with the Campions."

French hesitated. "You don't mean," he said at last, "that you suspect those two ladies of making away with the man?"

"I suspect no one," Sheaf returned. "But wait a moment. When Sheepshanks came in that Monday morning we had a talk about it. We considered these points. I told him to go out again and have another look round. As he's told you, he did so. I don't think he's told you all he got."

Sheepshanks looked up with a protesting expression.

"No, you didn't," the superintendent insisted, "but I will now. First of all he got what you've seen in the statements. From Mrs Earle, unwillingly, that she and her husband did not always see eye to eye about things. Then from the maid that relations were often very strained indeed, and Sheepshanks imagines that was putting it mildly. From Miss Lawes, the sister, that she was very fond of her sister and that she was a novelist, and of course that business in London from the visitor, Miss Stone."

"What has Miss Lawes being a novelist to do with it?" French asked, for the first time not seeing exactly where the other was leading.

"Probably nothing, but don't be in such a darned hurry. Now here's what Sheepshanks, for some reason best known to himself, didn't tell you. It'll throw light on what I've been saying. He got permission from Mrs Earle to look through Earle's papers. He found a will. Earle had left everything to his wife."

Sheepshanks, covered with confusion at his lapse, muttered an apology. French at once passed the affair off with a joke, thereby winning the sergeant's undying goodwill.

"I don't think anything follows from that, super," he continued, once again to draw the other. "It's not uncommon for a husband to make a will of the kind."

"Quite. And it's not uncommon for a man who is running another woman to change that sort of will."

French shook his head. "I don't follow exactly. Does that not mean that you do suspect Mrs Earle?"

"No, but I'll tell you what it means. It means that there is enough suspicion to make it necessary that we should be sure."

"I agree. And yet does it not occur to you that the mere improbability of the story tells in favour of the ladies? They would never surely have invented these unlikely details. They would have said nothing about the affair for a considerable time, then perhaps would have explained that Earle had gone to London for a few days, but that his return was overdue. It's the argument you used yourself about a deliberate disappearance: they would have waited till the scent grew cold."

"I realise that all right," Sheaf returned, "and you may be quite correct. That, however, is where the sister's writing *may* come in. If she is good at inventing plots she might have foreseen that argument of yours, and raised a fuss and advised us simply as a safeguard. If they had found a good place to hide the body, it would have been a pretty good safeguard too. I don't push that; it may be nonsense. All I say is, there's a case for enquiry."

"I agree," French repeated.

"On the other hand," Sheaf went on, "Earle may simply have deserted his wife for the other woman, and that is where your connection with the Yard comes in: we couldn't handle that part of it here."

"Right, super, I'll carry on. I think all I still want to know is what steps you've actually taken. You said you were having the cross-Channel boats watched?"

"Yes, we sent a description to the pier men; also a general description to all stations. You better check that; you may be able to get more details. That's all we've done."

"You haven't touched the man's finances?"

"No."

"It would be interesting to know if he had withdrawn any considerable sum recently."

"Quite; that's up to you. Any help you want you'll get to the best of my ability. Now if you want to have a talk with the sergeant, go ahead. Only take him away out of this."

"Come along, sergeant," said French, "we're not popular here any longer. I don't know that there's very much I want to ask you," he went on as they settled themselves in another room. "What's your own idea about the affair?"

"He's gone to that woman in London, if you ask me, sir. I don't think Mrs Earle and the sister have done him in, but of course it's possible. Tell you the truth, sir, I don't see where they could have hidden the body."

"You don't? I thought that might be a difficulty. Tell me, how complete was your search? Did you go over much of the wood?"

"I went over it carefully close to the house, say a hundred yards in from the boundary fence all round. It's a slow job, you know, sir; the place is full of thick undergrowth and it's hard to push one's way through. But I went along the paths for half a mile or more: further than those women could have carried the body."

"No sign of anything being dragged through the undergrowth?"

"No, sir, I looked particularly for that."

"Had the car been taken out?"

"I don't think so, sir. I felt the radiator and it was cold."

"Who is this man Campion?"

"One of the Godalming doctors, sir. He's a partner of this Dr Earle who's disappeared, though Earle has practically given up the practice. Campion took another partner some years ago who lives in the town and does the night calls, and Campion moved out to the country at Binscombe. I'm told they have a good practice between them."

French got up. "Well, sergeant, if there's anything else I want, I'll come to you. I'll go out to the place now and have a look round. Can you lend me a bicycle?"

"Certainly, sir."

French enjoyed his ride out through The Sands to Hampton Common. He was fairly familiar with the district, not only because of his previous visit to Farnham, but because these Surrey uplands from Leith Hill to Haslemere had formed the venue of many of his Sunday excursions with Mrs French. The more he had explored the country, the more it had appealed to him. He loved the tree-edged outlines of its successive ridges, showing up solid one behind the other like drop scenes in a theatre. He loved its quaint villages with their old red-roofed half-timbered buildings and their still older churches. He liked following the narrow twisting deep-cut lanes. But most of all he delighted in the heaths, wild and uncultivated, areas of sand and heather and birches and pines over which one could wander as entirely cut off from sight or sound of human habitation as if one was exploring a desert island.

On reaching St Kilda French began work by making himself familiar with the house and grounds. The house was set back some seventy or eighty feet from the road, from which it was screened by a thick belt of shrubs. It faced towards Farnham, that is, parallel to the road. The isolation of the place at once struck French, as it had struck Ursula on her first visit. On three sides was the wood, cutting off the view like an impenetrable curtain, while on the fourth side the outlook was equally impeded by the belt of shrubs. In the immediate proximity of the house the trees had been cleared and a small garden and lawn had been made.

The house was small and compactly planned. On the ground floor were four main rooms. The sitting room from which Earle was alleged to have vanished was in the angle between front and side. It was a good-sized room with a square bow giving on to the drive in front and a French window facing the road. Across the hall opposite to it was the dining room, behind which was a small study or den, used solely by Earle. The kitchen was in the remaining corner of the house, behind the sitting room.

French began actual work in the sitting room. First he turned his attention to the French window. It was unlocked, as it had been on the Sunday evening, and he found he could open and close it silently. Earle could therefore have passed out without being heard by the ladies.

"Were the curtains drawn?" he asked.

"Were they, Julia?" Marjorie repeated. "Yes, they were," she went on; "I remember. The curtains of the French window were drawn, but not those of the bow."

"That's correct," Julia confirmed. "We usually pulled the long ones, because you can see in a little bit from the road through the bushes. But no one can see in from the front, and we seldom covered up the bow."

French nodded. If then someone had called secretly for Earle, he could have seen that no one else was in the room before attracting the man's attention.

"And your kitchen?" French went on. "Were the curtains pulled there?"

"No; it looks out at the back towards the wood."

"Were this room and the kitchen the only two lighted up?"

"And the hall, yes."

"I'm afraid I shall have to have a look over the house, and, if I may, over Dr Earle's papers."

"You can go anywhere you like, and if you want us we'll be here."

After a hasty lunch of sandwiches French began a detailed search of the house. He was soon convinced that Earle's body could not have been hidden there on the Sunday night. Miss Stone had searched as well as the sisters, and it was impossible to conceive of all three of them being privy to a murder. If therefore Earle had been done to death by his womenfolk, they had managed to dispose of the body outside the house before the arrival of the Campion party at 10.10.

French did not waste time examining the grounds or wood. He felt that any improvement on Sheepshanks' search would involve a proper organisation and a considerable number of men. He therefore went to Earle's study, and began to go through the man's papers.

There was no safe, but in one of the drawers of the small roll-top desk French found a steel despatch box, the key of which was in another drawer. In it was the will, Earle's bank-book, a cheque-book, some miscellaneous papers, and fourteen pounds ten in notes.

Having checked Sheepshanks' statement as to the contents of the will, French turned to the bank-book. It had been made up to a fortnight previously and French put it in his pocket, intending to get the entries brought up to date. Then he went through the miscellaneous papers, but without coming on anything of interest. All he found, both in the bank-book and elsewhere, was just what he might have expected to find in the case of a man of Earle's position.

Seating himself at the study desk, he then called in each member of the household and formally took their statements. This unavoidably overlapped what Sheepshanks had already done, but French preferred to have the whole of his information at first hand from the start. Having satisfied himself that Sheepshanks' notes were correct, he proceeded to try to get some further information on his own account.

He began with Julia. "Now, madam, in this case I must consider various possibilities. And first there is the question of voluntary disappearance. I am sorry to suggest this, but it can't be overlooked. Do you consider Dr Earle left here deliberately?"

"I am sure he did not," Julia said decisively. "Surely if he had intended to do that he would have put on shoes and a hat? Besides, he had settled down for the evening."

"Quite so, but if for some reason he had wished to leave secretly, might he not have done these things as a blind?"

"I don't think so. It would have been most unlike Dr Earle, who was not at all secretive. Besides, why should he have wished to do such a thing?"

"Well, that's what I was going to ask you," said French. "Can you suggest no motive?"

"None whatever."

"Probably you're right, madam," French said smoothly. "Now tell me: Did you recently notice anything abnormal in Dr Earle's manner?"

Julia hesitated. "I think I did," she answered, without the decision of her former replies. "I scarcely like to say so, because I'm really not very sure, but it was my impression that for some days he had something on his mind."

"He seemed worried?"

"Yes, worried."

"When did you first notice the change?"

"I don't know; four or five days ago, I should think."

"Was it more pronounced on the Sunday than previously?"

"No, I don't think so."

"You noticed no difference?"

"None."

French nodded. "Now," he went on, "I'm sorry to have to refer to another unpleasant subject, but unfortunately it's my duty. You know that Dr Earle met a lady in Town on Thursday last?"

Julia's face grew harder. "Well, and why shouldn't he?" she asked aggressively.

"Did he tell you he had done so?"

"Why should he? He's not a child. Neither of us are children. Why should we tell each other every little trifle?"

"Did he tell you he had played golf that day?"

Julia hesitated. "I really didn't ask him," she said at last.

"Possibly not, madam," French said gravely, "but did he tell you?"

"I don't see what that has to do with his disappearance or that it's any business of yours."

"In that case, madam, I'll explain it to you." French's manner was firm but kindly. "It has been suggested, with what truth I do not know, that Dr Earle was tired of his life here and that he wished to give it up and start another establishment elsewhere. I must test this suggestion. I must know whether he told you he had been playing golf at the time at which he really was meeting the lady, as this may throw a light on his motives."

Julia was very unwilling to speak, but at last she resentfully admitted that she knew nothing whatever about the lady, and that Earle had stated directly on that Thursday morning that he was going to play golf, and in the evening that he had done so.

French intended his questions to be a little more subtle than they actually appeared. Not only was he anxious for the direct answers, but he wanted to see their effect on Julia. If she were party to her husband's murder, she might naturally be expected to make the most of any circumstance which would suggest his voluntary disappearance.

But Julia made no such attempt. She took the line that if her husband wished to meet a lady in London, he had a perfect right to do so without consulting her, but that in any case it was no business of French's.

"Was there, or had there been recently, any disagreement or unpleasantness between your husband and yourself?" went on French.

"Nothing of the kind!" Julia answered sharply. "If you think Dr Earle left home because he wasn't happy here you may put the idea out of your mind. You'll only be wasting your own and everyone else's time."

"That's really what I wanted to be sure of," French returned soothingly. "Very well, that's one point dealt with. Now another: what about money? Was there any financial trouble which might have been weighing on Dr Earle's mind?"

"I don't think so; not that I know of at all events. But I can't answer you there because Dr Earle looked after his business himself. Why don't you go to his bank? They'll tell you."

"I'm going to ask you, madam, for an authorisation to the manager to give me this information."

"Yes, I don't mind letting you have that."

"Thank you. Now I should like to know what letters or other messages Dr Earle received during the last day or two before his disappearance. Can you help me there?"

"I don't think so. I didn't notice his receiving any unusual letters, nor did he tell me of such. You can look in his desk."

"I have done so, madam, without success."

"Then I'm afraid I can't help you."

"You don't know if he received a telegram or telephone message?"

"Not to my knowledge."

"Then callers, madam. Can you let me have a list of everyone who came to the house, say on Friday, Saturday and Sunday?"

"To see him?"

"To see anyone, if you please."

"No one came to see him. I don't see how my callers affect the matter."

"I don't expect they do, madam, but it's a routine I am bound to go through. If this information was not given in my report, my superiors would want to know why."

"Oh, very well. On Friday there was no one. I don't suppose even you want details of the calls of the milkman and the various errand boys? That day we went to see some people at Eastbourne, and my husband came to drive, as I don't like driving in the dark. On Saturday" – she paused in thought or apparent thought – "on Saturday I don't think there was anyone either. Oh yes, Mr Slade, who lives next door, looked in for a moment with a book he had promised to lend me. He only stayed a minute or two. Then on Sunday the Campions came, Dr and the two Miss Campions."

"Thank you, madam, yes. I've heard of their call. That was all?"

"That was all."

"One last question. You said, I think, that Dr Earle was reading the *Observer* just before he disappeared. Do you happen to have the paper?"

"I think it's still in the sitting-room," Julia answered. "Nothing has been disturbed in any of the rooms, in deference to the request of the sergeant."

"Perhaps we might go in and look?"

They went into the sitting room and found the paper, still on the chair in which Earle had been seated.

"Thank you, Mrs Earle. That's all at present. Now could I see Miss Lawes?"

To Marjorie French repeated practically all the questions he had asked Julia. He made it a practice in all his cases to ask the same questions of everyone concerned. It was tedious, of course, but he believed there was always the chance of learning something fresh from the comparison of the different viewpoints, apart altogether from the possibility of exposing a lie. In this case, as it happened, he found his method justified. From Marjorie he obtained two involuntary hints.

The first was what Sheepshanks had already learnt: that conditions in the household were not of the happiest.

French seized on to Marjorie's injudicious remark like a leech and stuck to it till he had learned all there was to be known about it. When he had finished, he was satisfied that the Earles were no longer in love, if they ever had been, but now merely tolerated each other in the spirit of trying to make the best of a bad bargain.

The second hint which Marjorie involuntarily gave him was when he came to discuss recent callers. At once he saw that she did not like Reggie Slade. With an almost automatic reaction French seized on this point also. Who was Mr Slade? Had she seen much of him? Oh, as much as that? Then how often had he called, say, in the last fortnight? Seven times? To see Mrs Earle? H'm. He liked Mrs Earle? Yes, and she liked him? But surely if she didn't like him she wouldn't have seen him so often? Oh, if it was business, what had he called about? Something about his car on one occasion? Oh, his car? H'm. H'm. Quite so. Had Miss Lawes ever known Mrs Earle to go out in Mr Slade's car? Certainly, there was no reason on earth why she shouldn't, French was merely asking the question. She had? Yes, and when? Oh, on last Thursday? The day Dr Earle was in Town? And on different other occasions also? Yes, quite so.

When at last French knocked off and returned to Farnham, he felt satisfied with his progress. It looked as if at least the motive for the affair would present no difficulty. There was unhappiness at home, there was the matter of the lady in London, and it might well be that this Reggie Slade would prove a further factor in the case.

But was Earle the prime mover or the victim in the affair? Up to the present French had obtained no light on this fundamental question. As he went up to bed in the local hotel he fully realised that he was in point of fact only at the beginning of his troubles.

– 5 –

THE PROBLEM

Next morning French rode out again to St Kilda to resume his interrogations. This time Ursula was the sufferer.

As before he began by repeating the questions he had already asked. But from Ursula he obtained no fresh information.

"Have you met a Mr Reggie Slade?" he went on.

"Once I met him, yes."

"Only once. Where was that, Miss Stone?"

"In the garden here."

"Was Mrs Earle present?"

"Not at first, but she came up afterwards."

French had this elaborated, then continued: "You know, I suppose, that Mrs Earle and Mr Slade are very close friends?"

Ursula didn't know anything about that. French raised his eyebrows.

"This is a serious matter, please remember, Miss Stone," he said gravely. "You may have to swear in court to everything you are now saying. Do you really mean to tell me that you had no idea that those two were, to put it mildly, particularly interested in each other?"

Ursula was no match for him, and the whole scene in the garden came out; the look she had surprised on Slade's face, Julia's treatment of him, even Marjorie's remarks later on. French noted everything systematically, then went on to Ursula's visit to Town and her seeing Earle driving with the lady.

"You will see, Miss Stone," he explained when he had obtained her statement, "that we shall have to find this lady. She may be able to throw some light on Dr Earle's disappearance. Will you please describe her as best you can."

"She was rather ordinary looking, if the truth be told. Youngish; thirty, I dare say, or perhaps less. As far as I could see, she looked both pleasant and clever. Her nose was good – fairly long and straight with a high bridge – Grecian, in fact. Her chin was rounded. That's in profile; I didn't see her full face. I'm afraid that's all I noticed."

"What you've told me is quite helpful. How was she dressed?"

"She had a round grey hat with a red brooch in front; rather more of a toque shape than is worn now. Her coat was of grey cloth and she had grey shoes and stockings."

"Wealthy looking?"

"By no means: quite the reverse."

French was pleased. This description was better than he could have hoped for. That Grecian nose would be a help. It was something distinctive, not like the usual "medium height with dark hair and eyes", which covered about a third of the women in the country. And a lucky thing that she had been seen by a woman! A man might have vaguely noticed the grey clothes, but he would never have assimilated the semi-toque with the red brooch.

"That's excellent, Miss Stone," French approved. "Now can you tell me how Dr Earle was dressed?"

"As he left that morning: a sports hat and yellowish-brown overcoat."

From the servant Lucy Parr, whom French next interrogated, he obtained little except some further confirmation that relations between the master and the mistress were often a good deal strained. Her sympathies, French was interested to notice, were entirely with Earle and against Julia. According to Lucy, Earle was kindly and unassuming and always ready to smooth troubled waters, even to the extent of giving up his rights. Julia on the other hand was dictatorial and overbearing and very exacting. Evidently Lucy thought Earle had a pretty thin time with his wife. She also believed that he knew all about the Slade affair and was very much worried by it.

This completed the preliminary taking of statements, but before turning to the next business, French made sure that he had all the usual routine information; a detailed description of Earle and the other members of the household, with photographs; samples of Earle's handwriting; lists, so far as these could be compiled, of his friends and acquaintances; a note of how he spent his time and the places he was in the habit of visiting: in fact, all those commonplace sort of details which might at some future part of the enquiry become important. Earle's bank and his solicitor French already knew, from the bank-book and the will respectively.

The day was slipping quickly away, but there was still a good deal that French wished to do at St Kilda and he hurried on with his work. Going to Earle's bedroom, he made a rapid search, but without result. When, however, he continued this process with the overcoats hanging in the hall, he found a scrap of paper which he thought might be useful.

It was in the right side pocket of a yellowish-brown overcoat – the only yellowish-brown overcoat that was there

– and was rolled into a tiny ball, the result evidently of the absent-minded movement of the owner's fingers. French carefully unrolled it. It was of thin yellowish paper, about 2½ inches by an inch, clearly the torn-off end of some docket. Near the top was a number, printed by a stamp, not fount type, through which the paper had been torn, but of which the last four digits were 1153. Below that in faint pencil was the latter portion of a date, the current month, October, and the year being given, but the day of the month being torn off. Below in heavy capitals was printed the word "FEE", with after it in a little square and also in heavy black the amount "6d". In small type near the bottom of the docket were the ends of three lines of printing, reading respectively:

> wner's entire
> ponsible for any
> ough every care

evidently some note about liability.

What was it? Not a railway cloakroom ticket, as this would have been required to obtain the deposited articles. Not a ticket of admission to some show: it would have been handed up on entrance, besides such tickets were usually of thicker paper. A shop receipt? Somehow it didn't look like one.

French could think only of a parking-ticket. Most parks charge 6d. for two hours' parking, and the dockets bear a serial number, usually printed by an automatic hand-stamp. All bear a place for the date, and all a phrase about cars being left at the owner's risk. Moreover, its being a parking-ticket would fit in with its being found torn and rolled up in an outside coat side pocket. On parking Earle would naturally have thrust the docket in his pocket, because though the sum was small, it was a receipt for his money. In the nervous absent-minded way people do, he might have torn it up and rolled the pieces in little balls. In drawing out his hand some of these little balls might easily have been carried out, leaving the one which French had found.

As French put the fragment away in his pocketbook he felt particularly pleased. If he could find the park – and he was sure he could – it might prove a valuable clue. The chances that the ticket had been obtained on the Thursday of Earle's visit to Town were high. In the first place, less than a third of October had elapsed; Sunday was only the 9th. It was unlikely therefore that Earle had visited many parks during this period. Moreover, the fact that the fragment had been in a yellowish-brown overcoat – the coat the man was wearing on that Thursday – seemed more hopeful still.

French began to wonder what steps he should take to find the park. Then he thought the problem could stand. He must get on with his work at St Kilda before it got dark.

Having taken the number and description of Earle's car, a Morris-Cowley saloon, PE 2157, French turned to his next item. He had brought in his case a powerful electric light with flex and lamp-holder plug. With this he went from room to room, examining every inch of the carpets, rugs, chairs and other furniture, searching in the most thorough way for marks which might prove to be blood. But nowhere could he find any.

One thing puzzled him. Though Julia had said Earle was writing a book on some medical subject, he, French, had found nothing among the man's papers referring to any such activity. French again questioned Julia on the point and found she had not actually seen any of her husband's manuscript. She had taken it for granted that when he was working, it was at the book. French therefore found himself forced to assume she was mistaken.

It was close on eight o'clock when French, tired from his long day, rode back into Farnham. After a long-deferred meal, he settled himself in the lounge to complete the one or two things which still remained to be done that night.

From his notes he produced a revised description of Earle and a somewhat sketchy one of the London lady, and with a photograph of Earle, posted them to the Yard for insertion in the list of wanted persons. Then he turned to the parking-docket.

Miss Stone had seen Earle and the lady in Seymour Place. That was at 12.30 and they were going westwards. Earle arrived home that evening about seven or a few minutes after. Was there anything to suggest where he could have gone to in the meantime?

French ruminated, puffing slowly at his pipe. The only points he had were these hours and the fact that the car was heading west. Not much to go on, certainly! However, let him see what he could do.

In the first place had the pair left Town at all? French thought so, first because of the general balance of probabilities; and second, because the parking-ticket was paper. He remembered that the tickets of most London parks were printed on thin card. Neither of these arguments was conclusive, but both indicated a preliminary search outside London.

Falling back then on the question of time. From 12.30 to 7 was 6½ hours. What had to be fitted into that period?

Well, he thought it was not too much to assume that Earle had brought the lady back to Town before he left for home. Now Earle's return journey from London to St Kilda would take him about 1½ hours. Deduct that from the 6½ hours, and it left 5 hours from London to London.

Then what about meals? During this 5 hours it was pretty certain that the travellers had had lunch and tea. How long would these take?

Not less than an hour for lunch and half an hour for tea, and probably longer for both. However, say 1½ hours for meals. That from 5 hours would leave 3½ hours.

French smoked slowly on and then another point occurred to him. It seemed reasonable to suppose these meals had been taken in a hotel or restaurant. Earle might of course have bought luncheon and tea baskets, but most elderly men consider these a nuisance and prefer properly served meals indoors. On the whole French thought a hotel more likely. But if they had gone to a hotel, why had Earle paid for parking? Hotels and restaurants park free of charge the cars of customers. Therefore did it not look as if the travellers had, after lunching, driven on to some other place at which they carried out their business?

For some time French thought over this. It did not seem to be leading anywhere. Then he dropped it and considered another point.

It was unlikely that Earle would pay for parking for a shorter time than, say, an hour. This was of course guesswork; still, see where it led. An hour off the 3½ left would reduce it to 2½.

If then French were correct, 2½ hours only were left for the journey to and from London: or say, roughly, a little over an hour each way. This meant that the parking-place must lie within about an hour's run from London.

An hour's run in the crowded traffic of the suburbs would not mean much more than 30 miles. To the west this would include Windsor or Maidenhead, or at the outside Marlow or Henley, or places correspondingly situated more north or south. French decided to try these districts first. If a search of them failed, a more extended area could be embraced.

Finally he wrote another letter to the Yard, asking that a copy of the ticket fragment be sent to all the police stations within a radius of 30 miles of London, to the north-west, west and south-west. The police were to try to find the park from which it had been issued, and if they succeeded, were to check their work by seeing if the car No. PE 2157 appeared on any of the carbon blocks for the date in question.

Feeling he had done a good day's work, French went out to post his letter, then after a look at the evening paper, he turned in.

Next morning he was early at it again. The most urgent thing now was to try and get some light on Earle's finances, and as soon as the banks opened French presented himself at Floyd's in Farnham and asked for the manager. The letter which Julia Earle had given transformed Mr Clayton into a valuable ally. He made no difficulty about telling French all he knew.

Unfortunately this did not amount to a great deal, and yet it had its value. Everything Mr Clayton had to say was negative. Earle got most of his money from investments, though the small remains of his practice still produced a little. Dividends and warrants had been coming in regularly, ever since Earle had transferred his account from Godalming some six years earlier. Beyond the drop in values universal during the slump, there had been no recent change in his income. The man's outgo had also remained normal. In fact, from the financial point of view, there was nothing to indicate that Earle had contemplated any drastic or unusual action. His current account stood at some £100, and there was £700 odd on deposit receipt. In the ordinary course a fair sum was shortly due. Certainly no large sum had recently been withdrawn, as would have been likely had Earle intended to disappear.

Of course this did not prove that Earle had not realised his capital, but French had come across records of a number of dealings with a stockbroker while going through the man's desk, and none of these suggested anything of the kind. This of course was not conclusive either: Earle might have secretly consulted some other broker. But French did not see why he should. If the doctor had realised his capital, there was nothing to be gained by employing one man of business rather than another.

Systematically French turned to his next enquiry. Taking a bus to Guildford and thence to Merrow, he found the secretary of the Golf Club, and showing his credentials, asked for a little confidential information. Could he tell him whether Dr James Earle, of St Kilda, Hampton Common, Farnham, had been on the links on the previous Thursday?

The secretary knew Earle. He was not a member, but had played as a visitor on different occasions. The secretary did not, however, know whether he had been there on the day in question, but he would find out. He vanished, returned presently, and said that no one had seen Earle. It was impossible, he added, that the doctor could have been on the links unknown to his staff.

Up to the present the actions taken by French had either been dictated by routine or were such as were obviously required by the circumstances. But now he had reached the end of these enquiries. He felt therefore that the time had come to take a preliminary survey of the case, so that he might decide the most productive lines on which to continue working. Accordingly he returned to his hotel, lit the fire in his room, and settled down to take stock of his position.

So far as he could see, there were three possible solutions to the mystery: Earle had either disappeared voluntarily, or he had met with an accident, or he had been kidnapped or murdered.

The accident theory seemed to him most unlikely, but for the sake of completeness he summarised his conclusions on the matter.

According to this suggestion, Earle had left the sitting room by the French window on some possibly perfectly innocent business and while carrying it out he had had a heart seizure, or had fallen and hurt himself so that he could not return, or had been knocked down by a car on the road.

Any of these mishaps were of course possible, but French rejected them all on the same ground: that they did not account for the disappearance of Earle's body. The only exception was that if the man had been knocked down by a car, he might have been taken to hospital. But this was an exception in name rather than reality. If a motorist had stopped to run his victim to a hospital, he would have reported the accident to the police.

The only doubtful point under this heading was whether Sergeant Sheepshanks' search had embraced a sufficient area of the wood. French noted to go into the matter with the sergeant and if necessary to organise a further search.

Included under the heading of accidents was the possibility that Earle was suffering from loss of memory. This, however, seemed out of the question, as there had been nothing to suggest such a thing in the man's previous state of health.

French did not really believe in the accident theory and he passed on rapidly to what he considered was the real crux of the affair: Had Earle disappeared voluntarily, or had he been murdered?

When Sheaf had been discussing this point the arguments in favour of kidnapping or murder had seemed to French stronger than those for a voluntary disappearance. He therefore took murder first and began with the details of the actual happening.

In the first place Earle had made no apparent preparations for a voluntary disappearance. It was a cold night, but he hadn't taken either a coat or a hat. Still more remarkable, he was wearing thin slippers. These were not evening shoes – the Earles did not dress when alone, and never for supper on Sunday night. They were heel-less slippers of soft brown leather: quite unsuitable for walking on anything but a carpet or boarded floor. It was inconceivable that Earle could have intended to go any distance in that get-up.

This argument was strongly reinforced by French's researches into the man's finances. A voluntary disappearance meant starting life all over again in some new place. For such a start Earle would require money, a substantial and regular income. But all the evidence French had yet obtained indicated that Earle had made no such provision.

Then there was the argument which Superintendent Sheaf had used; that if Earle had intended to disappear, he would have gone off openly, saying that he would be back at a given time. The man must have known that the longer he could postpone enquiry, the safer he would be. He could have reached the Continent or even America before his disappearance was reported. Why then should he have adopted a plan which would have raised an immediate hue and cry? French simply did not believe that he would have done so.

Lastly there was the question of Earle's manner. If he had intended to take such a revolutionary step as to disappear, surely some excitement would have shown in his manner? All concerned had noticed that he had been depressed or worried for some days beforehand, but all agreed that this was not more marked on the Sunday than formerly. Could Earle have so completely hidden the fact that on that evening he was about to undertake something of tremendous importance? Here again French did not believe he could have done it.

Provisionally assuming then that Earle had been kidnapped or murdered, could French think of anyone who might have had a motive?

In this at least there was no difficulty. His wife, Julia Earle, had a double motive, if not indeed a triple motive. First, if she was really carrying on a serious flirtation with this man Slade, she would want Earle out of her way. Secondly, and this was even more convincing, if she knew that Earle was in love with the lady in London – and wives do know these things – she would be afraid that he might alter his will in this stranger's favour. Thirdly, Julia might have been utterly fed up with Earle and have hated the very sight of him. This of course was mere guesswork, and French gave it no real weight.

And if Julia had motive, she most certainly had opportunity. She was alone with her sister in the house. The servant was out; the visitor had gone over to these people Campion. What easier than to give her husband poison or a narcotic in his food at dinner, and when he should be helpless to carry him out into the wood and there where no marks would be left on carpets or chairs, kill him with some heavy tool and hide his body? Julia Earle was a strongly built woman and her husband small and of poor physique.

Alternatively, if Julia had not committed the murder, was it not possible that Slade had done so? If Slade were the kind of man he had been pictured, and if he were really so much in love with Julia as had been suggested, he would in all probability have murdered for her. And so far as French knew to the contrary, Slade would also have had opportunity. Could he not have come to the window on that Sunday night, and seeing Earle was alone in the room, have beckoned him out, knocked him on the head and carried him off, disposing of the body somewhere in the wood?

All this of course was the purest guesswork, but it represented a necessary line of research, and that was all French wanted at the moment. He noted that he must find out a lot more about Slade and check up his movements on the Sunday evening.

So much for the possibilities of murder. French turned next to consider the question of a voluntary disappearance.

As he did so he was surprised to find that most of the arguments which he had used to prove murder could be interpreted equally in support of a voluntary disappearance. He went over them in order.

If Earle intended to disappear he might well have tried to disguise the fact by creating the impression that he had been murdered. He might have left in slippers and without a coat or hat just for this reason. Walking-shoes and a coat and hat, specially bought for the occasion, could easily have been hidden close by, and could have been assumed on leaving the house.

French still thought that Earle would never have gone off voluntarily without having made sure of a proper income. But he now saw that this did not necessarily depend on Floyd's bank in Farnham. Earle might easily have had another account in some other bank, possibly under an assumed name. Here at all events was another line of investigation.

Sheaf's argument about the reporting of the affair also cut both ways. If Earle had been murdered, the murderer or murderers would never have called in the police on the night of the crime. Julia, if guilty, would have waited for ten or twelve days, and then when the trail was old would have come forward with a story of how Earle had gone for a week to Town.

With regard then to Earle's manner. Did the fact that the man had obviously had something on his mind for several days, not mean that he was contemplating a disappearance? It was at least more likely than that he was contemplating his approaching murder! And might the alleged lack of increase of excitement on the Sunday not simply be due to want of observation on the part of the other members of the household?

Lastly, there was the question of motive. Here at all events there was no difficulty. Earle was unhappy in his home. His wife was disagreeable and overbearing and had ceased to love him, if indeed she had ever done so. Moreover, she was in love with, or at least carrying on a flirtation with, another man. He himself had found elsewhere the comfort and the sympathy his wife had failed to give him. Why should he not go where he would get this sympathy and so give both his wife and himself another bid for happiness?

To the murder theory, moreover, French now saw two objections. The first was Marjorie Lawes. If Julia were guilty, or if Julia and Slade together were guilty, what about Marjorie? Was it conceivable that she would be a party to the murder? French could scarcely bring himself to believe it.

The other difficulty was the hiding of the body. Whether Julia or Slade were guilty, this difficulty obtained. French did not see how it could have been met.

On the whole, on trying to balance his results, French saw that as yet he had evolved nothing conclusive. His cogitations had brought him to the same conclusion as had Sheaf's: that either murder or voluntary disappearance was possible.

His time, however, had not been lost. Not only had he now got the problem he was up against clear in his own mind, but he had compiled a valuable list of the enquiries still to be made. He spent another half hour getting these in order of importance, then with a yawn he went up to bed.

ENQUIRIES

Up till now French had not had an opportunity of examining the *Observer* which Earle had been reading immediately prior to his disappearance, though he had brought it away with him for that purpose. Though unlikely, it was conceivable that the man had seen something in the paper about which he had wished to consult one of his neighbours, and had there and then gone off to deal with it. After breakfast next morning French therefore took half an hour to go over the two pages which had been exposed. However, a careful search revealed nothing interesting.

Referring to the list he had made on the previous evening, he saw that there were a number of local enquiries to be made, obvious enquiries of the routine type, and he wondered if he could shove these over on to the Farnham men. Making his way to the police station, he asked for Sheaf.

"Well, super," he greeted him, "I was passing and I thought I'd look in and have a word with you. I've been out to St Kilda and had a look round."

Sheaf took a cigarette from a box on the table, then pushed the box over to French.

"Got anything?" he asked, sitting back in his chair as if prepared for a chat.

"Nothing very startling so far. I've really been trying to get the thing into my head. There's another man in it."

"Another man?"

"Yes, a man called Slade. He and the missus have been going rather strong. He seems to have done seven calls in fourteen days, and besides that she's been out different times with him in his car. In fact there's been trouble all round. Earle and the wife don't pull, and he's running after this woman in London and Mrs Earle after Slade. It seems to me we're not going to have much difficulty about motive, at all events."

"Motive for what?" Sheaf asked innocently.

"For what's happened," French answered, with a twinkle in his eye.

Sheaf grinned. "And what's that?"

French grew serious again. "I'm hanged if I know," he admitted. "I had a bit of a think over the thing last night and I'm hanged if I could tell whether it was murder or a voluntary disappearance. You can make a tolerably decent case for either. We'll have to get a deal more information before we know."

"I thought so myself. What are the special points that struck you?"

"There are a lot of points which cut both ways," French answered, leaning his arms on Sheaf's desk. "That one of yours, for instance, about not arranging for a fortnight's grace before reporting the disappearance, and others of the same kind. But the two most important point opposite ways. Earle does not seem to have made financial provision for a new life, and if he didn't, he never disappeared voluntarily. On the other hand, if he was murdered, where's the body?"

Sheaf nodded without replying.

"If Mrs Earle and her sister and Slade were all in it," French went on, "the thing might be possible. The women might have drugged Earle and handed the body over to Slade to get rid of. Otherwise I don't see just how it could have been done."

"That means a deal of enquiry," said Sheaf.

"It does, and that's really what I called in about. Some of these enquiries are purely local and could be best done by men who know the district. Others I could do better, such as the finding of the woman Earle met in London. What I want to know is, can you take on any of the purely local ones?"

"I thought there was something behind all this palaver," Sheaf declared darkly.

"There's always something behind everything," French somewhat enigmatically explained.

"Yes, but what's the good of getting a dog and then barking yourself?"

"You needn't bark," French pointed out, "though I'm sure no one could do it better. All I want is one or two other little things. An enquiry or two along the roads and so on."

Sheaf made a hopeless gesture. "Let's hear the worst," he invited.

French opened his notebook. "I took it that the first point we had to settle was: Did Earle leave the neighbourhood that Sunday night? I jotted down a few enquiries that I thought we might make between us."

"Go on."

"First of all, there's the question of whether he was seen along any of the roads. Your people would know who might have been out on Sunday evening: your own patrols, doctors, domestic servants, perhaps members going to or from the golf club house. Will you do the local enquiries and I'll fix up a broadcast?"

"Right," said Sheaf, making a note.

"Then," French went on, "was he picked up by a road vehicle? I thought we might see the conductors of buses running in the neighbourhood, and perhaps owner drivers and chauffeurs of private cars."

Sheaf made another note.

"Then there are the railway stations. That's a big job: there are the deuce of a lot of them. You see, we'll have to cover a radius of the longest distance the man could have walked. Of course only the larger stations are likely. I should say Guildford was the most likely of all. Earle I suppose might be known at Farnham station?"

"He might not. I understand he generally travelled in his car. Well, we'll do our best."

"Good," French approved. "There is next a bicycle: Did Earle own or hire or borrow a bicycle? Can you see to that?"

"I suppose so."

"The question of his finances I'll undertake and also the broadcast. The watch at the docks and the general search through the country you arranged, but I have sent a more complete description than was available at first as well as photographs. Then the next point is Slade; can you tell me anything about him?"

"Is this what you call a division of labour?"

French looked up anxiously. "Do you think I'm taking more than my share?"

"I haven't discovered what your share is yet."

"The London lady," French said, with an air of a man who effectively uses a small trump. "I want to get on to tracing her, but if you can't see your way to look after these one or two little matters I've mentioned, I'll have to stay here and do them."

"Have you mentioned them all?"

"All I have a note of," French admitted. "Can you think of any other line we should follow up, super?"

"No, and don't you either. You've thought of quite enough things. Are you going back to Town now?"

"I'm going out to have a chat with Slade. If nothing comes of that I'll go back to Town. Now, super, you've not answered my question about Slade. Can you tell me anything about him?"

Sheaf pressed a button. "I don't know him myself, but Constable Black lives out there somewhere. We'll have him in. He may be able to help you."

The constable wasn't able to help very much after all. His father had a small farm at the edge of the wood, not far from Altadore, Colonel Dagger's house. Slade was Mrs Dagger's brother. He was not thought highly of in farming circles. He was a good judge of horseflesh, but there his excellences appeared to begin and end. He attended every race meeting in the country and was supposed to lose huge sums of money. He and Dr Campion from Binscombe, and Mr Gates from Polperro, near Compton, were a trio: all friends and all keen on betting and all believed to be hard up. Crime? Oh, that was a different matter. He didn't believe Mr Slade would stand for serious crime, though for all the constable could say to the contrary, he might take a short cut with cards if he saw the chance. Yes, the constable was only guessing about that: he knew nothing of the man's card-playing abilities. Yes, sir, he understood that he should only refer to what he actually knew as a fact.

None of this was very illuminating, but it did to some extent prepare French for his coming interview. He decided, however, he would first pay a call at St Kilda, and followed the constable from Sheaf's room.

Once again French enjoyed his ride out to Hampton Common through the pleasant Surrey scenery. It was an extraordinarily fine spell of weather for the time of year, and in the warm sun the scent of the pines was as aromatic as at midsummer. In fact, except for the changing colours of the leaves, it might have been midsummer. Birds were strongly in evidence, and twice French disturbed a rabbit as he rode past.

On reaching St Kilda he went to the garage. He had asked Sheepshanks whether the car had been taken out on the Sunday night, and Sheepshanks had said that he believed not, as he had felt the radiator and found it cold. It had since occurred to French that it is an easy matter to cool a warm radiator by changing the water. He now opened the drainage tap and looked at the water running out. It was brown and rusty, too brown and rusty to have been recently put in. Sheepshanks' evidence, then, was satisfactory and the car had not been out.

One other item he had omitted to check. He got Julia to take out the car, run along the road, come back, stop at the gate, and start away again, while he listened from the kitchen. The sounds were very distinctly audible. French was satisfied that no car could have stopped and restarted on the Sunday evening unheard by Julia and Marjorie.

French took the opportunity of asking Julia something about Slade. She was not communicative and French did not learn a great deal.

"Can you tell me the last time you saw him before the disappearance?" he went on presently.

"Yes, on Saturday after lunch."

"Where, madam?"

"Where?"

"Where, madam?"

"I don't see what it has to do with the case or what business it is of yours, but if you must know, it was here in the drawing-room."

"Thank you. Was anyone else present?"

Julia hesitated momentarily. "During our interview?" she said. "No."

French could not see why she had used the first phrase. He therefore questioned blindly. "Not necessarily during your interview. What I mean is did anyone else see Mr Slade?"

Again Julia hesitated, but as before, only very slightly. French imagined she was wondering whether or not to tell the truth, immediately deciding to do so. "My husband saw him for a moment."

"Oh yes?" said French. "When exactly was that?"

"This seems to me the most utter waste of time," she said resentfully. "However, since it is so excessively important, my husband was in the drawing-room when Mr Slade was announced. They were speaking when I entered, but my husband shortly went out of the room. Is that what you wanted to know?"

"Very nearly, madam. If you will tell me what they were saying when you entered the room, it will be all."

"I don't know what they were saying. I'm not in the habit of listening to other people's conversations."

"You couldn't have entered the room without overhearing something. I do not want the whole conversation, only what you overheard."

"I don't know what they were discussing," she replied frigidly, but with evident irritation. "They stopped speaking when I entered."

From her manner French imagined that she knew, but didn't wish to say. He decided, however, to let it pass for the moment, believing he could get the information more easily later. He nodded.

"Then, madam, when did you next see Mr Slade?"

She seemed relieved. "On Monday. He heard of my husband's disappearance and came down to offer help."

"Then you didn't see him on Sunday?"

"No. I should have thought that followed from my previous answer."

"In this sort of question and answer it's very easy for misunderstandings to arise," French said smoothly. "I am much obliged to you, madam. That is all I want."

He next went to the kitchen. He had been extremely polite to Lucy when taking her evidence, and the result now was that she smiled when she saw him enter.

"Well, Lucy," he said, with an equally satisfactory smile, "here I am to bother you again. Do you think you could give me a glass of water? It's a thirsty day."

"I can get you a bottle of beer," she answered, "if you wait half a sec."

"No, no, thanks; don't mind the beer. A glass of water's all I want. Very good of you all the same."

She let the tap run for some seconds to get, as she explained, the water cold. While she was doing so French continued chatting, but when he had had a few sips of the water he turned to her and spoke more seriously.

"I want you to tell me, Lucy, about the unpleasantness between Dr Earle and Mr Slade on Saturday last."

It was a barefaced bluff, and yet, he thought, a legitimate enough deduction from Julia's manner. But bluff or no bluff, it worked. Lucy stared.

"How did you know?" she asked, with something like awe in her manner.

"Oh," said French, "I know all about it. But you may be asked about it in court, and I want to be sure of what you're going to say. Start at the beginning and repeat your lesson like a good girl, then you won't be bothered about it again. You showed Mr Slade into the drawing room where Dr Earle was alone? Isn't that what happened?"

He completed her discomfiture by producing his notebook and writing at the top of a fresh page in large characters, "Unpleasantness between Dr Earle and Mr Slade on 8th October. Miss Lucy Parr's evidence." "Now, Lucy, if you please," he encouraged her.

Her story didn't amount to a great deal after all. Slade, it appeared, had asked for Julia, and Lucy had shown him into the drawing room in ignorance that Earle was there. She knew that Earle disapproved of Slade's visits and she always endeavoured to keep them from meeting. When she opened the drawing room door she did not see Earle; then she was horrified to hear his voice asking in very unpleasant tones, "Well, what do *you* want?" Slade had seemed taken aback and had not replied at first, but before she closed the door Lucy heard him stammering something about returning a book that Mrs Earle had lent. She could not bring herself to return instantly to the kitchen, and she therefore heard Earle's reply in an equally unpleasant but somewhat louder voice: "Well, you can put it on the table there and then get out." By this time Slade had evidently lost his temper, for she heard him replying angrily. Lucy was thrilled and listened eagerly for more, but at that moment she had heard Julia's step on the stairs, and fled to the kitchen. From the kitchen she could not hear what was said, but for some time the voices continued loud, and then the door opened and Earle went upstairs. By dinner-time the bad feelings seemed to have died down, for both Julia and Earle appeared quite normal. Slade had stayed about half an hour altogether.

Though French could not help smiling internally at the fact that Slade had found himself greeted on different occasions by both husband and wife with the same welcoming phrase, "Well, what do *you* want?" he could not but recognise the importance of this news. A row between Earle and Slade might well have been the last straw which precipitated the calamity. He asked a few more questions, and then with thanks for her help, took his departure.

A short distance down the road in the direction of Farnham was the Daggers' place, Altadore, as the plate on the gate indicated. It was a larger house than St Kilda, and evidently much older. The grounds were tastefully laid out and well kept. Here even the grass was good, which, as French had by this time learned, was something of a triumph on this sandy soil. Like St Kilda, the place was surrounded on three sides by the wood, and on the fourth was screened from the road by shrubs.

French was interested to see that the boundary between the two places was merely a fence of rough posts set far apart, and bearing only two wires. This ran through the wood and of course presented no barrier to persons, even if carrying heavy weights.

Going to the door, he asked for Slade, handing in a plain card bearing only the words "Mr Joseph French". He was shown into a small sitting room and asked to wait.

– 7 –

SLADE

Slade was in no hurry to make his appearance. For twenty minutes French sat in the little room, growing momentarily more impatient. Then the door opened and Slade lounged in.

"Sorry to keep you and all that," he murmured. "You wanted to see me?"

"I did, sir, but before I state my business I should tell you who I am." He handed over an official card.

"I know who you are," Slade returned, scarcely glancing at the card. "You're the Scotland Yard man. I heard about you next door."

"Then," said French, "you know my business. I'm investigating the disappearance of Dr Earle, and I called to ask you to kindly give me any information you may have which might help me."

"Not easy when I haven't any."

"You may unwittingly have some, sir, and it is that I want to get hold of."

"Well, you better ask what you want to know."

This being good advice, French took it, systematically working through the points on which he desired enlightenment.

The house, Slade said, was owned by Slade's brother-in-law, Colonel Dagger, a retired officer who was a figurehead director on a number of small companies. There were no children and Slade lived with them. Slade did not exactly say it, but French gathered that the Daggers were not too well off, and were glad of the addition Slade's residence made to their income. Slade had "some money" of his own, and was not engaged in any business, but he was interested in horses and attended the principal races, as well as belonging to some hunts. He had known the Earles since the Daggers moved into the house, some two years previously. Yes, he liked Mrs Earle, who was always very decent to him, though of course there was nothing in the slightest degree serious or improper in their relations. He did not care much for Earle, not because he had anything against him, but simply because he was not in his line.

He had seen Julia Earle on the Thursday and the Saturday before the disappearance. On the Thursday she had gone for a little run in his overhauled Bentley; just down to Arundel and Bognor. On the Saturday he had simply called to ask if she was all right after the run.

Yes, he had seen Earle on the Saturday's call. No, there was certainly no unpleasantness. He did not care for Earle nor Earle for him, but they were always polite to each other.

"Did Mr Earle ask you why you had come?"

As the interrogation proceeded, Slade was obviously getting more and more nervous. "Yes," he answered after a pause, "and what's wrong with that?"

"Nothing," said French. "Did he invite you to go?"

Slade was evidently most unwilling to reply. "I don't know what you're getting at," he complained. "Are you accusing me of kidnapping the man?"

"Don't be silly, Mr Slade," French returned. "You might know I'm accusing you of nothing. If I were doing so I should have cautioned you. But you've got to tell me what you can or else come round to the station and see the superintendent."

"You can't make me answer you if I don't want to."

"Not if you're under suspicion, I agree. But if in a possible murder case you hold back information, you'll find out we're not so helpless as you seem to think. Now please don't let us waste any more time. Did Mr Earle invite you to go?"

Though loath to admit it, Slade was evidently impressed. He sulkily admitted Earle had told him to get out, and that he had replied that he would do so when Julia asked him. Julia had then come into the room, had wanted to know what the trouble was, and had asked Earle if he was aware that this was her visitor. Earle had said in a nasty tone, "Your visitor, is he? Well, I hope you're proud of him," and had gone out of the room. Julia had then told Slade not to mind what Earle had said, that he got fits of bad temper, but would be all right presently.

French turned then to the Sunday evening. Where was Slade from 8.45 that evening until the next morning?

For the first time it seemed to dawn on Slade that these questions might be more significant than he had realised. His sulkiness disappeared suddenly and was replaced by an evident anxiety to please.

"Where was I?" he repeated. "I was in bed, the whole time."

"In bed at 8.40 in the evening?"

"I was in bed at half past eight. I wasn't well. I had a chill or something."

"Did you have dinner that evening?"

"Yes, I did. At least I turned up at dinner, but didn't eat anything."

"Were you all right next day?"

"No, I didn't get up next day till lunch-time."

"Did anyone go up to see you after you had gone to bed?"

"Not that night. When I didn't go down for breakfast next morning Elmina – that's my sister, Mrs Dagger – came up to see how I was."

"Then," said French, "from half past eight on Sunday evening till breakfast on Monday morning you were alone. You tell me that you were in your room, but can you prove it?"

Slade was obviously growing more alarmed, but now, either because he thought it a wise attitude or because his self-respect demanded it, he simulated indignation.

"Why should I try to prove it?" he asked truculently. "I resent your tone extremely. If you're accusing me of some crime you've already said yourself I needn't answer your questions. If you're not, I object to the questions."

"Now, Mr Slade," French answered quietly, "there's not the slightest use in your taking up that line. This may be a case of murder, and in a murder case everyone in any way concerned is asked to account for his or her movements at the time of the crime. You have told me you were in bed. Very good; I'm not disputing it. But I want proof. If you think for a moment you'll see that for yourself."

"Well, I can't give it to you."

In his painstaking way French went into the matter, seeing Slade's bedroom and the lie of the house, and interviewing the servants and Mrs Dagger. The servants could tell him nothing, but Mrs Dagger substantiated a good deal of Slade's story. She said that on the Sunday her brother Reggie was seedy all day. He ate scarcely any lunch and spent the afternoon in a chair before the fire. At dinner he had nothing whatever, and immediately after dinner he went to bed. Next morning, when he did not come down to breakfast, Mrs Dagger went up to his room and found him rather feverish. He got up for lunch, however, and gradually got all right, though for three or four days he was not up to the mark.

This was all very well, but it missed the point at issue. As a result of his enquiries French felt satisfied that Slade could have secretly left and re-entered the house at any time after half past eight. At the same time, there was not the slightest evidence that he had done so.

Suppose, French thought, he had left the house. Suppose he had committed the murder, either alone or in co-operation with Julia. What, in either of these cases, would have been his particular and most important part?

The hiding of the body, undoubtedly. How could this have been done?

French saw that the answer to this question hinged largely on whether Slade could or could not have taken out his car. If he had been able to do so, the body might have been disposed of anywhere within a radius of a hundred miles. On the other hand, if the car were not available, the body must have been hidden close by. French wondered if he could get any light along these lines.

Leaving the house, he walked round to the yard. It evidently dated from the days of horses, and there were ranges of stables, coach-houses and haylofts. The coach-houses had, however, been turned into garages, and the lofts over them into a dwelling house for the chauffeur and his wife.

There were three cars in the garage, a large Daimler, a Morris Minor, and Slade's sports Bentley. Bates, the chauffeur, was engaged in polishing up the last, a well-preserved but very old car. French bade him good morning.

"I've been admiring the condition you've got those cars in," he went on. "I wonder if you'd tell me what stuff you use for them?"

This was one of French's favourite gambits. Long experience had taught him that with certain types a word of judicious flattery was invaluable in the extraction of information. The ice thus tactfully broken, they discussed car polishes till French really began to know something about the subject. Then he turned to business. Explaining who he was, he went on to say that he was asking everyone in the neighbourhood if they could give him any help. He didn't suppose Mr Bates could tell him anything, but he was asking just on spec.

Mr Bates could tell him nothing.

"No," said French, "I didn't expect you could. At the same time you may be able to do more for me than you think. I am trying to find out if Dr Earle was seen on Sunday evening. Now while you may not have seen him yourself, you may have seen someone else who saw him. You follow me?"

Bates cautiously agreed.

"Good," said French; "then you won't mind telling me how you spent Sunday evening, say from 8.30 on?"

Bates didn't in the least mind. He had spent it in his home, above the garage, with his wife and little son.

French expressed disappointment, though he was inwardly delighted.

"I suppose," he went on, "you don't usually have much to do on a Sunday evening? Cars are not often wanted out at that time?"

The man agreed again.

"Were any of the cars out last Sunday evening?"

No cars had been taken out on Sunday evening.

"But how can you be so sure of that?" French persisted. "I don't doubt what you say, but I'd like to understand how you know."

"Why, because I didn't hear them," Bates returned a trifle impatiently. "You couldn't as much as open the garage door without me hearing it in the sitting-room, or for the matter of that, anywhere in the 'ouse. And as for starting them up, why, it would kinda wake the dead. If there was anyone about the garage I tell you I'd be down pretty quick."

"I suppose you would. And your wife, she didn't hear anything either?"

Bates regarded his interrogator with a sort of mild pity. "Well," he said, "you can ask her. 'Ere," he called up the stairs, " 'ere, Maria, 'ere's a gentleman wants to ask you a question. Will you come up?"

"Thanks," said French.

Mrs Bates proved to be a pleasant reliable-looking woman, whom French instinctively felt he might trust. She corroborated her husband's statement. She was quite positive no car had been out on Sunday.

"Good," said French. "I'm much obliged."

This seemed conclusive enough. All the same, French examined the cars, on the chance that if any of them had been used, some trace might remain. But he found nothing.

If, then, Slade were guilty, and if he had not used a car, the body must be somewhere close by. Where did murderers hide bodies?

In graves, under cairns of stones, under brushwood, in the sea and in deep pools of rivers, in disused mine shafts, quarry pits, caves, dene-holes, wells…But usually in graves.

Here on this Surrey common there were practically no stones; no water except the Tarn, a small lake in private grounds about a mile from St Kilda; no mine shafts, quarry pits, caves or dene-holes, and very few wells. There were, however, plenty of dogs, which would quickly find a body concealed beneath brushwood. French felt sure that if the body were anywhere in the neighbourhood, it must have been buried.

For grave-digging a spade would have been required. Did this suggest a line of investigation?

French turned into the garden and strolled round to where the gardener was turning over the soil in a recently cleared bed.

"I've been admiring your roses," he began, repeating his tactics with the chauffeur. "A splendid show you've got for this time of year."

The gardener rose to the bait and began to talk readily. French presently stated his business.

"Dr Earle may have been murdered that night," he went on, "and if so the murderer may have buried the body. I'm therefore wondering where he might have got a spade. Can you help me there?"

The gardener didn't think so.

"Where do you keep your tools at night?" French went on.

"In the tool-'ouse; that little 'ouse over there behind the laurels."

"I'd like to see it."

It was a substantial little brick-and-tile building. It had been locked during the entire weekend of the disappearance, but the lock was an ordinary stock lock, and French was satisfied that it would be a simple matter to get a key to open it.

"You didn't happen to notice on Monday morning whether any of the tools had been disarranged?"

No, so far as the gardener was aware, nothing had been touched.

"Very well," said French, "I'll try these spades for finger-prints. And I'll want to take yours also, because it's only prints other than yours which will interest me."

But nothing came of the experiment. No prints other than the gardener's were revealed. Nor did an examination of the blades show any foreign substance which might have formed a clue.

French walked back to St Kilda and rang up Superintendent Sheaf. Could the super spare a few men to assist in making a more extended search of the wood?

Sheaf agreed and in a short time a car arrived with Sergeant Sheepshanks and three constables. They got immediately to work, and placing themselves in a line, each some twenty feet from his neighbour, they walked backwards and forwards through the wood, examining a fresh tract each time. When as it was growing dusk they had finished, French felt utterly convinced that the body of James Earle had not been disposed of anywhere near his home.

Nor apparently had it been removed by car. None of the only four cars available to his suspects had been used, and had a car been borrowed, Sheaf's enquiries would almost certainly have revealed the fact. It looked indeed as if the body could not have been disposed of at all; in other words, that Earle had not been murdered.

Kidnapping French thought exceedingly unlikely, and his thoughts turned back to a voluntary disappearance. These discoveries had made it increasingly necessary to trace the lady Earle had met in London. If she could be identified, the chances were that the whole affair would be cleared up. It might not be necessary to find either herself or Earle. Proof that they had gone off together would probably end the case so far as French was concerned.

It was because he had reached this conclusion that French was so greatly pleased at the message which he found waiting for him at the police station in Farnham. It was from the Yard and read: "Parking ticket issued to car PE 2157 from Halloway's Park, Staines, on Thursday, 6th inst."

In a happier frame of mind than he had experienced for some time, French took a late train to Town. Tomorrow would be Sunday, but on Monday morning he would follow up this clue.

8

THE LONDON LADY

The fine weather of the last few days had held and the sun was shining with soft brilliance as on Monday morning French made his way to Staines. Travelling down in the train was like setting out for a day's holiday. French, thinking of his recent job at Whitechapel, congratulated himself on his good fortune. It was worth something to exchange the dreadful sordid streets of London's slums for this idyllic country.

As the train ambled gently forward he went over in his mind what he already knew of this phase of the enquiry. It did not amount to much. Earle had left St Kilda in his car on Thursday, October 6th, at about 10 a.m. At 12.30 p.m. he was seen by Ursula Stone picking up a lady in Seymour Place and then driving westwards across Edgware Road. About 7 p.m. he arrived home. That was all. But French felt with satisfaction that the Staines discovery justified his deductions as to the distance the two had driven from London, and with a good deal of eagerness he looked forward to testing the correctness of his other conclusions also.

On reaching the historic little town, he called at the police station, partly to express his appreciation of the work the local men had done for him, and partly to learn where

Halloway's Park was. Five minutes later he reached the park itself.

"Good morning," he greeted the attendant. "I'm a police officer from Scotland Yard. Was it from you the local police got some information about the parking of a car on last Thursday week?"

"Yes, sir."

"Good," said French, taking from his pocketbook the scrap of paper he had found in Earle's coat pocket. "Is that a bit of one of your dockets?"

"Yes, sir," the man repeated, producing his book for French's inspection. There was no doubt the fragment had been taken from it, and when the man turned over the leaves and found that the correspondingly numbered carbon copy bore the magic sign, PE 2157, French noted with delight that at least one point in this nebulous case was definitely fixed.

French had taken the precaution of providing himself with a number of photographs of persons as like Earle as he could find. He now handed the lot to the attendant, and had the further satisfaction of seeing him pick out Earle's without the least hesitation.

"When did the car come in?" he asked.

"You'll see that, sir, from the docket block," the man replied. "One-fifteen."

"Was the man alone?"

"No, sir, there was a lady with him."

"Can you describe her?"

The attendant hesitated. "I don't know that I can, sir," he said slowly. "You see, I wasn't speaking to her, but to the gentleman only. She got out while I was filling up the docket, and I didn't even get a good look at her."

"Never mind," said French. "They got out and I presume the man paid for his car. Then what happened?"

"Nothing more, sir; they just walked away."

"They asked you no questions nor made any remarks?"

"No, sir."

"Which direction did they go off in?"

"That way, sir, along the street."

"And where does that lead to?"

"Well, just the town, the railway stations, the hotels."

"Quite. Now tell me supposing they wanted lunch, where would people of that type go?"

"To the Queen, sir, I should think, or perhaps to the Romney. Those are the two best hotels."

"Good," said French again. "Then when did they come back?"

"The gentleman came back by himself, sir; I didn't see the lady again. He came back about, about a quarter to six, I should think. I'm not just sure."

"From what direction?"

"The same that he had gone in."

"I see. Well, I'm much obliged to you. You'd better give me your address in case any other point arises. By the way, what kind of mood did they seem in? Quite normal?"

"Quite, sir."

The time of arrival at the park worked in admirably with that at which Ursula Stone had seen the car in London. Earle and his companion must have run straight down to Staines. But French was puzzled by a point which had occurred to him when making his analysis. Why had they parked in a town park? They must surely have had lunch somewhere, and it would have been natural for them to park where they lunched. However, there might be some reason for it that as yet he couldn't see.

That they must have lunched, however, was pretty certain. French turned back into the town to try the hotels.

At his very first call he was successful. The head waiter, shown Earle's photograph, remembered his having been in for lunch and tea somewhere about the date in question. Earle had been accompanied by a lady and had engaged a private room. The head called the waiter who had served them.

This man also recognised Earle's photograph. More than this, he had noticed the lady and was able to give a reasonably complete description of her. She was an attractive-looking woman, about thirty, he imagined.

"Did you hear their names? What did they call each other?" French asked.

The waiter hadn't heard.

"Did you hear anything they said?"

The man shook his head. "They were talking together, earnestly, as you might say, but I didn't 'ear what it was about. They didn't speak when I was near."

One interesting and suggestive point was that the "parties" had appeared anxious to avoid being seen together. Earle had entered alone, shortly before half past one, and while he was making the arrangements for lunch, the lady had followed. She had waited in the lounge till the business was complete, and had then allowed him to precede her at some little distance to the private room. They had left in the same way, separately, Earle slightly before the woman. About five they had returned, gone back again singly to the private room, had tea, and left in the same way about half past five.

From this it was clear to French why they had used the public park. Evidently it was this fear of being seen together. The chances of being recognised were of course much greater in the case of a hotel than of a town park.

Between 5.30 then, when they had left the hotel together, and 5.45, when Earle had returned alone to his car, the friends had parted. Where had the lady gone?

French saw that if Earle was at Staines at 5.30 and had reached home by about 7, he would not have had time to drive via London. The lady must therefore have returned to London by herself – if she did return. Was there a train or bus between 5.30 and 5.45?

French found a timetable in the lounge. Two trains left for London at 5.45, a Southern reaching Waterloo at 6.16 and a Great Western reaching Paddington at 6.27. Buses left at 5.30 and at 6.30.

"How far is it from here to the stations for Town?" French asked the waiter.

"About seven or eight minutes' walk to each, sir."

"And how far from the stations to Halloway's Car Park?"

"About the same from the Southern station and perhaps half of it from the Great Western."

If, then, the lady had gone by train, the times would work in exactly. Five-thirty leave the hotel; 5.37 or 38 arrive at the station, take the ticket and get into the train; 5.45 the train departs, and about 5.50 Earle reaches the park. The bus times on the other hand wouldn't work in so well.

But by which line might the lady have travelled? Surely Great Western, if she were returning to where she had been picked up. It was a long way from Waterloo to Seymour Place, but Paddington was comparatively close. Convenience and economy suggested Paddington, and as far as time was concerned, French thought there would be little in it. He would try the Great Western line first. If that failed he could fall back on the Southern.

He walked down to the station and saw the stationmaster. He wanted to know whether a lady had travelled alone to London by the 5.45 train on Thursday, 6th inst. Could the stationmaster help him to find out?

The stationmaster laughed at the idea – very politely. How did the inspector think such a thing would be possible? There was no record of the passengers, and it was unlikely that after so long a time anyone would remember the lady, especially as there was not even a photograph of her.

"Well, let's see the booking-clerk at all events," said French, whose reaction was always to proceed in the routine way when no special clue exhibited itself.

The clerk could not remember any individual bookers, but had a record of the bookings. By that train he had issued six firsts and twenty-three thirds to Paddington, all returns, also one first and two third singles. At the singles French's heart leaped.

"Do you issue many singles?" he asked.

"Very few," the clerk returned. "Most of the bookings are returns, and one-day returns at that."

Though French could find no proof that the lady had gone by the 5.45 train, he thought that the balance of probability was in favour of her having done so – he put it no higher than that. But if she had, he might get on her track at Paddington. It was worth trying at all events.

He took the next train to Paddington and began one of his humdrum enquiries. There was no direct tube from Paddington to Seymour Place, and though the distance was not great, it was possible that the lady had taken a taxi. Very well; try the taxi drivers. It was a legitimate clue, though a rather long shot at best.

All that afternoon he worked away, questioning driver after driver, but without success. He was scarcely disappointed: clues of this nebulous type seldom yielded much result. All the same, when next morning came he could not bring himself to give up without a further effort. He would complete the interrogation of all the regular men at the station. If that failed, he would issue from the Yard a general notice to all taxi men, and if no result came from that, it would be time enough to turn to something else.

He carried on during the next day till the mere sight of a taxi man made him feel ill, and then in the afternoon he got some news which banished all his weariness. A man said he had been engaged by a lady, as near as he could remember, on the day and about the time the inspector mentioned. He could not tell anything about a grey hat, but he thought she had a grey coat.

"Where did you drive her?" French asked.

"To Bryanston Square," answered the man, "but I'm darned if I can tell you the number."

French's heart warmed with pleasure. It really looked as if this long shot was going to get a bull's-eye! Bryanston Square was just behind Seymour Place!

"Try and find it again," said French, getting into the vehicle.

In Bryanston Square the driver suddenly pulled in to the kerb and stopped. "It were in this 'ere block," he declared, "but I'm blessed if I can say which 'ouse."

"All right," French said after giving him time for thought, "if you can't, you can't. Try and fix limits for me. Go a little further in each direction than it could have been, so as to make sure it lies between the two places."

This was more successful, and French dismissed the taxi with the belief that the unknown lady had entered one of a group of nine houses.

A very familiar phase ensued. He began calling at house after house to enquire for a lady with a Grecian nose and a grey coat and hat, and who was away from the house between the hours of 12.30 and 6.30 on the 6th inst.

At the fifth or middle house, No. 129B, he struck oil, showing what an extraordinarily good guess the taxi man had made. Here the door was opened by an enquiring maid.

"I'm a police officer from Scotland Yard," said French, entering upon his little saga. "I wish to make some enquiries about a lady – "

The girl stared. "What's that?" she interrupted. "Surely not another! Why, the other man got everything."

It was now French's turn to stare. "I don't follow," he said. "What other man?"

"Why, the other officer," she declared. "Inspector Tanner his name was. He came and got all the particulars."

Here was something unexpected. His good old friend Tanner on the same job! Or was it the same? French concealed his surprise.

"I see that something has happened of which I am not aware," he explained. "Will you tell me what it is? Has anything gone wrong here?"

The girl tossed her head. "I thought you would have known, seeing you come from the same place," she said pertly, and then as French did not reply, went on: "It was the nurse; Nurse Nankivel. She's gone."

"A nurse? Gone? I didn't know of it. I'm evidently on another case. What do you mean by 'gone'? Left her employment?"

"I mean gone," the girl returned. "Left her employment, if you like. She's just gone and nobody knows where she's gone to."

"Oh," said French with a sudden thrill, "you mean disappeared?"

"Anything you like. I called it 'gone' and I calls it 'gone' still."

"You surprise me very much," said French with truth. "What was she like, this Nurse Nankivel?"

The girl looked at him pityingly. "Why, she were an or'nary-looking woman enough," she answered. "I suppose some people would have called her good looking, but I never thought much of that kind. Too much of a dresser, if you ask me. If you're a nurse, you should wear a nurse's uniform, so I say. But she would never go out without dressing herself up as a fine lady. Fine lady indeed!" Jealousy peeped out of her close-set eyes.

"As a matter of fact," French declared confidentially, "I quite agree with you. Just how did she dress when she went out?"

"Mostly in grey, as you said. Grey coat, grey hat, red brooch in hat, grey shoes and stockings, grey bag: oh," bitterly, "all very complete and like a nurse."

"It sounds like a nurse," said French to humour her. "Now can you tell me if she was out on the afternoon of Thursday the 6th; that's Thursday week?"

The girl nodded. "You've got it in one," she returned.

"Between what hours?"

"The most of the day. From half past twelve to half past six, as I'm a sinner. She wasn't here long before she was wanting time off. Different to other people who 'ave to do their work steady and not go gadding about as if they weren't being paid for their time."

"Well," said French consolingly, "it might have been better for her if she had stayed at home. When did she come here?"

"Saturday three weeks," the girl returned after thought. "The General was took ill on the Friday, and on Saturday they sent for a nurse."

"And how is he?"

"Pretty bad, but they think he'll pull through now."

"By the way, what's his name?"

"Hazzard. Brigadier-General Sir Ormsby Hazzard, CMG, DSO, no less."

"Ah, of course," said French, though he had never heard the name before. "Now tell me, when did Nurse Nankivel disappear?"

"Sunday week." French felt a further little thrill of interest. "On Sunday week she went out after lunch. It was her day out, I suppose, though after the Thursday anybody'd 'ave thought she wouldn't 'ave wanted another day so soon." She gave a contemptuous sniff. "She went out after lunch and she just didn't come back. Nice way to leave 'er ladyship! She was up all that afternoon and evening with the General, and then next morning she rang up the nursing 'ome for another nurse."

"And you never heard anything more of Nurse Nankivel?"

"Never another word."

"And who applied to Scotland Yard?"

"Ask me an easier one. 'Ow should I know? The next thing was this Inspector Tanner was 'ere and asking every kind of fool question that came into his head."

"Like me?" said French.

The girl looked at him sulkily, as if not sure whether this was a joke.

"I suppose you know your own business best," she answered at length.

"I hope so," said French, "but I'm not always sure. Well, miss, I'm much obliged for what you've told me. I'll say good-bye for the present." He smiled, raised his hat, and left her looking sulkily puzzled, as if this was the strangest specimen of a policeman she had ever seen.

As he took a bus to the Yard French was keenly delighted with this new development. There could now be little doubt as to what had happened at Farnham. Earle and this nurse had gone off together. On the Thursday they had met to complete their plans, and on the Sunday they had put them into effect. Now that he had identified the woman, proof should not be hard to get, and proof once obtained, his case would be done.

Though he could not refrain from putting the questions he had to Brigadier-General Sir Ormsby Hazzard's unpleasant servant, French was in hopes that no investigation would be necessary in so far as the nurse was concerned. Tanner was in charge of the case, and French knew Tanner. If Tanner had gone into the affair there would be nothing left for anyone else. He would know everything that there was to know.

It was with an eager spring in his steps that French ran up the stairs to Tanner's room. Once again his luck was in. Tanner was seated writing at his desk.

"Hullo, old son. What brings you here?" he greeted French, glancing up from his work. "Thought you were down at Farnham?"

"I was down at Farnham," French admitted. "I came up when I found you were sneaking my case."

"I like that," said Tanner, sitting back and putting down his pen. "I wouldn't touch your childish little case with a barge pole. What's bitten you?"

"Ever heard the name of Nankivel?" French asked, striding up and down in pleasurable excitement. "Oh you have, have you? Well, she's mine."

"Good Lord!" Tanner looked shocked. "And what about Mrs French?"

"On Sunday evening, the 9th instant," French went on, ignoring this question, "Dr James Earle of St Kilda, Hampton Common, near Farnham, disappeared. On Sunday evening, the 9th instant, Nurse Nankivel, employed at 129B Bryanston Square, disappeared. On Thursday, the 6th instant, three days earlier, Dr James Earle and Nurse Nankivel had a long and more or less secret interview at Staines. Now do you know what's bitten me?"

"Good Lord!" said Tanner again. "I say, French, that's very interesting."

"Of course it's interesting! Isn't it my story?"

Tanner took a cigarette case from his pocket and held it out. "Tell me," he invited.

"The very words I was going to use to you." French produced a lighter, operated it without result, cursed and struck a match. "There's never any petrol in this confounded thing," he remarked, continuing oblivious of Tanner's enquiry as to why he didn't occasionally fill it. "It's you who must tell the story, Tanner. I've finished mine. It's about the nurse we want to know. What happened about her?"

"I don't think this interest in the nurse is seemly for a married man," Tanner said severely. "However, I'll tell you all I know: it isn't much." He turned and took a loose-leaf cover from a shelf, turning to page 1. "Her name," he went on, "is Helen Nankivel and she comes from Cornwall, some little village near Redruth. She is aged 30, and trained in the usual way – details herein. Two years ago she went on the staff of Sister Austin's nursing home at 25 St George's Terrace, Redhill Road, Chelsea. She's a good nurse, competent at her job, no fool, liked by her patients and the staff. There was no trouble with her; no 'undesirable acquaintances', to give Miss Austin's phrase; a nurse with a future, if you understand me; the last nurse in the world to go and make a break with an elderly doctor. She nursed in the home at times, but was generally out on jobs. Miss Austin, in fact, looked upon her as one of her best nurses, and she was sent to important cases."

French chuckled. This was Tanner. He had known that if Tanner was in charge, the spadework would all be done.

"On Tuesday morning, a week ago today," resumed Tanner, "a 'phone came through from the nursing home to say that one of their nurses had disappeared, and they would like a man. I wasn't doing more than six or eight jobs at the time, so was sent. I saw Miss Austin, who seems a good enough sort of woman, and she told me that on Saturday, the 24th of last month, Saturday three weeks, a 'phone had come in from Dr Clark – address and qualifications herein – saying that General Hazzard, of 129B Bryanston Square, was ill, and to send a nurse at once. It happened that the Nankivel had just returned from a case, and she was sent. They had the usual reports, and everything seemed to be going swimmingly. I've seen Dr Clark, and he was satisfied with her in every way."

"A paragon," French suggested.

"In brief, a paragon," Tanner agreed. "All the same, there appears to have been something not entirely right about the woman. Some curious little incidents happened, which aren't very easy to explain. The first occurred five days after she went there. On that day something upset her. Up till then she had seemed slightly depressed or anxious; nothing remarkable; but from then she was undoubtedly a good deal worried. I tried, of course, to find out what had upset her, and I came to the conclusion it must have been a letter: at least, I couldn't find anything else. She had had a letter that day, the housemaid thinks. Unfortunately the girl's not sure. I had a look for the letter, but couldn't find it."

"Did that depression continue till she disappeared?"

"No," said Tanner, "it didn't. On Thursday week, 6th instant, she obtained leave of absence to attend to urgent private business. She left the house about 12.30 and returned about 6.30. I didn't know where she had gone, but you tell me it was to meet Dr Earle at Staines. That meeting cured her, or partially cured her, at all events. Lady Hazzard told me she noticed that after it a great deal of the depression and worry seemed to have gone, but instead that Nankivel was excited. She seemed to be on edge, expecting something to happen. Of course Lady Hazzard may have been talking through her hat, but that's how it seemed to her. This state of excitement continued till the nurse left after lunch on Sunday week: that is, left for the last time."

French took another cigarette.

"It doesn't seem so hard to account for that," he suggested. "She and Earle are in love. On that first day she gets a letter from him suggesting a mutual disappearance to a more salubrious clime. She hasn't made up her mind and it worries her. On the Thursday she meets him at Staines and they fix it up. Her main anxiety is therefore gone, though there still remains the excitement of the affair to look forward to."

Tanner nodded. "You may be right," he admitted. "I didn't think of that, but of course I didn't know about this Dr Earle. Another small point. On the Wednesday afternoon, about six, the parlour maid thought, the nurse was called to the 'phone. It was a man's voice, so the parlour maid said – a quite poisonous woman, by the way. She evidently tried to listen, but all she heard was Nankivel saying: 'Well, I'll arrange it somehow. Twelve-thirty.' Obviously the appointment for next day. No doubt you could now trace if the caller was Earle."

"No doubt."

"A couple more points," Tanner went on. "One day earlier in the week before she disappeared – the maid couldn't remember which day, but thought it was Tuesday – the nurse received an official-looking business letter. The maid didn't know what was in it, but she thinks it must have been something of importance, as nurse seemed very eager to get it. Of course that may be only the girl's talk. Then on the Saturday evening, just before dinner, a telegram came for her. You might get a trace of that, particularly if it was from Earle about Sunday."

"I might," agreed French. "You haven't gone into any of these things?"

"No. I put out a description and the chief thought we'd give it a chance first. I suppose you'll do it now?"

"I suppose so. We'd better see the chief, hadn't we?"

"Right. But it'll be you all the same."

French ground out the stub of his cigarette. "Let's see that I've got all that straight first," he said. "This woman goes to nurse in Bryanston Square. She is in a slightly depressed frame of mind on arrival, and this persists for five days, when she becomes seriously worried, as the result, so you believe, but you have not proved, of a letter. On the

Tuesday a business letter comes for her and she claims it with a great deal of interest. On the Wednesday evening she receives a telephone message, presumably from Dr Earle, to which she replies: 'Twelve-thirty. I'll arrange it somehow.' On the Thursday she spends the afternoon with Earle at Staines. On the Saturday evening she gets a telegram, and on the Sunday both she and Earle disappear. That right?"

"That seems to be the sequence of events," Tanner admitted.

"And what do you make of it?"

"What you make of it, I think. I imagine we're investigating the completion of plans for a departure in company for another and more congenial sphere."

French nodded. "There's motive for it so far as he was concerned. Unhappy at home: wife uncongenial and running after another man and all that. Come along and let's see the chief and I'll get started."

Ten minutes later Tanner was officially relieved of further participation in the case, and his folio was handed over to French.

9

FARNHAM AGAIN

French was tired as, after a call at the Yard to see if anything had come in, he made his way home. The last two days had seen real progress in his case, and he was correspondingly pleased. Though he did not fail to note that his results were chiefly due to his own skill and pertinacity, he had also to admit to a certain element of luck. Certainly his clues had worked out well. Without finding that bit of the parking ticket he did not see how he could ever have traced the nurse. Again, had she not taken a taxi from Paddington he might have lost the trail. Had he known that she was a nurse, he could no doubt have got on her track, but he had not known this important fact. French indeed felt very well satisfied as to the way things were going.

There could be little doubt, he thought, that Earle and this woman had decided to throw in their lot together and start life anew in fresh surroundings. The doctor's decision to do so he could readily understand. His professional career was over, and what he probably most desired was peace and a congenial companion, neither of which he appeared to have at his home. The woman's motives also were fairly obvious. She would doubtless want security. A nurse's life is both hard and precarious. If she were to fall ill she would have nothing to look forward to. The settlement of a reasonable sum on her by Earle – an almost certain condition of any agreement between them – would mean security, or as much security as is obtainable in this life. And in the nature of things she was unlikely to lose very many years of her freedom. At the longest, Earle could scarcely survive her own middle age. She had, in fact, much to gain and little to lose by the arrangement.

But likely as this theory was, it had not been proved, and until either it or some other had been placed beyond question, the case was not over for French. However, a very few more enquiries and he believed it would be complete.

Next morning accordingly he was early at work. His first call was to the house in Bryanston Square, where he asked to see Lady Hazzard.

He did not expect to learn much from her, and his anticipation was justified. In fact, she told him practically nothing. She had liked Nurse Nankivel, finding her efficient as a nurse, pleasant to speak to, and but little trouble in the house. Her husband, the General, had also liked her.

When the nurse had failed to turn up on the Sunday evening they supposed she had missed a train. Lady Hazzard sat with her husband till the night nurse came on duty. They fully expected that next morning the truant would return. When she did not do so they telephoned to the home and another nurse was immediately sent. They understood that the matron had reported the affair to the police.

All the information Tanner had obtained had apparently come from Gladys, the maid, who had evidently hated the nurse and jealously watched her every movement. French had a long interview with Gladys, but without adding to what he had already learned. He also had a look at the room which Miss Nankivel had occupied, but as Tanner had already searched it, he did not give it much time.

From Bryanston Square French betook himself to the nursing home in Chelsea. Here Sister Austin, the head of the home, saw him at once. As Tanner had reported, she seemed an efficient and kindly woman. Certainly she was genuinely upset about her missing nurse and asked French anxiously if the Yard had learned anything about her. When French tentatively mentioned the theory that she had gone off with a doctor, the sister ridiculed it. Nurse Nankivel, she said, was not that kind of woman. It was much more likely that some accident had happened to her; in fact, that was the only way Sister Austin could account for her absence.

The sister then repeated what she had told to Tanner. It was what French had expected to hear, and he would not have been disappointed if her testimony had ended there. But as it happened, his systematic enquiries produced something entirely unlooked for. Without in the least appreciating the importance of the question, he asked for a list of the recent cases on which Nurse Nankivel had been engaged.

"Her last case," the sister replied, "was rather a long one; she was at it for twelve weeks. A very nice place it was, at Compton, near Guildford. That was with a Mr Frazer. He died."

A sudden thrill shot through French. Compton! Frazer! This was a bit of all right! Things were working in better than he could have hoped. In his enquiries at St Kilda he had learnt that Earle had been called in as consultant in this very case. This was how he and the nurse had met. Doubtless they had been attracted to one another, and doubtless had had more interviews than at their patient's bedside. No more suitable country for clandestine assignations could have been conceived than that in which these two people found themselves, with its thick, almost impenetrable woods and its comparatively sparse population.

"That interests me a good deal," French remarked. "It happens that the doctor with whom it is suggested she went away was a consultant in that case."

The sister was shocked. She had not believed there could be anything in the police theory, and now here was something very like confirmation.

"I couldn't have believed it," she declared. "It just shows. You never know"; with which rather cryptic remark the interview closed.

It would now be necessary to try for evidence that Earle and the nurse had been in secret communication during Frazer's illness. That meant a return to Farnham. But French decided that before he left Town he would do what he could to trace the two messages, telephone and telegraph, which Nurse Nankivel had received.

He began with a visit to one of the Post Office departmental offices, where he asked for Mr Jordan. Jordan was a little man whom French had got to know over a case of burglary in which the tracing of a certain message had become an essential feature of the prosecution. It had turned out that he lived near French, and they had kept up the acquaintance, dropping in to see one another occasionally in the evenings. Before taking on his present job Jordan had spent some years in the postal service of India, and French loved to hear him describing his Eastern experiences.

"Hullo, French," said the little man. "Haven't seen you for a month of Sundays. What have you been doing with yourself?"

"What do you think?" French returned, taking the one chair available in the tiny office. "As usual working myself to death."

"I know," Jordan chuckled, "killing yourself careering round the best bits of the Continent on the pretence of following up some poor devil that you've got your knife into. How's Miriam?"

Miriam was French's ancient and feeble fox terrier, whose decease from senile decay was believed to be impending.

"Fine," said French; "but as a matter of fact I didn't come in to talk dogs. I want you to do me a favour, Jordan."

Jordan rose and made a little bow. "Honoured, I'm sure," he declared. "Whence this unusual politeness?"

"Pearls before swine, I know," French admitted. "What I want is to trace a telegram delivered to a certain nurse in Bryanston Square," and he gave the details. "Also a telephone message to the same lady. It occurred to me that you might be able to help me."

"Marvellous!" cried the little man, throwing up his hands. "These Scotland Yard men at work! How sound their methods! How subtle their proceedings! They succeed every time, *if* only they can find the man who knows and get him to do the work."

"Naturally; that's what people like you are for."

"I know. For the public the work: for you the sitting back and taking the credit." The little man continued making jibing remarks as he ran rapidly through a book of reference. Then he picked up his telephone and gave some cabalistic direction. A pause, then: "Could you put me through to Mr Hinckston?...Oh, Hinckston, I recognise your voice. Jordan speaking. No; Jordan...Yes. Look here, Hinckston...No, don't cut me off. Curse it, they've cut me o— Oh, Hinckston, I've got an inspector here from Scotland Yard making confidential enquiries. He wants to trace a telegram," and the details followed. "Thanks very much. No, I'll hold on if you can get it soon. You can't? Well, you'll ring up?…In a few minutes? Good. Thanks very much."

"You'll have time to talk about Miriam after all," Jordan remarked, turning to French. "What's this new tale of blood and horror you're on to now? I never knew anyone with such morbid tastes."

"It's what I call a 'thin air' case," said French. "At 8.40 on a Sunday evening a peaceable elderly gentleman is seated over his drawing-room fire, all settled down comfy for the evening and deep in his *Observer*. Three minutes later he has gone."

"Gone where?"

"Not gone where. Just gone. Vanished. Become thin air, whatever that is. Never heard of from that day to this."

Jordan whistled. "Earle?" he suggested, with a knowing look. "I read about it?"

French nodded.

"Skedaddled with the nurse, eh?"

French shrugged. This was putting two and two together too rapidly even for him.

"Nothing doing?" Jordan went on. "But I bet you know all about it all the same, you slippery old humbug. Why, I wouldn't mind betting – " The telephone bell cut short his remark.

"Yes; speaking. Oh, you've got it, have you? Good man. Then repeat, will you, Hinckston, and I'll take it down. Will you confirm to Inspector French, the Yard? Good."

He began writing. French, looking over his shoulder, grew better pleased with every word that came into being.

"Bless you, my son," he apostrophised. "You're the goods."

The message had been handed in at Seale Post Office and ran:

> To NURSE HELEN NANKIVEL,
> 129b Bryanston Square, W1
> Reference our conversation. Very urgent. Be at new bypass bridge, Hog's Back, at six tomorrow, Sunday. Will meet you there. Don't fail.
> JAMES EARLE.

"I said you knew all about it," Jordan declared, ringing off.

"I'm learning," French admitted, once again hiding his satisfaction. "Now what about that telephone call?"

This did not seem to be so attractive a proposition. Jordan hemmed and hawed, apparently unwilling to admit there was anything he couldn't do. At last, however, he came down to brass tacks.

"Unless you know the exchange from which the message was sent, I'm afraid you'll not get it. If you've any hint of the sender, try the exchange he'd be likely to use. You might get it there, but I'll not answer for it."

With this French had to be content. He got up. "You did that well, Jordan. I do like to come here and learn how business really ought to be carried on. When are you looking in?"

"I'll wait till Miriam goes the way of all flesh, I think. You come to me instead."

French departed with genial blasphemy, and after lunch and a visit to the Yard, he took an afternoon train to Farnham.

That evening he invited Superintendent Sheaf to dine with him at his hotel, and during the meal he reported the results of his London activities. Sheaf was obviously impressed, though he said but little. Indeed, his final question, "What are you going on with now?" was his longest single contribution to the conversation.

French had noted several lines of enquiry, and next morning he set to work on the first. He went to the post office at Seale, and showing the postmistress the copy of the Earle–Nankivel telegram, he asked if she remembered its transmission.

The postmistress remembered it very well, partly because she knew Dr Earle, but also because of the unusual way in which she had received the message. It had not, she explained, been handed in over the counter in the customary manner. The postman had brought it. He had found it in a pillar-box near the Hampton Common crossroads when making the usual five o'clock collection. The message, written on the proper form, was in the box, together with the money for its despatch. This method of sending telegrams was not unknown, but it was unusual enough to fix the matter in her mind.

French saw, however, that it was reasonable enough under the circumstances. From Earle's house to the post office was a matter of perhaps two miles, while the pillar-box was within five minutes' walk of his gates. Theoretically, of course, there was no absolute proof that Earle was the sender, for the simple reason that he had not actually been seen putting the paper into the box. But the thing had to be judged in harmony with the other factors of the case, and French had no doubt that Earle was his man.

It was easy also to understand why Earle should have sent a telegram in this way rather than telephone the message to the post office or even direct to the nurse. Earle's telephone was situated in his hall, and if any of the members of his household were about he could not have kept his message secret.

From the post office French rode to the telephone exchange. Here his rather wonderful luck held. When he showed his authority and gave the Hazzards' number in Bryanston Square, the operator was able immediately to turn up the number from which the call had come. A note of the trunk call had been kept for revenue purposes, and the bill on which it would eventually find a place would be sent to St Kilda. The operator, moreover, had recognised Earle's voice, he having attended her during a long illness.

Here, then, was the desired proof that the message had come from Earle. The discovery conveyed no fresh information – French had not doubted the call was Earle's, but its proof was a step further in the case he was so satisfactorily building up.

French looked at his watch. Quarter past eleven. Campions' was the next name on his list and he wondered whether he would find the doctor if he were to ride over to the Red Cottage. He put through a call from the exchange, and the answer being that Campion was out, but was expected home for lunch, he once again mounted the sergeant's bicycle.

He enjoyed the ride. It took him through Shackleford and almost into Farncombe, a suburb of Godalming – or indeed an adjoining town. Then turning back in the Compton direction, he reached the village of Binscombe. Here he slackened down, examining the names on the various gates.

Presently he found the Red Cottage. It stood on one of the few plots of quite level ground in that undulating country. This was a much less characteristic district than that in which Earle had lived. Here the land was agricultural and there were many more houses to the square mile. Campions' looked as if it had been built about the end of the last century. Its great feature was its gables, which jutted out in all directions from the main roof. The garden and grounds were tidy but commonplace.

French turned back into Godalming and had his own lunch, then when he thought Campion would have finished his, he rode out again. Campion was in his workshop.

"Come in," the doctor called in answer to his knock. "Oh, it's the inspector. Good afternoon, inspector. You want to see me?"

"If you please, sir," French answered, looking round with admiration at the beautifully appointed little shop. "You have a wonderful place here."

"Yes, it's not so bad. Can't get time to work in it though. Would you like to come in to the consulting-room, or will this place do?"

"This will do, sir, perfectly, so far as I'm concerned. It's just a few questions arising out of this matter of Dr Earle's disappearance. I won't keep you long."

"It's all right. I'm not in any special hurry. What is it you want to know?"

"It's a rather delicate matter, sir," French went on. "It's about a nurse named Nankivel. I understand she was nursing a patient of yours?"

Campion seemed to stiffen slightly. French noticed it with some misgivings. He hoped professional etiquette was not going to come in to make his task more difficult. The man, however, did not hesitate. He nodded, answering, "Yes, she nursed the late Mr Frazer."

"So I had heard. Would you tell me, doctor, what you thought of her?"

"As a nurse?"

"In every way, please."

Campion shrugged slightly. "That's a largish order," he answered. "As a nurse I thought highly of her. She was careful and attentive and got on well with her patient. I had certainly no fault to find with her. As to other information, I don't know that I can tell you much. She seemed a quite ordinary, nice sort of woman, but I saw nothing of her otherwise than professionally. Why do you ask?"

French bent forward. "You didn't know, sir, that she has disappeared?"

Campion stared. "Good Lord!" he exclaimed; "you don't say so? Disappeared! When did that happen?"

"On Sunday." French lowered his voice and spoke more impressively. "I'll tell you what I know, but please regard it as confidential." Campion nodded impatiently. "On Saturday evening Nurse Nankivel got a telegram from Dr Earle, asking her to meet him on Sunday on the Hog's Back. Whether she did so or not I don't know, but after lunch she left the house in Bryanston Square, where she was employed, and has never been heard of since."

Campion swore. He stood looking at French with amazement in his eyes, which rapidly turned to a question.

"I can tell you, inspector, that's a surprise," he said at last. "Earle! You're not suggesting, I suppose...?" He hesitated.

"I'm not suggesting anything, doctor. What I want to know, and what I'm going to ask if you can tell me, is whether Dr Earle and this lady were acquainted down here?"

Campion whistled beneath his breath. "They were acquainted of course," he answered, "if you mean by acquainted twice seeing each other while professionally engaged in the sick man's room. If you mean socially acquainted, I don't know. I never suspected or imagined such a thing, but of course I can't say definitely."

"You never observed anything between them of which at the time you thought nothing, but which now, in the light of what I have said, appears to you significant?"

"Absolutely nothing."

"I understand, doctor. Tell me, during what hours was this lady free?"

"She was on day duty. She had a couple of hours in the afternoon. We had a second nurse for the night."

"The name of the other nurse, please, doctor. She might have seen something."

"Most unlikely, I should say: however, it was Henderson."

"From the same home?"

"Yes."

"Can you say how often Dr Earle visited the case?"

"Yes, I said so: twice."

"And perhaps you'd tell me the circumstances which led to his being called in?"

Campion seemed a little unwilling, but his hesitation was only momentary.

"I've no objection to telling you, inspector, though I don't fancy many medical men would do so. You probably know that Dr Earle and I are partners?"

"I've heard so, sir."

"The practice was Dr Earle's. It's a fairly good practice in Godalming and the surrounding districts. Some six years ago Dr Earle came into a little money. He never cared for general practice, but wanted to do research work. He had a theory connected with germ cultures about which he wanted to write. He therefore advertised for a partner, and I answered and we came to terms. He moved out into the country and I took over the work. But he did not entirely give up the practice. Certain of the older patients preferred him and he always attended those. Also, in serious or important cases I asked him to come in to check my opinion. This case of Mr Frazer was a serious case – the man, as a matter of fact, was dying – and I asked him to come in: not that I had the slightest doubt as to the treatment, but simply as a satisfaction to the members of the family."

"Thank you, doctor, that's all very clear. It doesn't affect my case exactly, but out of curiosity, would you tell me what the old gentleman died of?"

"Well, he had gastro-enteritis. But it was really old age and a weak heart that finished him off. He was sixty-nine."

French made a move to go, then stopped. "By the way," he said, "you told me that Dr Earle had intended to write a book on his germ theory. You don't know if he ever did so?"

"He had begun it: in fact, he had written a considerable part of it. I've seen his manuscript and we've talked it over."

"It's a funny thing that when I was looking over his things I never came across any papers connected with it. Where did he keep them, do you know?"

Campion shook his head. "I've no idea. When I saw the manuscript it was on the table in his study, but where he put it I don't know."

"This book and this theory of his meant a good deal to him, I suppose?"

"They did," Campion answered. "He was very keen." Then his face changed and he favoured his visitor with a swift, questioning look.

French saw that the doctor had divined his own thought. If at the time of Earle's disappearance this beloved manuscript had vanished also, was it not the final proof that that disappearance had been voluntary?

The more French thought of this, the stronger the argument appeared. If the man had been so keen on his theory and his book, he would never have left the manuscript behind. On the other hand, if he had been murdered, the manuscript should be at St Kilda. The fact that it had gone undoubtedly settled this extremely knotty point.

This, then, was all that was required from Campion. French slowly made a move to go. Then suddenly he started as an entirely new idea flashed into his mind. Did this matter of the manuscript not mean something very different?

– 10 –

POLPERRO

The idea which like a whirlwind had upset all French's previous assumptions was very simple. Was it possible that Earle's theory and Earle's book were really valuable, so valuable that they would make the name of their author? Was it possible that Campion should have known this and *stolen the manuscript*? And to enable him to get the benefit of his theft, could he have killed Earle?

Campion guilty of Earle's murder! Here was something to think about! Surely the idea was too far-fetched? Campion was a reasonably successful man, comfortably off now and with an assured, if not a very brilliant, future. He had surely too much to lose to run the terrible risks of committing murder simply to gain professional fame?

French was not so sure. The man might be vain, and vanity is one of the most potent springs of human action. To have his name handed down reverentially, like Harvey's or Pasteur's, he might risk a great deal.

French rapidly considered, while to cloak his concentration he took out and laboriously consulted his notebook, "to make sure he had asked everything and would not have to come back and trouble the doctor again".

He saw at once that this theory raised again the old problem of the nurse. If Campion had murdered Earle, what had happened to Miss Nankivel? It was absurd to suppose that Campion could have murdered her too.

In three seconds French decided that he could leave this problem over for the present. There was probably nothing in his new idea, but he mustn't miss this opportunity of finding out more about it.

"Well, Dr Campion," he said, "I'm very much obliged for what you've told me. That's everything except just for one technical point which I require in order to complete my report. In a murder case, as I'm sure you know, it is the duty of the investigating officer to ask everyone concerned where he or she was at the time of the crime. We don't know that this is a murder, but it conceivably might be so, and if in your case you will give me that information, it'll probably save my troubling you again."

Campion looked keenly at his visitor, then smiled wryly. "I've heard you did that," he replied, "but I don't quite see how I am one of those concerned."

"Only, sir, in the sense that you were a person – how shall I describe it? – in Dr Earle's environment. You were his partner. The thing is a matter of form. If I went to London without such information I should be sent back to get it."

"It's all right," Campion said resignedly. "I don't mind telling you. Where do you want me to begin?"

When he was about it French might as well cover six o'clock, when the nurse was supposed to reach the Hog's Back.

"Oh, I don't know," he answered, as if to make light of the question. "Say from lunch-time. What time did you have lunch?"

"The usual time, I believe – half past one."

"Very well," French agreed; "that gives us a start. What happened after lunch?"

"I'm sure I don't know what you want this for seeing Dr Earle was alive and well for another six or eight hours. However, I suppose you know your own business." He took a small engagement book from his pocket and turned over the pages. "After lunch: I'm really not sure. I think I sat and read for a time, but I may have come out here. I had to pay some calls and I went out – I'm not sure: after three, I think. I paid – one, two – four calls in all, and then came back here. Miss Stone was spending the afternoon here and I went into the drawing-room at once. Then – "

"About what time did you get back here? Can you remember?"

Campion paused in thought. "I can't," he said at length. "Somewhere about half past six, I should think, but I'm not sure."

"Where did you have tea, sir? That might bring the time to your mind."

"With the Slaters near Puttenham: that was the last call I paid. They were going to tea as I was leaving and they asked me to join them. I did so and sat for half an hour chatting."

"So that you drove home somewhere between 5.30 and 6.30?"

"Yes, so far as I remember."

"Very good, sir. Then you came back here, and went to the drawing room. What happened then?"

"I can tell you that," Campion declared. "I remember it all very clearly. Miss Stone was spending the evening with us, as I said. Well just before supper she asked me if I would show her my workshop; my sister had been bumming about the cost and the splendour of my tools. I agreed, of course. Now while I like Miss Stone personally, I abominate hen parties and I looked round for some excuse to keep out of the drawing-room after supper. I noticed a packet of parts for a dolls' house which I had intended to make up for a small patient who had died, and I offered to make them up for Miss Stone. You know, I suppose, that she's connected with a children's hospital in Bath? She was pleased with the idea, so after supper I assembled the thing. When it was finished I went to the drawing-room, and almost at once we started off for St Kilda: the whole party of us."

"They're very good, those dolls' house packets. Which one did you choose?"

"The Handicraft people's Romeo Special."

"A beautiful model," French commented. "Now can you tell me, doctor, about what time you came to the workshop and returned to the drawing-room?"

"I came here immediately after supper; I suppose that would be about eight. I reached the drawing-room at – Let's see now, I don't know that I can tell you that. About half past nine, I think. No; earlier, because they took a solid quarter of an hour to throw wraps round their shoulders, and we arrived at St Kilda at quarter to ten. I noted the time as soon as I heard about Earle. I must have reached the drawing room about quarter or twenty past nine."

From 8 to 9.15 or 9.20. And Earle disappeared at 8.40. Could Campion possibly...?

"From eight o'clock to 9.15 is the critical period, doctor. I'm making no insinuations, but can you prove that you were in your workshop during that time?"

"No, of course I cannot," Campion rejoined irritably. "And why should I? Are you accusing me of kidnapping Earle?"

"I told you, sir, I was accusing you of nothing. All the same, if you can prove where you were during that time it would be so much to the good. Did no one see you at any time between those hours?"

Campion moved jerkily. "What the hell difference does it make whether anyone saw me or whether they didn't?" he asked angrily. "If you don't suspect me, it doesn't matter. If you do, I'm not going to answer you. I don't see what you're getting at."

French shrugged. "Well, sir, you can take that line if you like. At the same time, I don't see why you should mind answering. If you refuse, of course I automatically suppose you have something to hide. However, it's a matter for yourself."

French's moderation cooled Campion down. "I've not the slightest objection to telling you anything I know," he declared. "What I dislike is the insinuation behind your question. However, I can't help that. No one came into the workshop, and no one can tell whether I was here or not. On the other hand, I went into the house. I went in to consult Miss Stone on how she would like the dolls' house finished."

"What hour was that, Dr Campion?"

"I don't really know. Somewhere about halfway through the time, because the job was about half done. But I couldn't tell you exactly."

"That would be somewhere about twenty minutes to nine?"

"I expect so."

"Well, sir, if you can't go nearer to it, you can't. Then you drove over to St Kilda?"

Campion made a sudden gesture. "Your saying that reminds me," he declared. "When I went into the drawing-room the question arose of how Miss Stone was returning to St Kilda. She had wanted to go by bus and I had said I would run her over. I remember now thinking that if she was going by the bus she would have to start at once. The bus passes the end of our road about five minutes past nine, and it takes about a quarter of an hour to walk to the end of the road. She would have had to leave about a quarter to nine. I must have gone in about twenty-five to nine, or a minute or two later."

French saw that if this were true Campion could scarcely have had anything to do with Earle's disappearance. Not indeed that he had really seriously suspected Campion, but still...Better to be sure than sorry.

"Very good, sir. That seems to clear the thing up. Then you drove over to St Kilda?" And he pursued his enquiries.

Presently he thanked Campion for his information and went back to the house. Could he speak to Miss Campion for a moment?

Alice Campion saw him at once. He explained himself and put his questions, then sat waiting while the spate of talk flowed over him. He had asked for details of what took place in the drawing-room between supper and the departure for St Kilda, and he certainly got them. Full measure, pressed down, running over.

Her statement, which French implicitly believed, confirmed Campion's on every point. There was no doubt that Campion had been in his own drawing-room at the time at which Earle had left his house, over five miles away. And Flo Campion, whom French next questioned, told the same story with equal conviction.

This testimony satisfied French. However, to make assurance doubly sure, he stopped at the first call office he came to and rang up Handicrafts Ltd. to know how long it should take a skilful carpenter to assemble their Romeo Special dolls' house set. When he was told about an hour and a half, the last doubt vanished. Without a pang he abandoned his theory that Campion had killed Earle for the manuscript. Indeed, he now saw that he had never really believed in it.

Returning to Farnham, his way led past St Kilda, and he called for a few minutes to try to find out where James Earle had been about six o'clock on the Sunday afternoon of his disappearance. He was the one most likely to have met the nurse, and proof that he had done so would be very acceptable.

French, however, was unable to obtain any information on the point. Mrs Earle thought the doctor was in his study, Miss Lawes believed he was out, and neither Miss Stone nor the servant knew anything about him.

French was disappointed. However, as he rode back to Farnham he told himself he could not expect always to score a bull's eye. Better luck tomorrow!

Next morning was once again fine, and in a mood of reasonable optimism he turned into the police station to see Sheaf.

"Tell me," he asked after the usual greetings, "something about these Frazers: the old man who died recently and his family."

"What's the trouble about them?" the super grunted.

"Only that this Nurse Nankivel was there for the twelve weeks previous to Frazer's death, and I want to find out if she was meeting Earle during that time."

Sheaf nodded, sat back in his chair and produced the inevitable box of cigarettes. "I don't know much about them," he said, "except what's pure gossip. If you want anything definite, you'll have to get it for yourself. Compton's a good distance away, and quite out of my district."

"I understand that of course, super."

"Well, as you know, the old man lived near Compton; between Compton and the Hog's Back. He had a nice place there; fine garden and all that. Mrs Frazer, I believe, was his second wife, and so far as I am aware there were no children by either marriage. The old boy is supposed to have led her a pretty dance; a crotchety, miserly old ruffian, according to the tales going about, and she seems to have had a hell of a time nursing him and looking after him and running messages for him. Pretty well-to-do old boy too: presumably that's why she married him. He's supposed to have left about a hundred thousand."

"To her?"

"Partially, according to the stories. I heard she got the house and about two-thirds of the income during her life. There is a nephew; he lives there and potters about the place. Apparently he gets the other third of the capital now, and all the rest at the wife's death. But you mustn't take any of this for gospel. If any of it matters, you'll have to check it up."

"I don't think it does matter," French returned, "except to give me a general idea of the sort of people I'm likely to find. Right, super. Many thanks. Will you be busy this evening before quitting time?"

"Not specially."

"Then if you don't mind, I'd like a chat about the case. I've an idea I've gone far enough."

The super nodded and French went out. Once again commandeering the sergeant's bicycle, he set off along the winding road through Seale and Puttenham to Compton.

Before reaching the latter village he found himself reminded of his Dorset case. Here earthworks were in progress, first parallel to, and then crossing, the road and disappearing in the direction of the Hog's Back. The Whitness Widening on a Lilliputian scale! The new bypass road, this must be. This work which he was looking at must continue to the new bridge under the Hog's Back, a bridge he had noticed many times: the bridge at which Earle and Nurse Nankivel were to meet on the Sunday of their disappearance.

French was a good deal more interested in the bypass than he would have been before his Dorset visit. He remembered what he had heard of it. It was to run from just north of Guildford to just south of Godalming, cutting out both towns. A very much-needed improvement, he thought, from what he had seen of the traffic in both of them. In a way he would have never dreamed of doing a year earlier, he now looked at the work: almost indeed from the point of view of an engineer!

He found that the workings ran parallel to the road from Compton Corner to the Hog's Back, and he cycled slowly along, dismounting at intervals to walk across the field to the left and have a look at what was going on. First he came to filling. A small locomotive was bringing down trucks of material which was being dumped to form a bank across some low-lying ground. French observed with interest that side tipping was in progress; that is, that a narrow bank of the proper height had first been made, and that this was now being widened to the full width of the new road.

Though he had by this time reached the gate to the Frazers' place, he could not resist pushing on past it for a short distance to see some more of the workings. Soon the filling ran out and cutting took its place. This got deeper, running first through soil, then bringing to light a bed of heavy yellow clay, and finally reaching chalk. For a few moments French stood watching a steam shovel taking out great bites of the clay, each bite filling a wagon. This clay was going down to widen the bank he had first seen.

With a half-sigh – French had an Irishman's love of doing other people's jobs – he turned back, and passing through an ornate gateway, bearing on each pillar the name "Polperro," he rode up the Frazers' drive. Sheaf had certainly not exaggerated the beauty of the place. Its great glory was its trees. There were elms fringing the drive at either side, and oaks standing at intervals in the green sward, which looked as if they might have been growing there in the days of Elizabeth. Probably they were. The place gave that impression of peace and security which so many of these old English estates bear, the suggestion that time and shocks were powerless to alter its placid and unhurried existence.

The house, when it came into view, was unexpectedly small and unexpectedly old. French was not an expert in such matters, but he had seen through some of the more famous of the old Kent and Surrey houses, and guessed it fifteenth century. It had a tower in the façade, nearly, but not quite, in the centre, with a gateway which would have taken, if not a carriage and pair, at least two horsemen riding abreast. Two wings stretched out on either side of the tower, of different heights, different window spacings and different lengths. The walls below were old rubble masonry, with half-timbering above of black and twisted oak, leading up to a high-pitched roof of mellow brown tiles. It looked to French like the front portion of a square surrounding a courtyard, and he found afterwards that it had been so, but that the other three sides had been destroyed by fire in the reign of the second Charles. In front, replacing the old moat, was a sunk garden, and to the right of the building French could see a large range of glasshouses.

Ringing at the door he sent in his official card, asking if Mrs Frazer could see him. He was shown into a room panelled and ceiling-joisted in old black oak, with whitewashed rubble between the two. Only the windows and the electric light pendants seemed modern, the former having been evidently enlarged at some comparatively recent time. The fireplace was like a small ante-room, and an electric fire shone like a beacon beneath the huge stone chimney opening.

French had not more than time to observe these details when the lady of the house entered. Mrs Frazer was tall and fair and good-looking. "Forty, if she's a day," thought French, "and knows her own mind." She invited him to sit down and shortly asked his business.

"I'm engaged on this case of the disappearance of Dr Earle," he answered, "and in the course of my investigations I have discovered that a nurse who was with you here, during the illness of the late Mr Frazer, has also disappeared: Nankivel, her name was."

Mrs Frazer registered mild surprise, but not much interest and no feeling.

"Very remarkable and unfortunate," she commented. "Yes?"

"I wished, madam, to make some enquiries about Nurse Nankivel. I am, of course, now trying to trace her as well as Dr Earle."

"Naturally, but I'm afraid I cannot give you much help. I met the nurse frequently while she was here, but that was invariably in her professional capacity. I know nothing of her in her private life."

"Quite, madam. You also knew Dr Earle?"

"I have met him, but only in the same way."

"Then you cannot, I suppose, tell me whether these two met otherwise than professionally during the nurse's stay here?"

"No," said Mrs Frazer, coldly and finally.

"The nurse gave satisfaction while she was here?"

"Oh yes; I had no fault to find with her."

French expressed his thanks, adding that he was afraid he would have to ask similar questions to her staff.

She agreed with the same cold lack of interest, and ringing, told the butler to answer anything French might ask him, and to see that the other servants did the same. Then with a slight bow she left the room.

The butler, Marks, lost the rigidity of an automaton which he had assumed in his mistress' presence, indicating that he did not consider French had any pretentions to social position. He answered all his questions with readiness, but without conveying much information. Most of what he did tell was about the family and practically nothing about Nurse Nankivel. It seemed that he for one was sorry about the old man's death. Frazer had evidently been a crotchety and fault-finding employer, but Marks clearly believed Mrs Frazer would be worse. Obviously he actively disliked her.

Nor did he seem to care much for the nephew, Gates. Gates had a small suite on the first floor, and since his return from Australia some four years earlier, had lived at Polperro. He acted as a sort of secretary-agent for his deceased uncle, who liked him and was believed to have paid him a considerable salary. The work he did, however, was a mere bagatelle. His real interest in life, so the butler indicated with knowing winks, was horseflesh. He and his friend Mr Slade attended all the races in the country, and betted heavily on them all. Indeed – the butler lowered his voice and became extraordinarily confidential – Mr Gates was believed to be in low water. He had been, so Marks said, touching his uncle for every penny he could get out of him. They had had some pretty serious disagreements, if not actual quarrels, on the subject. Marsden, the chauffeur, had heard one of these quarrels when passing outside the library window, and Frazer had then threatened to disinherit the nephew if he did not pull himself together. But they had apparently patched the affair up, for Gates was left a handsome slice of the old man's money, besides being residuary legatee. Mrs Frazer was left the interest on £60,000 and the house for her lifetime, Gates getting the rest, some £30,000. About Nurse Nankivel, except that she was a "nice girl", the man knew little, but he recommended French to apply to the gardener's wife, with whom she seemed to have struck up an acquaintance. She was on duty during the day, but usually went out from four to six, when sometimes Mrs Frazer and sometimes Gates watched in the sickroom. He had mentioned a Mr Slade? Yes, it was the gentleman who lived at Altadore, Colonel Dagger's brother-in-law. He had been a frequent visitor, both to Gates and the Frazers.

All this was told with a very convincing air, but when French asked Marks how he knew it, it lost a great deal of its force. Apparently most of it was gossip, founded on the not necessarily sound deductions of the staff. French, however, knew how well up servants usually are in the affairs of their employers, and he imagined that a considerable substratum of truth underlay the statements.

In his painstaking way he went on interviewing member after member of the staff, till he had questioned them all. He did not, however, learn much more. The chauffeur,

Marsden, repeated the story of the conversation he had overheard between uncle and nephew. Mrs Frazer was liked by no one, and Gates' sporting proclivities were common property. All had a good word for Nurse Nankivel, but except for the fact that her afternoon walks had been usually taken outside the grounds, no one knew much about her.

With one exception. When in the course of his investigations he interviewed the head gardener's wife, she told him a little more. Mrs Carling had evidently been fond of the missing woman, and seemed glad to give any help she could towards her discovery. Nurse Nankivel, she said, was a pleasant jolly girl, and she, Mrs Carling, had enjoyed her frequent afternoon visits and the walks they had together. The nurse had been in good spirits all the time she was at Polperro, until about a week before Mr Frazer died, when she suddenly became depressed and anxious-looking. Mrs Carling had asked if anything was wrong, but Miss Nankivel had replied evasively. When she was saying good-bye she had begged Mrs Carling to write to her and keep her posted in the Polperro news. Mrs Carling had done so, once, but she had had no reply. Mrs Carling was greatly distressed about her friend's disappearance and did not for a moment believe that the girl's own actions had in any way contributed towards it.

The mention of a letter at once interested French. Tanner had told him that the nurse had certainly received one, and was believed to have received two, letters while at Bryanston Square. The first one, the doubtful one, she was thought to have had on or about Thursday, the 29th of September – that is, ten days before her disappearance. The second she had undoubtedly received on the Tuesday following, four days before the disappearance. Of these, the first was believed to have added a good deal to her perturbation of mind. The second she seemed to have been anxiously expecting.

"When did you write your letter, Mrs Carling?" asked French.

The lady was afraid she could scarcely tell him; she thought five or six days after the nurse had left, but she wasn't sure. French thereupon got down to it.

By dint of painstaking suggestions he fixed the date. She had really written to tell the nurse about the funeral, and she had described this and the reading of the will and Mrs Frazer's and Mr Gates' reactions on becoming wealthy: all as described to her husband by the butler. This proved it was written on or after Tuesday the 27th, the date of the funeral. On the other hand, she had not mentioned a slight accident to her little son which had taken place on the 29th, and she certainly would have done so had it then happened. The letter must therefore have been written on the 27th or 28th.

This certainly looked as if it might have been the letter believed to have been received by the nurse on the 29th, and which had so much increased her anxiety. On the other hand, try as French would, he was unable to discover anything in Mrs Carling's letter which could have so upset her.

Taking leave of Mrs Carling, French went back to the main house and asked to see Gates. He was laid up with bronchitis, it appeared, and in bed. French, however, sent up his card, thinking that as the man was probably bored he might see him. Whatever the reason, French's action was justified, for he was asked to go up to the bedroom.

As he entered Dr Campion was leaving.

"Hullo, inspector! Still at it?" he called as French stood aside to let him pass. "Got any further?"

"Getting on, doctor," French returned. "Slow, you know, sir, but terribly sure."

Campion laughed. "I always back the snails and tortoises myself," he declared as he went downstairs.

Gates, who was sitting up in an armchair at the fire, was a big man, about the same height as Campion, but of a heavier build. His fiery red hair and long moustache were greying, and his eyes were blue and dancing with intelligence. His rough-hewn features and massive chin suggested strength, and his manner gave French the impression of a man who would not be easily turned from his purpose.

"Very good of you, sir, to see me when you're not feeling well," said French. "I just want to ask a question or two on the chance that you may be able to help me."

"Sit down," said Gates in a deep booming voice. "I'm all right. I'll be out tomorrow. What did you want to ask me?"

French explained about Nurse Nankivel and said he was trying to find someone who had seen her on her daily walks or at other times when off duty. "I want to find out if she had made any local acquaintances," he went on, "and it occurred to me that you might possibly have seen her talking to someone."

Gates hadn't. He knew nothing about her. He had seen her of course, as he had frequently gone in to the sickroom to sit with his uncle. The nurse had been there, though she usually left them alone together. She seemed "all right", but he had never taken much notice of her.

French did not take to the man. He spoke in a loud blustering way, and French was sure that if he was crossed, he would be nasty. After the subject of the nurse had been exhausted, French stayed for a moment chatting. "You must have seen life in Australia, sir?" he suggested, and Gates, rising to this, told a few of his experiences. He had, it appeared, worked at most things out there. He had farmed sheep, he had dug for gold, he had knocked about on the waterfront of Sydney, apparently at one time being next thing to down and out. French would have liked to hear his story, but as his curiosity was only idle, he could not well ask for it. With a polite word of thanks he therefore took his leave.

His enquiries at Polperro had not been particularly productive; in fact, he could scarcely have learned less than he had. He wondered if the second nurse, Nurse Henderson, could tell him more.

From the nearest call office he rang up Sister Austin at the Chelsea nursing home. Could she tell him the present whereabouts of Nurse Henderson? Oh, at Bramley, was she? Thanks very much.

French felt he could not but take advantage of so wonderful a stroke of luck. Bramley was close by, not more than five miles from where he was standing. Without further consideration he pedalled off.

He had no trouble in running Nurse Henderson to earth. She was on day duty and saw him at once. On hearing his business she at once grew keenly interested, and he saw that she had been much attached to her missing colleague. She was younger than Helen Nankivel, probably by four or five years. French sized her up as a pleasant unaffected girl, and by no means a fool.

He thought it better to take her into his full confidence, and therefore told her of the suspected understanding between the missing woman and Dr Earle. Nurse

Henderson was scornful, indeed utterly sceptical of the idea.

"Oh no," she said, "nurse was not that kind of woman. You've made a mistake there, inspector, I'm certain."

"You may be right," French admitted. "I'm only trying to get information to build a theory on. Tell me, have you got any theory as to what might have happened?"

Nurse Henderson had none. To her the disappearance was a tragedy. Terribly upset as at a personal loss, she admitted her dread that her friend must be dead.

"Oh," said French, "don't say that. We have no information so far to warrant such a conclusion."

"You have her disappearance," the young woman returned. "How else can you explain it?"

French did not repeat his explanation. He busied himself without much success in trying to get further information about the missing woman.

According to Nurse Henderson, Helen Nankivel was happy and contented in her job. She had a little money, not enough to live on, but enough to make her reasonably comfortable when added to her nurse's salary. She had no worries, or none of any magnitude. Her health was good. She was not unhappy through any affair of the heart. In fact, she had no reason to take any drastic action with a view to changing her lot.

French was slightly puzzled as he rode back to Farnham to have his talk with Sheaf. No one who had known Nurse Nankivel accepted his theory of her having gone off with Dr Earle, but none of these people gave any reason for their belief other than that they did not think she was that kind of woman. Moreover, while he had expected to have been able to trace communications between the two missing persons, he had so far failed to do so. On the other hand, no theory other than his own had been put forward, nor could he himself think of an alternative.

Having fortified himself with a cup of tea – it was just five o'clock – French reached the police station and went in to see Sheaf.

11

WHAT SHEAF THOUGHT

The superintendent was expecting him. "Well, French," he greeted him, "you want to have a talk about the case?"

"Yes," said French, sitting down and producing a new box of cigarettes, which he absent-mindedly opened as he spoke. "I'm not sure that I haven't gone far enough with the thing, and I wanted to discuss the point with you. I admit the affair is not properly finished, but it seems to me so clear what has happened that I question if it's worth spending any more time and money on it."

Sheaf took and lit a cigarette, nodding heavily as he did so. "Go ahead," he said briefly.

Slowly and with extreme care French in his turn selected a cigarette, while he marshalled his facts in his mind. Then he began to speak. He briefly recounted everything that he had done and learnt since he took over, but without commenting on the facts. "Now, super," he went on, "it's your shot. Will you let me know what's been done locally?"

For answer Sheaf pressed a bell. "Find Sheepshanks, will you," he directed.

The sergeant was evidently in the building, for he turned up in a few seconds. "The inspector wants to know what you've done, sergeant," Sheaf said. "You might repeat what you told me a little while ago."

"We've made enquiries on the lines you suggested, sir," Sheepshanks answered, turning to French, "but we've got nothing. We've done the roads and the buses and any cars we could hear of and the railway stations and the houses in the neighbourhood. We've made all the enquiries we could possibly think of, without a single result. If Earle went away by road, either voluntarily or involuntarily, no one saw him. Of course that's not so surprising as it looks at first sight. St Kilda is a lonely place and he might have left a dozen times without anyone being a bit the wiser."

"Yes, French, that's quite true what Sheepshanks says," Sheaf agreed. "Because the man wasn't seen is really no argument that he didn't walk away openly from the house. I agree that we had to make the enquiries, but I'm not surprised at the result. I didn't hope for anything different."

"I suppose you're right," French agreed. "All the same, it does seem a bit surprising that no one saw him. But of course what you say is correct. The place is very exceptional."

Sheaf moved impatiently. "Well, you wanted to discuss it," he grunted. "Suppose you go ahead and let's hear your ideas. Then if there's anything left to discuss, we'll discuss it."

French grinned. "I like your suggestion that when I've dealt with it there'll be nothing more to say," he declared, then as Sheaf opened his mouth to reply, he went on hastily: "Very well, I'll give you my conclusions, and if you think I'm not right, stop me."

"You'll not get far on those terms," the super muttered, while Sheepshanks grinned painfully.

"I'll go on as long as I'm allowed." French became serious. "So far then as I've been able to see, there are four possibilities in this case, which I, or rather we, have investigated to some extent. I say 'to some extent' because admittedly these enquiries are not complete. I suggest we take these possibilities in turn."

Sheaf settled himself in his chair with an air of virtuous resignation, and Sheepshanks, who had been told to sit down, with one of interest.

"I begin with Earle," French went on, "and to make the statement complete, I presume you agree that we may eliminate accident and suicide and confine ourselves to voluntary disappearance and murder?"

"I agree. That's proved by the disappearance of the body."

"Quite. Then let's take murder first, in which of course I include kidnapping, because frankly it's the case I don't believe in."

Once again Sheaf nodded.

"Now as to possible murderers. Julia Earle is the first. I don't know that I need go over the case against her; you know it as well as I do. The home was unhappy; she was running after this man Slade; the husband presumably was after this Nurse Nankivel; there was a very real fear that he might change his will and leave her comparatively poor: you know all that?"

Sheaf put in his customary nod.

"Then she had opportunity. She could have drugged her husband at supper and she could have knocked him over the head in the drawing-room or outside. Or she could have poisoned him. All that was possible, *but* there were two snags. First, Could she have murdered him without the sister's knowledge? and second, Could she have got rid of the body? I decided, rightly or wrongly, that she could have done neither. That's my first possibility.

"My second is, Could the sister, Marjorie Lawes, have been party to the thing? On the whole, I thought not. She didn't seem to me to have the character for it; she had no motive, and even with her help I did not believe the women could have got rid of the body. It is true that if they had taken out their car they might have disposed of it, but you, sergeant, felt the radiator when you got out and it was cold, and I made sure the water hadn't been changed. So they hadn't taken the car out. I came to the conclusion Marjorie Lawes was also innocent. That's my second possibility."

"I never believed those two were guilty," Sheaf declared, while the sergeant nodded his approval.

"I'm glad you both agree," French returned. "My third possibility was Slade: Slade either alone or in partnership with Mrs Earle. Slade had motive. He was running after Mrs Earle, and doubtless he wanted Earle out of the way. And if he had had any hint of Earle's goings on in London, as almost certainly he must have, he also would want to prevent Earle altering his will. Moreover he was on bad terms with Earle: they had had at least one quarrel. Again, Slade had the necessary opportunity. He could have left his house unseen and knocked at the window of Earle's drawing-room, got Earle out and killed him. But in Slade's case the same snag arose: what could he have done with the body?"

"A car," Sheaf suggested.

"No," said French, "that's just the point. I went into that and Slade could not have got a car," and French recounted the evidence of the chauffeur and his wife. "So I eliminated Slade, my third possibility. That covers, so far as I can see it, the case for murder."

"Then, by elimination, voluntary disappearance only is left?"

"I think so, but there's more in it than that. Take it conversely. Suppose Earle was murdered. Very well then, what about the nurse?"

Sheaf grunted. "There's something in that," he admitted.

"There's a good deal in it," French declared. "I take it that no one's going to suggest that the nurse was murdered too? Even if Mrs Earle or Slade or both were guilty of killing Earle, they could have had no animosity against the nurse. Then where does she come in? Why should she disappear? I can conceive no reason."

"Nor can I."

"On the other hand," French went on, "if Earle disappeared voluntarily, the nurse's action is accounted for at once. If they were attracted to one another, they might easily go off together. It's not hard to make a case for their doing so: he would want peace and she security. I needn't labour the point: you'll both see it as clearly as I can."

"Yes, that's all right." Sheaf was lounging back in a bored manner, but his expression showed that he was listening with the keenest attention and interest.

"Now," went on French, "the more we consider this theory of voluntary disappearance, the more confirmation we find. First take the question of the absence of shoes and hat and coat and the failure to secure an uninterrupted period before the hue and cry is raised. From one point of view these may be eliminated, because they remain unchanged on any theory. I mean, whether the affair was murder or voluntary disappearance, these difficulties have to be met.

"At the same time their most *likely* solution is that Earle previously hid shoes and a hat and coat outside his house and put them on as soon as he left. He would only have had to carry the house slippers, which he could easily have put into his pocket. Knowing the district, he could have made his way unseen, say, to Guildford station, where he was unknown, and where by mixing with the crowd, he could have reached the London train unnoticed. And of course he might have taken these precautions to make it seem unlikely that he had gone off with a woman."

"Same with the raising of the hue and cry?"

"Same with the raising of the hue and cry."

"That's all obvious," Sheaf agreed. "If the man had wanted to get away on the quiet, he could have done it. What do you say, sergeant?"

Sheepshanks, delighted to be asked, emphatically agreed with his chief.

"Then there's another strong point for voluntary disappearance: Earle's book. Apparently this was an important work about which he was extremely keen. I told you the manuscript had vanished. Now if Earle were murdered, should the manuscript not be there? On the other hand, if Earle went off secretly, would he not have taken it with him?"

"I suppose, sir," Sheepshanks said diffidently, "it's out of the question that the doctor could have been murdered for the manuscript?"

This was evidently a new idea to Sheaf. He nodded approvingly. "Yes, what about that, French?"

"I thought of it," French returned. "As a matter of fact, I wondered if Campion could have killed him for it. But Campion was in the drawing-room with his sisters and Miss Stone at the time of Earle's disappearance. I couldn't think of anyone else who might have done it."

"Besides," Sheaf added, "there remains the nurse. For the moment I forgot her."

149

"That's right, super. To say that either Campion or anyone else murdered Earle doesn't explain what happened to the nurse."

"Very well. Then, as I said, if we eliminate murder, only voluntary disappearance is left?"

"That's my view," French agreed. "So far I think the thing may be summarised by saying that there's no direct evidence for murder, and that the murder theory creates certain rather grave difficulties, while there is evidence for voluntary disappearance, and this theory fits all the facts and meets these difficulties. Do you agree so far, super?"

"I do, but there are difficulties in the disappearance theory too," Sheaf pointed out.

"I know there are: I'm coming to them. There are no less than five as I see it, but only two of them are serious."

"Let's have 'em, anyway."

"Well, the first is financial. I've not been able to trace that Earle got any money to go away with. There's nothing surer than that if he went off with the nurse he had money to do it: not merely a lump sum, but a steady income arranged somehow. As I think you know, I put out a circular with a photograph of Earle to all banks in the hope of tracing a second account in some other name, but without any success. I feel sure that if Earle had had such an account, I should have heard of it. Then I made enquiries from the companies in which Earle had his money. His holdings had not been sold out. Moreover, the man was not known to have had other resources."

"You're right about that being a difficulty," Sheaf declared, grinding out the stub of his cigarette and lighting another. "If you ask me, it's a pretty hefty snag. And the nurse had no money either?"

"No, not so far as I can learn."

Sheaf nodded again. "Right; go ahead."

"The second difficulty is that neither of these two sent any message to their respective friends. To me, super, this is an even greater difficulty than the first. It doesn't seem to me in the character of either of them. Mrs Earle was convinced that if her husband would have let her know his movements, he would have done so, and that sister at the nursing home said exactly the same about the nurse. One can understand that they mightn't say anything about it beforehand, but when the thing had actually been done, there could be no reason against, and many for, relieving their friends' anxieties."

"Curse it," said Sheaf, "you're right about that. I hadn't thought of it. Well, never mind; go on."

"The other difficulties are of less importance, but still I think they must be taken into account. The third is that no one who knew the nurse will believe that she would have acted as we are supposing: they all say she 'was not that kind of woman'. Incidentally the same applies to some extent to Earle also. These general opinions may not perhaps be very convincing, but they should have some weight."

"Not a great deal," Sheaf declared.

"Not a great deal, but some. The fourth difficulty is that no information as to their leaving can be obtained. The entire police force of the British Isles is on the look-out for these two persons, and neither has been seen."

"Nothing in that, French. All sorts of people disappear and are never found, in spite of police search. You should know that better than I."

"I do know it," French admitted, "but this should count when added to the other facts."

"Very well, let it go. Next point?"

"Passports," said French. "Earle had a passport but he had not taken it. I found it in his desk. And Nurse Nankivel had never applied for one. Of course they might both have applied under false names, but they would scarcely have succeeded in getting them. Police supervision over this matter may not be very rigorous, but it would be enough to stop that. And neither would have known how to get a forged copy. I take it then that they did not mean to go abroad. But if they remained in this country, their identity would be almost certain sooner or later to become known."

Sheaf rubbed his forehead. "I don't think there is much in that. What do you make of it, Sheepshanks?"

The sergeant held definite views. He thought they might remain hidden in London or some other big city. "Earle could fake an illness," he pointed out, "and grow a moustache. He'd probably never be recognised then. And if people have only seen the nurse in her uniform, they mightn't recognise her in ordinary clothes."

The others looked at Sheepshanks with approval. Right or wrong, his view had been worth putting forward. "Then that's the other side of it," Sheaf said heavily and the trio relapsed into silence. At last Sheaf made an impatient movement.

"I will admit, French," he declared, "that for a man who was proving this was a disappearance, you've been fair to the opposition."

French shrugged. "Take care of the cons and the pros will take care of themselves," he retorted. "You know that as well as I do, super. I've been as clear as I could about these difficulties, because the disappearance theory depends on them. If they can't be met, the theory's false: that's all."

The superintendent grunted. "Can they be met?" he asked. "What do you say, sergeant?"

This time Sheepshanks was not certain. It did not seem to him a clear case. On the balance he thought the facts pointed to a disappearance, but he didn't think this was conclusively proved.

"I declare, French, I agree with Sheepshanks," the superintendent said at last. "You've made too good a list of difficulties. Tell me, would you really be satisfied yourself to leave the case as it is?"

French laughed. "That's a nasty one." He thought for some moments. "I don't mind confessing," he went on, "that I'd rather have the thing cut and dry, and all these ends that seem to be over tidied away. But it's going to mean the deuce of a lot of work, for which, I presume, you'll pay. Under the circumstances, I think it's up to you to call the tune."

Sheaf appreciated that, but he didn't want anything afterwards to come out which would indicate that the Farnham police and their superintendent had been caught napping. "I would suggest, French, if you're agreeable, that you stick it a little while longer. Let's see, this is Friday night: that's less than a fortnight since the thing happened. What about trying for another week, and then if nothing fresh has turned up, we can have another talk about it?"

French agreed readily, indeed almost with enthusiasm. It was exactly what he wished himself. There was nothing he hated more than to leave a case incomplete.

"Right then," he finished up. "I'll go up to Town now and tomorrow try and tighten up the general search, and on Monday I'll come down and have another shot here."

Before Sheaf could reply his telephone bell rang out. "Yes?" he grunted into the instrument; "speaking. Oh, it's you, super? Yes? Oh, you have? Good!...Well, Inspector French is here now and I'll tell him. Hold on a sec." He turned to French. "Guildford super speaking. He has news of your nurse. He wants you to go over in the morning."

"Not tonight?"

"Not tonight, super?..." Then again to French. "No, he thinks nothing would be gained. Fact is, he doesn't think what he's got will be much help to you."

"Right," said French. "I'll go in the morning on my way to Town."

"He'll be with you first thing in the morning, super," Sheaf repeated and rang off.

"He didn't say who saw her?" went on French.

"No; no details."

The tracing of the nurse's possible arrival at the Hog's Back being a local enquiry, French had asked Sheaf to put it in hand; and Sheaf, on the grounds that the area in question was outside his district, had passed the matter on to the Guildford authorities.

Next morning French took an early bus to Guildford and in ten minutes had heard the superintendent's news. It appeared that the nurse had kept her appointment for that Sunday afternoon. Careful enquiries had led to the discovery of two persons who had seen her. The first was the conductor of a bus running from Guildford to Farnham. He said that a lady answering the given description and whom he recognised from the accompanying photograph, had boarded his bus, the 5.50 p.m. from Guildford, at the Technical Institute in Guildford, the regular stopping place. She had travelled with him up on to the Hog's Back to where the road to Compton branched off. There she had got out. It was dusk at the time and he had not seen in which direction she had gone. She had seemed perfectly normal in every way and not at all excited, though as his bus was well filled, he had not observed her with any special care.

The superintendent had not been content with this result, and had continued to press his enquiries. These at last had resulted in the discovery that a Mr Kenworthy, of Guildford, had also been at the place just before six o'clock and had also seen the nurse. Mr Kenworthy had been walking along the Hog's Back road in the direction of Farnham, and was just approaching the Compton road junction, when a bus overtook him and stopped at the junction. A lady got out, and he was just near enough to see that she was dressed in some lightish colour such as grey. The bus passed on towards Farnham and she walked in the same direction, Mr Kenworthy following some distance behind. At the Farnham side of the bypass under-bridge, some hundred yards farther on, a car was standing. As the lady reached it a man got out and spoke to her. Then she got in and the car moved off towards Guildford. Mr Kenworthy had not, however, observed whether when it reached the road junction, it went on towards Guildford, or turned down the hill towards Compton. Presumably, however, it had gone towards Compton, as the nurse would scarcely have been taken back to the place from which she had just come.

"Fine, super," French said warmly when he had assimilated these details. "That's bound to be a help to us. This man Kenworthy wasn't able to describe the car?"

"No, but I didn't push him very hard. I thought you would probably like to see him yourself. As a matter of fact he was with me here last night when I rang Sheaf up, and I told him you'd be over this morning and asked him to keep in touch. He said he'd be at his house all day," and the super gave the address.

The house was up on the hill at the back of the old High Street. A delightful position, French thought it, as fifteen minutes later he knocked at the door. Mr Kenworthy was elderly, evidently a retired business man. But he could not tell French more than he had already told the super-intendent. There is a footpath over the bypass bridge on the right side, facing Farnham, and he, Kenworthy, was walking along this. When the lady got out of the bus on the far side of the road she crossed and walked along the footpath a few yards in front of him. The car was standing at the same side of the road, facing towards them as they came up. The lady had got into the car, and the car had just started as Kenworthy came up.

As to the man who had got out and spoken to the lady, Mr Kenworthy could give no particulars. It was dusk, nearly dark, in fact, and he had only seen him as a smudge. No, he couldn't be certain that it was not a lady. Someone got out, and that was really all he knew.

Nor could he tell anything about the car except that it was a saloon. He had not observed the make or the size; in fact it had not attracted his attention in any way. French, seeing he could get no more, thanked the man and walked slowly down to the station *en route* for Town.

As he thought over what he had heard, he swore. This information about the nurse was damnably puzzling. His next step, he supposed, must be to find the car which had met her. But that wasn't going to be so frightfully easy. It meant the usual elimination. He must find out where all the possible cars had been at six o'clock. And the possible people also...

And where had the nurse gone?...

Curse it all! He was sick of the whole confounded business. French realised that he had gone stale and that what he wanted was a weekend away from the case. Well, he was on his way home now and until Monday morning he wouldn't let another thought of the darned affair into his mind. Sufficient unto the day!

12

URSULA STONE

That Saturday night a severe rainstorm passed over the whole country. French, wakened by the downpour, had listened to it with actual distress. For in furtherance of his design for achieving a complete change of thought, he had planned one of his usual Sunday excursions with Mrs French. It was to be a rather special occasion, inasmuch as they proposed to go farther afield than usual, or at least farther than was usual at this time of year. They had decided on the Romney Marsh. Neither of them had ever been there, though both had read about it, and both were looking forward with keen pleasure to seeing this stretch of new and distinctive country.

When morning came, however, they were both delighted to find that the wind had fallen, the clouds had vanished, and the sun was shining as if it were May. As they looked out of the express they saw that everything simply looked the fresher for the rain. Taking a bus from Hastings, they drove through Winchelsea to Rye, explored the streets and church of the quaint old town, and ended up with a long tramp along the shore towards Dungeness. They enjoyed every minute of it and found the breath of sea air invigorating and wholly delightful. These excursions counted for a good deal in both their lives. Though married for more years than French cared to contemplate, he and his wife remained as good pals as ever they had been. Healthily tired and pleased with themselves and life, they reached home in the evening in time for a late supper.

When the meal was over French settled down in his arm-chair before the fire, determined to end a day of relaxation with a couple of lazy and luxurious hours over a novel. But Fate willed otherwise. About nine o'clock, before he had read a dozen pages, his telephone bell rang.

It was the Yard. A message had just come through from Farnham. The officer on duty read it in a dull unemotional way which threw French into a paroxysm of impatience. "From Superintendent Sheaf, Farnham, to Inspector French, Scotland Yard. Ursula Stone disappeared. Please come at once. Will have car to meet 9.30 from Waterloo at Guildford."

French gave vent to an oath which surprised even Mrs French. "That Farnham case," he cried; "I've got to go down," and running to his room he packed his bag and hurried off to the Yard. There he picked up the suitcase containing his notebooks, and such apparatus as he used in his work, and went on to Waterloo. Fifty-one minutes later he left the train at Guildford.

"What's gone wrong now?" he asked the constable who was driving the waiting car.

"I don't know, sir, except that there was a 'phone through from St Kilda about nine o'clock saying that Miss Stone had disappeared. The super and Sergeant Sheepshanks have gone out. I was told to repeat the message to the Yard and then meet you here. There are better trains to Guildford than to Farnham at this hour."

French felt as if the bottom had been knocked out of his world. The bottom had certainly been knocked out of his case. What he was up against, he now saw, was infinitely bigger than anything which up till now had entered his mind. He had been working on some neat little theory to cover the vanishing of Earle and the nurse, but the vanishing of Earle and the nurse was only a part of what was going on. What terrible and sinister agency could be behind these manifestations?

One thing at least seemed to leap out from them, clear and unmistakable. Ursula Stone could scarcely have disappeared voluntarily. In her case there could surely be no motive for such a step. Besides, the coincidence of three voluntary disappearances coming so close to one another would be too remarkable to be accepted without the most overwhelming proof. No; this time it looked, at first sight at all events, a definite case of murder. And if so in Ursula's case, what about the others? Must it not follow that they also…? French had seldom felt more bewildered.

So much at all events for his theory. The one alleviating feature in the affair was that he had not pressed his theory unduly and had agreed to continue working on the case. But it had been a narrow shave. He had been tempted to take up a much stronger attitude.

They drove quickly up on to the Hog's Back, then turning left, passed down through Puttenham and round the corner at the Tarn to St Kilda.

Here French found a tense atmosphere. Sheaf was very obviously in command, and round him, pale faced and trembling, were Julia Earle, Marjorie Lawes, and Alice and Flo Campion, while Lucy, the maid, hovered in the background. A little distance away Dr Campion was discussing something with Sergeant Sheepshanks. A constable stood at the door.

"Oh, here you are, French," said Sheaf heavily. "It looks like Miss Stone this time. She's been missing since five o'clock."

"Since five o'clock?" French repeated in surprise. Why in Hades had they waited for four hours before giving the alarm?

"Yes, she was last seen at five o'clock, but it wasn't till nearly eight that it was suspected she was missing. Mrs Earle will tell you. Will you take over from now? I've done nothing except to have the woods and road searched."

"Very well," French returned. He crossed the room and drew Sheepshanks into a corner. "Have you felt the car radiator?" he whispered.

"Directly I got here, sir. It was quite cold."

French addressed the company. "First of all, ladies and gentlemen, I'd like to hear just what has happened. Perhaps, Mrs Earle" – he turned to Julia – "I might begin with you. Would you mind coming into the dining-room and sitting down and telling me about it?"

Julia was pitiably shaken and nervous. Her face was drawn and livid, her teeth chattered, and she kept jerking restlessly about. French did not at all like her appearance.

"You've had a nasty shock," he said kindly. "Perhaps I might suggest a drop of whisky. I think you'd feel better for it."

"We all want a pick-me-up," Julia admitted. "You see, we were so upset we didn't really have any supper. What can it all mean, inspector? If anything has happened to Miss Stone, I think after the other it will kill me."

French beckoned to Lucy. "Mrs Earle wants some wine or whisky. Will you bring something. You'll excuse me, madam," he went on to Julia, "but you can't tell me a proper story unless you're feeling fit yourself."

A whisky and soda made Julia feel a new woman, and while the others were helping themselves, she told her story.

"Miss Stone, you know, was here when my husband disappeared," she began. "She had intended to leave on the following day, the Monday, but I persuaded her to remain on with us, and she did so. She agreed to stay an extra fortnight, and was intending to leave tomorrow.

"After tea this afternoon she went up to her room to lie down. She frequently did so in the afternoons, though not always. I was upstairs myself and I looked in to see that she was comfortable. That was just about five o'clock, and she was then lying down with a book and seemed quite all right in every way. I came back to Miss Lawes here in the sitting room. We were doing nothing particular, just reading and chatting a little. Then the Campions looked in to see how we were, the doctor and his two sisters. After they left I think my sister and I fell asleep; I did at all events. About seven I went out to get supper: cold supper we have on Sundays because Lucy is out. It was ready about half past seven and I rang the bell. Miss Stone didn't come down, and after a few minutes I said, 'Ursula can't have heard the bell. I'll ring again.' My sister told me not to ring, saying that she would go up. She did so and I heard her moving about upstairs. Then she called me. There was a kind of urgency in her voice and I ran up quickly. 'Ursula isn't here,' she said. 'She's taking a bath before supper,' I said, but my sister said no, that she had looked everywhere upstairs and she wasn't there. For a time we didn't realise that anything could be wrong, though there was a sort of fear at the back of our minds. We searched the entire house, but she wasn't anywhere in it. Then we thought she had gone out for a breath of air before supper and we looked in her room for her things. All her outdoor things were in her

room; her hats and coats and outdoor shoes. By this time it
was getting on towards eight o'clock, and of course she
knew supper was at half past seven. We looked at each other
in a sort of horror: it was all so like this day fortnight. We
had a quick look round the hall to see that no wraps had
gone, and also a look round the grounds. We could find
nothing unusual, and then we rang up Dr Campion. At first
Dr Campion made light of it. He was like ourselves at first,
he could not believe anything had gone wrong, but when
we told him we had found that none of her outdoor clothes
had been taken, he thought more seriously of it. You know,
it's a cold night. They came over at once, he and his sisters,
and they've been here ever since."

"About what time did they arrive?" French asked.

"They came at once. They must have got here about
eight or a few minutes past: I didn't really look. Dr
Campion spoke of ringing up the police immediately, then
we thought we'd have a look round ourselves first. Perhaps
we were wrong about that, inspector, but you know how
people feel about that sort of thing. Dr Campion was
splendid. He organised a search, just as had been done this
day fortnight, giving everybody an area to search. We
looked for some time, then shortly before nine we all met
again and Dr Campion said we could not delay any more
in ringing up the police, and he did so."

Julia had shown evidences of strong emotion all the time
she was speaking, and it was with an obvious effort that she
had compelled herself to remain calm and tell her story
consecutively.

"That's all very clear, Mrs Earle," French said. "Now I
want you to wait here for a moment till I speak to
Superintendent Sheaf, then there are just one or two
questions that I should like to ask you."

Sheaf was waiting for him in the hall. "I'm going now, French," he said. "Is there anything you'd like us to do?"

"That's what I wanted to discuss with you before you left," French answered. "You say you've had the roads and wood searched?"

"Yes, as far as torches would allow. I don't believe much can be done in that way till we get daylight."

"I agree with you, super. Can you let me have some help in the morning for this purpose?"

"Yes, I'll send you half a dozen men as soon as it's properly light; say at seven. Now is there anything else?"

French hesitated. It was scarcely his place to detail jobs for the Farnham men.

"Don't you think we should make the same enquiries that we did in the case of Earle?" he asked. "I mean enquiries along the roads, at the stations, from bus conductors, and so on?"

The superintendent dropped his voice. They had strolled out to Sheaf's car and were alone.

"I'm afraid we must do so," he returned, "but I don't believe we'll learn anything. This is no disappearance, French. This woman wouldn't have wanted to disappear. This is murder. All these enquiries were based on the possibility of Earle's having disappeared voluntarily."

French nodded. "That's what I thought coming down in the train," he agreed. "But we might come on some trace of the murderer."

"Not a chance, I should say. The man that's done this thing knows his way round too well to be caught napping. All the same, I agree we daren't omit these local lines and I'll take them on, same as I did in Earle's case. That'll leave you free to follow up anything special you get on to. How's that?"

"First rate, super. Nothing could be better. Just let's get out a description of Miss Stone, and perhaps you would 'phone it up to the Yard for circulation? Then I'll stay here all night and give those fellows a hand to make their search in the morning."

The description complete, Sheaf drove off with his men, while French returned to the dining room. It seemed to him that nothing could be done out of doors till the morning, and that he could best spend his time in getting the fullest details possible from the members of the household.

"Now, Mrs Earle," he said, "just two or three questions if you please. I'll not keep you long, but I want to know everything you can tell me in as great detail as possible. And first about Miss Stone herself. Did you notice anything unusual in her manner recently?"

"Absolutely nothing whatever."

"You think she didn't foresee that anything – er – out of the common was about to take place?"

"I'm positive of it."

"No signs of excitement?"

"None."

French nodded. "Did she get any message today which might have led her to go out this afternoon?"

"Not as far as I know. In fact I may say definitely that she didn't. There's no post on Sunday, and I've been about all day and would have heard the telephone."

"No caller?"

"No."

"Nor note delivered by hand?"

"No."

"Were there no other callers today except the Campions?"

"Only Mr Slade."

"When was that, Mrs Earle?"

"About three. He only stayed a few minutes."

"Any special subject under discussion at tea?"

"No," Julia answered again. "So much so that now, half a dozen hours afterwards, I couldn't tell you what we talked of."

French paused. That seemed to cover all he could hope to get about Ursula Stone. He thought for a moment, then went on.

"It was about five o'clock, you say, when Miss Stone went to lie down and you saw her in her room. When did the Campions arrive?"

"About quarter of an hour later; say quarter past five."

"Did Miss Stone know they were here?"

"If she were awake she must have heard them," Julia replied. "Her room is in the front of the house and she would have heard the car and then their voices."

"Would she not have come down if she had heard them?"

"Not necessarily, I think. It's true she was a friend of the Campion sisters, but after all it was to me that they were paying the visit. I couldn't say, she might reasonably have come down or not come down."

"She had intended to leave tomorrow?"

"Yes."

"Then would she not have come down to say goodbye?"

"She might: I couldn't tell."

Again French paused, whistling tunelessly below his breath.

"Nothing occurred, I suppose, during the Campions' call? Was anything special talked about?"

"I don't think so. The only thing I remember indeed was admiring the furniture for Miss Stone's dolls' house."

"Furniture?"

"Yes. Dr Campion had made furniture for the house and he brought it over with him. Indeed he nearly forgot to give it to us. We were in the drawing-room when he suddenly said, 'Oh, I've brought something for Miss Stone. It's in my coat pocket.' He disappeared for a moment into the hall, then came back with the most lovely little tables and chairs and bedsteads. You never saw anything so wonderfully done. I'll show them to you; they're beautiful. We handed them round and admired them. I wanted to call Miss Stone down, but he wouldn't hear of her being disturbed."

"I follow," said French. "I'm afraid that doesn't help us very much. What I was really trying to get at was whether anything was discussed which Miss Stone might have heard as she was coming down to join you, and which might have caused her to change her mind?"

Julia shook her head. "Oh no, nothing of the kind. We just chatted about nothing in particular."

"And how long did you say the Campions stayed?"

"They left about six, I think. About three-quarters of an hour. I think Miss Campion would have stayed longer, but Dr Campion was anxious to be off as he said he wanted to call at the golf club to see someone about going to Town tomorrow. In the end he went out and started up the car. When she heard that she made a move."

Once again French paused. None of this was very productive, but he didn't think anything more was to be learnt from Julia.

"Now let me see that I've got these times right," he went on. "The Campions left about six, then you and Miss Lawes remained sitting in the drawing-room and had a little sleep. About seven you went to get supper and about half past seven you rang for Miss Stone. It was then you discovered she was missing?"

"Yes, that's correct."

"You looked about until nearly eight, and then rang up Dr Campion. He and his sisters came at once, arriving a few minutes past eight, and then you carried out your search?"

"Yes," said Julia again.

"Tell me about your search. Where exactly did you look?"

"We divided up between us what was to be done. My sister and I again searched the house, the outbuildings and the grounds, the Campion sisters took their car and drove over the roads, while Dr Campion went through the wood. It was really repeating what had been done before."

"I understand. And how long did your search last?"

"Till nearly nine. I suppose we were forty minutes or three-quarters of an hour looking. My sister and I were done soonest, then the ladies came in with the car, and then Dr Campion. The wood took longest, as the doctor searched among the trees as well as along the paths."

"Quite," French agreed. "That's all, I suppose, you can tell me?"

Julia's manner suggested that it was a great deal more than she would have volunteered. French then thanked her for her clear statement and asked to see Miss Lawes.

One after another he interviewed the others; Marjorie Lawes, Lucy, and the three Campions. But practically the only fresh information he obtained was from Lucy. She said she had seen Ursula Stone in the hall as she was going out that afternoon. It was then just half past three. She was sure of the time, because she had caught the bus which passed the house at 3.35.

"I think, Mrs Earle," French said when he had finished, "that nothing more can be done tonight. I should like to have a look at Miss Stone's room and then with your permission I shall have a sleep here on this drawing-room couch. I suggest that at your convenience everyone may go to bed."

This was arranged. The Campions drove off and Julia and Marjorie retired to their rooms. French made a provisional search of Ursula's room, though without finding anything bearing on the mystery. Then he went down to the drawing-room, turned off the light, and lay down on the sofa.

He was tired, but he could not sleep. This utterly unexpected development filled his mind and kept it working actively. How on earth did Ursula Stone, a visitor to the household, and so far as he had been able to learn, not a very close intimate of any of its members, how did she come to be mixed up so vitally with whatever dreadful activities were going on below the surface of things in this quiet country retreat? And what was in effect going on? Why had first Earle and the nurse and now Ursula Stone been spirited away in this uncanny fashion? What was at the bottom of it?

The only thing in the whole case of which French felt sure was that his conclusions on the previous disappearances were false. These three cases were so much alike that a common origin was irresistibly suggested. It was absurd to suppose that Ursula had disappeared voluntarily. The question reiterated itself, therefore. Did it not follow that all three, she and Earle and the nurse, had been abducted or murdered, or both?

French turned to details. If Ursula had been murdered, how could she have been induced to go out? In the case of

Earle it was possible to conceive of someone coming to the drawing-room window and beckoning him. But this could not have happened in Ursula's case. She was upstairs. Her room was over the dining-room and it had two bow windows, one looking out in front and the other at the side away from the road, that is, the side on which the study gave. But from neither could she see anyone beckoning unless she was actually in the window. Lying on her bed it would have been out of the question. Moreover, it didn't seem possible that anyone could have called her unheard by those below stairs.

Apart from this, the similarity of this case with that of Earle struck French more and more forcibly, the longer he considered them. Both the missing persons had settled down for what would normally have been a considerable time, Earle with his paper, Ursula with her book. It was probable indeed that both would have dozed before they moved. Both had vanished without making a sound or leaving a trace and without the slightest suggestion of a reason. Both had worn house shoes with thin soles, unsuitable for walking even a little way outside. Though on each occasion the weather was cold, neither had taken any wrap or hat. Neither had left any note or message explaining their absence.

French swore mentally as he thought of it. In such circumstances one would have thought that only a perfunctory enquiry would have been needed to clear up the affair. And yet as he thought of what he and Sheaf had done in Earle's case, he realised grimly that nothing could be farther from the truth. The solution was very far indeed from being obvious. On the contrary, it was as hard to reach as any he had ever yet come up against.

His thoughts turned back to the witnesses he had just questioned. *Both* Julia and Marjorie were looking extremely shaken and upset. He began to wonder...Had the fate reserved for the husband been meted out also to the guest? Could it possibly be that these two women were responsible for what had taken place?

In considering this idea French began slowly to grow sleepy. Gradually his thoughts became nightmarish. Dark pictures invaded his mind of dreadful ways of disposing of bodies. The thrilling tale of "The Lodger" recurred to him. But here was no stove like that in the kitchen of that awful house. What, however, might not be found beneath the concrete of the cellar floor? He had read of a body being built into a pillar of a house or an entrance gate, be couldn't remember which. That pillar would never dry out...There was a well-known cave where the fish ate anything thrown in...Quicklime had been used...Who could say what ghastly things lurked in quarry holes or the shafts of disused mines?...Had not the remains of what had once been bodies been found –

A sudden knock awoke French. Daylight was streaming into the room and at the door stood Sergeant Sheepshanks and five policemen.

– 13 –

THE TWO DEPRESSIONS

A few minutes sufficed to settle a programme for the search which would cover all the ground. As soon as each man was allotted his area he started off, and soon work was in full swing.

It was a fine morning, but cold and slightly cloudy: a good morning for their task. There was plenty of light to see anything that was to be seen, but no bright sunshine to throw dark shadows in which small objects might be missed. French took the area immediately surrounding the house. He had measured Ursula's shoes on the previous night and now he began hunting for, among other things, footprints which these might fit.

For some time the monotonous work went on, then a constable called to French.

"I'd like you to have a look here, sir," he said. "There are some traces which might interest you."

He led the way through the wood behind the St Kilda grounds, till in a few yards he struck one of the many paths or tracks leading through the trees. Fifty yards along this path he stopped and pointed into the undergrowth.

"Something's been in that clump, sir. If you go round that way, so as not to disturb these bushes, you'll see."

French followed the advice. Making his way round the clump as the constable directed, he saw that at one point the rough grass was beaten down as if by a weight.

He approached still closer and stood looking down at the marks. Yes, there was no doubt: a weight had lain there, a long narrow weight, perhaps five feet by a foot or fifteen inches, a weight of the shape and size of an average woman's body.

" 'Pon my soul, it's suspicious enough," said French at last.

"You'll notice also, sir," the constable went on, "that someone has passed from the thicket to the path. That's why I asked you to go round and not straight across."

"Good man," French approved. As he examined the place he realised that the officer was right. There was a general appearance of grass and leaves having been dragged lengthwise by the passage of feet. When very close this was not visible, but by going back and stooping he could see the slightly lighter colour of the grass, due to its lying at a flatter angle than the rest.

It certainly looked as if someone had carried a weight along the path, something which he wished temporarily to hide. Seeing this thicket, he had doubtless turned aside and hidden his weight behind the shrubs. Then at a later time he or some other person had come back and removed the object. What was the weight which had been carried?

French went down on his knees and began a meticulous search among the leaves and grass. If a body had lain here, some little object might have dropped out of one of its pockets. Or out of the pockets of the bearer. Or a fragment of cloth might be sticking to a twig. French decided that if there was anything of the kind, he wouldn't miss it.

For some time he worked away, then as he moved some leaves at one end of the depression, he felt his pulses quicken.

"See this," he grimly invited the constable. "You've got on to something right enough."

Beneath the leaves were traces of blood; slight traces, not more than three or four drops. But as far as French was concerned, they were as significant as a lake. That Ursula Stone had been murdered and that her body had lain here, seemed now to be beyond possibility of doubt.

Though French was only too well accustomed to murder and sudden death, he nevertheless could not repress a feeling of horror as he contemplated these sinister tokens. Ursula Stone was more to him than a mere name, the peg on which an investigation was hung. He had interviewed her on more than one occasion and in a mild way he had admired her. She had come up to his ideal of a lady: straight, generous, dignified, kindly; in fact in his own word which covered all the virtues, *decent*. The last person, he would have said, to have been associated with murderers or to have incurred enmity so bitter that it could only be appeased by murder. If this gentle harmless lady had indeed been done to death it meant that something was in progress evil beyond anything he had up to the present imagined.

But an inspector of Scotland Yard engaged on a case cannot allow his feelings to cloud his judgment. Soon the tragic side of the affair gave place to the professional.

He nodded to the constable. "You've done well," he said. "I'll not forget it. Now carry on and finish your area, then come back to me. I'll be between this and the house."

The constable, delighted at the unwonted praise, saluted and withdrew, and French turned once more to his examination of the ground. Because he had found four drops of blood it did not follow that there was nothing else there.

Having marked the place of the bloodstains with a peg, he put the stained leaves in a tin box and dropped the box into his pocket. If the case came to court it would be well to be sure that this was human blood, and not merely a record of the death of some animal.

He continued his researches out to the path in the same patient and thorough way, passing neither shrub nor tuft of grass till he was certain it bore no traces of quarry or victim. Just before he reached the path his care was rewarded again. On the ground was another drop of blood.

Well pleased, he worked on towards the house. Twenty yards farther he found still another drop. It certainly looked as if the body had been carried from the house.

The path was approaching the St Kilda grounds at an angle of forty-five degrees. It did not actually reach the grounds, but passed round the corner behind the house and so to the road. There was, however, a very faint track from it to the grounds, a track made probably by Earle himself. This track reached the grounds at a point nearly opposite the study window. The boundary fence was merely two strands of fencing wire, and served only to mark position, being practically no obstruction to passage.

When French reached the faint track he turned along it towards the house. At the fence, again on a leaf, he found another drop of blood.

He was about to pass through the fence when he happened to notice marks on a small patch of sand behind a furze bush. He went over. This sand, which had evidently been thrown up by a rabbit, was the only sand in the immediate neighbourhood. It lay on the farther side of the bush from the house, the bush being about twenty feet from the building and almost exactly opposite the study window. The marks were undoubtedly footmarks, and fresh at that. They had obviously been made on the Sunday, because they were free from water pitting and Saturday night had been very wet. The sand was too soft to hold details. All that seemed clear was that they had not been made by high-heeled shoes. This, however, did not prove they were a man's, as many women wear low heels in the country. French, pleased with his progress, thought whimsically that if now he only had the great Sherlock's luck, he would find the end of a cigar which would lead him direct to the person who had waited behind the bush. But though he looked everywhere about, he found neither a cigar-end nor anything else.

With renewed zeal he began searching round the house. If he could find blood actually at the house it would show that Ursula had been murdered, or at least attacked, inside, whereas if no further trace were visible there would be nothing to prove that she had not walked out and been killed in the wood. It was a more important point than appeared at first sight, as if the murder had taken place in the house, it would be difficult to exonerate Julia – and perhaps Marjorie – from complicity, while if Ursula had somehow been enticed out into the wood, the chances were the sisters were innocent.

The most meticulous search all round the building, however, revealed no further traces and French transferred his operations to the inside. He began in the hall, connecting the flex of his powerful electric lamp to the ceiling holder. Here, though he was extremely careful, he had no luck. He moved on to the drawing-room, again without result. Then he thought that of all rooms in the house, Ursula's own bedroom was the one most likely to have been the scene of the tragedy, and he went up and made a much more thorough examination of the floor and furniture than he had on the previous evening. But again he found nothing of interest.

A good deal disappointed, he turned his attention to the stairs. No result. Then doggedly he set to work to complete the house. He did the dining room. Again no result. Next he moved to the study. And here, almost immediately, he found more blood!

Locking the door, he began systematically crawling over the floor with his lamp. Yes, here was a drop of blood. And another. And another. Three drops of blood on the carpet!

The study was a small oak-panelled room about ten feet by twelve. In one of the shorter sides was a bow window, the centre portion forming a double-doored French window. Facing into the room from the window, the fireplace was in the middle of the right side and the door to the left of the wall opposite. On the left wall, opposite the fireplace, were bookshelves.

Two of the drops were close together in the corner between the fireplace and the door; the other was just inside the French window. French stood gazing down at them, thinking deeply.

Was there not something suggestive in the position of these drops? The single one near the French window was easy to understand: it had probably fallen while the body was being carried out. But the other two were not, as might have been expected, in the line between the door and the window. They were much too near the corner. They had certainly not fallen while the body was being carried through the room.

Did it not rather look as if the murder must have been committed in the study itself? For a few moments French continued standing in thought, then registering the idea for future consideration, he continued his search. But almost at once he stopped again and began whistling tunelessly.

He had withdrawn to the corner of the room and was glancing about in the hope of seeing something suggestive, when he noticed what he thought were sandy footmarks on the carpet. When bending over the carpet with his lamp he had missed these, but now looking from a distance they showed faintly. Stooping down so as to look along the surface brought them out more clearly. Yes, there was no doubt someone with sandy shoes had walked across the carpet from the French window to the corner where the two drops had fallen. He examined the marks as carefully as he could, but they were very vague and he could not even tell whether they had been made by a man or a woman. He brushed up some of the sand and put it in an envelope, also taking a sample of that behind the bush for comparison.

His first thought was that these traces had been made by the murderer when entering to attack Ursula Stone, but in a moment he saw that the discovery was not necessarily so significant. The footprints need not have been connected with the murder at all. They might have been made in a hundred perfectly innocent ways. However, it was a matter to be borne in mind.

Before turning from this general inspection to examine details French got out his dusting apparatus and went over everything which he thought might bear fingerprints, particularly the handle, key and edges of the French window and of the door between the study and the hall.

On the latter he got prints, several of them, but the handles and key of the French window were absolutely clean. With his little flashlight camera he made records of all the prints he had come on.

The French window next secured his attention. It was locked, but the key was in the door. French unlocked it and opened it. The second half of the door was fastened at top and bottom by running bolts which engaged with the lintel and step respectively. All the fittings were of strong construction and in good order.

French closed and relocked the window, then going out through the hall door, he tried to open it from the outside. It was as he had thought. No one could have entered without a key.

He had just returned to the study when Lucy knocked at the door. She understood he had had no breakfast, and if he liked she would bring him in something on a tray.

French was really grateful, and said so. Breakfast was becoming quite a problem. He didn't want to take the time necessary to go into Farnham for it, but he knew that when he grew hungry the quality of his work fell off. On the other hand, he did not like to ask for anything in a house in which he was a potential enemy.

He seized the opportunity of Lucy's arrival with the tray to make some enquiries. She had, she said, gone over the floor with the vacuum sweeper on the Friday, and she was satisfied that no sand could possibly have been left on it then. At the same time she had dusted the furniture. It was her business to see that the window was secure every night, and she had always done so. The study was now but little used, and so far as she was aware, the French window had not been unlocked for a week. Yes, she had looked at the window on Saturday night, and it was then locked. She had not actually touched it; it was not necessary. You could, as she pointed out, see the bolt of the lock between the two doors. No, she had no objection to French taking her fingerprints to see whether they were the same as those on the door to the hall.

His meal finished, French interviewed the other members of the house. At once the obtained important information. Julia told him that she had both opened and closed the French window on the previous day, the Sunday of the disappearance. She had gone into the study during the morning; she could not say the exact time, but she thought about twelve; and it had seemed to her stuffy and unaired. She had therefore opened both halves of the window. She had gone in again just before lunch, and she had then closed and locked both halves. She had not actually passed out through the window; she had merely opened and closed it.

French then enquired if any other member of the household had passed in or out through the window since the floor had been swept on the Friday. No one appeared to have done so, except possibly unhappy Ursula Stone herself. This, however, was considered unlikely by everyone. French agreed with them for the simple reason that all Ursula's shoes bore fairly high heels, and it was therefore improbable that she was the person who had left the sandy traces.

All this, if true – and French had no reason to doubt it – was significant. If Julia had opened and closed the window about lunchtime on the Sunday, her fingerprints should still be on it. As they were not, it followed that someone afterwards had opened and closed it and, moreover, that this person had either worn gloves or had taken the precaution to wipe the handles after use.

French, rapidly thinking over his next step, decided that he should spend no more time in the house. If other traces of the tragedy remained, they would last longer under cover than they would in the open. Better to see first if he could pick up anything more outside.

Suppose Ursula had been murdered in the study and her body carried out and hidden in the thicket: were there any indications as to the direction in which the remains might afterwards have been taken? French thought there were.

If Earle had been murdered and the method of this latter crime were the same as that of his case, the bodies would have been disposed of in the same way. Now French did not believe that Earle's body had been hidden in the wood. The search had been too thorough. It must then have been removed by car, for the fact that he had been unable to find a possible car was not really evidence that one had not been used. The same considerations would obviously apply in Ursula's case.

The path past where the body had been laid ran out on the road just at the back of St Kilda. Here the starting of a car would be clearly heard by anyone within. It was unlikely therefore that that end of the path had been used. Nor did French think the other end would have been employed, as this debouched on a road more than a mile away: too far to have carried the body. But French remembered that another path crossed this one at right angles a little farther into the wood, and came out on the St Kilda road four or five hundred yards nearer Farnham. This was surely the most suitable place. These were the only paths near the house.

French decided to try the end of this cross path before going farther afield. He therefore retraced his steps to opposite where the depression in the grass had been found, and continued along the path in the direction of Farnham.

Though he did not examine the ground so meticulously as before, he kept a sharp look-out for bloodstains or other marks. But without result. He saw no signs of blood, and though there were plenty of footprints in the patches where the grass had given place to sand, these were so poorly defined as to be useless.

He reached the cross path, and, turning to the right, continued till he came within a few yards of the road. Then once again he began his thorough inspection of every inch of the ground.

His search was soon rewarded. Behind a clump of bushes, in a place hidden both from road and path, was another depression in the grass similar to that found by the constable. French was delighted. This was the kind of achievement which always filled him with satisfaction. He had thought what might have occurred, he had tested his idea, and now his investigations had proved that his guess was correct. That was the way to use one's imagination! And that, he told himself, was where most of his *confrères* came short.

The body then had been carried here from its first resting-place, and here it had lain till its removal by car had been made possible. So far French felt no doubt as to the sequence of events.

He spent a solid hour searching the ground about this second depression, but without result. There were no further traces of blood and no one concerned seemed to have dropped anything. The absence of blood he could understand. The body, immediately after the murder, had been carried to the first thicket. But it had lain there for some time, during which all bleeding would have ceased.

He was about to give up and return to St Kilda when he made a further discovery. On a branch of furze at the side of the road he found a tiny strand of light green wool.

Light green wool! He remembered that in the description of Ursula sent to the Yard one of the items was, "dressed in light green woollen jumper". An important find!

This discovery practically proved his assumption that the body had been removed in a car. French began searching for wheel-marks. Yes, there they were! A car had pulled in towards the edge of the road where the path debouched. But unfortunately the marks were too blurred to be of any use in identifying the vehicle.

Well satisfied with his progress, French returned to St Kilda to find that Sheepshanks and his helpers had completed their work and were waiting to see him before taking their departure. They had found nothing of interest.

"Well, I've got something," said French, and he told the sergeant about the second depression, the wool and the wheel-marks. "You might report to the super and get all enquiries pushed on about cars seen on the roads last night. The super'll know what's wanted. I'll follow you into Farnham presently."

When the police had gone French re-entered the house. One or two small points still remained to be seen to. He asked for Julia.

"Sorry to trouble you again, Mrs Earle, but I wanted to get a little further information, this time about Miss Stone. Can you tell me anything of her general history and circumstances?"

Julia told him what she knew: that Ursula had been at school with herself and her sister; that she was the daughter of a clergyman long since dead; that she had a little money;

that she lived in a small cottage on Bathwick Hill, Bath, and that she interested herself in the local children's hospital.

French, having noted these details, turned to his next point. Going once more to the garage, he examined the car with scrupulous care. He wondered whether it could have been the vehicle used. Sheepshanks had told him that one of the first things he had done on arriving at St Kilda had been to feel the radiator. It was then cold. That had been at a few minutes past nine. As once again French made sure that the water had not been changed, he wondered how long it would take to cool.

He did not know. It depended on many factors: the level of the water, how hot it had been, how cold the night was, how far the garage protected it; all superimposed on some kind of constant for the make of car. He guessed from three to four hours, but he had no idea if this was correct.

Three to four hours would mean that the car could have been used up to about six o'clock and still show no traces of heat. Supposing Julia – and possibly Marjorie – were guilty, when could they have used it?

Lucy had gone out at half past three and had testified that at that hour Ursula was alive and well. How long would the murder have taken?

French did not believe the sisters would have made a move till Lucy had gone some time, lest the girl should have forgotten something and come back. Suppose they had waited for half an hour and at four the fateful blow had been struck. Ursula's body could have been carried to its resting-place in the first thicket inside five minutes, and the two criminals could have been back at the house by 4.15. When could the body have been taken on the second stage of its journey?

That it had lain in that first thicket for some time seemed evident from the condition of the grass, and also because if it had not lain there for some time it was difficult to see any reason for its having been put there at all. Suppose it had lain for half an hour. It could then undoubtedly have been carried on to the second halting-place, and Julia and/or Marjorie could have returned to St Kilda before the Campions' arrival at 5.15. After their departure at six the car could have been taken out and the body finally disposed of.

French saw that while the suggested timing was tight this theory was possible, and yet as a theory he was not pleased with it. It did not somehow seem likely. As a matter of fact, while he didn't feel so sure about Julia, he could not picture Marjorie Lawes as a party to such a crime.

Did the two women, he wondered, know the Campions were coming that afternoon, so as to fit their operations in with the visit? This seemed an important point and he asked both. They denied it, convincingly enough. He took a note, however, to see the Campions on the matter.

Reserving judgment on the possible guilt or innocence of the sisters, French decided that his most pressing line was the tracing of the car by which the body had been conveyed. He would slip into Farnham for some lunch while he considered how this could best be done.

SLADE'S SUNDAY

As French drove through the pleasant Surrey lanes his thoughts switched over from the Lawes sisters to another of his former suspects, Reggie Slade. Could Slade have had anything to do with this second mystery?

He had, of course, thought of Slade directly he had heard of Ursula's disappearance, just as he had thought of Julia and Marjorie. But now the possibility of Slade's guilt must be seriously considered.

That Slade alone should have encompassed the kidnapping or death of Ursula he didn't think likely. For one thing, he did not see how Slade could have entered the study. Nor did he believe Slade could have prevailed on Ursula to meet him there. But if one assumed that Slade and Julia had been acting in concert, these difficulties vanished.

Suppose Slade and Julia had agreed to murder Ursula – leaving the possible motive out of account for the moment. Suppose they worked out a plan by which Julia was to get Ursula down to the study and there murder her and carry her body out to a prearranged place: the first thicket. This would be Julia's part in the affair. Slade would then come into the picture. He would carry the body from the Thicket No. 1 to Thicket No. 2, where he would leave it while he went for his car. Returning, he would lift it on board and run it to its final destination.

This theory at first sight seemed to cover the facts. But further thought showed that it didn't quite. It didn't account for the footprints both behind the bush and on the carpet.

French puzzled over this; then suddenly he saw a possible explanation. If the crime were carried out jointly, would not Slade, rather than Julia, have committed the actual murder? In this case, would not Slade have waited behind the bush for Julia to let him in, Julia then calling Ursula down to the study?

To French this seemed extremely likely. Moreover, it accounted more satisfactorily for the two halts during the passage through the wood. Slade, on getting the body away from the house, would secrete it in the first hiding-place he could find, so that he might return to make sure that Julia was all right and that no traces of the crime remained. He would then carry it to the second thicket, again leaving it hidden while he went for his car.

French was pleased with his progress. His theory was taking shape. Three points, however, remained unaccounted for, and on these he now concentrated.

The first was the motive for this second crime. Why should anyone desire the life of this pleasant, kindly, harmless lady? Of all people in the world Ursula Stone seemed about the last to inspire feelings of fear or hate.

But wait a minute. Was she so harmless as he had supposed? Suddenly French saw that she might be anything but harmless; so dangerous indeed to these two people that they would have a very adequate reason for wishing her dead. Suppose in some way Ursula had discovered the truth about Earle's disappearance? If Julia and Slade were guilty of Earle's murder, this would mean nothing less than the hangman for both of them. If so, small wonder that Ursula was sacrificed!

The second difficulty was comparatively trifling: the fact that he, French, had come to the conclusion that both these people, Julia and Slade, were innocent of Earle's death. But this did not weigh very much with him. His former conclusion was not divinely inspired. He might even have made a mistake.

The third difficulty, however, was overwhelming. What about Nurse Nankivel? If Earle had been murdered, what had happened to the nurse? It was inconceivable that she also had been murdered. There could have been no motive.

As French considered this argument it seemed to grow slowly stronger and more unanswerable. Did it not mean that Earle had not been murdered at all, but that he and the nurse had gone off together, as French had originally concluded? Why, he asked himself, had he changed his mind on this point? Simply because of the possibility that Ursula Stone had been murdered. Was this really convincing?

On second thoughts he believed not. Ursula's death – if she had died – might not have been connected in any way with Earle or his disappearance. Her murderer – again, if she had been murdered – might purposely have made the crime look like a voluntary disappearance, with the very object of its being erroneously connected with Earle's.

Then French saw further that if Earle had not been murdered, it invalidated the only motive he had been able to think of for Ursula's death. Therefore *had* Earle been murdered after all?

French swore. The thing was a regular dilemma. If Earle had not been murdered, there was no motive for Ursula's death: if he had, there was no explaining the nurse's fate.

French turned into the hotel for lunch. As he sat over his roast beef and greens it occurred to him that it might be wise to broadcast for news of Ursula. It was evident that the murderer had not intended suspicion of murder to arise, and it might be no harm to let him think his ruse had been successful.

Accordingly, having sent the necessary application for the broadcast to Scotland Yard, he once again returned to the seat of war. Calling at Altadore, he asked for Slade. The young man was at home, and this time did not keep French waiting. He appeared at once, wishing French good morning in an almost obsequious manner.

"Sorry to trouble you again, Mr Slade, but it's the same business over again. This affair of Miss Stone is so like that of Mr Earle that we have to go on the same lines in each case. I hope you'll help me all you can."

Slade nodded. "I understand, inspector. I'll help you all I can and all that. But I expect it won't be much. Don't know anything about the affair, you know."

"I don't suppose you know anything directly," French returned smoothly, "but you may be able to help me indirectly. You were at St Kilda in the afternoon, quite possibly only a short time before Miss Stone disappeared. Though you may not have seen her, you may have seen someone else who did, and from whom I might get my information."

"Didn't see a soul. I'd tell you at once if I had, but I met no one."

"Just what time were you at St Kilda?"

" 'Bout three. Don't know exactly, not within a few minutes, you know; but about three."

"Quite. And what did you do after you left?"

"Went to Petersfield. I'll tell you." Slade was speaking almost eagerly. "Dagger and my sister went over to spend the day with some people at Arundel, so I was by myself for lunch. It was pretty ghastly all alone, and after lunch I took out the Bentley and went over to St Kilda to try and get Mrs Earle to come out for a run. That was why I went over, you know." He paused expectantly, but French not replying, went on. "But she wouldn't come. So I was at a loose end again. I thought I'd go over to Petersfield and see some people. So I did. The man I wanted to see was out, but I did find a couple of chaps I knew. We had some drinks and so on. I soon got fed up with it, so I came back, back here. I had a wash-up and a change and then I went back to the golf club. It wasn't so bad there. I found some chaps and we had a spot of bridge. We dined together and played on till the place closed at eleven. Then I came home and went to bed. That all you want?"

"Very nearly," French returned. "That statement is perfectly satisfactory to me, and all I require is a bit more detail. Now first" – And he began in his painstaking way to dissect the evidence. Amplified, the statement amounted to the following:

Slade had reached St Kilda about 3 p.m. and left about 3.15. He had seen Lucy, who had opened the door, and Julia, Marjorie and Ursula, who were in the drawing-room. He had driven to Petersfield, reaching his friends about four. He had stayed about an hour, leaving about five. The drive back took another three-quarters of an hour and he was about a quarter of an hour changing. That brought it about six. As soon as he had changed he went to the club, only of course two on three minutes in the car. He parked his car at the club and drove home about eleven. Then followed a list of persons who might witness on his behalf.

French was a good deal impressed by the statement. So much of it could apparently be vouched for that he scarcely saw how it could be false. All these people could not be accomplices. And if the statement were true it looked as if Slade must be innocent.

What had French to check? First the time of Slade's arrival in Petersfield. French had an idea of the distance and he felt sure the run could not have been made in less time than Slade had said. If Slade therefore had arrived about four, he couldn't possibly have committed the murder *before* his trip.

Again, if he had filled in his time even approximately as he had said, he would not have had time to dispose of the body between his return from Petersfield and his departure for the golf club. And he would scarcely have attempted it after eleven, when he would expect the search to be in progress.

It would be necessary, of course, to get these key hours checked, and French decided that he would take this on next. Accordingly next morning he went out again to Altadore and asked to see the servants.

As on the day of Earle's disappearance, only the cook had been on duty on this Sunday. When he had previously interrogated her French had been impressed with her straightforwardness. Now as he talked to her again he received the same impression.

When therefore she told him that Slade had been out all Sunday afternoon and had returned at quarter to six, leaving again in some fifteen minutes, French believed her. All the same, he asked how she remembered the hour so clearly. She had, she explained, supposed Mr Slade would be in for dinner, and at six o'clock she would have begun preparations for the meal. She was therefore watching the time, and noted exactly when the young man had arrived. When she had heard him go out it had occurred to her that it was just the time she would have been starting work, had he not done so. The cook also stated that during the fifteen minutes Slade was changing, she had seen the Bentley standing at the door.

French then went on and saw his friends the chauffeur and his wife. The chauffeur could not entirely answer his questions, as he had been at Arundel with Colonel and Mrs Dagger on the Sunday. They had left about midday, and up to that time all three cars had been in the garage. When he returned about 10.30 in the evening the small car was there, but the Bentley was out. Mr Slade brought in the Bentley about eleven, and he, the chauffeur, put it away.

The chauffeur's wife, however, was able to give further information. She had been about the premises during the entire day and stated positively that no cars could have been taken out or left in unknown to her. Mr Slade had come to the yard about three, and had taken out the Bentley. The small car had not been taken out at all, and the Bentley had not been brought back till the time her husband stated – namely, eleven.

"Well, that's pretty useful to me," French declared cheerily. "Have you cleaned the Bentley since Sunday?"

The chauffeur looked slightly shocked. He had been cleaning the Daimler and adjusting its brakes on Monday, and it surely wasn't expected that he could have dealt with the Bentley as well? Besides, the Bentley wasn't dirty. He had been over her thoroughly on Saturday, and she was quite all right.

French saw that he had been injudicious. He agreed that the Daimler was more than enough for anyone, and then said he would like to have a look at the Bentley. If Ursula's green wool would catch on twigs, a strand might stick to the cushions of a car.

But no strand had done so. French was very thorough in his examination and he found nothing suggesting Ursula's presence. The only thing he noted was that Slade at some time must have been walking on muddy ground, as traces of yellow clay showed in the pile of the carpet at the driver's seat.

So far everything that French had learned corroborated Slade's statement. French, however, could not be content with corroboration of a part of the statement; he must check it all. The golf club was close at hand and he would take it next.

The clubhouse was situated on the road running between Hampton Common crossroads and the village of Seale. It was a low rambling house of mellow red brick walls and mellower red roof tiles, with half timbering on the upper story. It looked genuinely old, as if two or three cottages had been knocked into one. There was a U-shaped drive, forming an entrance, a sweep before the door, and an exit. Round at the side of the building, hidden by a screen of trees both from the windows and the road, was a macadamised area used as a car park. Between the drives was a grass plot with flowerbeds and shrubs. At the other side of the building from the park was the first tee.

It happened that the secretary was in his office when French arrived, and he saw him at once. French had to put his questions delicately. He wanted to check the alibi of a man who was not under suspicion. Making official red tape the scapegoat therefore, he besought the secretary's good offices.

Curiously enough it happened that the secretary himself had seen Slade's arrival on the Sunday evening. He happened to be on the steps in front of the building when Campion drove up. Campion went into the clubhouse, remaining for a couple of minutes only. On his reappearance the two men exchanged a few words, and while they were doing so Slade arrived in his sports Bentley. He parked and entered the building. As he passed the others he asked if certain other members were in the club, saying he had come for an evening's bridge. Campion then drove off and the secretary went home. The latter reached his house a few minutes past six, and as it was only seven or eight minutes' walk, Slade must have arrived at the club about six.

Though this was all the secretary knew personally, he continued to be extremely helpful. He called waiters and attendants from whom French was able to get conclusive testimony that Slade had remained in the clubhouse till it closed at eleven.

There remained now only the enquiry at Petersfield, and in the afternoon French took a bus thither. Here the information he obtained was equally conclusive. He interviewed two members of the family on whom Slade had called and they confirmed the young man's statement on every point. He had turned up almost exactly at four o'clock and had stayed for just an hour.

All this testimony seemed to French to constitute overwhelming proof of Slade's innocence. At no time before eleven would he have had an opportunity either to commit the murder or to dispose of the body. And French could not bring himself to believe that he would have left any part of the dreadful scheme over till this hour, as he would have foreseen the presence of police in the neighbourhood. Besides this, of course, there was the testimony of the chauffeur and his wife that all cars were in the garage by eleven o'clock and remained there all night.

No, Slade was out of it. And if Slade was out of it, French believed that Julia was out of it too. And he had never believed that Marjorie was in it. This whole line of suspicion must be erroneous and the truth must lie in some totally different direction. What possible direction could that be? French recognised creeping over him that dreadful baffled feeling which had so often oppressed him when a promising clue petered out.

He sighed. Curse it all! If Julia and Slade were innocent, who was guilty? French really suspected no one. But someone must have done it. What had gone wrong with him was that he was so bankrupt of ideas. He might not be able to obtain proof of guilt, but he should at least know whom to suspect.

In the hope of something having resulted from the local men's activities, he went in to see Sheaf. Their results, however, could be covered by the one word, Nil. No one, either walking or driving a car, had been seen on the roads or in the vicinity of St Kilda, nor had anything affecting the case been discovered.

Pessimistically French returned to his hotel to write up his notes.

– 15 –

OAK PANELLING

A night of sound sleep and a bright sunny morning raised French's outlook once again to the optimistic level. To be held up in a case was no new experience. Again and again in the past he had reached a deadlock and always (or at least, very nearly always) these checks had proved temporary. He would find a way out, as he had so often before.

Moreover, as he considered his day he saw that he had been wrong on the previous night. He was not really held up at all. A deadlock was not yet in sight. It was true that progress on the Ursula Stone problem had been checked. But fortunately or unfortunately, the Ursula Stone problem was only a part of the case. He had still to trace the car and driver who had met Nurse Nankivel on the Hog's Back at six o'clock on the Sunday on which she had disappeared. He would get on to that at once. A bit of luck with it might solve all his problems.

When he came down a letter was handed to him. It was from the Yard and stated that the samples which he had sent up had been examined. The blood in Thicket No. 1 was human blood, and the sand from the study floor was the same as that from behind the bush. Somehow this letter, giving a firm foundation to at least part of his case, still further increased his wave of optimism.

But when he came to examine his immediate problem, the wave became somewhat dissipated. This line of finding out who met the nurse was not so promising after all. French had already had a try at it and had failed to learn anything. Because of the telegram and the journey to Staines, Earle was the likely man, but no one had been able to tell him where Earle was at the time in question or whether the St Kilda car had been out. Earle therefore remained a possibility, though there was no proof that he was anything more. Julia, Marjorie and Ursula Stone, French had checked up, satisfying himself they were all at St Kilda.

On the other hand, Campion by his own admission might have been near the bypass bridge at six o'clock, and therefore could have met the nurse. But there was no reason to suspect Campion.

Nor did French believe there was any reason to suspect Slade. He had not, however, enquired into Slade's whereabouts at this time, and he decided to do so at once.

Once again he rode out to Altadore and looked up his friend the chauffeur. Would the man carry his memory back to Sunday fortnight, when Dr Earle disappeared...?

The chauffeur and his wife both carried their memories back. Their effort, however, didn't help French. Both were positive that at six o'clock on that Sunday afternoon all three cars were in the garage.

This was only what French had expected. He had never been able to see why Slade should have desired the nurse's death.

As he rode out of Altadore gate on his way back to Farnham he saw Miss Campion. She was strolling slowly along the road and signed to him to stop.

"I've just been at St Kilda," she said, "and I'm waiting for the bus. I wondered how you were getting on. I don't know whether I should ask or not, but I feel this dreadful affair so much that I'd like to know."

"I can understand, madam," French returned sympathetically. "It must have been a blow to you. The poor lady was your friend, was she not?"

"A lifelong friend. I knew her as a child at Bath, where we were both brought up. It does seem to me the most terrible affair. If ever there was a kindly and innocent and harmless individual in the world, it was Miss Stone. Really *good*, you know, without any nonsense about it."

"I understand, Miss Campion. It was just my own estimate of her, though of course I hadn't your opportunities of judging."

"That's why I feel it so dreadfully. I'm afraid something must have happened to her. She never would have gone away like that of her own accord; never. What do you think, inspector? You haven't said anything."

"I'm afraid because I don't know anything, madam. I admit that the idea you've mentioned occurred to me, but I've got no proof of it."

"Proof? You don't want proof. Her character was proof enough. Something has happened to her; some accident or something. I'm convinced of it."

"I'm glad to have your opinion," French declared. "I suppose you can't form any idea of what might have happened?"

Miss Campion made a gesture of despair. "Absolutely none. The thing's an insoluble mystery to me. I can't think of *anything*."

"You don't know if she had any enemies?"

She looked at him in horror. "Is that what you fear?" she said, almost in a whisper. "Not *murder!* Oh poor Ursula! How unspeakably dreadful!" For a moment she seemed overwhelmed, then went on: "But good heavens, inspector, who would do such a thing? What could anyone have against her? She who never hurt anyone in her life!"

French shrugged. "I appreciate the difficulty, Miss Campion, but there seem to me only the two ways out of it. Either she disappeared voluntarily, or she – didn't. Which is the more likely?"

Alice Campion was obviously deeply shocked and grieved. "I couldn't have believed that either could have happened," she declared. "Oh, if someone is to blame for this, if someone – " she boggled over the word, then forced it out – "if someone has murdered her, *how* I hope you'll get him. I'd go gladly to see him hanged, and I'm not vindictive. But there: I don't believe anyone could have done it."

For a moment they walked on in silence, then Miss Campion spoke again. "Do you think this affair is connected with the other? I mean Dr Earle's disappearance?"

French moved uneasily. "To be strictly truthful," he said at last, "I don't know. What do you think, madam?"

"I don't see how it could be, and yet it's strange that the two cases should be so alike. My brother was talking about it. I said they were so alike that they must be connected, but he said it didn't follow, that the second case might have been intentionally copied from the first."

French nodded. "I agree with Dr Campion. It's possible they were connected, or it's possible that the perpetrator of the second was simply trying to make it look like his predecessor's work. I'm obliged to you, Miss Campion, for talking like this. Your ideas may be a help to me. And there's another thing that might help me. Perhaps while we're talking you'd tell me in as full detail as you can, what you know about last Sunday. The statement you gave me that night was necessarily short. If you wouldn't mind repeating it with plenty of details, some chance phrase might give me an idea."

"I don't think I know anything which could help you," she returned. "However, there's nothing I wouldn't do to get the thing cleared up. We spent that afternoon very quietly. From lunch till tea the three of us, my brother and sister and I, sat reading and chatting in the drawing-room. Then after tea my brother got out the car and we went over to St Kilda. There was nothing abnormal there; I can assure you of that, inspector. Mrs Earle and Miss Lawes were just as usual. I asked where Miss Stone was, and Mrs Earle said she was lying down. She offered to call her, but I wouldn't hear of it. Well, nothing happened during the visit; absolutely nothing out of the common. We stayed three-quarters of an hour or so and then drove back. Or no; I'm wrong there. We didn't drive directly home. We went round to the golf club, where my brother wanted to see one of the members. But that only took a minute or two. Then we drove home. I prepared supper and my brother and sister sat and read in the drawing-room. It was while we were at supper that Mrs Earle rang up."

"You went over at once?"

"We went over at once. Mrs Earle told us what had happened. She seemed very much upset and of course I didn't wonder. Howard – my brother – suggested ringing up the superintendent at once; then he agreed with us we might have a look round ourselves first. I think we all see now that we were wrong, but you can understand – I don't mean any discourtesy – that application to the police is distasteful and is usually made as a last resource."

"It's natural, madam," French said smoothly.

"We organised a search, or rather my brother did. But when we met without having made any discoveries, we agreed that an application to the police could no longer be delayed. We rang up Farnham, and I think you know the rest."

"I think so," French agreed. "Well, madam, I'm glad we met here and much obliged for your ideas."

The bus turned up presently and French saw the lady into it. She had not really told him anything he had not known before, and yet it was interesting to find her so convinced that only foul play could account for Ursula Stone's disappearance.

French had by this time completed all those obvious and local enquiries which the tragedy of Ursula Stone had suggested. He was worried by the question of whether or not he should run down to Bath and have a look over the missing woman's house. He did not think there was the slightest chance of learning anything useful from such a visit, and yet he doubted the propriety of omitting it. Finally he decided to go, and after sending a wire to the Bath police, he set off to Reading to get the afternoon express.

A thorough search revealed just what he had expected: nothing whatever, and with only the consciousness of work well done, he returned to Farnham on the following evening. During dinner that night and afterwards as he sat smoking in the lounge, he brooded sombrely over the case. What he particularly wanted was to have his programme for the next day settled. But for the life of him he could not see on what line to concentrate. Every direction in which he turned seemed to lead to a deadlock.

At last, wearied and disgusted, he picked up a novel which he had brought down to finish, but with which up to now he had made but little progress. He found, however, that he could not concentrate on the story. Again and again his thoughts strayed back to the case, and presently he threw the book down and gave himself up to a renewed mental search for other lines of attack.

It was while he was thus desultorily reviewing the evidence that he found himself trying to picture just what must have taken place in the study at St Kilda at the time of Ursula Stone's murder. There were one or two points about that study business which were not altogether clear. Why the study, in the first place? Why had the murder taken place there, if it had? Was it simply because that from the study there was a convenient exit to the wood? On the other hand, was the choice accidental? If so, how had Ursula been induced to come down there from her bedroom? And most puzzling of all, if neither Julia, Marjorie nor Slade had been concerned in the murder, who on the face of the earth had been?

As French sat smoking and pondering these conundrums, he began to wonder if there was not in this selection of the study some deeper and more fundamental motive than he had as yet contemplated? Could there be here something that he had missed, or was he just wasting his time in fanciful nonsense?

The line of sandy footsteps recurred to him. Whose were these? How disappointing it had been that he had been unable to learn something more about them! If he had even been able to say whether they belonged to a man or a woman it might have been a help. But they showed no detail.

Wait a minute though. Did they not? They had position. Was not their position at least interesting?

French recalled exactly where they had appeared. Their owner had evidently entered by the French window and had walked across the room. To what part?

So far as it had been possible to ascertain, to the corner to the left of the fireplace. Was there a reason for this, or was it a mere accident? French recalled the furnishing of the room. There was no furniture at that place, nor was there anything on the wall. What could the visitor have gone there for?

Just an accident, he thought. And yet he was not wholly satisfied. Had there been a table or a bookcase it would have been easier to understand, but there was neither.

Impatiently French dismissed the affair from his mind and turned again to his novel. But a mental picture of the study seemed to intrude between his eyes and the page. With a muttered oath he threw the book away and let his thoughts roam where they would.

And now he recalled a fact which he had noted at the time with some small feeling of surprise. The walls of the study were expensively panelled in oak. It had struck him then, and now it struck him again, that this elaborate decoration was a little out of keeping with the remainder of the house. In fact, the decoration in the study must have cost more than that of the whole of the rest of the house put together. Why?

Well, there had often been a reason in the past for panelling. But, of course, such a reason would not apply today. All the same, French could not get the idea out of his mind.

Wondering if he was altogether a fool, he determined that, as he was at a loose end, he might as well run out once again to St Kilda and have a look at that panelling. As soon as he reached this decision his subconscious self seemed satisfied, thoughts of the case vanished from his mind and he became immersed without effort in his book.

Next morning he was early at St Kilda, and going into the study, he locked the door and settled down to his problem. He had measured exactly where the footsteps had gone and he now marked the place with a couple of books. Yes, he had been right. They went close to the wall, but at the place there was neither furniture nor pictures: only the panelling.

He moved across and began to examine the panelling. It was an exceedingly good job, with fine, well-fitting joints. French took out his lens and began slowly passing it along these joints.

In most of them the wood touched, and where it didn't they were full of dust. Clearly no movement had taken place since they were made.

Then suddenly a little tremor of excitement passed through French. Here, just opposite where the footsteps had stopped, was a joint entirely clear of dust. It was very narrow, not more than a sixty-fourth of an inch in width, but quite clean.

French followed it along, and as he did so his excitement grew. The joints around a complete panel of some twelve by eighteen inches were clean!

French was immediately tempted to indulge in an orgy of pressing, pulling, shoving, squeezing and twisting, but he restrained himself. Before touching anything he got out his powdering apparatus and dusted a large area of the panelling for fingerprints.

His forethought was rewarded. Certain portions of the panelling bore prints. But as French examined them he became conscious of something even more interesting.

Practically none of the prints were whole. There were half-prints and quarter-prints and narrow strips of prints. Little round or oval patches of the markings had been wiped out, and French had no difficulty in guessing the cause. Gloves! Someone who wore gloves had been feeling over the panelling!

There seemed little use in photographing such prints as remained, but French was taking no chances, and he made records of all the marks. Then he gave himself up to manipulation. For a considerable time he worked upon the area covered by the prints, but without result. Then it occurred to him that many secret panels were opened by a simultaneous pressure on the panel and on another point perhaps four or five feet away. He therefore began searching with his lens for clear joints at some other part of the wall.

At last he found a decoration on the oak mantelpiece which also was surrounded by clean joints. At once he began a new orgy of pressures and twists.

And then a wave of delight shot over him, for the decoration moved. Moreover, pressure on the panel now had its effect. It slid backwards and then to one side, revealing in the brick wall behind a small steel safe!

French felt that at last he was on to something material. This was what the murderer had come for! This probably was what Ursula had seen him operating, and for her knowledge she had paid with her life!

The safe was locked. French remembered, however, having seen a number of keys in Earle's desk. He took these out and tried them one after another. None of them would enter the lock.

He wondered if Julia knew of the safe. Without a search warrant he daren't break it open, but Julia might give him permission. He stepped out into the hall and called her.

Her amazement when she saw the safe was so obviously genuine that French couldn't doubt it. She emphatically denied ever having seen or heard of it before.

"It's his book!" she exclaimed. "You were asking where he kept it and I didn't know. He was very secretive about his book. Except that it was about some medical subject, he never would give any information. Certainly you may have it opened. Indeed, if you don't, I shall do it myself."

"When was it put in, Mrs Earle?" French asked.

"It must have been when we took the house and before we moved in," she answered. "The panelling of this room was done then at all events. I remember I wasn't very pleased about it. It seemed a waste of a lot of good money. If all the sitting rooms had been done I shouldn't have said a word. But only this study! Dr Earle said it was because of the damp. It never occurred to me to doubt that, but now I remember that I was in this room before it was done and I never saw any damp."

When Julia had gone French telephoned to the Yard to send down an expert to open the safe. Then he returned to the study, determined not to leave the room till he had seen the contents.

While waiting he had another orgy with his dusting powder: with the same result. Obviously the last person to open the safe had worn gloves.

Scotland Yard put its best foot forward and in five minutes less than two hours a car drove up with two efficient-looking men and a formidable kit of tools. A short inspection told them that the lock could not be forced, and they rigged their oxyacetylene plant and began playing a high temperature flame on the plates. Presently the hard steel burned away and soon a small circle of plate was lifted out. Then came a delay while the remaining metal cooled sufficiently to be touched; but eventually, working through the hole they had made, the experts were able to disconnect the lock and the little door swung back. Eagerly French gazed in.

Julia Earle was right! Here was the book! There were scores, probably hundreds, of quarto sheets covered with Earle's rather untidy handwriting: these sheets – and nothing else!

French turned them over. Yes, they were about medical subjects: so far as he could see in a rapid glance, the production of disease from cultivations of bacilli.

He swore bitterly. Seldom had he had so great a disappointment. This discovery of the safe, reached by a process of reasoning and investigation which he felt did him immense credit, should surely have led to something really helpful. And what had he gained from it? Nothing!

Less than nothing! It had removed from the possibilities one theory of the crime and one criminal! French had never very seriously suspected Campion of stealing the book, but now here was proof that the doctor had done nothing of the kind. So much time wasted!

Automatically French worked on, testing the inside of the safe for fingerprints: again with the same result. Gloves had been at work within as well as without. Then he sat down at Earle's desk and gave himself up to thought.

There was in this whole matter something which he was quite unable to understand. A secret safe was a very unusual thing. What was it for? It could not have been put in because of anything which had recently happened. Obviously the panelling had been undertaken as a mask for its installation; six years ago; before the Earles' moved into the house. Had Earle's disappearance, then, to do with some long-standing secret?

Or was the safe simply to hold the manuscript of the book? French did not think so. An ordinary safe would have held it all right. It was not as if there had been any secret about the book itself. Everyone knew Earle was writing it. Was there something more in Earle's life than he had yet suspected? Things were beginning to look very like it.

French, having obtained Julia's permission, parcelled up the manuscript to send to a doctor who sometimes did police work for the Yard and who had become rather a friend of his own. He did not think it was important, but it would be well to be sure it could have had no bearing on the affair.

Apart from its *raison d'être*, the existence of the safe did certainly clear up some of the detail of Ursula's murder. It seemed obvious that she had in some way become suspicious and come down and discovered the thief in the act of burglary. In self-defence he had killed her – defence, that is, from the legal consequences of his act. But if so, why had he not removed the book?

Then French saw that he was being stupid. Why limit the contents of the safe to the book? The book didn't fill it. Had there not been something else more vital to the thief?

At once French's previous idea recurred to him. Was it something which, if found, would prove that the thief had murdered Earle? It might well be. Even it might prove that he had murdered Nurse Nankivel also. French was puzzled and for the moment he didn't see how he was to settle the point. The whole affair was confoundedly exasperating.

Then still another idea flashed into his mind. What if the space in the safe had been filled, not with proof of the murder of Earle, but with *money*? What if here had been what he had so long sought under the guise of a second banking account? What if Earle had not been murdered at all, as he, French, had just been supposing? What if, taking from this safe a large sum of money or negotiable securities, Earle had after all gone away with Helen Nankivel? Was there any evidence for his death? There was not. French had assumed it, partly because Ursula had been murdered, but principally because he had taken no money with him. Suppose he *had* taken money with him. How would the question then stand?

Again, was there any evidence of Helen Nankivel's death? There was not. Was there any motive for it? None. Why had he ever thought of such a thing? Simply because he had been driven to assume Earle's death. Now was that assumption not invalid?

French swore. Instead of clearing up the case, this discovery of the safe was making it a hundred times worse confounded! Its foundations were cracking. He now knew no more what had happened to Earle than on the day of his first visit. And if this idea of the money were correct, what had the thief been after, and why had Ursula been killed? Damn it all, *had* Ursula been killed? For all the evidence there was, she might merely have been rendered unconscious in the study and then kidnapped. She mightn't be dead at all.

Overcome with exasperation and disappointment, French rode dejectedly back to Farnham.

– 16 –

FRENCH ARRANGES AN EXPERIMENT

French's mood lasted all evening and all evening his thoughts remained busy with the case. What was to be his next move? Rack his brains as he might, he couldn't think of any line which he had not already explored.

Worried beyond measure, he sat smoking in his room, where he had lit the gas fire, gazing vacantly into space and pondering on the eternal problem of what was truth.

Idly he wondered which of the two phases of his work – one or other of which he was usually up against – was the more exasperating: to have to make endless wearying repetitions of some small enquiry with consistently futile results, or not to see the way ahead at all. "Ough!" he groaned in disgust. "Who would be a detective?"

Carefully he began to go over for the thousandth time the facts of the case. Was there nothing that he had missed? No line of research still unexplored? No stone – he smiled whimsically to himself at the pompous cliché – still unturned?

Mechanically he got out his notebook and began more seriously and systematically than ever to review the entire circumstances.

The thing had got on his nerves, and his bedtime came and went, leaving him still seated in his armchair turning over the pages of his notebook, reading an item, remaining motionless as he considered it from every point of view, reading another item...But nowhere could he get any light.

Again and again he told himself that he must give up for the night, but his mind was so restless that he could not do so. Surely to goodness there *must* be something that he had missed? There was necessarily a complete and satisfying explanation to the whole affair. Why could he not find it? What men had imagined, men could imagine again. What had gone wrong with him lately?

He sat in his chair. He paced the room. He threw himself on his bed. He paced the room again. He sat in his chair and bent forward. He sat in his chair and leant backward. But no change of position helped him. He could think of nothing fresh.

It was past one o'clock. He must really go to bed. This sort of worrying over the affair just upset him and didn't lead anywhere.

He was refilling his pipe for one last smoke when suddenly he paused and sat motionless, while an expression, first of interest and then of actual excitement, grew slowly in his eyes. Was it possible that he had missed something after all; something which might well be vital?

He put down his pipe and began whistling softly under his breath. That clay in Slade's car! Was not that his clue? Was it not the most important thing he had yet discovered, or was he merely being more silly than usual? That clay: where had it come from?

He recalled exactly what he had seen. In the pile of the carpet before the driving seat were traces of yellow clay: evidently from the shoes of the driver. Where had it come from?

French considered the country soils, so far as he knew them. There were large areas of sand – black sand, white sand, yellow sand. There was on the Hog's Back ridge chalk, white and greasy. There was a light brown loam. There was a kind of peat. But yellow clay?...

There was only one place in which French had seen it, and it was the memory of this which had given him so furiously to think. On the bypass! When he had walked up towards the Hog's Back along the Compton road on his visit to Polperro he had had a look at what was going on, and he had seen yellow clay passing in the contractor's little trucks. Yellow clay on the bypass! Yellow clay in Slade's car! Was there any connection?

For a time French was filled with excitement. Then came the natural reaction. The thing must, of course, have some quite natural explanation. Perhaps Slade knew the engineers, or was merely having a walk over the workings to satisfy his curiosity. It might be so. And yet French didn't imagine that dull and humdrum engineering of the cut and fill type would have appealed to Slade.

While determined not to be disappointed if nothing came of it, French decided that unless he thought of something better in the meantime, he would have another look at that clay on the bypass. If it did no good, it could at least do no harm.

Next morning his enthusiasm had waned still further – waned indeed till nothing was left of it. However, he took a bus along the Hog's Back, and alighting at the bypass bridge, set off to walk towards Compton. As before he penetrated to the right at frequent intervals, examining the workings. There at all events was where the yellow clay was coming from. Beneath the summit of the Hog's Back the cutting had been through chalk, but here on the south side of the ridge the chalk ran out and was succeeded, a dozen feet or more below ground level, by yellow clay. This clay was being loaded by a steam shovel into wagons and run along a narrow-gauge line to be dumped lower down.

Full of interest, French walked along the side of the cut. He wanted to see again where that clay was being unloaded, and presently he came to the place, not so far away. As he had noted before, the work was being carried out very similarly to that of the Whitness Widening. A bank was being formed across some low-lying ground; a bank some fifteen feet high. In some way which was not now obvious, a narrow strip of banking of the proper height had first been made along the centre line of the new road, and this was now being widened by side tipping. Yes, there was where the yellow clay was going to all right.

French walked up and down the bank, first on one side and then on the other. On the right side, facing towards the Hog's Back, the bypass kept fairly close to the road, though it was screened from it by shrubs. On the left side the bank ran through a field in which were straggling clumps of bushes and small trees. Across the field and at some distance were isolated houses.

For an hour French continued to move about, sighting the directions of the various houses and clumps of bushes. Finally he walked up to the foreman of one of the gangs of workers and asked for the address of the chief engineer.

" 'E's to be dahn 'ere on Monday morning," the man replied. "You be 'ere abaht ten an' you'll see 'im."

This suited French admirably. It was now Saturday, and the fact that an appointment for Monday morning had been made would secure him a free weekend.

He walked up again on to the Hog's Back and took the first bus back to Farnham. There he saw Sheaf, explained his ideas, obtained the necessary local backing for his plan, lunched, and took the next train to Town. His weekend passed all too quickly and at ten o'clock on Monday he was once more with the foreman.

"There 'e is," said the man when he saw French, pointing to a little group at some distance along the workings. "The big man in the grey coat an' 'at."

With the engineer were three men, one obviously the foreman of a squad, the others young fellows in waterproofs and big boots and with plans under their arms. French waited till they had finished discussing their business and were turning away, then he went forward.

"I should like to have a word with you, sir," he said, handing over his official card.

The engineer smiled when he read it. "What you want is an international conference," he declared. "My name's English and my assistant here is Welsh. Unfortunately this other gentleman is Bradbury and not Scott, as would be seemly."

"That's a pity," French returned. "We have a sergeant at the Yard called German, and we get ragged. They call us 'The Foreigners' and pretend we can't understand English. Often we can't too," and French smiled in his turn.

"Yes, I dare say that would happen more often in your job than in mine. You wanted to see me?"

"Yes, sir, I wanted two things from you. I should explain that I'm down here looking into the disappearances of Dr Earle and Miss Stone from Hampton Common."

English was interested at once. He had read the case in detail, so much as was known to the papers, and seemed full of theories about it.

"Gone off with that nurse," he said, with a knowing wink. "What do you think, inspector? Or is it part of your religion not to say?"

French laughed. "I'm glad to discuss any case with anyone," he declared. "There's always the chance of my getting an idea."

"Well, there's an idea for you."

"It certainly is," French admitted. "But I'm afraid it's not what one might call exactly new. It has been discussed, I should say, several hundred times."

English laughed in his turn. "Well, if I can't help you with ideas, what can I do for you?"

"Two things, as I said. First, I want to know whether you, or any of your assistants or underlings, are acquainted with a man called Slade, living at Hampton Common, or whether such a man has been having a look over the workings?"

"Never heard of him," English returned. He drew a whistle from his pocket, blew a piercing blast and waved his arm. Messrs. Welsh and Bradbury, who had been strolling away slowly, turned and began to approach.

"Either of you know a man called Slade?" English asked when they came up.

Neither knew him. Nor had Slade, so far as they knew, ever been on to the workings.

"It's in this particular stretch that I'm interested," French explained. "If you've had any men working just here, perhaps you'd ask them?"

Detailed enquiries revealed the fact that Slade had never been about the place, at least not in working hours.

"That is what I rather expected to hear," French went on, "and it leads me to my second point, which I'm afraid may give rather more trouble. I'd like to explain, but first I must ask you to keep what I say as strictly confidential. If my suspicions were to leak out, it might be a very serious matter."

This beginning was not calculated to damp the engineers' interest, and all three gave the required undertaking.

"I want," French went on, "the toe of this bank opened at certain points," and he explained his idea. "It may cost a bit of money, but I'm authorised to say that the Surrey police will stand for that."

The three men showed an interest almost approaching excitement.

"I'm sorry," said English, "that I can't be here personally to see it done, but Bradbury will do all you want. Better let's have some further details."

"Certainly. If you gentlemen will come down to the toe of this bank, I'll show you what I mean."

Rain had fallen during the night and the heavy clay was greasy from the water. As with some difficulty they climbed down the rough slope of the dump to the "toe" or bottom edge, French went on explaining.

"You understand, of course, that at best this whole affair is only a guess. My entire idea may be a washout. But there's a chance of its coming off and I daren't neglect the chance."

The engineers grinned. They fully appreciated French's point. Indeed, their looks of admiration indicated something more than mere appreciation.

Having reached the surface of the field on the side remote from the road, French led the way to the place he had already selected.

"Here," he said, "is the only part of this entire piece of banking which is out of sight of houses. As you see, it stretches for about a hundred feet. Its being hidden is due to those clumps of bushes. And of course from the road it's screened by the bank itself."

"Yes, that's right enough," English admitted. "Then it's here you want the toe opened?"

"Yes, sir. But not the toe of the bank as it is now. I want it where the toe was on Sunday week."

"Naturally: I follow that. Well, we'll do our best. Let's see now." English turned to his assistants. "You measured this up for the certificate, didn't you, Bradbury? When was that?"

"We both measured it," Bradbury answered. "I took the levels and Welsh the measurements. That was last Friday week."

"That should give it to us, inspector," English declared. "Cross sections were taken on the previous Friday, and there would be little change between Friday and Sunday." He turned back to his assistants. "I want you to peg off where the toe was on Friday week. It'll be as near Sunday's position as doesn't matter. Understand?"

They understood and would get at it at once.

"Then cut back to it. The stuff can simply be thrown forward into the field. You have to widen a good deal here, haven't you?"

"About twenty feet."

"Exactly; anything you do will be covered. Then carry on as the inspector wants, not forgetting to charge him. He's paying for it, so it doesn't matter how long it takes. That right, inspector?"

"That's right, sir. But I'm afraid it may have to be opened for the whole hundred feet."

"Doesn't matter so long as we can charge you the damage. But you'll have to get me a chit about it before we start. Not that I doubt your word. It's just a matter of business. That is, Bradbury, if I'm not here, you mustn't begin any work till you get an official letter promising to pay, and if there's a maximum sum mentioned, you must see that no more than that sum is spent. Warn the ganger to keep the time separate. Well, we must be getting along if we're to see Bridge 15 before I go back. That everything, inspector?"

"Yes, thank you, sir. Where can I find you, Mr Bradbury?"

"I have an office about half a mile farther on. A note there'll find me if I'm out."

French, having obtained from Sheaf the necessary undertaking to bear the cost of the experiment, returned to the workings and sought the engineer's hut. The visit brought back once again his experiences on the Whitness Widening. These engineers' huts were all alike, except in the matter of size and fittings. As the Whitness Widening was an enormously bigger job than this bypass road, so the huts of Bragg and Carey and Lowell were bigger than this one of Bradbury and Welsh. But they had the same atmosphere, and these two young men were of the same type as Ashe and Pole.

Bradbury was in the hut when French arrived. "The chit Mr English wanted," said French, handing over his letter.

Bradbury glanced over it. "Right-o, inspector. When would you like us to start? We can do it any time."

French did not answer directly. "Tell me," he said, putting his head on one side, "do you think there'd be any chance of doing this job secretly? If there's nothing in my idea it doesn't matter. But if there is, I'd rather no one knew about it. You can understand, Mr Bradbury, that it would be wiser not to put anyone on his guard."

Bradbury was obviously thrilled. It was a new experience to be taken into the confidence of an officer of the Yard engaged on a murder case, and the young man reacted suitably. He was out, he said, to help the inspector and he would do the work as unostentatiously as he could.

"I don't think, you know, that we can keep the thing quiet if your man is about and watching developments," he declared. "If he's there he'll see it. But I believe we can prevent our men smelling a rat. I'll tell 'em a roll of essential plans were forgotten here and got covered and we have to find them. But of course if we get what you're looking for the fat'll be in the fire."

"That's just what I'm considering, Mr Bradbury," French said slowly. "I'm inclined to think it would be better to do the work with policemen and at night."

Bradbury looked disappointed. "Could they do it?" he asked doubtfully. "Shovelling this heavy clay is no joke if you're not accustomed to it."

"That's the very thing that's bothering me," French admitted. "I want your men to do the work, but I don't want them to find anything. Look here, couldn't you clear it back to where it was on Sunday and let us do the rest?"

Again the young man showed disappointment. French saw what was wrong. "Of course," he added, "if you yourself could see your way to come out and give our men the benefit of your advice, I'd take it kindly. But I'd like to keep anything we might find absolutely to ourselves."

Bradbury was radiant. All he had wanted was to be in on the affair. He agreed at once to cast forward the recently tipped clay, leaving the slope as it had been on the previous Sunday week. He would then have a number of small lamps filled and set aside for the night work, and would meet French and do anything he could to help.

"Very good of you, I'm sure," French declared. "When do you think we can get to work?"

"Tonight, I should think. I'll put some men into it now. You'd like to stay and see us start? Then see here." Entering with zest into the experiment, he turned to the corner of the hut and pointed to a filthy old waterproof, stained with clay and oil. "Put that on and those leggings and stick that plan under your arm and they'll mistake you for an engineer. That's better. Except for the glory of your hat you look fine."

They went out of the hut and along the workings, tramping heavily through the sticky mud, just as French had tramped with Clifford Parry down at Whitness. Just as Parry would have done, Bradbury called a ganger and gave his instructions.

"I say, Bates, I want you to bring your men down to Peg 188 and shift a bit of stuff. We've lost some plans and we've got to find them if we dig up the whole of Surrey. They were put down on the slope and the tip's gone over them. Start in here and clear it back."

The men, obviously unsuspicious, began to work along the hundred-foot stretch, quickly throwing the clay forward into the field, and roughly trimming the slope as Bradbury directed, that is, as it had been on the Sunday in question. Having seen the work started, French excused himself on the ground that he wished to make arrangements for the night, and leaving his borrowed plumage in the hut, he returned to Farnham.

Sheaf was not pleased at the idea of turning his constables into navvies, but he raised no serious objection, and a squad of a dozen men was got together and instructed to be ready at eleven o'clock. Having arranged the necessary commissariat and transport, French returned to his hotel for dinner and a rest.

– 17 –

AND CARRIES IT OUT

That night three cars left the police station at Farnham and took the road leading to the Hog's Back. In the leading one sat French with beside him Sergeant Sheepshanks. The remaining seats were filled with constables. Short intervals separated the cars.

French was more nervous than he would have cared to admit. He had taken a biggish risk, staking a good deal of his reputation on this throw. What they were about to do would cost money, and if it led to no result he would have to stand the racket, a racket admittedly not of censure, but of ridicule and loss of prestige.

He ran over again in his mind the steps which had led him to his conclusion, and as he did so he took comfort. He believed, whether his conclusion should turn out right or wrong, that his present action was justified. The chance of success was sufficient to make the effort worth while.

First, he had suspected Slade of the murders, or one of them, either acting alone or with Julia Earle. Slade had the necessary motive and, so far as French could form an opinion, the necessary character for the crime. French was inclined to gloss over the question of whether he had the opportunity: assume he had. Now it was practically certain that Ursula Stone had been murdered on Sunday afternoon and her body removed in a car. The great difficulty, however, was, Where could it have been removed to? Where could it have been hidden? An exhaustive search had failed to find it. Then suddenly French had thought of the most perfect hiding-place conceivable. If the body could be buried in the freshly tipped earth on this bypass road, it would be hidden for good. In the first place the surface of the tip was so rough and uneven that the disturbance of making the grave would never be seen. Then on the very next day the grave would be covered by fresh deposits of clay, and by the time the bypass was finished, the body would be buried under some fifteen or twenty feet of clay. This perfect hiding-place was not only the only one known in the entire district, but it was close – within five miles of Earle's house – and was secret: away from the track of people and screened from the sight of houses.

So much was theory – and, French felt, good theory at that – but the case was not confined to theory. On the floor of Slade's car were traces of clay, this same yellow clay which was tipped at the perfect hiding-place. It was, so far as was known, the only yellow clay in the entire district. Moreover, Slade was not known to have been at the bypass on any legitimate business.

All this seemed entirely convincing, but French could not forget Slade's alibi. He had undoubtedly tested it pretty thoroughly, and had found it watertight. Alibis, however, were notoriously unreliable. While French did not think that the existence of the alibi should prevent the experiment being tried, he was a good deal worried by it.

It was a perfect night for their work, at least from one point of view. Pitch darkness and a fine rain driven by a bitter wind from the southeast would keep every self-respecting person indoors. No one was likely to discover what they were doing. On the other hand it wouldn't be very pleasant. Everything would be wet and the clay specially sticky and hard to work.

Having discharged their passengers at the nearest point, the cars were driven a mile or so along the road, so that their appearance should not lead the curious to inopportune explorations. Not wishing to show lights on the Compton side of the embankment, French led his little band out in the darkness on to the uncharted wastes of the field. They reached the bank, with many a slip and stumble managed to climb it, splashed across the top, and slid down the other side. In the field at its base was Bradbury, and with him a dozen hurricane lamps.

French found that a perceptible portion of the bank had been trimmed back, the clay removed being thrown forward into the field. On the ground was a little pile of shovels and picks.

"You're ready for us, Mr Bradbury?" he greeted his friend of the morning. "Fine!" He turned to Sheepshanks. "Now, sergeant, get the men to work, will you? The sooner we begin, the sooner we'll be through."

"I could have got you a couple of acetylene flares," Bradbury explained when the men had started, "but they're very bright. They would have lit up the whole country and I thought you'd rather be private even if it meant going a bit slower."

"That's right," French agreed, going on to point out that he considered the young man's arrangements perfect.

Bradbury took out a pipe and pouch, and bending forward with his back to the rain, began to fill the bowl.

"I suppose this is a bit out of your line, inspector?" he went on. "About as much as if I set to work to find the taxi man who had picked up a certain fare?"

French also began to make preparations for smoking.

"Not so much as you might think. Curiously enough my last big job was on works like this; bigger than this."

Bradbury looked as if he was slightly doubtful as to whether any works could have been bigger than his. "Where was that?" he grunted.

"Redchurch–Whitness; a railway widening."

"Oh gee, yes, I know about that. Do you mean to say you were on that case? Ever come across a chap named Pole?"

"Dozens of times. I knew Mr Pole quite well."

"We were at college together. Good chap, Pole."

"They were a very good crowd of men altogether," French declared.

"Well, perhaps, except – ?"

"Well, perhaps, except. There are exceptions to every rule, Mr Bradbury."

"I suppose there are. I'd like to see the work down there. Tell me something about it."

French did his best. His descriptions of things did not seem quite right to himself, but this keen young man seemed to understand them all right. "It's really a very interesting job," he went on. "You should go down and get Mr Pole to take you over it. You'd enjoy it."

They chatted on till presently Bradbury made a move. "I'm cold," he declared. "I'm going to have a whack at this job." He seized a pick and began thrusting it vigorously into the soft clay.

French somewhat gingerly took a shovel and began shifting stuff. It was harder work than he had bargained for. The clay was just in its most unpleasant and obstructive state. To get the shovel into it wasn't easy to start with, and then it wouldn't cast. It stuck to the shovel and had to be carried to where it was to be placed, and scraped off. And all the time it was slippery and abominable to walk on. The men were doing their best, but progress was slow, and once or twice French found himself regretting that he had not used the bypass labourers instead of police. Very little work was enough for French. He soon resigned his place to a burly constable and stood back to regain his breath.

The scene was slightly weird. The faintly illuminated strip of earthy bank showing up out of the black darkness surrounding, the moving figures of the men taking up all sorts of distorted and unnatural positions in the dim radiance, the grotesque shadows dancing drunkenly, the driving rain, the melancholy sough of the wind. It recalled an episode in French's life, when several years earlier in Thirsby, in Yorkshire, he had stood by a reopened grave and watched the coffin of Markham Giles being uncovered and raised to the surface. That was in that horrible case at Starvel Hollow. Then his deduction had been justified. Would it be justified on this occasion?

French paced up and down, lost in thought. A cut of more than two feet had now been made along the whole hundred-foot stretch, and no signs of anything unusual had been come on. However, a couple of feet wasn't a great deal. It was indeed too soon to hope for anything.

He looked at his watch. It was just half past two. The men had been working for three hours. It was time for a rest and a snack.

Half an hour later work was resumed. French made an alteration in his dispositions, concentrating the men at the centre of the stretch. It had occurred to him that the middle or place of greatest concealment was most likely to have been selected, if indeed any place had been selected at all.

Towards four o'clock the wind died down and the rain turned from a driving mist into a steady downpour. Everyone was tired and wet and in a slightly uncertain temper. French was beginning to feel very depressed. His chances of success seemed to grow less and less with every moment that passed. He forgot that they were approaching that period of the night when health and energy are at their lowest ebb, the time when the outlook on life seems most hopeless, the time when the end comes to the sinking, the hour at which suicide is most common. He forgot in fact that the darkest period comes before the dawn.

So it happened at all events on this occasion. It was just a little past five when one of the men gave a shout. French hurried up.

"Something 'ere, sir. See." The constable held up the end of some dark object like the large leaf of a rooted plant. French turned his electric torch on it and gasped.

It was a piece of cloth, the end, French imagined, of a lady's skirt.

"Clear away here," he said in a low tone. "Carefully does it now, men."

The atmosphere grew tense as the men worked. Slowly the clay was removed, and as the object was cleared, the last lingering element of doubt disappeared. The outlines of a body became revealed: a woman's body, buried there in the clay without shroud or coffin. The only faintest sign of reverence or decency shown was that the jumper – of light green wool – had been torn off and laid over the face. When it was removed French found himself gazing with some emotion into what had been the features of Ursula Stone.

But what features! Dreadful, swollen, distorted. And the cause was not far to seek. Round the neck there was a crease, and when French examined it he found it was caused by a string. Ursula had been strangled! Poor, kindly, harmless Ursula!

French was accustomed to murder and its awful results, but when he looked down on that face and thought of how it had been brought into that state, his anger grew hot against the criminal. There would now, he told himself, be something personal in his efforts to track down the author of so fiendish a deed. It was as if this outrage had destroyed one of his own friends. If the murderer were not caught and if the murderer were not hanged, it would not be French's fault.

But moralising over the remains, however natural, would not produce this result. French pulled himself together and became official once more.

"Some kind of a stretcher?" he asked Bradbury.

"Over here," the young man pointed. "There are planks and rope. We'll tie a couple of planks to a couple of fence posts: they'll make a hurdle. Rough, but good enough. Here, officer," he explained.

"I suppose there's not a disused hut that we could leave the body in?" went on French.

It seemed that there was. A hut had been used as a powder store during the blasting through the chalk ridge of the Hog's Back. This work was now finished and the hut was empty. It was close by, within a few hundred yards.

"That'll do," French agreed. "Come on, men, as soon as you're ready with that hurdle."

The remains, cleared now of clay, were with rough reverence lifted on to the improvised stretcher, and borne along the bypass formation to the hut. There they were laid, a policeman being left in charge. Another policeman was stationed at the place where they had been found, with orders to let no one approach. French wanted in daylight to turn the clay over again, in the hope of finding some trace of the criminal.

"You'll stop work at this particular point for a day or two, won't you, Mr Bradbury?" French asked. "I fancy I'm not through yet with all I want."

The young man raised his eyes and nodded significantly. "Of course, inspector. And if you want to dig farther in, we can do it for you at any time."

"That's what I shall want," French agreed. "Well, sir, much obliged for your invaluable help. I'll push off now, but I'll be back later. We needn't hope to keep this matter secret now, but the less of it gets out, the better."

"That's all right, inspector. Trust me."

French had sent the drivers for their cars, and soon the party of tired but excited men were on their way back to Farnham.

"I'm going for a wash-up and a bit of breakfast," French declared, "and all of you men do the same. If you're a bit late turning up I'll stand for it with the super."

French, clothed and in his right mind, was at the police station when Superintendent Sheaf arrived.

"Well, I hear you've pulled it off," Sheaf greeted him, with slightly less pessimism than usual. "Sheepshanks looked in on his way home. That should be a help."

"I hope so, super. It was that trace of clay in Slade's car that put me on to it. But it was a bit of luck finding the body so soon. Sheepshanks told you that she'd been strangled?"

Sheaf grunted assent. "Well, now you've got it, what do you propose to do next. Want to pull Slade in?"

French glanced at his companion. Was Sheaf just a little bit jealous? For a moment French thought so, then he felt sure he was mistaken. It was just Sheaf's manner. Sheaf had been very decent and considerate to him. In fact he had done everything he possibly could to help him, and French meant himself personally and not merely the case. However, he thought it no harm to be diplomatic.

"That's one of the things I came in to consult you about, super," he said. "Slade has a rather awkward alibi. It may be faked: probably is. But so long as it stands I'm not sure that we shouldn't hold our hand. Personally I'd rather be a bit surer of my ground before I burned my boats, so to speak," French added, feeling his metaphor was slightly strained. "I'd stand for keeping him under observation, but I don't think I'd favour an arrest."

Sheaf nodded. "I agree. Do you want me to do the shadowing?"

"If you will, super."

"I'll put a couple of men on to it. What about the body?"

"I would suggest that we have it brought in to the mortuary here," French answered. "We can't leave it in that hut."

"I agree. You want the ambulance?"

"Yes, please. Then I'll have that clay turned over again. Might find something useful."

Sheaf nodded again.

"Also I want to go back farther into the bank," continued French.

Sheaf looked at him keenly. "Yes," he rejoined slowly, "I should have thought you probably would." He paused. "Well," he went on presently, "that should be easy. But now that the thing's going to be known, I don't see why those bypass men shouldn't do the work. What's the point of our doing it ourselves?"

"None, super. That, I'm afraid, was a mistake on my part. I wanted to keep private anything we might find. I think we need scarcely worry about that now."

"That's all right. You were justified. Will these engineer people do what you want?"

"Oh, yes, they've got quite a good young man in charge there and he's keen to help."

"Something amusing for him," Sheaf grunted. "Very good, inspector, that seems all right. When will you have the body in?"

"As soon as you can let me have the ambulance."

"Right; I'll arrange it now. And I'll have the doctor at the mortuary in an hour."

French nodded. "One other thing, super. I'd like a relief to put on the bank. I don't want anyone messing round till I've had a further search."

"One man?"

"One man, super."

Sheaf pressed a bell. "Tell Black to go out with Inspector French and to act under his directions all day."

Twenty minutes later Constable Black had relieved the man who had been left on the scene of the excavation and the latter was helping the ambulance driver to lift all that remained of unhappy Ursula Stone into the vehicle. French returned with it into Farnham. As they reached the mortuary the police doctor appeared. French introduced himself.

"I'll hand you over the clothes presently, inspector," said Dr Peters. "Then I'll make my examination."

French went carefully through the clothes, but beyond satisfying himself that the strand of wool found in No. 2 Thicket was the same as that of the deceased's jumper, he learned nothing. Then while waiting for the doctor's report, he took a car and drove out to St Kilda to inform Julia Earle of the discovery.

Both she and Marjorie were terribly upset by the news. French could hardly doubt that their distress was real. Moreover, he felt sure they were genuinely surprised. The discovery had of course revived his suspicions, of them as well as others, but he had to admit there was no suggestion of guilt in their deportment.

By the time he reached Farnham Dr Peters had finished his preliminary examination. Ursula, he reported, had received a severe blow on the point of her chin which had probably rendered her unconscious. Some slight bleeding had taken place from her mouth and nose. This doubtless accounted for the drops French had found. But the real cause of death was strangulation. A cord had been tied tightly round her neck, and she had probably never recovered consciousness. There was the cord. As the inspector would see, it was a perfectly ordinary piece of cord, which anyone might have in his or her pocket.

"Then you don't think it was premeditated?" French asked.

"I didn't say that," returned Peters. "I don't know whether it was premeditated or whether it wasn't. I say it needn't have been. A man can use his fists at any time without premeditation, and given an unconscious woman and a piece of string – which anyone might have in his pockets – murder could be carried out without any further preparation."

French nodded. This worked in with his theory that Ursula had disturbed the thief as he was working at Earle's safe.

"You'll make a post-mortem, doctor, won't you?"

Given time to look round him, Dr Peters would do so. The inquest could, if the police authorities so desired, be held on the following day. He would be ready.

231

French went in to talk to Sheaf about the inquest. While the coroner would have to be advised immediately, he suggested that the actual inquest should be postponed for a day or two.

Sheaf raised his eyebrows. "More evidence?"

"It's possible, super."

"Right; well, I'll see the coroner, and you get ahead out at Compton."

French's luck in minor matters was less in evidence than usual when he reached the bypass. Bradbury was down near Milford, and nearly an hour passed before he was run to earth. French's immediate difficulties, however, were then over. Bradbury agreed to put a dozen men and a ganger at his disposal, who would do whatever he wanted. If he would come back to Compton, Bradbury would arrange it at once.

French first had the whole of the clay surrounding the spot at which the body had been found turned slowly over in the hope of finding some object dropped during the interment. This was a tedious job, but important. Unfortunately it yielded nothing.

While this search was in progress Bradbury was obtaining further necessary information, namely the precise line to which the toe of the slope had stood a fortnight earlier than that he had already given: on the date, in fact, not of Ursula's, but of Earle's disappearance.

This was some four feet farther into the bank, and French set his gang to open back to it.

"We'll not get it done today," the foreman told him.

"I don't suppose you will," French agreed. "You can go on again tomorrow, and I'll have a man to watch it tonight."

Next morning the work was resumed. By lunchtime the line of the previous bank was reached, and the men, who were fully alive to what was going on, worked with more eagerness. French stood beside them, watching with an eagle eye each shovelful as it was cast aside.

Keenly occupied though he was with his inspection, French's philosophical mind could not but be struck by the overwhelming effect of an idea. Here he was, watching one of the most commonplace and prosaic operations imaginable, the shovelling of clay; and yet he found the process exciting to an almost painful degree. He was thrilled to the marrow every time a workman had difficulty in driving in his shovel or paused to examine the ground he had uncovered. And why? Simply because of the idea he had in his mind.

He had concentrated operations on a stretch of a few feet on either side of where Ursula Stone's body had been found, and the men were placed as close together as they could work. Progress was consequently as rapid as was possible with such sticky clay. Fortunately the rain had ceased on the previous day and there had since been over twenty-four hours of dry weather. The clay was therefore in a slightly more workable condition than when the Farnham police had tried navvying. The bank had now, half an hour before quitting time, been cut some two feet in beyond the line of the slope on that eventful Sunday when Earle had so mysteriously vanished.

French was much too excited to stand still. He kept impatiently walking up and down, dancing on one foot at a time, jerkily lighting and throwing away cigarettes. It must be, he thought, now or never. He wondered if the men would work a little late and if the necessary lights could be obtained. There were the lamps they had had on the previous night, if these had been filled. He decided to send a man to ask Bradbury.

But before he could do so, history suddenly repeated itself. One of the men gave a cry, and when French hurried over, it was to find that the shovel had struck some cloth-covered object. French stooped and scraped away the clay. The cloth was stained and muddy, but as he lifted a fold he saw the other side. It was grey!

Even his nerves, case-hardened by the discovery of many a similar record of crime, were not proof against this one. A shock of physical horror ran through him. Earle's body he had expected to find, yes. But this body was not Earle's! Earle had been dressed in brown on that fatal Sunday. Surely this body must be, could only be, the nurse's!

"Clear away the clay," he said in a low voice. "Carefully does it now!"

The men did not need to be told. With the utmost care, even reverence, they dug away the surrounding material. Very little work was needed to confirm French's suspicion. Here indeed lay the body, not of Earle, but of Nurse Helen Nankivel.

It was with a furious anger against the diabolic author of the crime, that French saw the manner of her death. Here were the same dreadful, swollen, distorted features and the same terrible line round the throat that had appeared in Ursula Stone's case. The chin also was bruised. French did not need the doctor's report to know what had been done.

Once again French registered a vow that he would not rest till the devil who was guilty of this ghastly crime had paid for it on the scaffold. That this light-hearted, cheerful, kindly young woman, who had spent her short life trying to ease human suffering, and who had the reputation of having never willingly injured anyone, that she should have been done to death in this revolting way, demanded the heaviest penalty that the law allowed. French swore to himself that that penalty should be paid to the uttermost.

In a subdued voice he gave orders. This time he had brought a stretcher, and the remains were lifted upon it and borne to the same hut where those of the other unhappy victim had rested. French, hastening to the nearest telephone, rang up Sheaf, asking for the ambulance.

But unless he was greatly mistaken, the ghastly affair was not over. He hurried back to the men, who had stopped work and were conversing in eager knots. "Carry on," he said grimly. "I'm afraid we're not done yet."

They had scarcely set to work again when the expected happened. Another workman cried out and French hastened over...

Once again the same dreadful scene was enacted. Just beside where the body of the nurse had lain cloth was again found, brown cloth this time. The clay was removed. A human form was uncovered: Earle's. There, murdered in the same awful way as the two women, was all that remained of the missing doctor.

French found his horror grow as he contemplated the magnitude of the crime. Three murders! Three persons done to death to gratify someone's greed or lust or hate or fear! And no clue to the perpetrator – except a little patch of clay on the floor of a car. Well, that could wait.

For the third time the ghastly ritual was gone through. Earle's body was taken to the hut, and when the ambulance arrived, the remains of both victims were carried off together. French went with the vehicle into Farnham and saw Sheaf. Dr Peters was advised. Then French rode out once more to St Kilda and carried out the terribly distressing duty of telling the news to Julia and Marjorie.

Next day the inquests on the three bodies were opened. Formal evidence of identification was taken and in each case the proceedings were adjourned to enable the police to make further enquiries. Till this had been done French was too busy to sit down and think over the position with the necessary detachment. But as soon as the immediate requirements were over he set himself to consider what still remained to be done.

He almost smiled as he remembered his suggestion that he should drop the case. Drop it! No matter what time and labour were involved, he must not now rest till he had found the criminal and till justice had been satisfied.

– 18 –

THE CASE TWISTS

It did not take French long to settle on his first line of investigation. This dreadful discovery of the three bodies had been brought about in a very simple way: by his observation of the clay in Slade's car. Obviously the first question to be gone into was, How had the clay got there?

He wondered if Slade could account for it. If he could, there was no case against him, but if not, the inference was damning.

After a deal of thought French came to the conclusion that he must ask Slade the question. This would have the unfortunate result of putting Slade on his guard, were he guilty, but French did not see how he could help that. He could not risk wasting a lot of time on what Slade might be able to clear up in a sentence.

He looked at his watch. It was still early in the afternoon. No time like the present. In half an hour he was knocking at the door of Altadore.

Once again he was lucky in finding Slade at home and once again the young man's manner was obsequious.

"It's just one more question, Mr Slade," French began. "You will understand that points keep arising in a case like this, and it is not always possible at a single interview to cover all you want to know."

"That's all right, inspector. What is it?"

"I'll tell you, sir. I understand you did not take your car out on Saturday week at all. Is that correct?"

"Saturday week? Day before – er – Miss Stone was killed?" He paused, apparently in thought and evidently anxious. "That's right enough. I stayed in both the morning and the evening and had a round of golf in the afternoon. Walked to the club, you know."

"Quite so, sir. On the Sunday you had it out from about midday till about eleven at night?"

"Yes."

"That was the only time on the Sunday you had it out?"

"Yes, the only time."

"Now on the Sunday did you happen to give anyone a lift?"

"No, I did not," Slade declared.

"This is rather important, Mr Slade, important to you as well as to me: excuse me therefore for stressing it. You're quite sure you had no one in the car, either when it was in motion or stationary at any time on Saturday or Sunday?"

Slade was obviously growing more and more uneasy. "Absolutely. Perfectly certain. No one entered the car but myself."

French nodded. "All I wanted, sir, was to be sure you understood what I was asking," he explained. "Now another question, please. On that Sunday did you walk in any dirty clay soil?"

Slade stared while the expression of his eyes changed. "No," he said, shaking his head.

"You're quite sure?" French persisted.

Slade moved uneasily in his chair. "Absolutely," he repeated earnestly. "Wasn't off the road anywhere."

"Then," said French quietly, though watching the other keenly, "how do you account for the fact that on that

Sunday yellow clay was deposited in your car on the carpet in front of the driver's seat?"

Slade did not reply. He sat staring vacantly at French while the blood slowly drained from his face, leaving it a horrible mottled grey. French remained motionless with his eyes fixed on that unwholesome countenance. "Well, Mr Slade?" he said at last.

Slade roused himself. "My God, I don't know," he stammered in a low troubled tone, and then: "I can't believe it! It isn't true! There *couldn't* have been clay in the car. You don't really mean it, inspector?"

"There was certainly clay there, Mr Slade."

Slade gave a sort of inarticulate moan. Then the words came quickly. "I don't know anything about it," he exclaimed eagerly. "Never saw any clay. Didn't know it was there. Don't know how it could have got there. You believe me, inspector? I tell you it's the truth."

More than this French could not obtain. For a moment he wondered had he enough evidence to risk an arrest. Then he saw he had not. He therefore expressed himself as satisfied with Slade's statement, reassuring him as best he could. "I may have to question the servants," he added. "I take it you have no objection?"

Slade had no objection and French, wishing him good afternoon, turned his attention to the parlour maid. Who cleaned Slade's shoes? Who had cleaned them on the dates in question? Had there been any trace of yellow clay on any of the shoes?

He made as complete enquiries as he could, but with only a negative result. No one had seen yellow clay on either Slade's or anyone else's shoes. Then he examined for himself all Slade's shoes, believing that even if cleaned, minute traces of clay might remain. But he could find none.

French was puzzled as he rode back to Farnham. If he were to judge by Slade's words and manner alone, he would have assumed him guilty. Slade certainly was frightened, and he unquestionably realised the significance of the clay. On the other hand the matter of the shoes undoubtedly supported Slade's statement.

But, French saw with exasperation, even if Slade were lying, the matter was far from clear. There were two additional reasons why it was hard to visualise the man's guilt.

Of these, the first was his alibi. Unless French could find a flaw in his alibi, Slade could not be taken into court. His defence would be overwhelming. And French couldn't find any flaw, at least he had not been able to do so up to the present. But this matter of the alibi was fundamental to his progress. He must establish it beyond doubt or break it down.

He went up to his room and settled down to work on it. Item by item he went over the thing again in his mind, with the sole result of becoming more puzzled than ever. Slade and his car were definitely at Petersfield at 4.00 p.m. Of that there could be no doubt; it was checked by the people he had visited. From St Kilda to Petersfield was something like 21 miles, part of it over narrow and twisting roads. It would be *impossible* to run the distance in half an hour. But at 3.30 Ursula was alive. The servant, Lucy, had seen her just before going out. And Lucy had unquestionably caught the bus which passed the house at 3.35. There was her own evidence, and that of the friends to whom she was going, as also of the bus company as to their service, all of which points French had checked. It was certain, therefore, that Slade could not have committed the murder *before* reaching Petersfield.

That Slade stayed there till five was also proven beyond possibility of doubt. It was at least as certain as human testimony permitted. Two of the friends he had met had particularly noted the hour of his departure, as they had considered what they would do between then and dinner.

Again there was definitely no time for Slade to have made the interment between five o'clock, when he left Petersfield, and six, when he reached the golf club. Every minute of that hour was satisfactorily accounted for. Besides, it was not as if the thing were a matter of minutes. To have conveyed Ursula's body from Thicket No. 2 to the bypass bank, and there buried it, would have been a matter of an hour or more. Slade simply could not have done it before six. Nor could he have done it between six and eleven. The evidence that he was at the club during the whole of that period was too convincing to be doubted.

There was then left only the time after eleven. Here came in the evidence of the Dagger chauffeur and his wife. They were positive, firstly, that Slade's car was returned to the garage at about eleven, and secondly, that neither it nor any other was taken out till the next day. And all French's instinct and experience told him that they were speaking the truth. Besides, after eleven St Kilda and its surroundings were in the hands of the police. It did not of course follow that Slade would have been seen had he then attempted to dispose of the body, but French did not believe he would have attempted it. He would have known that both the paths in the wood and the roads were being searched, and the chances of his being seen would be considerable. This admittedly was not convincing, but the evidence of the chauffeur and his wife was.

But if the alibi made a difficulty in the theory of Slade's guilt, French's second consideration involved an even greater difficulty. He believed that if Slade had murdered Ursula, whether assisted by Julia or not, it could only be because Ursula had got hold of evidence that one or other was guilty of the first murder. Now Slade – and Julia – might have had a motive for murdering Earle, but what possible motive could either have had for killing Helen Nankivel? French couldn't imagine any.

Did it mean, then, that Slade was out of the affair? It would seem so. But then there was the clay! French swore.

Presently he put Slade out of his mind and turned to reconsider the whole problem from a broader standpoint.

He had so often fruitlessly wondered who could be guilty, that he felt there was no use in spending more time over the problem. Rather he thought he should concentrate on motive. What could have been the motive for these three crimes?

Taking Ursula's case first, he went over the theory which had already occurred to him. Had she been murdered because she had discovered someone burgling Earle's secret safe, and was the burglar removing evidence that he had murdered Earle?

At once French thought of an important point which up to now he had overlooked. It was practically certain that the burglar *had* murdered Earle, for the simple reason that there was no other way in which he could have obtained Earle's keys to open the safe. That he had opened the safe was proved by the indications that someone wearing gloves had been fingering the inside. And it had certainly been opened with a key.

The assumption then was that the burglar *had* murdered Earle and that French's theory of Ursula's death was correct. Admittedly it did not prove that incriminating information about the first murder had been hidden in the safe, but proof of this point was not immediately material to the investigation.

But what was material, and what had so far been left entirely out of the picture, was the murder of the nurse. Obviously the three crimes were intimately connected. Where did unhappy Helen Nankivel come in?

In the light of his subsequent discoveries, French's original theory of an intrigue between Earle and the nurse seemed scarcely tenable. Was there any other possible reason for their association?

At once an idea which he had already frequently considered recurred to him. Could their association have been professional? They were both, as it were, in the same line of business. Could some medical question, something possibly about Earle's book, have arisen, which had led to their dreadful end?

Then French remembered that there had been another point of contact between them connected with their professions. Had they not recently been consultant and nurse on the same case? Could anything in connection with the Frazer case account for what had happened?

French turned to his notes of that case, taken incidentally and without much detail. He was no doctor, but he had picked up a few isolated medical facts. As he re-read his notes a new and startling thought leaped into his mind and he began to whistle soundlessly beneath his breath.

He got up and began to pace the room as he turned the idea over. Was it a possibility? Was he at last on to the root of the whole affair? He could not tell. His knowledge did not enable him to say. He must have advice.

For a few moments he hesitated. Then he went to the telephone and rang up the London police doctor to whom he had already sent Earle's manuscript.

"A hypothetical case, doctor, if you please," he said. "A man of nearly seventy gets – " and he passed on all the information he had about Frazer and his illness and death.

At once his own idea was confirmed. *Arsenic!*

"If you're suspicious and if those are the symptoms," said the doctor, "then try arsenic. I don't say it was arsenic. Those symptoms are the symptoms of arsenical poisoning, but they are also the symptoms of the disease the man was supposed to be suffering from. All I'm giving you is a hint as to what you may look for."

French rang off, his brain whirling. Could it be that he had not yet reached the end of the horror of this ghastly case? His nerves were pretty well hardened, but a case with four murders was a bit too much even for him. Could this wild idea of his really be the truth?

If so, what could possibly have happened? Why, that Earle and the nurse had tumbled to the thing, that the murderer learned that they were preparing to act and in self-defence murdered them both. That the proof they had procured – why, yes, of course! – was in Earle's safe. That the murderer was trying to recover this when Ursula interrupted him and that he therefore had to kill Ursula too!

Here at last, French was convinced, was the truth! For the first time all these dreadful isolated events fell into line and became unified. Here at last was a satisfying theory of what might have happened.

Once again he began to pace the room, too much excited to remain still. If this idea were correct it opened up a complete new field of investigation. Who could have murdered not only Earle, the nurse and Ursula, but also old Frazer? Surely not more than one person could have had the necessary opportunities!

If so, French's task became instantly easier. He had only to find this one person and his work would be done. And elimination should lead to him directly. All he had to do was to make a complete list of the apparently possible, and detailed investigation should unquestionably rule out all but one.

He determined that not even to Sheaf would he breathe a hint of what he suspected, until he had looked into the matter further. And then and there he began to do so.

Once again he looked over his notes. Frazer had evidently been a trying old man. Sheaf had said his wife had had a hell of a time with him and suggested that she could only have married him for his money. The information French had picked up at the house and from Campion and Nurse Henderson tended generally to confirm this view. And it seemed indubitable that Mrs Frazer stood to gain a very large sum of money, put by the butler at £60,000, by her husband's death.

Here at once was motive, and strong motive at that. To change a life of bondage and worry and fear of being disinherited, for freedom, a charming place and £60,000, was something for which it would be worth running a risk.

He had of course met Mrs Frazer only once, but in that short interview he had obtained a very definite impression of her character. She was, he guessed, selfish, efficient and probably cruel. He did not think that qualms of conscience would hold her back from anything she might undertake. Undoubtedly Mrs Frazer was a suspect.

This seemed progress, though when he began to consider how Mrs Frazer could have murdered Ursula

Stone, he didn't think he had progressed so far. However, let him take his fences when he came to them. On a fresh page of his notebook, under the heading "Possible Suspects", he wrote, "1. Mrs Hermione Frazer."

Equally obvious as a suspect was the nephew, Gates. Gates so far seemed to him somewhat of a dark horse. He had evidently led a rough life among a rough crowd in Australia. Why when he was heir to much money he should have done so, was not clear, but it looked as if there had been some early trouble in his life. Hearsay told French moreover, first, that Gates was hard up, and secondly, that he was due a large sum on his uncle's death. Under Mrs Hermione Frazer's name French wrote, "2. Arthur Gates."

But when he came to consider a third suspect, French's facility deserted him. So far as he could tell from the information in his possession, no one else had any motive at all.

He decided to get hold of the Frazer will and see for himself just how the money had been left. For the moment, then, he might leave this point.

But money was not the only motive for murder. Could anyone have been in love with Mrs Frazer? Could she have been in love with anyone? Here was something to be looked into at once. And also another point: Who could have got at the medicine and the food? If these questions were answered, and the results tabulated and compared with lists of those who could have murdered Ursula, Earle and the nurse, the main problem should be solved.

And then, as in warfare an attack is followed by a counter-attack, French saw the inevitable snag. Earle and Helen Nankivel could scarcely have suspected that Frazer had been poisoned, as if they had, they would never have acquiesced in the burial. They would never have kept silence about their doubts for so long a time as seventeen days after the old man's death.

At the same time the mere fact that a rich man had died with symptoms similar to those of arsenical poisoning, was in itself suspicious. French decided that there was sufficient doubt on the point to demand an enquiry. For some time longer he considered whether he could proceed with this unknown to Sheaf. Finally he decided that he could not.

Next morning therefore he had a talk with the superintendent. Sheaf at first was sceptical, but on thinking over French's arguments, he also agreed that the matter could not be left as it then stood.

"What will you do?" he asked.

"I thought of trying to get some more details about conditions in the Frazer household, and the possibilities of tampering with food or medicine. If I come on anything suspicious I thought then of going to Campion and getting his views."

"He'll not admit much," Sheaf grunted. "Didn't he give the certificate."

"He mayn't be able to help himself. However, I'm afraid that's going a bit too fast."

Then began one of those nebulous enquiries which French loathed; the search for motives and possibilities rather than facts. He wanted to find out if anyone besides Mrs Frazer and Gates had an interest in Frazer's death, and also who could have administered the poison. And this when the possibility of poison could not be hinted at.

French found the job tedious and disappointing. His veiled enquiries at Polperro roused antagonisms and the assurances that his questionees knew nothing. And indeed he was forced to the belief that at least in most cases, that reply was true.

He began by seeing Mr Hunter, the senior partner of Hunter, Newnes & Hunter, the late gentleman's solicitors. He made an impressive start by producing his Yard credentials, but Mr Hunter was not impressed. The only information the solicitor would give was that he was now acting for Mrs Frazer. As to Mr Frazer's will, that would be made known in due course, but was now confidential. If the inspector wished to see it and produced the necessary authority, it would at once be handed over. In the meantime if that was all the inspector wanted, he wished him a very good day.

At Polperro practically the only thing he learned was that both Mrs Frazer and Gates had had ample opportunity of tampering with the deceased gentleman's medicine, as one or other sat with him while Nurse Nankivel was out in the afternoon. Apparently, however, any other member of the household could have done the same, as in the course of their business both nurses occasionally left the sickroom during their periods of duty and towards the end old Frazer was too exhausted to observe who might enter.

The same pretty well applied to the question of food. The cook and the nurses could of course have doped it, and French believed so could anyone else. There was, moreover, in the tool sheds any amount of weed-killer containing arsenic, and any member of the household could have secretly helped him or herself.

But French learned nothing to indicate that any of these things had been done.

He thereupon widened the mouth of his net. Since coming down to Farnham he had made a number of acquaintances; local people at the hotel, shopkeepers, postmen, occupants of houses near Hampton Common. Now he made it his business to meet these people accidentally. When he did so he was expansive, ready to give information – information due in any case for the newspapers. In the hope of getting further details these people willingly prolonged the conversations, which somehow always turned on the Frazers. French was extraordinarily skilful at what might be called the painless extraction of information, but here his most persistent efforts brought him little result.

One thing which seemed certain was that there had been no illicit love affair in the case of Mrs Frazer. At least if there had, she had been extraordinarily discreet.

About Gates French found it easier to obtain information. Gates was a well-known member of the sporting community and plenty of comment had passed on his doings. Judicious enquiries revealed the fact that he had had pretty expensive dealings with moneylenders. One of these gentlemen, anxious to remain on good terms with the police, produced documentary evidence that a part of Frazer's money was entailed and that Gates was expecting its reversion. In fact his testimony bore witness to the accuracy of Constable Black's incidental statements, when he was asked about Slade.

French was much dissatisfied with the result of his enquiries, though he did not see how he could have done better. He had obtained nothing positive. Suspicion against Mrs Frazer, and still more against Gates, was possible, but there was no positive evidence against either.

Moreover, he had to remind himself sharply that the same doubt applied to the fundamental question of Frazer's murder itself. To suspect poison was possible, but the suspicion was not backed up by the slightest scintilla of real evidence.

Yet French could not leave the matter in its present state. He decided that he must approach Campion. The interview would, he was afraid, prove embarrassing, for it practically meant accusing Campion of giving a false certificate. However, there was nothing else to be done, and once again he rode out to the Red Cottage.

– 19 –

CHEMICAL ANALYSIS

Campion was out when French called, but he was expected at any moment, and French was shown into the consulting-room to wait. It was not the first time he had called on a doctor to suggest that the latter had been professionally remiss, and these interviews had never been happy. Campion, however, seemed a sensible sort of man and he would probably be able to see something besides his own dignity.

The servant's expectations were justified, and French had not waited more than five minutes when the doctor appeared. He seemed surprised to see French, but greeted him civilly enough.

"I wanted a word with you, sir, but I'm not in a hurry and can wait if the present is not convenient."

As French had hoped, this mild beginning appeared to impress Campion favourably. He sat down and said that in all business there was no time like the present.

"It's rather a serious matter," French went on. "A certain suspicion has been aroused in my mind by the events which I've been investigating, and I wanted to consult you about it before proceeding any further. I may say that I have mentioned my idea to no one except Superintendent Sheaf of Farnham, and that only in the strictest confidence. There is no question therefore of any whisper of the thing having got out."

"That's a good mysterious beginning," Campion returned. "What's it all about?"

"I'll tell you, sir. It's about the late Mr Frazer, of Polperro. Not to beat about the bush, may I ask you, Are you, and were you at all times, quite satisfied as to the death of Mr Frazer?"

Campion stared. "Satisfied?" he repeated. "What do you mean by that? Explain yourself."

"I mean, doctor, satisfied in your own mind as to the cause of death?"

Campion continued to stare. "Even now, inspector," he said slowly, "I'm not sure that I've entirely grasped your meaning. Are you suggesting that I gave a certificate the correctness of which I doubted?"

"No, sir," French answered promptly. "I'm not questioning your good faith for a moment. But you know as well as I that many a certificate has been signed in the best of good faith, which owing to later information has proved not entirely correct."

Campion made a gesture of irritation. "For goodness sake, inspector, get down to it. What are you questioning? Are you suggesting the certificate was wrong?"

"Not necessarily, sir. I'm coming to you, as the doctor in charge of the case, to ask your opinion and advice upon certain suspicious circumstances which have come to my knowledge, but which may not have come to yours."

Campion looked bewildered as well as exasperated. "As I said, you're very mysterious. What are these suspicious circumstances you speak of?"

"The first one is – and this is where I want your opinion and advice – the first one is that the death had all the symptoms of arsenical poisoning. Now tell me doctor, am I right or wrong in that?"

A light seemed to dawn on Campion. "Oh, so that's it, is it? Poison, no less." He laughed shortly. "I'm afraid, inspector, you've allowed your calling to run away with your imagination." Then more gravely, "But that's a very serious suggestion you're making. I take it you're not by any chance pulling my leg?"

"I'm afraid the matter is serious, sir," French said directly. "At all events I should like an answer to my question."

For the first time Campion seemed impressed. "Well, I take it you wouldn't say that unless you had something to back it up. It's a very nasty suggestion." He paused, then went on: "As to the symptoms, of course they were like those of arsenical poisoning. That is because Frazer had gastro-enteritis. Everyone knows the symptoms are similar. But that's a very different thing from saying the man was poisoned."

"Quite so: I appreciate that, doctor. But I should like to ask this, Was there any symptom inconsistent with death from arsenical poisoning?"

Campion sat back in his chair and squared his shoulders. "The man was suffering from gastro-enteritis," he said firmly, "and had been for a considerable time. He died from gastro-enteritis, *plus* old age and a weak heart. There were no symptoms inconsistent with death from arsenical poisoning: there aren't in that disease. But as I said before, that's no reason to suspect poisoning. Why" – he warmed to his subject – "the whole idea is ludicrous. Do you mean seriously to tell me that there's no such disease as gastro-enteritis? That everyone who is supposed to have died from it was poisoned with arsenic? Because that's really what you're arguing. Unless" – his manner changed suddenly –

"you've got some further information up your sleeve. Have you?"

French shrugged. "My other points are really confidential," he returned. "Just as I came to you about the symptoms and kept this point secret from everyone except the super, so I do not think it fair to discuss with you what may concern other people. But two points you can see for yourself. The first is that Mr Frazer was wealthy and had to leave his money to someone; the second, that mysterious death has overtaken two of the persons concerned with that illness. Come now, doctor, you can see for yourself that without mentioning names or other facts, of which there are a few, that I am justified in making enquiries. In any case the matter is out of my hands; Superintendent Sheaf has agreed it must be gone into."

Campion was visibly impressed. "That's all very disquieting, inspector," he said anxiously, "very disquieting indeed. If you're right, it means that I've given a false certificate. Not a very pleasant thing to contemplate. But I can't and don't believe it. I need scarcely say such an idea never for a moment occurred to me, and looking back now, I can't see anything about the case in the slightest degree suspicious." He moved uneasily. "The idea's damnable. But I don't believe it; not for a moment. You're on the wrong track; unless you know a darned sight more than you've told me."

Campion paused, then before French could speak, went on again. "And there's another thing. Dr Earle saw Mr Frazer twice – the last time just two days before he died – and Dr Earle was satisfied. If he had had the slightest doubt he would have raised the question. He would never have allowed the burial to take place if he had suspected poison. The same applies to the two nurses." He sat back as if relieved. "No inspector, I'm afraid this time you're barking up the wrong tree. Besides, who would do such a thing? No one!"

French gave a crooked smile. "Now you're going a bit too fast for me," he declared. "I've not got the length of considering possible criminals. But I suppose I may take it from your question that poison is not impossible?"

"My God!" Campion cried, twisting about in his chair and striking the table a heavy blow with his fist, "of course it's not impossible! But there was no evidence and is no evidence that it was anything but gastro-enteritis. I said gastro-enteritis in the certificate and I stick to it. There's no reason to think anything else!"

"I agree, sir," French declared smoothly, "that at the time there was nothing in any way suspicious. I suppose every other doctor would have acted exactly as you did. But now things are different. Information has been obtained which was not at your disposal, and this information makes all the difference."

"But bless my soul, inspector, who could have done such a thing? You speak of legatees. But there were only two, Mrs Frazer and Mr Gates, and I know them both. And anything more absurd and iniquitous than attributing murder to either, I never heard!"

"I'm very far from attributing murder to either," French returned. Suddenly it occurred to him to try a bluff and he leant forward and sank his voice impressively. "What about the nurse?" he asked knowingly.

Campion stared and French continued. "Might not the nurse have slipped a little arsenic into the old man's medicine?"

"But what for?"

"For a consideration. If, for instance, the nurse proves to have come into money, it might be worth tracing where it came from."

Campion laughed contemptuously. "What about your superintendent?" he asked with heavy sarcasm. "Have you thought of him? If probability's not to be considered, Sheaf's as likely as anyone else."

"The super has an alibi," French said smoothly. "But seriously, sir, I want any information I can get. You said you knew Mrs Frazer and Mr Gates. Do you mind telling me anything you know about them?"

This proved too wide for the mark. French, as conversationally as he could, narrowed his enquiries down.

Campion could not, or would not, tell him much. According to the doctor, Mrs Frazer had been a model wife. Admittedly Frazer had been sometimes hard to bear; people with stomach troubles were often depressed and cantankerous. She had been unfailingly good to him, and it would be stupid as well as wicked to suspect her of such a crime.

As to the innocence of Gates, which French next touched on, the doctor was equally emphatic. Gates was well known to the doctor. They had met, Campion told him, on many racecourses. Gates was a bit rough in his manner, but as good-hearted as they were made. Campion did not believe he was hard up, as he could have got all the money he wanted because of his expectations.

In the end French left the Red Cottage convinced that Campion might have made a mistake and that the man knew it.

For some time the case dragged. It was indeed nearly a week before French made his next discovery. During that week he was by no means idle. He worked as hard as he knew how trying to pick up information about the Polperro household, and particularly about Mrs Frazer and Gates. Gates he saw on two occasions, on each seizing the opportunity to have a long chat. But he could learn nothing in the slightest degree helpful.

His next discovery came from a quite different line of enquiry. He had returned to Town on the Saturday intending on the Monday to start a more complete investigation into Nurse Nankivel's life, in the rather desperate hope of coming on something which might give a new lead to his ideas. He began by a call at Bryanston Square.

Lady Hazzard herself saw him. She appeared genuinely interested in the nurse and horrified as to her fate. With some eagerness she asked French whether there was any hope of the murderer being brought to justice.

French did not so far know, but trusted this end would be duly attained. In the meantime had anything of the nurse's been left behind at Bryanston Square?

Only, Lady Hazzard returned, a letter which had come by that morning's delivery and which she had been about to send to the nursing home. French, glancing at the address, "Miss H Nankivel, c/o Brig. Gen. Sir Ormsby Hazzard, CMG, DSO", said that he was going to the nursing home and would take it.

Instead of the home, however, he went into Hyde Park, and sitting down on an empty seat, carefully slit open the envelope.

It contained a bill for three guineas from Messrs Morgan & Winterton, who described themselves as analytical chemists, and whose address was Room 174, Ocean Buildings, Tabbilet Street, WC2. There were no items, the charge being merely, "To a/c rendered."

Tabbilet Street, French knew, was in the neighbourhood of Covent Garden. In two minutes he was in a taxi on his way thither, and in another fifteen he was knocking at Room 174 in Ocean Buildings. Mr Winterton was disengaged and saw him at once.

"I called, sir," French began, "in connection with this account," and he handed over the contents of the envelope.

"Ah yes," said Winterton, "we shall be glad to have it settled. But how, inspector, has it become a matter for the Yard?"

"I'm afraid, sir," French returned with a faint smile, "I've not come to settle it. Unhappily I am the bearer of bad news. I have to tell you that this Miss H Nankivel has been the victim of a serious crime; in fact, I may say at once that she has been murdered."

"Bless my soul!" Winterton exclaimed. "Did I hear you say *murdered*?" He was tall and thin and curved his long back forward over the table, blinking at French like a draggled old bird.

"I fear so, sir," French answered. "I am in charge of the case, and I am anxious to get some information from you as to the transaction for which this debt was incurred."

"Quite so. Very natural. But dear me, murdered! How very dreadful! Very dreadful indeed!" He cleared his throat pompously. "I shall of course place any information I may have at your disposal."

Presently he came to the point. He sent for a file, turned up a letter, and handed it to French. "We received that on the 30th of September last, as you will see, together with the enclosure. Better read the letter before I go on."

French did so. It was written in a feminine hand, which French at once recognised as that of the dead nurse. Above the printed legend, "129B, Bryanston Square, W1", was written, "c/o Brig. Gen. Sir Ormsby Hazzard, CMG, DSO" It was dated 29th September and read:

Messrs Morgan & Winterton,
Analytical Chemists.

DEAR SIRS,
I send you herewith a small bottle containing a solution, and should be obliged if you would kindly analyse same and let me have a note of the contents. If you let me have your account, I will send the necessary amount.

Yours faithfully,

(MISS) H NANKIVEL.

"Yes?" said French.

"We carried out the analysis as requested," went on Winterton. "Unfortunately the bottle contained too small a quantity of the solution to enable a really accurate quantitative analysis to be made. Our work, however, was very close to the truth. We then wrote the following report." He delved in his file and handed across another document. It was a carbon copy of the letter and read:

3rd October

DEAR MADAM,
In reply to your communication of 29th ult. we have to inform you that we carried out an analysis of the liquid sent us. We regret that the quantity was too small to enable completely accurate results to be obtained, but the figures given on the attached sheet are approximately correct. Trusting that this will meet your requirements,

We are, etc.,

MORGAN & WINTERTON

Per J W

From another file Mr Winterton handed over an analysis sheet, which French read with an air of profound wisdom, but of which he could make very little.

"I'm not a chemist, Mr Winterton," he explained. "Could you not put this result into ordinary language which I could understand?"

Winterton shrugged. "Well," he said, "I on my part am not a doctor. However, I shall do my best. The liquid seemed to us to be a medicine for indigestion or stomach ulcer or enteritis; something about the stomach, I don't know what. But it contained one unusual ingredient: an appreciable quantity of arsenic."

At this French metaphorically sat up and took notice. "That interests me quite a lot, sir," he declared. "Now if you would kindly tell me the effect of that addition, I should be even more obliged."

"A doctor could do better than I," Winterton returned. "Obviously, however, the effect depends on the amount taken."

"Suppose for argument's sake it amounted to one whole ordinary-sized bottle."

Winterton shrugged. "Even that, I'm afraid, is not sufficient information. As you doubtless know, different people have a different tolerance to drugs. The harm done would depend on the constitution of the recipient."

French, mentally cursing the limitations of the scientific mind, tried again.

"I understand, sir, that you can only speak very generally. Assuming a purely hypothetical case with a normal tolerance to the drug, could you tell me what might be expected?"

"Hypothetically, I believe I'm safe in saying that the arsenic would certainly disagree very seriously with anyone taking it."

"Would it poison him?" French asked directly.

"That," the old man replied, "is an extremely difficult question. One dose, I should say, certainly not. The whole bottleful" – he shrugged impressively – "probably."

"I see, sir. Then did that end the transaction? You sent the analysis to your client. Was there an answer?"

"That most assuredly did not end the transaction," Winterton declared, and French saw that a ponderous joke was intended. "The transaction will end when we are paid our fee, which, as you know, has not yet been done. You may say, Why did we not demand prepayment? Because of General Hazzard's name. We checked up on the address as being really his, and felt quite safe. Now if I may ask, inspector" – the old man became solemn once more – "I should like to know something about our client."

"Your client was a nurse, Mr Winterton," French answered. "Her name was Helen Nankivel, and her murdered body was found buried along the new bypass road near Guildford."

The bird-like old man was thrilled. He had read the account of the discovery in the papers, but had never connected the "H Nankivel" of the analysis with the murdered nurse. "If we had had the slightest idea of her identity," he declared again and again, "we should instantly have communicated with New Scotland Yard! A really dreadful affair, inspector!"

He would have kept French talking about it for hours, but French had other fish to fry. Accordingly, after thanking the old man, he took his leave.

That he was now on to an important link in his case French had no doubt. Though he didn't see exactly how it worked in, he believed a little thought would show him the connection. But first to make sure of his facts.

On his way back to the Yard he called on Dr Randal, the police doctor with whom he had already consulted about the case.

"Just one question, doctor, if you don't mind," he said, laying the analysis down on the consulting-room desk. "I wish you'd tell me what this is."

Dr Randal glanced at the paper. Then he shook his head. "I don't know," he admitted. "A medicine made up by an imaginative lunatic, I should think. What about it?"

"Might it be an ordinary medicine with one extra ingredient added?"

"Ah," said Randal, "now you're talking. Yes, without the arsenic it would be a quite ordinary medicine."

"For what complaint, doctor?"

"Internal inflammations, stomach troubles, intestinal troubles: anything of that sort."

"Gastro-enteritis?"

"The very thing. You'll soon be qualifying if you go on like this, French."

French grinned. "And what would the effect of the addition be?" he persisted.

Dr Randal practically repeated what Mr Winterton had told him. Assuming one bottleful of the medicine had been taken, the arsenic, particularly to anyone with a complaint of gastro-enteritis or anything like it, would be a serious matter. One dose would not do a great deal of harm, but the bottleful, even taken in normal doses at normal intervals, would certainly kill. No, there would be no great change in the symptoms, except that these would become more marked. Yes, if such poison were secretly admini-stered, the doctor attending the case might easily give a cer-tificate without the slightest suspicion that all was not right.

"What about the nurse attending the case? Do you think she ought to have been suspicious?"

"My dear man, how in thunder could I tell? It would depend on how the stuff was administered, I mean in what quantity, also on the patient's health: matters of which you haven't seen fit to inform me."

"It's because I don't know myself. But what I want to get at is this: Suppose the patient was getting that medicine regularly without arsenic. Then suppose the arsenic was added. Suppose the patient continued to get it regularly. Should the nurse notice a sudden marked difference in the patient from the time the arsenic was put in?"

Dr Randal did not answer for a moment. "Yes, I think she should," he said at last. "It's not easy to be quite sure, as the effect of drugs of this kind is cumulative. Besides, if the patient had been having the usual ups and downs, she might naturally take this as a 'down'. On the whole, however, I think she should notice something. That, mind you, is a very different thing to saying that she would have become suspicious of poison."

This was what French expected to hear. The usual indefinite opinion. The nurse might have noticed something, but then again, she mightn't. That was the way! There was nothing that he could absolutely bite on to and say, "Here is fact!" He had been hoping that the direct question to Nurse Henderson as to whether she had noticed any sudden change in her late patient's condition, would have told him whether or not the old man had been poisoned. But apparently he had been hoping too much. All the same, to run down to Bramley would only take three or four hours. It would be worth putting the question.

French rose to take his leave, but the doctor motioned him to sit down again. "I've read that manuscript you sent me," he remarked.

"Oh yes," French returned. "I intended to ask you about it, but with this other thing it slipped my memory. What did you think of it?"

For a moment the doctor did not answer, then he glanced curiously at his visitor. "It's a very remarkable piece of work, French," he declared. "I was much impressed!"

French laughed. "That tells me a lot, doesn't it? Is there anything in it that would impress me?"

Randal did not laugh. "I think there is," he said seriously. "I want you to take it away from here with you now, and if you take my advice you'll get an escort with it to the nearest fire and burn it there."

French stared. "Bless us all, doctor, but you're mysterious! What's wrong with the darned thing?"

"Just this," Randal said grimly. "Do you know that that manuscript is nothing more nor less than a child's guide to murder? Real murder, murder that could never be found out? It's a remarkable piece of work; very original and clever, but very dangerous."

French whistled. Then he swore. Then he asked for further explanations.

"Well," Dr Randal answered, "it's very simple – to talk about. This Earle has found a way of simplifying the making of cultures – cultures of the bacilli of fatal diseases – so as to bring this within the reach of any intelligent layman. With this book in his hand practically anyone could produce a serum which when injected would cause death; death, that is, through the ordinary medium of disease.

How the disease was contracted would no doubt remain a puzzle, but there would be nothing to arouse suspicion."

"Good Lord, doctor! But how could such a book be published?"

"That's more than I can tell you. But do you know Earle meant to publish it?"

"Well, there's not much use in writing a book just for the fun of it."

"I'm not so sure," the doctor said slowly. "People do queer things. However, didn't Earle take precautions it shouldn't get into anyone else's hands? I think you mentioned something of that kind?"

French slapped his thigh. "You've got it, doctor! I never thought of it! That's what the safe was for. You know, he had a secret safe hidden behind oak panelling. Regular medieval affair with sliding panel and all the rest of it. As secret as you like. And behind the panel a modern steel safe. That's it!"

"That's it, as you so truly say. The man would recognise that he had only to be a bit careless with his keys, and an ordinary safe would become no further protection. The secret panel idea was good, and in my opinion justified."

Here was the answer to one of those minor problems which had worried French in his conduct of the case. He had been bothered as to whether, owing to the time at which the safe had been put in, Earle's disappearance had been due to some long-standing secret. Now this was cleared up. The safe had been put in to hold the manuscript, and the manuscript had nothing to do with Earle's decease. Presumably he had simply taken advantage of the existence of this very secret receptacle – the only really safe place in the house – to hide the proofs of Frazer's murder.

With an effort French switched his thoughts back to his motive in calling on Dr Randal. The death of Frazer! His next step was to see that nurse at Bramley. Well, he must get on with it.

He travelled down to Bramley, found Nurse Henderson, and put his question. "Tell me," he said, "did you notice any more or less sudden change in the old man's condition? Suppose he had been going on on what I might call a certain level of ill health, did he suddenly drop to a lower level and continue on it? Tell me anything you can about his variations of health."

The nurse didn't know that she could do that. As she was sure the inspector knew, invalids were variable in health. They had good days and bad. There was no accounting for these changes.

"You can't remember the changes in the case of Mr Frazer?"

She was afraid not. Mr Frazer had been going on on the level, as the inspector had put it, and he certainly had suddenly changed for the worse. Then he had seemed to go rapidly down the hill, and his death followed quickly.

This was more than French had expected. He thought quickly, then very impressively swore the girl to silence.

"Suppose," he said, "that Mr Frazer had been given a course of arsenic, would that account for his varying condition?"

Nurse Henderson was very much excited and upset at the idea. At first she denied the possibility of poison, then gradually came round to the idea and admitted that French's suggestion might well be the truth.

"Was Mr Frazer quite clear mentally up to the end?"

"He was as clear as you or I till he got that change for the worse. After that he got duller and finally became unconscious."

"Clear, that is, until he was given the poison – if my suspicion is correct. Tell me, nurse, who dispensed the medicine?"

"Malcolmson, the chemist in Guildford."

French decided to return to Farnham via Guildford and call on Malcolmson. He saw Mr Malcolmson, who produced Campion's prescription for the medicine. This was in accordance with Morgan & Winterton's analysis, except that, as might be expected, there was no mention of arsenic. As might be expected also, Mr Malcolmson was positive that there was no arsenic in the medicine when it left his shop. Both the receipt of the prescription and the despatch of the medicine had been by post. From this it seemed to follow that the arsenic had been put in by some member of the Frazer household.

As he drove in a bus to Farnham, French tried to modify his theory of the case to include all these new facts. Suppose Nurse Nankivel had noticed that Frazer's condition varied according to whether he did or did not take certain medicine. If she had become suspicious, she might have experimented by giving him the medicine or withholding it. Suppose she had withheld it and had sent the equivalent doses to Morgan & Winterton for analysis. She had received in reply the proof that the medicine did contain arsenic. Very well, what would she do then?

Ah, but wait a moment: that wouldn't work. The medicine had been sent to Morgan & Winterton on the 29th of September, exactly a week after Frazer had died. Why should it have been sent then? If the nurse had been suspicious it must surely have been during the old man's lifetime. If she was not suspicious then, why should she have become so after his death? Had this medicine after all any connection with the Frazer case?

Then French saw that it almost certainly had. Morgan & Winterton's reply was posted on the 3rd of October, which meant that the nurse received it on that day or the next. But the 5th of October, two days later, was the day on which she had received the telephone message to which she had replied, "Well, I'll arrange it somehow. Twelve-thirty." That message was obviously from Earle, arranging the Staines trip. It looked uncommonly like as if Nurse Nankivel had written to Earle on receipt of the analysis, asking for an appointment.

When French reached the hotel he sat down to try to get the dates straightened out on paper. He was pleased with the result, which he thought promising.

Thursday (22 Sept.)	:	Frazer dies.
Friday (23 Sept.)	:	Nurse Nankivel leaves Polperro.
Saturday (24 Sept.)	:	Nurse goes to Bryanston Square.
Tuesday (27 Sept.)	:	Frazer's funeral.
Wednesday (28 Sept.)	:	Mrs Carling writes to nurse.
Thursday (29 Sept.)	:	Nurse receives Mrs Carling's letter and sends medicine to analysts.
Friday (30 Sept.)	:	Winterton receives medicine.
Monday (3 Oct.)	:	Winterton posts analysis.
Tuesday (4 Oct.)	:	Nurse receives analysis and presumably writes Earle.
Wednesday (5 Oct.)	:	Nurse receives Earle's telephone.
Thursday (6 Oct.)	:	Nurse and Earle at Staines.
Saturday (8 Oct.)	:	Nurse receives telegram to go to Hog's Back on Sunday.
Sunday (9 Oct.)	:	Nurse goes to Hog's Back and is murdered.

These dates seemed to French fairly well to clear up what had occurred. His tentative theory now stood as follows:

During Frazer's illness Nurse Nankivel becomes suspicious that her patient is being poisoned, but cannot prove it. After reaching Bryanston Square her suspicions are somehow increased, and she sends the doubtful medicine to be analysed. The analysis confirms her suspicions and she feels she must share the responsibility. Campion has signed the certificate and she therefore funks going to him; probably also she has found Earle more approachable. She writes to Earle, hinting her news and asking for an interview. Earle, realising that for many reasons the meeting should be kept secret, arranges the Staines affair. At Staines she unburdens her soul and hands over the analysis and possibly other evidence. Earle puts it in his safe. Frazer's murderer somehow gets to know what is going on and sends the telegram in Earle's name asking the nurse to go down on Sunday – to her death.

This theory, while a distinct advance, had some pretty wide gaps. What, for instance, had suddenly increased the nurse's suspicions after reaching Bryanston Square? The dates suggested it was the letter from the gardener's wife, Mrs Carling. Could this be?

Then French suddenly saw that it might very well have been the letter. For the moment he had forgotten what that letter contained, but now he remembered. In it Mrs Carling had described the reading of the will and Mrs Frazer's and Gates' reactions on becoming wealthy. There it was! A motive! The girl had been suspicious that the old man was being poisoned, but she probably couldn't supply a satisfactory motive. She must have known that old Frazer had money and that his wife would get some of it, but she probably didn't imagine that such a large sum was involved, nor that Gates also stood to gain.

This of course was a pure guess, but it worked in. French added it to his tentative theory and passed on to that fundamental question: Who had learnt what had been discovered, and that the proofs had been hidden in the secret safe? In other words, Who was the murderer?

French felt that though minor parts of the case might be yielding to his treatment, on the major issues he was as much in the dark as ever. One major fact, however, seemed to stand out clearly from this analysis business, and that was that Frazer really had been poisoned. It would be too great a coincidence to have suspected arsenic, and then to have come across the track of arsenic in the case, unless there was a connection between the two.

Tired but not discouraged, French went out after dinner to try what Farnham could do in the way of amusement. He saw a first-rate film about a trainload of persons who were held up by bandits in the disturbed East, but who after surprising adventures safely reached their journey's end, and much refreshed in mind, he went up to bed.

– 20 –

DISAPPOINTMENT

French awoke jubilant next morning. At last his case was progressing! All that business of the analysis, with its overwhelming suggestion that Frazer had been poisoned, was a gigantic step forward. By means of his work four appalling murders had been brought to light. And so far as he could see, to bring home the crime to the guilty party should be a fairly quick and straightforward job.

But this matter of the arsenic raised urgently a very delicate question. Should the manner of Frazer's death not be placed beyond the possibility of doubt? In other words, Should his body not be exhumed?

French went in and discussed it with Sheaf. Sheaf, though impressed with French's discoveries, was unwilling to apply for an exhumation order unless absolutely unavoidable. "Suppose you're wrong," he urged. "Where would I come in? You know it's a serious matter to exhume a body, particularly the body of a man of Frazer's position. If we make a bungle over it, what's going to happen to me?"

French pointed out that the same considerations applied to himself, but urged that neither he nor Sheaf had anything to fear. He argued that it was inconceivable that the medicine analysed could have been other than Frazer's, and if so, that poison had not been used. Finally he declared that failure to exhume would hold up the case.

Sheaf could not refute his arguments. So much so that then and there he rang up his chief constable and asked him if he could see him on the matter.

The chief constable happened to be in Farnham, and he shortly appeared at the station. He listened to French's arguments, and was convinced by them.

"I think we'll have to do what he wants, super," he declared. "We're human beings and can only do our best. If this proves a mistake, I'll stand for it. Go ahead and get your order."

Two nights later with as much secrecy as possible the exhumation was carried out, and in due course the report of the analyst on the contents of the deceased's organs was received. French was justified! Frazer had died of arsenical poisoning.

French in this case thought little of the dreadfulness of murder. Murder was always terrible, but here his professional keenness outweighed any feeling for the deceased. This discovery meant full speed ahead again for him. Fortunately his path was clearly defined. He had already considered the way, and he had nothing to do now but follow it. He had noted the obvious point that the person he wanted must have killed Frazer, Nurse Nankivel, Earle and Ursula Stone. Only a very restricted number of persons could be guilty of these crimes, and he had merely to eliminate from the apparent possibles, in order to solve his problem.

As he had seen, the first two of these possibles were Mrs Frazer and Gates. Could Mrs Frazer have murdered Frazer, Nurse Nankivel, Earle and Miss Stone? If not, could Gates have done it? If not, and French didn't believe this contingency would arise, Who else could have done it?

First then, Mrs Frazer.

It was obvious that Mrs Frazer could have administered the poison. She usually sat with her husband while Nurse Nankivel was out, and nothing would have been easier than to slip the arsenic into the medicine. Moreover, she worked in the garden, where there was any amount of arsenical weed-killer.

So far as Frazer was concerned, then, Mrs Frazer remained a possible. Next came Nurse Nankivel. Could Mrs Frazer have murdered the nurse?

French soon learned that on the Sunday of Earle's and Nurse Nankivel's murders Mrs Frazer was at Budleigh Salterton in Devon. On that day fortnight, when unhappy Ursula Stone met her death, Mrs Frazer's cousin, Mrs Hampton, had been staying in the house, and the two ladies had spent the afternoon and evening together. Though French noted that these statements must be confirmed, in the face of them he had no doubt of Hermione Frazer's innocence.

Believing that he was on to a more likely proposition, he turned his thoughts to Gates.

So far as the murder of Frazer was concerned, Gates was quite as much a possible as Mrs Frazer. His motive was just as strong, or stronger, and his opportunities of obtaining and administering the poison equally good. He also sat occasionally with his uncle during the nurse's afternoon walk, and he was actually in charge of the gardens. The test of Gates' guilt would lie rather with the other three cases.

French had not succeeded in finding out where Gates had been on the two Sundays in question, and he saw that his first job must be to do so.

With a definite programme in his mind, therefore, he set off after breakfast for Polperro. Gates, he had learnt from judicious pumping of the butler, had acted as a sort of agent for his uncle. He had supervised what farming was done on the little estate, looked after the tenants and their properties, kept a general eye over the gardeners and other outdoor servants, and attended to the old man's correspondence. He was down now at the farm buildings, where French could see him.

He didn't seem to be doing very much when French found him, all the same French apologised courteously for interrupting his business. French had been bothered by the question of how to approach Gates. He could not very well ask him to account for his time at the critical periods without giving away that the police had connected in their minds all these four murders, which he didn't wish to do. He therefore determined to bluff.

"It's just a little matter of routine," he went on; "a little misunderstanding or error on someone's part, which as a matter of routine must be cleared up. You can do it for me, I have no doubt, in a moment. The point is this. On that Sunday when Nurse Nankivel and Dr Earle disappeared, well, sir, not to put too fine a point on it, you are supposed to have been seen with a car meeting the nurse on the Hog's Back. That was about six o'clock in the evening. Now, sir" – he held up his hand as Gates would have spoken – "I do not believe this story, because I feel sure that if you had seen her you would have come forward and said so. At the same time there is the statement, and it has got to be met. I want you, sir, to be good enough to meet it for me."

As French spoke Gates seemed to be getting fuller and fuller of suppressed fury, and when French reached his peroration, the storm broke. Gates cursed and swore with a picturesque richness of expression, finally wanting to know the name of the blanked blank who had told this blanked lie against him. French let him get off steam, then brought him to earth by suggesting quietly that if there was all that difficulty about it, Gates must have something to hide, and he would have to ask him to come in to the police station to make a formal statement before the superintendent.

"Better let's have the whole thing, Mr Gates, when you're at it," French went on quickly, before the effect of his remark had worn off. "Put it this way: Where were you on those two Sunday afternoons; the Sunday on which the doctor and the nurse disappeared, and the Sunday fortnight, when Miss Stone vanished? Sorry to trouble you, but I must have answers. If you give them to me completely, I hope you will not be troubled again."

In spite of French's pacific approach, Gates made a great show of resenting the questions. He asked if French suspected him of the murder of these three persons. If he did, he, Gates, was not going to answer, for the Lord knew how his replies might be twisted. If on the other hand French did not suspect him, the questions did not arise.

French, in reply to this, took up the attitude of the official in one of its most asinine manifestations. These were the questions that he was accustomed to ask. It was the regular routine, hallowed by tradition: he couldn't contemplate or visualise any other course but to ask them. If they did not apply, he couldn't help it; enquiries were made in this way. Tradition was better than reason because it saved thought and because those in high places preferred it.

As he had hoped and expected, this attitude so infuriated Gates, that after cursing French and the British police and institutions bell, book and candle, to get rid of him he told him what he wanted to know.

It seemed that on the first Sunday, the day of the murder of the nurse and of Earle, Gates had left Polperro in his car, a small Riley, about midday. He had driven alone to Winchester, where he had arrived about or shortly before half past one. He had there lunched with some friends, people named Hutchinson. He had remained with them for tea, leaving about half past five. He had driven straight home, arriving at Polperro about seven.

This, French saw at once, would if true have made it impossible for him to meet the nurse on the Hog's Back.

"And what, sir, did you do then?" French went on.

On reaching home Gates had dined alone, Mrs Frazer being at the sea in Devon. After dinner he felt a bit stale from sitting about all day and he went out for a walk. He walked about five miles, then read for a couple of hours and went to bed.

French, naturally interested in the walk, made further enquiries.

Gates had left Polperro after dinner. "It happened," he explained, "that I was without a book, and as I like to read for a while after I go to bed, I thought I'd kill two birds with one stone and walk round to my friend, Owen Galbraith, and borrow one which he had promised me. Then it occurred to me that he usually went out on a Sunday evening, so I rang him up and asked him if he was going out to leave the book with his housekeeper and I'd call for it. He said he was going out, but would leave the book. So I walked over, got the book and walked back again."

French pressed for still further details.

"When did I start and when did I get back?" Gates repeated. "How in Hades do I know? Think I go about with a notebook recording everything I do? Ask me an easier one."

"This is the one I'm asking you," French declared doggedly, "and this is the one I want an answer to. Come on, Mr Gates, put your mind into it and no doubt you'll get it all right."

After some more blasphemy, which seemed to be the normal accompaniment of his conversation, Gates put his mind into it. As a result he was able to state the times fairly accurately. He had dined at half past seven. He was a quick eater, especially when alone, and he had finished before eight. He went out as soon as he had rung up Galbraith. If the time were fixed at eight o'clock, it couldn't be more than a minute or two wrong.

As to the hour of his return, he was not so certain. He would say about 9.30. The butler might possibly be able to help there, for the first thing he did on reaching home was to ring for a whisky and soda.

"Where does Mr Galbraith live, Mr Gates?"

"About halfway between Farncombe and Shackleford."

French brought out his map. "That would be about two miles from here?"

"Nearer three."

"I suppose it would," French agreed, as he scaled along the roads. "That would be a walk of between five and six miles?"

"If it's nearly three miles away and I walked there and back, it would seem so," Gates returned with heavy sarcasm.

"Quite," French admitted. "Now who did you see at Mr Galbraith's?"

"The housekeeper. There's no one else there. He's not married."

French thought quickly. This seemed to be all the information he required. If this tale was true, Gates was also innocent of Earle's murder.

"Thank you very much, Mr Gates," he said. "That's all I want about the first Sunday. Now if you'll just give me similar information about the second Sunday, when Miss Stone disappeared, that will complete all I want to ask."

For some reason this seemed to re-arouse all Gates' annoyance. "I suppose you think I murdered the lady?" he growled with a choice string of oaths.

French stolidly repeated his platitudes on the subject of routine. Gates shook his head with a hopeless gesture.

"You and your routine and your red tape and all the rest of your blanked tommy-rot," he jeered. "Can you never do anything except what you've done before?"

"Not very often," French admitted. "What were you doing on that Sunday, Mr Gates?"

"That's right. That's the question to ask. Precedent lays it down and therefore irrespective of the circumstances the question's asked. Have you asked the Lord Chief Justice what he was doing on Sunday afternoon?"

"No," said French, "but I will if you prove he knows anything about this job."

"Why drag that in?" Gates returned with bitter scorn. "What has knowing anything about the thing got to do with it? He knows as much about it as I do. I don't see why you don't go up to Town and ask him now."

After a good deal of rather stupid blustering Gates came to earth sufficiently to answer French's question. It seemed that after lunch on that second Sunday he had read the *Sunday Times*, enjoying a little sleep at intervals. Shortly after four he had tea with Mrs Frazer and her cousin who was staying in the house. He went out for a walk, getting back about half past six. From then till dinner he sat with the ladies. After dinner he took a gentle stroll in the grounds while smoking a pipe, say from half past eight till nine or thereabouts.

Pressed for details of his afternoon walk, he gave with unwillingness the itinerary. He had taken a round, out along the Hog's Back and borne by Puttenham and Compton. The distance was about five miles.

In accordance with precedent the usual search for confirmation followed. French took the first Sunday first. A visit to Winchester confirmed beyond question Gates' statement about his call on the Hutchinsons'. The man therefore was definitely innocent of the murder of the nurse.

The critical time in the case of Earle was in the evening, the doctor having disappeared about 8.40. Gates' statement was that he left Polperro about eight o'clock, returning about 9.30. If Gates had not walked to Galbraith in that period he might have committed the murder. Was his statement true?

From the butler French learned that dinner on that first Sunday had been at 7.30, and that Gates had eaten it quickly, as was his habit when alone, and had gone out after it. The butler had heard him telephoning before he did so. He didn't know what the conversation was about, but he had overheard Gates say, "Well, leave it with the housekeeper and I'll call for it." Gates had returned at or before half past nine. The butler did not hear him coming in, but he had rung for a whisky and soda and half past nine had struck while the butler was crossing the hall.

So far, so good. The next question was: Had Gates really walked as he said, or had he taken out a car?

French went out to the yard and saw the chauffeur. This man, Potter, was not nearly so communicative as the butler, but French gradually overcame his scruples and at last he answered his questions.

Just as at the Dagger-Slade establishment, there were three cars, a large and a small one belonging to Mrs Frazer, and Gates' Riley. On that first Sunday of Earle's and the nurse's death, Mrs Frazer had taken the small car to Devon, driving herself and her cousin. The large one had not been out. Gates' Riley had been ordered for twelve o'clock, and Potter had taken it round to the front door at that hour. Gates had brought it back about seven and it had not been out again on that day. Oh yes, Potter was positive of that. Like the Daggers' chauffeur, he lived beside the garage, and he was absolutely certain that neither car had been out on that Sunday evening.

There then remained the question of whether Gates had really walked to Galbraith's house. This would be French's next enquiry.

Then French became doubtful that this information was really required. If Gates had not had a car on that Sunday night, he could not have run Earle's body to the bypass. There was a bicycle in the establishment certainly – he had seen it in the yard – but even with a bicycle he could not have carried the remains. Moreover, that bicycle, though obtainable in the daytime, was locked up in the yard about half past seven, and the chauffeur declared it had so been locked up on that Sunday evening. However, to put the thing beyond doubt, he would go over and see this housekeeper of Galbraith's.

It occurred to him that when he was about it, he should confirm the time it took to walk the distance. He therefore left the sergeant's bicycle at Polperro, and set off on foot.

A delightful walk he found it, and a base temptation assailed him to forget the sergeant's bicycle when he came into these parts in future, so as to have more walks. He had no difficulty in finding his objective, and soon he was knocking at Mr Galbraith's door.

It was opened by a little white-haired old woman, with a pair of the most intelligent eyes French ever remembered to have seen. A determined little woman, too, from the strength of her jaw and the set of her features. She looked at French dubiously.

"Can I see Mr Galbraith?" he asked.

Mr Galbraith was at his business in Godalming and would not be home till the evening, and her manner seemed to suggest that anyone who was any good would also have been at his business at that hour.

"Perhaps then, madam, you could tell me what I want to know," French went on, producing his official card.

"You'd better come in," she said, leading the way to an aggressively tidy sitting room and pointing to a chair. French sat down.

The old lady made no difficulty about answering his questions. Yes, she was Mr Galbraith's housekeeper. Mr Galbraith was a lawyer in Godalming and lived here alone. Yes, she remembered the Sunday night of Dr Earle's disappearance. Mr Galbraith usually went out on Sunday evenings to play cards with some friends. She didn't hold with cards, particularly on a Sunday evening. However, that wasn't what the inspector wanted to know. Before Mr Galbraith went out he gave her a book; one of those trashy novels, it was; and told her that Mr Gates would call for it later. Mr Gates did call and she gave it to him. She went then to bed at her usual time, but before she was asleep she heard Mr Galbraith letting himself in with his latchkey. In fact, everything that evening passed as usual.

"That's just what I wanted to know," French said, complimenting her on her clear statement. "I suppose you couldn't say just what time Mr Gates called?"

Not to a minute, she couldn't, but approximately she could. She had finished all the work of the house for that evening at about half past eight, and had settled down with a book to enjoy a comfortable read. She hadn't been reading more than ten or fifteen minutes when Mr Gates came. That would make it about a quarter to nine: say from twenty minutes to ten minutes to nine.

This clinched the matter. Gates had left home about eight. He had returned about half past nine, or an hour and a half altogether. From French's own experience it took about three-quarters of an hour to walk between the two houses. Two three-quarters of an hour, there and back, would just make up the time. As in addition to this Gates had called at his objective at the middle of the period, confirmation was complete.

Not only so, but there was even more convincing proof of Gates' innocence in this little old lady's statement, than the mere confirmation of his story. At almost the very time that the murder of Earle had been committed, Gates was on the doorstep of Galbraith's house, some four miles away.

French was by this time tired of Gates and all his works, as he had worn round to the belief that he was not his man. However, there still remained the checking of Gates' statement as to how he had spent the second Sunday, the Sunday of Ursula Stone's death. French felt a little inclined to get these two Sunday afternoons mixed up, and he therefore consulted his notebook to make sure he was clear on the matter.

On that second Sunday Gates had stated he had gone out for a walk immediately after tea, which he had with Mrs

Frazer and her cousin. He had returned about half past six, and he had given the itinerary of his walk.

French had recourse once again to his friend the butler, and once again he got adequate confirmation. The man distinctly remembered Gates having tea with the two ladies on Sunday. Tea was at 4.15, a little earlier than usual, as supper was earlier on Sundays. He had not seen Gates after tea till about 6.30, when the man had come in. As to Gates' statement that he went for a stroll in the grounds after dinner, the butler was able to confirm that he was out for certainly not more than an hour. The chauffeur stated definitely that on that Sunday none of the cars were out.

French sighed as he turned away. He had now checked up his two most promising suspects, and in each case he had drawn a blank. At least he had no doubt he would do so, for he had yet to confirm the visit of Hermione Frazer to Budleigh Salterton.

This, however, was soon accomplished. A run down to Devon, armed with a description and photograph, set the matter at rest. Mrs Frazer had unquestionably stayed there during the critical weekend.

Once again feeling rather up against it, French sat down in the hotel to post his notes to date.

– 21 –

ACTION AT LAST

French was getting tired of working in that bedroom at the hotel. Not so much tired either of the room itself, nor yet of work, of which he was not afraid, but tired of the thankless and unprofitable and unsuccessful work with which the room had become associated. Now as he turned once again to this problem which had so long baffled him, he vowed he would not stop wrestling with it until it had yielded up its secret, or if not its whole secret, at least some vital part of it.

During the progress of the case he had successively suspected and acquitted in his mind no less than six persons: Julia, Marjorie, Slade, Campion, Mrs Frazer and Gates. Beyond these six he had been unable to think of anyone who might be guilty, and now, reconsidering the point, he found himself still unable to do so. Going slowly over the names of all the other persons he had come in contact with since his arrival, he felt satisfied that not one of them could be involved.

He felt thrown back therefore on his six former suspects. Had he made a mistake? Could it be that one or more were guilty after all?

As a sort of desperate last resource he decided he would once again go over the case against these six and satisfy himself absolutely of their innocence.

However, second thoughts left him precisely where he was before. So far as he could still see, not one of the six could be guilty. It was out of the question that either Julia Earle or Marjorie Lawes could have poisoned old Frazer, though conceivably (but most improbably) they might have been guilty of the other three crimes. French did not for a moment believe they were guilty of even these, but of Frazer's death they were innocent beyond yea or nay.

Slade was the next possibility. French had not been thinking so much of Slade lately owing to his preoccupation with the Frazer affair. Slade he recognised as the most likely member of his band of suspects, though even Slade by no means filled the bill.

In the first place he had been unable to think of any reason why Slade should have desired old Frazer's death. Nor could he obtain any evidence that Slade had been in the old man's room during his illness and therefore could have administered the poison. Admittedly the young man had been several times in the house at Polperro since Frazer had became seriously ill, but this in itself proved nothing.

Slade, moreover, had alibis in the cases of all three other victims. Admittedly those covering the deaths of the nurse and Earle were not very convincing and conceivably might be broken down, but that for the day of Ursula Stone's murder seemed absolutely watertight.

On the other hand the most suspicious item of the entire case was against Slade: the clay found in his car. There could be no question that it indicated a visit to the bypass, but French could not prove that Slade had paid it, nor could he break down Slade's rebuttal of the charge.

Incidentally he wondered whether a search for clay on the shoes of all his suspects – or at least those who might have killed Ursula Stone – would be of any use. None, he decided. Too much time had elapsed since that fatal Sunday. However, he noted the idea as a last resource.

Deeply dissatisfied as to the part Slade had played in the affair, French turned to his next possible, Campion.

Campion he had suspected of stealing the manuscript of Earle's book, and of murdering Earle to allow him to obtain the benefits and fame of Earle's discoveries. But the case against Campion had broken down for five reasons:

1. The book had not been stolen.
2. Campion was with his womenfolk at the time, or almost at the time, of Earle's disappearance.
3. Campion was with his womenfolk *all* the afternoon and evening of Ursula Stone's disappearance and could not conceivably have murdered her.
4. Though Campion could have met the nurse on the Hog's Back, he could not possibly have had time to bury the body.
5. Campion might conceivably have sent the nurse out of the room during a visit to Frazer, while he put arsenic into his patient's medicine. This, however, was most unlikely for two reasons. First, if the nurse were afterwards to suspect poison, she would be almost certain to remember the incident: which would doubtless give her to think. Second, it looked as if before taking the poison Frazer's faculties were quite clear, and if so, it would be impossible for Campion to tamper with the medicine unknown to him.

French saw that Campion might be ruled out. Since the book theory had collapsed there was no reason to suspect him, while there was definite proof of his innocence of at least two of the murders.

His next suspect had been Mrs Frazer. She could have poisoned her husband, and *might*, though it was most unlikely, have murdered Ursula Stone. But she was unquestionably innocent of the deaths of Nurse Nankivel and Earle.

Lastly French had suspected Gates. Gates could have poisoned old Frazer and *might*, though again it was most unlikely, have murdered Ursula Stone. But he could not have killed either the nurse or Earle.

Not one of his suspects could possibly have killed all four victims. Nor could any combination of them have done so, for so far as he could see, none of them could have killed Earle.

And once again, if these six were innocent, he couldn't think of anyone else who might be guilty.

All that evening his difficulties weighed on French's mind. He tried very hard to dismiss the case from his mind while he was dining, but found that even then he could not do so. And when after the meal was over he withdrew to the lounge, he remained silent from preoccupation; morose, his manner was considered by certain other visitors who essayed light conversation.

Bankrupt! That was the proper word for his condition. All the promising strings he had had to his bow had failed him and he was left without any. He simply did not know where to turn or what further investigations to make.

It was not good enough, he told himself. The thing had an explanation. He was not like an inventor working on what might really be an insoluble problem. He was more like a man trying to solve a crossword puzzle, the antecedent condition of his work being that the puzzle had a solution. Equally certainly, this case had a solution: more certainly, in fact, because in the crossword there was always the possibility of a misprint. In real life there was no possibility of error, unless such error as he had made himself.

His stalemate worried him terribly, though he kept on trying to assure himself that the affair was taking its normal course. Other cases he had been held up in, many of them, but always temporarily. (Or very nearly always.) But he could not afford to be held up in this. It was an important case. It had fired the imagination, not only of the British people, but of those of the Continent and America. In an age when murder was unhappily far too common, it stood out as a notable case: one of those big cases which for some reason best known to itself the public exalts into tests by which it may measure the efficiency of the police. French had not only his own reputation in his keeping, but that of his entire service. Was he going to let both down?

All the evening he wrestled unhappily with the problem; wrestled till he felt himself stale and tired to death of the whole thing. He went out hoping to achieve a change of thought, but the advertisement of the Eastern train was still on the boards at his customary cinema and he felt he could not summon up the energy to find another picture-house. For some time he walked, through an unpleasant drizzle, then returned to the hotel and his puzzle.

He went to bed at his usual time, but still he could not get rid of the gnawing uneasiness. Up till this stage in the case he had always had something to fall back on. Whatever point he was engaged on, there was another line to turn to if it failed. Now that was so no longer. His last hope had petered out.

The more French tried to compose himself, the farther sleep seemed to go from him. His mind was vividly alive and full of energy. His imagination also was abnormally active. Ideas poured out, ideas of all kinds. He marvelled at their range and originality. For a time he found himself wishing he were a novelist, so simple did the provision of the necessary matter seem.

But all this wealth of mental picture and imagery had one outstanding feature: it did not help with his case. None of these brilliant ideas solved his problem or suggested where he might profitably search for a solution.

He remembered vividly a similar experience through which he had passed some years previously. In Glasgow in the smoking-room of the St Enoch Hotel he had spent hours wrestling with the Sir John Magill problem: agonising over it would rather describe his state of mind. He had been up against blank despair and – he had pulled through! He had got his idea and his case. How he wished that on this occasion history might repeat itself!

It was well on into the small hours and French was growing tired of tossing and turning and thinking at a white heat of irrelevant matters, when something happened. A still further new idea flashed into his mind: an idea this time about his case. For a moment he toyed with it, then with an intense shock he realised that this was something different, something vital. He grew rigid, as if afraid that movement might dispel the thought, while he lay wondering, wondering, *had he got his solution?* Did he really see the end of his case? Were his troubles over?

He sweated with excitement as he turned this precious idea over in his mind. Had he got his solution? Fearfully he allowed himself to admit it looked like it!

Quietly he got up, switched on the light, and slipped on some clothes. Then he lit the gas fire, poured himself out a stiff drink from his pocket flask, and drawing the most comfortable chair up to the fire, sat down with a writing-pad to consider systematically the great thought.

He soon reached the conclusion that while he had stumbled on something of the utmost value – nothing more nor less than, he believed, the actual truth of what had happened – he had by no means cleared the affair up. His main idea, he could swear, was sound, but several of the details wouldn't work in. There were discrepancies and there were contradictions; fundamental discrepancies and contradictions which he couldn't reconcile. He made a list of these so far as he could visualise them.

After continuing his broad survey of the case till he thought he had extracted from it everything that it could be made to yield, he changed his method. Taking up the difficulties one after another, he began trying to find ways of overcoming them. In this, it must be admitted, he had little success.

About half past four he suddenly grew sleepy. Well satisfied with what he had accomplished, he got into bed again and a few minutes later he was slumbering as peacefully as an infant.

Next morning he settled down with the dossier to consider systematically the difficulties of his new theory. He was a profound believer in the motto: Take care of the cons and the pros will take care of themselves. Obviously on its objections the theory would stand or fall.

Hour after hour he sat racking his brains, turning the facts about, looking up details of time or place or action from the dossier, considering possibilities and alternatives and generally going through the slow tedious work of those who solve problems. But all without result.

Presently feeling stale, he went out for a sharp walk, then after a light lunch with plenty of strong coffee, he set to work again. For two more hours he worked, then suddenly his experience of the night was repeated.

His first difficulty was no difficulty at all! There was a solution to it, an obvious solution, so simple that he was now lost in amazement that it should have baffled him so long!

This discovery, he felt, practically proved his new theory, and it was with renewed zeal that he set himself to deal with the remaining objections. Though minor in character, these proved no easier to meet than the first, and night came before he had any more progress to record.

However, he was now convinced that success was merely a matter of time, and happier than he had been since he started the case, he resolutely put it out of his mind, dined and went to the pictures. Next morning, however, he was at it again, and almost at once he had another success. A second difficulty was overcome.

The clearing away of this second difficulty seemed to have removed the dam which was holding up the stream, and with an ease and speed which delighted French, further fact after further fact dropped into place. In an hour his theory was complete. He spent another hour noting his facts and deductions in logical sequence, then turned to consider what, if any, confirmation he could get.

At once he found his ardour checked. The possibility that certain happenings had taken place was one thing; the proof was quite another. His theory was good, but if he couldn't prove it, it was no more use to him than if the whole thing had been a fairy tale. At present he had no case to take into court: he doubted if he had enough even to justify an arrest.

Then at last he saw that there was one point, admittedly a secondary and incidental point, which he might be able to establish. It would, he thought, provide "moral" proof of the whole affair, though unquestionably it would not be sufficient for court. However, moral proof was better than none.

It hinged on one question, a question which could only be answered by a certain firm with a headquarters at Kentish Town. French immediately walked down to the station and took the first train to Town. In due course he found the firm's office and saw its principal.

To him he put his question. The principal sent for an assistant. Books were looked up. The assistant answered the question. Satisfactorily.

Full of a great happiness French returned to Farnham. No longer was there any doubt as to the correctness of his theory! All the same he would give a good deal for some more direct proof. Was such quite unobtainable?

His theory postulated that a certain car had passed along certain roads at certain hours on the night of Earle's murder. If so, surely someone must have seen it?

He thought the matter would be worth a further effort. Part of his hypothetical itinerary lay outside the area Sheaf had already explored, and fresh enquiries might produce something of value.

French put his back into it and on the third day he received his reward. He found a young man who had been keeping a tryst behind some bushes along one of the roads in question. This man had seen a car – *the* car; he had noted its number – drive up and stop fifty yards beyond the gate of a certain house. A man, whom he believed he had recognised, had alighted and gone up to the house, returning in three or four minutes and driving away.

This French considered complete confirmation, though still he knew his case was thin for court. However, he had no doubt that further proof would become available.

With deep satisfaction he walked to the station and called on Sheaf. Sheaf would be a surprised man! On the last occasion on which they had discussed the case, French had been unable to hide his despondency. Sheaf, French knew, believed that he, French, was going to fail in the case. How delightfully his mind would be disabused! French was looking forward to the interview with delight.

Sheaf nodded his greeting as French entered. "I'm glad you came in," he said; "I wanted to talk to you about one or two things. But take your own business first. You wanted to see me?"

"As a matter of fact I did, super. I've got something to tell you."

Sheaf looked up, struck by something in French's manner. "Well?" he grunted distrustfully.

"The result of two days and two nights of solid thinking: I should say, just sweating myself with thought. No sleep and all that sort of thing." French grinned. "Do you know, super, that I had in my possession every single bit of information that was required to solve this problem; and until a couple of days ago I didn't know it! And what's more, super, from my reports you have in your possession at this moment every single bit of information that you require to solve it too! And as for proof: I went up to a certain firm in Town and asked them a question, and the answer gave me all the proof I wanted. More than that, a certain car was seen in a certain place at a certain time, which clinches the thing."

Sheaf stared as if he couldn't believe his ears. He blinked at French, then he said heavily: "But I don't know your question and its answer, nor yet about your car; so these won't help me."

"You've enough without them to work out what must have happened. You'll then think of the question and want to ask it yourself. And when I tell you now that the answer is satisfactory, you'll know what it is. Same about the car." French paused for a moment grinning. "Listen to me, super." He bent forward and began to speak rapidly and in a low tone, as if imparting the most profound secret. Sheaf, disparaging at first, grew more and more interested as the tale progressed, until finally a suspicion of actual excitement appeared on his somewhat heavy features.

"I declare, French," he said at last with a strange but efficient sounding oath, "that's a neat bit of work! You're right; you've got the thing at last! And you're right also that I knew everything you've used to get it; everyone connected with the case knew it, but we just didn't think of what the facts involved. Congratulations, and all that!"

"Just a bit of luck, super. I got it because I had nothing to do but think of it, while you and the others were busy with your ordinary work. However, we're not out of the wood yet. I take it, you've got to decide now what you're going to do."

"I guess," returned Sheaf, "I know what I'm going to do. I'm going to act. With all that information of yours I daren't do anything else."

French nodded. "I hoped you would take that view. You realise that my proof would scarcely do for court."

"You'll get the rest. What about going out as soon as possible?"

"I'm on."

"Then I'll get some men and we'll go." Sheaf looked as nearly excited as French believed he had it in him. "This'll cause a sensation, French," he declared. "I tell you it will."

He pressed his bell and gave some orders. "That'll do," he went on, "I'll get the papers. Well, French, the sooner we get started, the sooner we'll be there. What about ten o'clock from here?"

"Right, super. I'll be ready."

It was with difficulty that French possessed his soul in patience while Sheaf was making his arrangements. He hated what was coming, and yet it was an experience with which he was only too familiar. Many a time the climax of a case had come under more difficult and dramatic circumstances. He recalled his expedition up the Cave Hill with the Belfast Police on that dreadful night of storm, when in the inky darkness of the dripping trees he and his friends fought for their lives against the Sir John Magill gang. He remembered also standing in the saloon of a launch in Newhaven Harbour, in an atmosphere charged with petrol vapour, expecting every moment that a shot from his quarry's automatic pistol would turn the whole air into flame. And he seemed even yet to feel the desperation with which he had clung to a Mills bomb, from which the pin had been extracted, while the wanted man struggled further to dislodge his grip so that both might be blown to atoms. Tonight there would be nothing of this kind. What they had to do would be done quietly, if equally relentlessly.

Ten o'clock arrived at last, and presently two cars left the police station at Farnham. In the first were French and Sheaf, in the second Sheepshanks and three men. All were in plain clothes and all were excited and on the stretch.

Though French did not lack the courage of his convictions, his excitement was not unmixed with uneasiness. This expedition was being undertaken at his suggestion, and though the final decision necessarily lay with Sheaf, it was French who would be primarily held responsible if anything were to go wrong. He was the expert. He had advised Sheaf, and Sheaf was only carrying out his advice.

Sheaf also felt doubts gnawing at his mind. French's theory sounded well and was probably true, but Sheaf was now realising more and more that it hadn't been proved, and well, unless a thing is absolutely proven, there is always the chance of error. And if error occurred it would not help with that promotion to which Sheaf was so anxiously looking forward.

The night was dark but fine as they took the now familiar road along the Hog's Back. French sat watching the black road as it streamed towards them in the beam of the headlights. To the left the white concrete curb and the grass edging quivered as they rushed past. Outside the area of the lamps was impenetrable blackness. They were running at a good speed on this stretch of straight smooth-surfaced road. No one spoke. Each was fully occupied with his own thoughts.

Reaching the bypass bridge, they slackened speed and turned down the Compton road. A little short of Polperro they drew up and the two officers and two men descended. They walked up to the house and French rang.

The butler opened the door. He recognised French with apparent surprise.

"I want a word with Mr Gates," said French. "Is he in?"

"Yes, sir, he's in the study. I'll tell him."

"And Mrs Frazer?"

"Gone up to Town, sir."

French nodded. "Thanks, we'll just go in."

Paying no attention to the man's somewhat scandalised expression, French and Sheaf pushed past him, and tapping at the study door, threw it open and entered. Gates was reading at the fire and as he looked round and saw the intruders he swore a blustering oath.

"Damn you, inspector, that's not the way to walk into a man's house. What in hell do you mean? And who's this you've got with you?" He rose slowly to his feet and scowled at them.

Sheaf stepped forward closely followed by French, while the forms of police constables became visible in the hall.

"Arthur Gates," Sheaf said solemnly, "I am a police officer. I hold a warrant for your arrest on a charge of conspiring to murder John Duncan Frazer, Helen Nankivel, James Earle and Ursula Stone on the 22nd September and the 9th and 23rd of October respectively, and I have to caution you that anything you say will be used in evidence. Be a wise man, Mr Gates, and come with us quietly. There are four of us here."

For a moment Gates seemed stupefied with surprise, standing staring with wide-opened eyes at the others. Then instantaneously he roused himself. Like a flash his hand flew to his pocket, came out and rose to his mouth. Like flashes also French and Sheaf threw themselves on him. French gripped his wrist in both hands, while Sheaf, throwing his arms round him from behind, sought to pinion him. Gates, however, had the strength of a giant. He shook Sheaf off, big man as the superintendent was, and turned to grapple with French. But French held his grip of the wrist, and before Gates could transfer what he held to the other hand, Sheaf was on to him again. At the same moment a constable laid hold, and in a few seconds Gates was handcuffed and helpless. From his hand they took a tiny sealed package of some powder.

"Potassium cyanide, I expect," French panted as he put the unbroken package into his pocket-case.

Sheaf was panting too. He nodded briefly, then turned to Sheepshanks. "Take him back with two men in one of the cars," he ordered. "The inspector and I want the other."

Gates, now pale and broken, was led out. French called the butler.

"Tell Mrs Frazer, will you," he said in a low voice, "what has happened. We're very sorry, but what could we do? Tell her he'll get every chance to prove his innocence. You better ring her up if you know her address."

"What – what's it for?" stammered the man, himself pale and trembling.

French hesitated. "Well," he said, "it's this case of Dr Earle," and hastened out after the superintendent.

"Come along, French," Sheaf called from the car. "This is a beastly business; let's get it over as soon as we can. Go on, driver."

The other car had driven up again towards the Hog's Back, but French and Sheaf, with the third constable, moved off in the opposite direction. Through Compton they went along the Peasmarsh road, turning presently to the left towards Binscombe. At the Red Cottage they drew up.

Here the same distressing scene was enacted. French, enquiring for Campion, was told he was in his workshop. He and Sheaf and the remaining constable went round there at once, and after getting so near Campion as to prevent any attempt at suicide, Sheaf arrested him for conspiring with Gates to commit the four murders. Campion grew very pale but made no reply. But in the car he tried the same trick as Gates. Unnoticed his hand stole slowly to his pocket, was withdrawn, and was flashing towards his mouth when French seized it. Handcuffed, Campion had no chance against the two officers. From his fingers was taken a little paper package of powder similar to that Gates had tried to swallow. French's guess was afterwards found to be correct – it was potassium cyanide; a dose large enough to kill a dozen persons.

So to an end came the dreams and the schemes of two miserable men.

– 22 –

FRENCH PROPOUNDS A THEORY

(NOTE – For the benefit of the reader who takes his pleasures sadly, references have been inserted into the following exposition, indicating the pages on which have been given each fact that French used to build up his conclusions.)

A couple of days later a little party assembled in Sheaf's room at police headquarters at Farnham. French was there and Sheaf, and at French's special request, Sergeant Sheepshanks. Also there was no less a person than Chief Inspector Mitchell of the Yard. Mitchell had been down on business at Alton, and on his way back to Town had halted at Farnham with the express object of being present at the gathering.

Its purpose was to hear French tell the story of how he had arrived at the truth. He had already given a rough synopsis of his results to Sheaf, but now he proposed to recount the actual steps of the reasoning by which he had reached his conclusion. All four men were eagerly looking forward to the coming demonstration, French with the desire of the artist for recognition, the others with keen personal and professional interest.

"Now, French," said Mitchell, when pipes and cigarettes had been lit and trial and error had revealed the best way of dealing with the superintendent's somewhat spartan chairs, "I don't know about the others, but I want to get home tonight. Wire in and get the thing off your chest. The sooner you begin, the sooner you'll be done, and the sooner we can relax and enjoy ourselves." His eye twinkled. "What do you say, super?"

Sheaf, if the truth were to be told, was so much interested in the case that he didn't care how long French took. However, he stolidly agreed with the chief inspector, thus indicating that the elucidation of a complex murder mystery by Scotland Yard experts was one of the normal experiences of his life.

French, on his part, knew that these preliminaries were mere camouflage to conceal the eagerness of both men, which it would not be proper to reveal in the presence of a professional inferior. He smiled internally therefore and took up his parable.

"I need not go over the early history of the case: you all know it as well as I do. I will pass over its gradual unfolding, as shown in the disappearance of Earle, the identification of Nurse Nankivel, the discovery that she also had disappeared, the vanishing of Miss Stone, the finding of the secret safe, the discovery of the bodies, and finally the proof that Frazer was also murdered. Instead of dwelling on these, I will start where I started a few days ago, and give you the steps of the argument as they then occurred to me. I shall of course have to go back on facts and arguments previously mentioned, but only as required to build up my case."

At this beginning the chief inspector assumed the painfully cheerful air of the conscientious martyr. He tried another experiment with his chair, but did not speak. French went on.

"I explored every line of argument I could think of again and again and again, but without success. Though I knew that there was necessarily a perfectly complete explanation of the facts, I couldn't find it.

"Before I go on to explain how at last I began to make progress, I should like to remind you of two sets of facts, as these, though not appreciated at the time, afterwards proved fundamental.

"The first set concerned the murder of Ursula Stone in the study and the finding of the safe. You remember the details? The depressions in No. 1 Thicket (p. 173) and the trail of blood leading to the corner of the study beside the safe (pp. 174 – 177), the sandy footsteps in the same corner (p. 178) and behind the tree (pp. 175 – 176), the fact that from Miss Stone's window a watcher behind the bush could be seen from the house (pp. 169 – 170), the finding of the safe (p. 205), and finally of No. 2 Depression (p. 182) and the marks of the car in the road near by (p. 183). You remember also my theory that Ursula Stone, looking out of her window, had seen the watcher behind the bush approach and enter the study and had gone down to give the alarm; that she had found him at the safe, and to hide his actions he had struck her on the chin, carried her insensible body out to the nearest thicket and there murdered her (pp. 208 and 231). Probably he had returned to the study to see that all was right, and had then carried the body to No. 2 Thicket, where he or an accomplice afterwards removed it in a car (p. 183). Also, of course, you remember that I assumed that Miss Stone's murderer was also the murderer of Earle, and that when discovered he was attempting to remove from the safe proof of that former murder (p.242)."

"Even I remember all that," said Mitchell, "and I'm sure the super is sick of the sound of it."

"I've heard it before," Sheaf admitted.

"Must just mention it, gentlemen," French pointed out with a grin, "as it leads on to what I'm coming to. Well, that was one set of facts. The other was about the finding of the clay in Slade's car (p. 193), leading to the discovery of the bodies (pp. 212 – 235)."

"We remember that too," the chief inspector said hastily.

"Yes, sir. Well, it was from this point I began to go ahead. First of all I was at a deadlock. The clay in the car proved that Slade had run the body to the bypass, but he had an alibi which proved he hadn't. This was of course the usual alibi deadlock and I expected I had been diddled over the alibi. But I couldn't see how. I stuck at this point for a long time, then the simplest idea occurred to me. This was the idea which put me on the right track."

French here made the first of those pauses which afterwards brought down so heavily the shafts of Mitchell's wit. However, this time none of the others made a remark, and presently he resumed.

"This idea was simply that my dilemma didn't exist. Both premises might easily have been true: that the body had been carried to the bypass in Slade's car, and that Slade's alibi was sound. Suppose the car had been borrowed by the real murderer, borrowed without Slade's permission?"

"You think that possible?"

"I think so, sir. I admit that such a thing would have been impossible before six o'clock. From the time that Slade got it out, until he reached the golf club at six, the car was either under observation or there would not have been time to borrow it. Similarly after eleven it could scarcely have been taken without the chauffeur's knowledge. But between six and eleven the circumstances were different (pp.190 – 191).

"Slade, as you know, reached the golf clubhouse at six and stayed till eleven (p. 194). I wonder, sir, if you remember my description of the place? The cars are parked in a space at the side of the building. They are not overlooked and in the dark anyone could have removed and returned one unseen (p. 193). But was there, I asked myself, a potential murderer available at that time?

"Obviously my next step was to go over the whereabouts of all my possible suspects between six and eleven, or rather, between eight and eleven, for until dinner was over I thought there would have been too much movement for tricks to be tried. I reached a very surprising and unexpected result. One of my former suspects and one only could have done it. This was my first great step towards a solution."

French once again paused and shifted his position.

"French always waits at this sort of stage in a story, super," the chief inspector remarked. "Dramatic effect and all that. Artistic, you know. Get along, French. We're too old birds to be caught with that sort of chaff. Let's hear the thing and get home."

"I don't know, chief inspector," said Sheaf with heavy humour, "that we don't want a bit of relief from such concentrated wisdom."

Both French and Sheepshanks stared at this attempt to play up to the chief inspector's lead. Then French grinned tactfully and resumed.

"Julia Earle and Marjorie Lawes were at St Kilda (p.162). Slade was at the club (p. 194). Mrs Frazer was with her cousin, Mrs Hampton (p. 273). Gates gave me a little thought. He dined with the ladies at 7.30 that evening and admitted going out into the grounds from about half past eight till nine (p. 279). This the butler had substantiated, and though he couldn't say the exact length of the walk, he was positive that Gates had not been out more than an hour (p. 283).

"But in an hour Gates could not have used Slade's car. To start with, he would have had about eight miles to walk, because I found the chauffeur locked the yard gates about half past seven, and neither car nor bicycle could have been got out without his knowledge (p. 280). And Gates would never have risked being seen in a bus. In fact it would have taken him two and a half hours to do what was done. Gates therefore was out of it.

"That left only Campion of all those who had at any time been on my list. Could Campion have borrowed the car?

"At first glance this seemed out of the question. Campion had been with his womenfolk all that afternoon and evening (pp. 162 – 168, 200). He had driven over with them to St Kilda, then had come the search for Miss Stone, and then he had rung you up, super. But suddenly in thinking this over, it occurred to me that I was wrong. Campion had not been with his womenfolk all the evening. He had been alone for something like forty minutes.

"It was Campion who organised the search. He set Mrs Earle and Miss Lawes to work in the house, and his sisters to go over the roads in the car, while he himself did the paths in the wood. By himself, mind you (p. 168). Could he not have borrowed Slade's car during that period?

"The more I thought over this, the more likely it seemed. Two considerations indeed seemed to prove it. You know that country, super. How long do you think it would have taken him to go over all the paths concerned?"

Sheaf nodded. "That's a point, certainly. I should say he could have done them all, good and plenty, in quarter of an hour (p. 181)."

"Just what I thought. He spent about twenty-five minutes too long. That's the first consideration and the second's the converse. If he had done what I suspected, it would have taken him the whole time. I worked it out. He would have had to hurry from St Kilda to the clubhouse, start up Slade's car, drive to Thicket No. 2, get the body on board, drive to the bypass, carry the body to the grave, drive back to the clubhouse, park the car, and finally walk back to St Kilda. He couldn't very well have run on the last stage of the journey, as he daren't arrive breathless. Well, I estimated how long all that should have taken. It came to forty-three minutes. Not a bad shot for the forty he actually took."

"But look here, French," Mitchell interrupted. "Aren't you going a bit too quick? How would Campion have known that Slade's car was there at the clubhouse waiting to be borrowed?"

French nodded. "Quite, sir. That bothered me at first, but I saw there was nothing in it. Campion was a member of the club and on his way home with the ladies from having tea at St Kilda, he called there to see a man about going up to Town on the following morning. He spoke to the secretary, who was at the door. As it happened, at that moment Slade drove up. Slade called to the secretary that he had come for an evening's bridge, and Campion must have heard him. He would know then that the car was to be had (p. 194)."

"And you think he would have taken all that risk with another man's car when he had his own available?"

"I suggest, sir, that his own was not available. I suggest that one of the ladies insisted on accompanying him in it, so that both sides of the road should be examined. You remember they did this in Earle's case (pp. 34 – 35). If so, Campion couldn't refuse without rousing suspicion. I suggest he acted on a brilliant inspiration. Of course this is guesswork and I don't insist on it. My case is simply that he took Slade's car."

"Very well, we'll pass that. But Campion couldn't have committed the murder, nor could he have buried the body. He could only have supplied transport?"

"Quite, but my point is that no one but he could have supplied transport. The thing at least was suspicious, suspicious enough to make me concentrate on Campion. I switched off to consider again whether he could have taken any part in the other murders.

"I did not see how he could possibly have killed Frazer without arousing suspicion. But it was clear that if someone else had put the poison into the old man's medicine, Campion could have played an equally vital part in the murder. He could have prevented suspicion arising, by treating the death as natural and signing the certificate.

"There was of course no proof that he had done so – fraudulently, of course, I mean. On the other hand, there was nothing inconsistent in it. The suspicions of the nurse, the analysis, the interview at Staines, and the locking of the evidence in the safe; all this would be perfectly consistent with Campion's guilt."

"Yes, that's right enough so far," Sheaf admitted gloomily, "but go on. How does Campion know that the evidence is in the safe?"

"I was just going to ask that," put in the chief inspector.

French nodded. "That bothered me for quite a while, but I think it's simple enough. Even if the nurse should have suspected Campion, she doesn't say so to Earle. It would be too dangerous without absolute proof. She simply tells him the facts and leaves it there. Now Earle will never believe Campion guilty. He is his partner and he has worked with him for years and so on. He tells Campion the whole thing and consults him as to who the real criminal could be. Even suppose Earle does suspect him, he still tells him the facts, so as to put Campion on his guard and give him every chance of proving his innocence."

"But you've not explained how Campion knows of the secret safe?"

"I suggest that Earle has shown it to him. According to Campion's own story, they read over and discussed Earle's book (p. 123). Very well, Campion would see for himself the danger of Earle's discovery becoming public. They would undoubtedly speak of the need for keeping it secret. It is impossible to believe that the safe should never have been mentioned."

"Yes, I dare say you're right."

"Very well, sir, that left me believing that in spite of certain obvious difficulties, Campion might have been party to Frazer's murder. Nurse Nankivel was the next victim. Could he have murdered her?"

"Another chapter," said Mitchell with a significant glance at the superintendent.

French laughed.

"As you say, sir, it's the artistic method. Campion according to his own story might have met the nurse on the Hog's Back at six o'clock. He had, he said, and I checked the statement, had tea on that Sunday afternoon with some people called Slater at Puttenham. After tea he had driven home somewhere between half past five and half past six (p.127). He could unquestionably have picked up the nurse, and no doubt could have murdered her and disposed of her body. I didn't see exactly how, but I felt sure it could have been done.

"Next I went on to consider whether Campion could have murdered Earle. I had gone into this when I had suspected him of stealing the manuscript, and I had found Campion had an alibi. You remember it, I'm sure. He was with his womenfolk at the time, or within a minute or two of the time of the murder (pp. 129 – 130). I thought over the thing for long enough and I felt I couldn't break the alibi down. There was too much independent evidence.

"This was my second great difficulty and it stuck me for a long time. Then like the first, I saw that it was no difficulty at all."

French paused again and Mitchell seized on the delay. "A short chapter, that! Short but pithy, hey, super?"

"He feels all these tricks are necessary to make it go," said Sheaf, continuing to be heavily humorous.

"Of course. Well, what was the great idea that put you on the right track for the second time?"

"Simply," French went on, "that again there wasn't any contradiction. I'll tell you how I got on to that. I dropped this question of Earle's murder and went back to that of Ursula Stone. Now in Ursula Stone's case, Campion could have provided transport, but could neither have committed the murder nor buried the body. Hence obviously Campion must have had an accomplice. Now I asked myself, Could this accomplice have murdered Earle?"

The others nodded appreciatively. "And were you able to answer it?" Mitchell asked.

"Yes, sir, though not quite in the way I thought at first. This idea involved going over once again everyone who could possibly be suspected, because the conditions of suspicion were now altered. Could there be anything between Campion and Mrs Frazer? There might, but I had never heard such a thing whispered. I took a note to make enquiries. An entanglement with Mrs Earle would not account for Frazer's death. Nor would dealings between Campion and Miss Lawes, Miss Stone or Slade. Gates was left, and when I thought about Gates he seemed to fill the bill.

"Gates was hard up. Gates would benefit to the tune of £30,000 or thereabouts by his uncle's death. What was more, Gates was associated with Campion at race meetings. Campion was reported to be hard up (pp. 79 and 249). I asked myself whether these two had conspired to murder Frazer and to share the proceeds, and had been forced into these other three murders to keep their secret from leaking out."

"Quite good theory," Mitchell approved, "but still only theory."

French agreed. But he held that it was progress, because it gave him something to test. He had, he pointed out, from nothing reached the definite opinion that Campion and Gates were guilty. That was the first half of his analysis. He would now go on to the second, the proof that this opinion was the truth.

AND ESTABLISHES IT

"I think," said Sheaf slowly and unexpectedly, "that this occasion merits some more than ordinary notice. Let us mark the starting of the second half in suitable manner." He took a bunch of keys from his pocket, and going to a cupboard, unlocked it and took out a bottle, three glasses and a cup. "I don't do this every day, chief inspector," he went on, "but then we don't have private entertainments like this every day. Some water, Sheepshanks. I can do a good deal here, but I can't run to soda at a moment's notice. Say when, chief inspector."

Mitchell said when in satisfied tones and French, who in his excitement had allowed his pipe to go out, now refilled and lit it up again. He was delighted with the reception his story was receiving. When Mitchell descended to anything like what might be called sublimated ragging it showed he was pleased, and Mitchell's pleasure, if caused by French's activities, was an important matter to French. When Sheepshanks returned with a large jug of water, they said that here was to the story and for French to get on with it, as they didn't want to sit on those blessed chairs all night. French accordingly got on with it.

"With this theory of the guilt of Campion and Gates in my mind, I turned back to reconsider the murder of Miss Stone. If my idea was correct, Gates must have murdered

Miss Stone. I assumed this had happened and tried where it would take me.

"Gates, then, upon this theory, must have stood behind the bush and watched the study, and presumably been seen by Miss Stone. Why should he do so? Obviously, I thought, to wait for the window to be opened for him. If so, who would open it for him? Obviously again, his accomplice, Campion. Had Campion done so?

"If Campion had, it must have been during the visit to St Kilda, between 5.15 and 6.00 p.m. But Campion was with the others during that visit. This bothered me for long enough."

"Even I," murmured Mitchell, "can see the way out of that."

"Yes, sir: I saw it myself after a while. I was wrong in thinking Campion was with the others all the time. He had left them twice, once at the beginning of the visit and once at the end. The first time he had 'forgotten' some doll's furniture that he had made for Miss Stone. He went to the hall to get it out of his coat pocket (p. 167). Plenty of time to slip into the study, unlock the French window and give a sign to Gates outside. Incidentally I thought, was it likely a man like Campion, who was so frightfully keen on his hobby, should *forget* the furniture? I didn't think it was likely at all.

"The second time Campion left the others was just before they came away. He went out to start up the car (p. 167). That would have given time to lock the window again, which, though perhaps not quite necessary, would prevent attention being concentrated on the study. It must be noticed here that there was not the slightest necessity to start up the engine before they were ready to leave. The engine was warm. They had come from the Red Cottage and it must then have been hot, and it couldn't possibly have cooled in the time. So that this leaving the others to start up the engine on the face of it was only an excuse."

French stopped to finish his whisky, which he had been slowly eking out as he talked. Once again his pipe had gone out, and once again he went through the formality of lighting it. The others sat smoking in silence. The attention they were giving to the story showed how much they thought of it, and French was profoundly satisfied.

"Then something else occurred to me," he went on, "which, if it had happened, would have drawn all this together. I was wondering how Miss Stone could have come to see Gates. When Mrs Earle had left her she was lying reading on her bed. Why should she have got up just at the precise moment that Gates should have been at the bush?

"Because, I realised, she would have heard the car. She would have got up to see who was arriving, so as to know whether or not to go downstairs. From her window she would have seen both Campion and Gates, Gates perhaps creeping into the study in a stealthy way (pp. 169-170). She would naturally go down to find out what he was about."

"Why should she not have gone to Mrs Earle?"

"I suggest that she realised from the behaviour of both men that they were in league in something underhand. She wouldn't then go to Mrs Earle, because Campion was with Mrs Earle. I suggest she did not intend to reveal her presence, and I suggest further that when Gates saw that she had learned his secret he murdered her because he had no option."

"Then you think her murder was not premeditated?"

"I imagine not, sir."

"Then how did Campion know his part?"

"I'm just coming to that, sir."

"Shall we pass that, super?"

"Provisionally I think so, chief inspector. We can go back on it if necessary."

There was a gleam in Mitchell's eye which pleased French, but all he said was: "Very well, French. Go ahead."

"This led to a further step. If I was right, Gates must have been engaged in the plot during certain hours. I next considered whether Gates' statement would work in.

"Gates had the choice of three cars, but none of them were out (p. 283). He had, however, access to a bicycle (p.280). The use of this bicycle seemed to make the thing possible.

"According to the theory, Gates must have reached St Kilda about 5.10 or 5.15 (p. 166). At, say, twelve miles an hour he would therefore have had to leave his own house, Polperro, about 4.40, and this was just about the time he said he had done so (pp. 278 and 283). He would have entered the study, rifled the safe, murdered Miss Stone and carried the body away. Then he would be faced with a nasty problem. Here was the body on his hands: how was he to get rid of it. He would instantly think of the bypass, as presumably he had helped to bury Earle there. But how was he to get the body to the bypass? Campion's car would be needed: he must therefore see Campion. I suggest he put the body down in the first secluded place he came to, Thicket No. 1, and then hurried back to St Kilda in the hope of being able to communicate with Campion. Whether or not he did so there I don't know, but it seems evident that he saw him before supper. He might have ridden to the Red Cottage and seen him there. At all events he saw Campion, fixed up a plan with him, went back to the wood, moved the body to Thicket No. 2, where it could be easily picked up by Campion, and rode home.

"Here again I worked out how long all this should take. I made it a little short of two hours, and a little short of two hours was exactly the time Gates said he spent on his walk (pp. 278 and 283). So that again worked in. And you remember also that no proof that he took that walk was forthcoming."

Mitchell moved sharply.

"But look here, French," he interrupted. "Earle was murdered on Sunday, the 9th of October. Why did those two wait a whole fortnight to get the analysis? Wasn't that running rather a risk?"

"Yes, sir; very much so. It was important that the safe should be cleared at the first possible moment, and so it was."

"But it wasn't. I don't see that."

"It was, sir. You're evidently not aware that Gates was ill during that whole fortnight: an attack of bronchitis (p.139). Sunday was the first day since Earle's murder that they could have tried the safe. It had to be a Sunday owing to the servant being out. I thought that important, because it also worked in."

Mitchell nodded. "I believe I did read your note about Gates' illness. Yes, that's all right. My objection has turned in my hand and become confirmation. That's as it should be. Very well, French?"

"There was then the question of the burial," went on French. "If my timetable was correct Campion could not have carried that out. He would only have had time to bring the body to the bypass. The theory therefore demanded that Gates should have dug the grave and carried out the interment.

"In working out Campion's suggested movements, I had estimated that he must have reached the bypass about 8.35

(pp. 168). Now Gates admitted leaving his house about 8.30 and returning about nine (p. 279), and my researches showed that he might have been nearly an hour (p. 283). That would have enabled him to meet Campion and bury the body."

"But not, surely, to dig the grave?" Mitchell put in.

"Yes, I think so. Remember the clay was freshly cast and loose and the grave was very shallow."

"Very well. I think we must agree, super, that all that works in. But we'd like that bit of proof that you've promised us, French. What about it?"

"Not quite ready for it yet, sir, I'm afraid."

"Did you ever hear what hope deferred does to the heart? Ah, well, we can't help it. We'll enjoy it all the more when it comes."

French dutifully grinned. He gave a hurried glance at his notebook, then went on.

"I think, that given an adequate motive in the papers in the safe, that covers the murder of Ursula Stone, and it's obvious that Campion and Gates in partnership could have murdered Frazer. But there were a good many points about the murders of Earle and Nurse Nankivel still to be cleared up. Of the two, the case of the nurse seemed easier and I took it first.

"It began with the telegram she received, asking her to go to the Hog's Back on the Sunday evening. As you remember, the message and money was dropped into a letterbox at Hampton Common: it was not taken to the post office (p. 118). Obviously either Campion or Gates could have dropped it in.

"Now we know that the nurse reached the bypass bridge at six o'clock (pp. 154–155), the hour of the rendezvous, and drove off in a saloon car (p. 155). We know also that she was buried that night or shortly afterwards. Further we know – ”

“How do you know when she was buried?” Chief Inspector Mitchell interrupted.

“I’ll prove presently, sir, that Earle’s body was buried that Sunday evening. The nurse’s was in the same grave (p.235), hence must have been buried at the same time. Besides, the position in the bank proves it approximately. Both bodies were just below the surface of where the tip extended to on that evening (pp. 232–233).”

“Very good. Go ahead.”

“As I’ve already stated, Campion could have met the nurse on the Hog’s Back at six o’clock, murdered her and hid her body. I cannot prove he did so. I simply show that he could have, and let the proof hinge on the general circumstances of the other murders.”

“Where could he have hidden the body?”

“In the bushes between the road and the bypass. I’ve been over the ground and there are lots of suitable places. Remember it was dark about six and the burial must have taken place about nine. The body would only have to remain hidden for about three hours.”

“It’s certainly possible. I suppose we might provisionally pass that, super?”

“Pending the proof we’re waiting for, I think so.”

“Ah yes, we must have that proof. Well, French, let’s hear what you have to say about Earle.”

“I found the murder of Earle a much tougher proposition, because both Campion and Gates had alibis and I had tested those alibis and found them watertight.

“I started working at them again, and the more I thought of them, the more watertight they seemed. You remember, sir, what they were? Campion was actually in the presence of his womenfolk and Miss Stone all the evening, except for a short time he spent in his workshop building a dolls' house (pp. 25–40); and the whole of the time he spent on the work would have been required for it (pp. 130–131). Besides that, at the actual hour of the murder, or within a minute or two of it, he was in the drawing-room with the three ladies (p. 129). Of this there was ample confirmation. Then as to Gates. Gates walked from his own house to Galbraith's and back (p. 277). The time he took would all have been required for the walk (p. 282). Moreover, he actually was at the door of Mr Galbraith's house at, or within a minute or two, of the hour of the murder (p. 282). It seemed impossible that either of these two could have been guilty. However, by this time I was satisfied that somehow or other both alibis had been faked, and I felt it was up to me to find out how.

"The first thing I went into was the question. Must the hour of the murder necessarily correspond with that of the disappearance?

"I came to the conclusion that it must. It seemed to me to be proved by Earle's clothes. If he had been going any distance to keep an appointment, he would have put on outdoor shoes and a coat and hat. He went out of the sitting room, I felt sure, because someone came to the window and beckoned him, and I felt equally certain he had then been knocked senseless. Obviously he had expected to be out for a moment only.

"There was then no relief from the difficulty that way, and I just settled down to it.

"I took Campion first, and at once I saw a difference in what I might call the strength of his alibi at various times. Before eight o'clock on that Sunday night, Campion was at dinner with his household. After 9.20 he was again with the three ladies. Also for five minutes from about 8.30 till about 8.35 the same thing applied (pp. 128–129). This alibi, I felt, simply could not be broken. All three ladies were sure of the facts.

"But I saw that the alibi for the intermediate periods was not so overwhelming. From 8.00 till 8.30 and from 8.35 till 9.20 Campion was not actually in anyone's presence. He was alone, ostensibly in his workshop, making a dolls' house. The only proof he had of his presence there was that it would have taken him all the time to carry out the work.

"It therefore occurred to me to wonder, Had he done the work at that time?

"I concentrated on this dolls' house affair, and presently two things occurred to me which made me suspect I was on the right track. The first was that the thing was entirely Campion's own suggestion. Nothing had occurred to lead up to his offer. And there was no real reason why he should have done the work then. The house could have been sent after Miss Stone. Admittedly Campion himself had given me a reason: that he was tired of the ladies' society and wanted an excuse to get away from them, and this of course might be true (p. 127). At the same time the mere fact that he had thought it necessary to give me this explanation was in itself suspicious.

"The other consideration was more convincing. Campion had first shown the separate parts to Miss Stone, as they had arrived from the Handicrafts people. He had then brought the partially assembled house into the drawing-room at half past eight, when he went in ostensibly to consult Miss Stone on the outside finish. And finally of course he had taken the completed house to St Kilda when they went to run Miss Stone back. Did this, I asked myself, not show evidences of design? Was it not done to establish the fact that that work at the house had really been in progress at that period? I thought it looked fishy. And I noted incidentally that the conversation about Miss Stone's returning in the bus looked very like an attempt to fix the hour at which he had been in the drawing-room."

French made his little pause, but none of the others commented. They were indeed paying him the compliment of a very close and undivided attention. French began to experience the first fruits of his reward.

"By this time I had no doubt at all that I was on the right track, though I still couldn't see how to break down the alibi. Then I thought, Suppose for argument sake that dolls' house affair was faked and that Campion had been free during those two periods 8.00 to 8.30 and 8.35 to 9.20, what could he have done?

"Obviously he could not have murdered Earle. Earle was murdered at 8.40 (p. 30), and Campion couldn't possibly have got to St Kilda in time. Assume therefore that Gates, in spite of his alibi, had carried out the actual murder, how could Campion have helped?

"This bothered me for long enough, then I thought I saw it. Transport again! Gates was at his house at eight o'clock (p. 277), and if he was to get to St Kilda in time, he must have been taken there in a car."

"Wait a minute," Sheaf interrupted. "What about the bicycle?"

"I thought of that, super," French answered. "In the first place the bicycle was locked up at that hour (p. 280), but there was more in it than that. The body had to be taken back to the bypass, and that could not have been done on the bicycle: it meant a car. But if a car was going with the body in any case, wouldn't Gates also go in the car? For this hurry job, to get the body buried before about half past nine (p. 277), the bicycle would be too slow. Therefore Gates couldn't have taken the bicycle to St Kilda, as he would have had no way of getting it back. Therefore he would have needed a car.

"Could Campion, I thought at last, in his first workshop period have run Gates to St Kilda, and in his second have run both Gates and Earle's body to the bypass?

"Here at once I was on to a snag. It was impossible to take the car out of the garage at the Red Cottage without its being heard from the house. I cursed over this for a while, and then I remembered that the drive was level (p.119), and that it would be possible with the Campions' light car (p. 28) to push it in and out of the garage by hand."

Sheaf made a movement. "I think this tale deserves another toast," he rumbled. "Say when, chief inspector."

"When," said Mitchell, again in satisfied tones. Then to French: " 'Pon my soul, French, it's going like a Sexton Blake. What do you say, super?"

"He should give up his job and take to writing for the films," Sheaf said heavily. "More money in it than working for the Yard anyhow, chief inspector?"

"There could scarcely be less," Mitchell agreed smoothly. "Well, French, what about the next chapter?"

Fortified by another tot, French went on with his tale.

"Thinking over the thing in detail, I saw that Campion would just have had time to take out the car, pick up Gates near Polperro, run him to near St Kilda, return to the Red Cottage, park the car somewhere close by, and take the dolls' house to the drawing-room. I estimated that he could do it in 28 minutes, and he actually had occupied half an hour. After Campion then had made his alibi he would have taken the car again, gone back to near St Kilda, picked up

Gates and the body, run them to the bypass, and returned home. Was there time for this?

"I went into it as carefully as I could, and I found myself bothered by something quite unexpected. Campion had occupied too much time. Not a great deal of course, about five minutes. But I thought that where every minute would count, a discrepancy of this kind meant something. I puzzled over it for some time and then suddenly I saw it."

"I think I see it too," Mitchell put in, "but I admit only because of all you've said. I didn't see it till you led up to it. You see it, super?"

"I see it now," Sheaf returned. "You mean Gates' alibi?"

"Of course. That's what you're coming to, isn't it, French?"

"Yes, sir."

"Well, go on in your own way. Tell us as if we didn't know. We may have overlooked some point."

"I saw after a long time what you and the super have seen in a moment," French resumed tactfully, "that that five minutes would have enabled Gates' alibi to have been established. Gates of course could not have called at Galbraith's house, but Campion could. The house was actually on his way from the Red Cottage to St Kilda. All that was necessary was to stick on a false moustache, pad up his clothes, and speak in a low rumble (p. 140). His height was about right; it was dark; Galbraith would be out so that only the housekeeper would see him; and most important of all, she was expecting Gates to call. I was satisfied Campion could have carried out the deception, and I was just as satisfied he had done so."

"Quite good, French," Mitchell approved. "You deserve a leather medal. Now let's see if I've got it all right. Campion and Gates start from their respective homes at the same time, Campion in a car and Gates walking. They meet somewhere near Gates' home. Campion picks up Gates, drives to near St Kilda, and sets him down there. Campion drives home, establishes his own alibi in his drawing-room, starts off again, establishes Gates' alibi at Galbraith's, and drives back to near St Kilda and picks up Gates. Gates in the meantime has enticed Earle out of St Kilda, murdered him, and got the body placed ready to put in the car. The two men drive with the body to the bypass, and while Campion goes home, Gates buries the body. That right?"

"Dead right, sir. I've got out a little statement which I think makes it pretty clear."

French handed over a sheet, reproduced here, and the other pored over it. "The sketch is not to scale," French explained, "but the positions are roughly as shown."

"Ah yes," said Mitchell, "this is it exactly." He pondered over the document.

Campion and Gates. Alibi

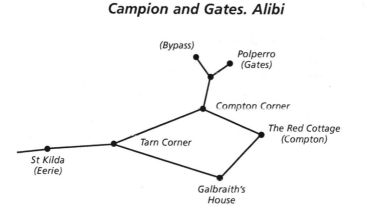

Time		Campion	Gates
8.00	:	Reaches workshop.	Leaves home to walk to Compton Corner.
8.02	:	Leaves workshop. Pushes out car.	
8.07	:	Starts car.	
8.10	:	Picks up Gates at Compton Corner.	Is picked up by Campion at Compton Corner.
8.15	:	Sets down Gates at Tarn Corner.	Is set down by Campion at Tarn Corner.
8.24	:	Reaches the Red Cottage and parks car.	
8.27	:		Reaches St Kilda and awaits opportunity.
8.28	:	Regains workshop.	
8.30	:	Enters drawing-room, completing own alibi.	
8.35	:	Leaves drawing-room. Makes up as Gates.	
8.38	:	Leaves workshop.	
8.40	:		Commits murder.
8.41	:	Starts car.	
8.44	:	Calls at Galbraith's.	
8.48	:	Completes faking of Gates' alibi.	Has body on road, ready to load up.
8.56	:	Picks up Gates and body near St Kilda.	Is picked up with body by Campion.
9.08	:	Leaves body in grave.	Assists to leave body in grave.
9.14	:	Reaches the Red Cottage and puts car in garage.	
9.20	:	Reaches drawing-room.	Reaches Polperro after burying body.
9.30	:		

8.40. Time of Earle's disappearance (murder).
Campion's Alibi:
8.30 to 8.35. Is in drawing-room with ladies.
Gates' Alibi:
8.44 to 8.48. Is at Galbraith's door.

"That's quite good, French," Mitchell commented, handing back the paper. "Now I wonder if I've got your theory of the entire crime? Just let's see. Campion and Gates, a pretty pair of scoundrels, get into financial difficulties by backing their ill luck on the racecourse. They thereupon get together and devise a scheme to repair their fortunes. Gates has reliable expectations of £30,000 when old Frazer pegs out. Frazer is nearly seventy, in frail health, and only a slight push will be necessary to help him into the next world. No one will be the worse of it. His wife hates him and so does everyone who comes in contact with him. Between them they give him the push. Probably Campion gives Gates the poison to put in the medicine, or Gates gets it from the weed-killer, which he could easily do. Campion's job is to sign the certificate. Somehow, we may take it, the responsibility is divided.

"This all works very well, and Frazer is got rid of. Unfortunately for our friends, however, the nurse is too wide-awake. She suspects, abstracts some of the doubtful medicine, has it analysed, thus having her suspicions confirmed. She tells Earle – very naturally: who else can she tell? But then what happens? Earle, as you suggest, tells Campion the whole story. Campion is naturally upset. He induces Earle not to make an immediate move. Then he meets Gates and fixes up his plan, which he has probably worked out beforehand as a precautionary measure.

Campion sends the telegram to the nurse, meets her on the Hog's Back, murders her and hides her body. The murder of Earle is carried out as you have described. Everything then is complete and satisfactory except for the destruction of the dangerous evidence. Now, French, here's a point. Why didn't Campion, as Earle's partner, simply go to the study in St Kilda, on the plea of looking for papers concerning the practice?"

"I thought of that, sir," French answered. "From what I have seen of Mrs Earle, I doubt if she would have allowed any investigation at which she was not present, and I suggest Campion realised this. Campion might have proposed conducting a secret search, but if the lady demurred, he could not press his request without suspicion."

"Very well. Campion had to wait for Gates' assistance, and Gates was ill. Then came the distressing advent of Ursula Stone to the study at the critical moment, and the necessity for silencing her. I'm sure your reconstruction of what happened is the truth. Now, for the third and last time of asking, your proof."

French moved uneasily. "I hope you gentlemen will consider it sufficient when you hear it. It's two-fold and the first point is about the dolls' house. As I pointed out, the construction of the dolls' house was Campion's proof that he had been in his workshop all the time he was away from the ladies. Well, I guessed he might have tried an old trick and I went up to Town and called on the manager of Handicrafts Limited (pp. 25 and 292). Enquiries proved that on Saturday, the 8th of October, the day before Earle's death, a man called at the shop and bought three sets of parts for this particular house. The assistant remembered the affair because there were only two sets in stock of the house the customer had asked for, and rather than wait while a third set was being obtained, the man had taken three sets of a quite different pattern. This was all right, but I was better pleased still when the assistant picked out the customer's photograph from a bundle I gave him. It was Campion."

"Good!" said the others in a breath. "The defence will find it hard to explain that. Campion had the three sets prepared beforehand?"

"That's what I'm going on, sir. As I understand it, Earle got to know of the Frazer affair on the Thursday and told Campion either that evening or next day. Campion saw Gates and fixed up his plan on the Friday, going up on the Saturday morning for the houses. Before the Sunday evening he had prepared them, leaving one set untouched, half finishing another, and completely finishing a third. He showed the appropriate set at the time required, and when the murder was over, destroyed the first two. And this very day," French added triumphantly, "in the ashes in the fireplace in Campion's workshop, I found the little door hinges and other metal parts of these two extra sets!

"The second part of my proof was connected with the car. I could not believe that Campion had done all that running without being seen by someone. I worked on this and at last I found a young fellow who on the night in question had waited for his girl close to Galbraith's house. While there he saw Campion's car drive up – he was a native of Binscombe and knew the number – and he observed a man whom he thought was Campion get out, call at the house for three or four minutes, and then drive off. That, gentlemen, was just at quarter to nine, and it seems to me to clinch the entire case."

With the air of a man who has worthily completed that which he set out to do, French drained his whisky. He was exultant, not only in his own achievement, but in the approval of his companions. Mitchell indeed directly congratulated him.

"Not bad that for proof, I will say," he declared. "The more you think of those two points, the more convincing they become."

Then, however, he took a little of the wind out of French's sails by adding: "Now that's all excellent and you've justified the arrests. But I'd like something more for court. You'll have to go ahead and scrape up some more direct proof."

As a matter of fact only a very few days later French succeeded in obtaining what he wanted. From his estimate of the character of Nurse Nankivel, based on her actions throughout the affair, he doubted that she would have handed over important documents to Earle without keeping a copy for her own use in case trouble arose. On the chance that such papers might exist, he called first at Bryanston Square, then at the nursing home, to re-examine the deceased's rooms, going on to her home near Redruth, where her effects had been sent. It was in Cornwall he made his discovery. In the lining of the nurse's somewhat antique suitcase there was a tear, a frayed slit which might easily have come through use. Pushed under the lining through this slit he found a folded paper. It read:

Copy of statement sent to Dr Earle, St Kilda, Seale, at his request, after interview at Staines on 6th October.

Dear Dr Earle,

In accordance with your request, I am putting in writing what I told you today at Staines.

As you are aware, there is an ante-room from which the late Mr Frazer's bedroom opens. On the wall of this ante-room hangs a mirror, and it just happens that if the door between the two rooms is open, a person entering the ante-room from the lobby can see through the mirror into the bedroom.

On the afternoon of 16th September, on unexpectedly entering the ante-room about five o'clock to get a letter I had forgotten to post, I saw through the mirror Mr Gates, who was sitting with his uncle, hastily corking and setting down a bottle. I kept my eye on the bottle and saw that it was one of Mr Frazer's medicines. Mr Frazer was asleep. At the time I thought nothing of the matter, but from then I noticed that after taking that medicine Mr Frazer grew rapidly worse. It had occurred to me how like the symptoms of Mr Frazer's disease were to those of arsenic poisoning, and though I didn't exactly suspect anything, I experimented with the medicine. Once or twice I didn't give it, pouring the doses into another bottle, which I determined to keep for analysis, should such seem necessary. On these occasions Mr Frazer seemed better than when he had the medicine. I didn't know what to do, and was very unhappy.

Then before I could do anything, Mr Frazer died. Again I didn't know what to do. I suspected, but I wasn't sure, and to make a mistake in such a thing would have ruined me. I did nothing. Perhaps I was wrong. I'm not trying to justify myself, only to say what happened. Dr Campion gave the certificate and I left Polperro and got another job.

On Thursday, 29th Sept., I had a letter from the gardener's wife, with whom I had made friends. Among other things she told me Mr Gates was reputed to have come in for £30,000. This made me think, and all my suspicions came back. I didn't know what to do, but at last I felt I should not be justified in withholding what I knew. I sent the bottle of medicine to be analysed, and on Tuesday, 4th Oct., got the analysis.

I thought first of telling Dr Campion, but somehow I never liked him and I was afraid he might not be sympathetic. Then I thought of you, Dr Earle, and I thought I should be safe in your hands. So I wrote you that letter asking you to meet me.

This, I think, covers all I told you, and I am sure that if you take any action, you won't let it injure me.

Yours sincerely,

HELEN NANKIVEL.

But one more incident remains to be told, an incident which gave the authorities any further proof they required and incidentally demonstrated the true nature of Howard Campion. When he saw how things were going he attempted to turn King's evidence, declaring that Gates, to whom he was heavily in debt, had put the poison into the medicine unknown to him, and that when he, Campion, had become suspicious, Gates had insisted on his giving the certificate, as the alternative to ruin.

On this statement Campion could be questioned, and French by a searching interrogation succeeded in breaking it down and establishing that Campion himself had been the moving spirit in the affair. Campion had used arsenic, partly because the symptoms fitted in with the disease Frazer actually had, but also because in case of discovery the use of this poison would not be attributed to a doctor, but probably to Gates, who had ready access to the weed-killer. Actually he had given the arsenic to Gates, who in his turn had put it into the medicine. Campion's attempt to save himself at the expense of his accomplice therefore failed.

Neither man could deny the motive, which French's further investigation fully established. Campion was in debt about four thousand pounds, and Gates about seven. The scheme to murder Frazer had been broached in a conversation on their joint troubles. Neither man, however, felt he could carry through the affair alone, and they formed a criminal conspiracy to commit the deed, sharing the spoils. After a trial of worldwide interest, both men suffered the extreme penalty of the law.

As a result of the case two unexpected alliances materialised. Mrs Frazer, seized with a loathing of Polperro and everything connected with it, sold it and went to the Argentine, taking with her as companion no less a person than Alice Campion. Alice had always hated her brother, and had kept house for him solely for financial reasons. Julia Earle, much softened by what she had gone through, married Slade and went after them.

For French what remained? At first he thought the consciousness of work well done. But then came congratulations from his chief and friend, Sir Mortimer Ellison, Assistant Commissioner at the Yard, with – ah no, it couldn't be! – a hint that the next vacancy...

But it was!

Freeman Wills Crofts

The Box Office Murders

A London box office clerk falls under the spell of a mysterious trio of crooks. Assisted by a helpful solicitor who directs her to Scotland Yard, she tells Inspector French the story of the Purple Sickle. But when her body is found floating in Southampton Water the next day, French discovers that similar murders have taken place and determines to learn the trio's secret and run them to ground...

Inspector French's Greatest Case

A head clerk's corpse is discovered beside the empty safe of a Hatton Garden diamond merchant. There are many suspects and a multitude of false clues to be followed before a tireless investigator is called in to solve the crime. This is a case for Freeman Wills Crofts' most famous character – Inspector French.

Freeman Wills Crofts

Man Overboard!

In the course of a ship's passage from Belfast to Liverpool, a man disappears and his body is later picked up by Irish fishermen. Although the coroner's verdict is suicide, murder is suspected. Inspector French co-operates with Superintendent Rainey and Sergeant McClung once more to determine the truth, whatever the cost...

> 'To me, Inspector French is the most human sleuth
> to be found in the detective novels of today.'
> – *Punch*

Mystery in the Channel

The cross-channel steamer *Chichester* stops halfway to France. A motionless yacht lies in her path and when a party clambers aboard it finds a trail of blood and two dead men. Chief Constable Turnbill has to call on the ever-reliable Inspector French for help in solving the mystery of the *Nymph*.

Freeman Wills Crofts

Mystery on Southampton Water

The Joymount Rapid Hardening Cement Manufacturing Company is in serious financial trouble. Two young company employees hatch a plot to break into a rival works on the Isle of Wight to find out their competitor's secret for undercutting them. But the scheme does not go according to plan and results in the death of a night watchman, theft and fire. Inspector French is brought in to solve the baffling mystery.

The Sea Mystery

A crate is washed-up containing the body of a murdered man. As there is no evidence to determine who the man is or where he came from, Inspector French has to use his imagination and dogged persistence to trace the clues and uncover a solution to this most ingenious of crimes.

OTHER TITLES BY FREEMAN WILLS CROFTS AVAILABLE DIRECT FROM HOUSE OF STRATUS

Quantity	£	$(US)	$(CAN)	€
☐ THE 12.30 FROM CROYDON	6.99	12.95	19.95	13.50
☐ THE AFFAIR AT LITTLE WOKEHAM	6.99	12.95	19.95	13.50
☐ ANTIDOTE TO VENOM	6.99	12.95	19.95	13.50
☐ ANYTHING TO DECLARE?	6.99	12.95	19.95	13.50
☐ THE BOX OFFICE MURDERS	6.99	12.95	19.95	13.50
☐ THE CASK	6.99	12.95	19.95	13.50
☐ CRIME AT GUILDFORD	6.99	12.95	19.95	13.50
☐ DEATH OF A TRAIN	6.99	12.95	19.95	13.50
☐ DEATH ON THE WAY	6.99	12.95	19.95	13.50
☐ THE END OF ANDREW HARRISON	6.99	12.95	19.95	13.50
☐ ENEMY UNSEEN	6.99	12.95	19.95	13.50
☐ FATAL VENTURE	6.99	12.95	19.95	13.50
☐ FEAR COMES TO CHALFONT	6.99	12.95	19.95	13.50
☐ FOUND FLOATING	6.99	12.95	19.95	13.50
☐ FRENCH STRIKES OIL	6.99	12.95	19.95	13.50
☐ GOLDEN ASHES	6.99	12.95	19.95	13.50
☐ THE GROOTE PARK MURDER	6.99	12.95	19.95	13.50
☐ INSPECTOR FRENCH AND THE CHEYNE MYSTERY	6.99	12.95	19.95	13.50

ALL HOUSE OF STRATUS BOOKS ARE AVAILABLE FROM GOOD BOOKSHOPS OR DIRECT FROM THE PUBLISHER:

Internet: www.houseofstratus.com including synopses and features.

Email: sales@houseofstratus.com
info@houseofstratus.com
(please quote author, title and credit card details.)

OTHER TITLES BY FREEMAN WILLS CROFTS AVAILABLE DIRECT FROM HOUSE OF STRATUS

Quantity		£	$(US)	$(CAN)	€
☐	INSPECTOR FRENCH AND THE STARVEL TRAGEDY	6.99	12.95	19.95	13.50
☐	INSPECTOR FRENCH'S GREATEST CASE	6.99	12.95	19.95	13.50
☐	JAMES TARRANT, ADVENTURER	6.99	12.95	19.95	13.50
☐	A LOSING GAME	6.99	12.95	19.95	13.50
☐	THE LOSS OF THE JANE VOSPER	6.99	12.95	19.95	13.50
☐	MAN OVERBOARD!	6.99	12.95	19.95	13.50
☐	MANY A SLIP	6.99	12.95	19.95	13.50
☐	MURDERERS MAKE MISTAKES	6.99	12.95	19.95	13.50
☐	MYSTERY IN THE CHANNEL	6.99	12.95	19.95	13.50
☐	MYSTERY OF THE SLEEPING CAR EXPRESS	6.99	12.95	19.95	13.50
☐	MYSTERY ON SOUTHAMPTON WATER	6.99	12.95	19.95	13.50
☐	THE PIT-PROP SYNDICATE	6.99	12.95	19.95	13.50
☐	THE PONSON CASE	6.99	12.95	19.95	13.50
☐	THE SEA MYSTERY	6.99	12.95	19.95	13.50
☐	SILENCE FOR THE MURDERER	6.99	12.95	19.95	13.50
☐	SIR JOHN MAGILL'S LAST JOURNEY	6.99	12.95	19.95	13.50
☐	SUDDEN DEATH	6.99	12.95	19.95	13.50

ALL HOUSE OF STRATUS BOOKS ARE AVAILABLE FROM GOOD BOOKSHOPS OR DIRECT FROM THE PUBLISHER:

Tel:

Order Line
0800 169 1780 (UK)
International
+44 (0) 1845 527700 (UK)

Fax:

+44 (0) 1845 527711 (UK)
(please quote author, title and credit card details.)

Send to:

House of Stratus Sales Department
Thirsk Industrial Park
York Road, Thirsk
North Yorkshire, YO7 3BX
UK

PAYMENT

Please tick currency you wish to use:

☐ £ (Sterling)   ☐ $ (US)   ☐ $ (CAN)   ☐ € (Euros)

Allow for shipping costs charged per order plus an amount per book as set out in the tables below:

CURRENCY/DESTINATION

	£(Sterling)	$(US)	$(CAN)	€ (Euros)
Cost per order				
UK	1.50	2.25	3.50	2.50
Europe	3.00	4.50	6.75	5.00
North America	3.00	3.50	5.25	5.00
Rest of World	3.00	4.50	6.75	5.00
Additional cost per book				
UK	0.50	0.75	1.15	0.85
Europe	1.00	1.50	2.25	1.70
North America	1.00	1.00	1.50	1.70
Rest of World	1.50	2.25	3.50	3.00

PLEASE SEND CHEQUE OR INTERNATIONAL MONEY ORDER
payable to: HOUSE OF STRATUS LTD or card payment as indicated

STERLING EXAMPLE

Cost of book(s):...................... Example: 3 x books at £6.99 each: £20.97
Cost of order:....................... Example: £1.50 (Delivery to UK address)
Additional cost per book:.............. Example: 3 x £0.50: £1.50
Order total including shipping:.......... Example: £23.97

VISA, MASTERCARD, SWITCH, AMEX:

☐ ☐ ☐ ☐ ☐ ☐ ☐ ☐ ☐ ☐ ☐ ☐ ☐ ☐ ☐ ☐ ☐ ☐

Issue number (Switch only):

☐ ☐ ☐

Start Date: **Expiry Date:**

☐ ☐ / ☐ ☐   ☐ ☐ / ☐ ☐

Signature: _____

NAME: _____

ADDRESS: _____

COUNTRY: _____

ZIP/POSTCODE: _____

Please allow 28 days for delivery. Despatch normally within 48 hours.

Prices subject to change without notice.
Please tick box if you do not wish to receive any additional information. ☐

House of Stratus publishes many other titles in this genre; please check our website (**www.houseofstratus.com**) for more details.